FANTASY ADVENTURE

ELMINSTER:
THE MAKING
OF A MAGE

Ed Greenwood

ELMINSTER:
THE MAKING OF A MAGE

Cover art by Jeff Easley

First Printing: December 1994
Printed in the United States of America
Library of Congress Catalog Card Number: 94-61675
First paperback edition: December 1995

9 8 7 6 5 4 3 2

ISBN: 0-7869-0203-5

TSR, Inc.
201 Sheridan Springs Rd.
Lake Geneva, WI 53147
U.S.A.

TSR Ltd.
120 Church End, Cherry Hinton
Cambridge CB1 3LB
United Kingdom

To Jenny

For Love
And Understanding
And Being There
... As Always

There are only two precious things on earth:
the first is love; the second, a long way behind it,
is intelligence.

Gaston Berger

Life has no meaning but what we give it.
I wish a few more of ye would give it a little.

Elminster of Shadowdale

verba volant, scripta manent

Prelude*

"Of course, Lord Mourngrym," Lhaeo replied, gesturing up the stairs with a ladle that was still dripping jalanth sauce. "He's in his study. You know the way."

Mourngrym nodded his thanks to Elminster's scribe and took the dusty stairs two at a time, charging urgently up into the gloom. The Old Mage's instructions had been quite—

He came to a halt, dust swirling around him mockingly. The cozy little room held the usual crammed shelves, worn carpet, and comfortable chair . . . and Elminster's pipe was floating, ready, above the side table. But of the Old Mage himself, there was no sign.

Mourngrym shrugged and dashed on up the next set of stairs, to the spell chamber. A glowing circle pulsed alone on the floor there, cold and white. The small circular room was otherwise empty.

The Lord of Shadowdale hesitated a moment, and then mounted the last flight of stairs. He'd never dared disturb the Old Mage in his bedchamber before, but . . .

The door was ajar. Mourngrym peered in cautiously, hand going to his sword hilt out of long habit. Stars twinkled silently and endlessly in the dark domed ceiling over the circular bed that filled the room—but that resting place hadn't been slept in since the dust had settled. The room was as empty of life as the others. Unless he was invisible or had taken on the shape of a book or something of the sort, Elminster was nowhere in his tower.

Mourngrym looked warily all around, hairs prickling on the backs of his hands. The Old Mage could be anywhere, on worlds and planes only he and the gods knew of. Mourngrym frowned— and then shrugged. After all, what did anyone in the Realms— besides the Seven Sisters, perhaps—really know about Elminster's plans or his past?

"I wonder," the Lord of Shadowdale mused aloud as he started the long walk back down to Lhaeo, "where Elminster came from, anyway? Was he *ever* a young lad? Where . . . ? And what was the world like then?"

It must have been great fun, growing up as a powerful wizard. . . .

Prologue

It was the hour of the Casting of the Cloak, when the goddess Shar hurled her vast garment of purple darkness and glittering stars across the sky. The day had been cool, and the night promised to be clear and cold. The last rosy embers of day glimmered on the long hair of a lone rider from the west, and lengthening shadows crept ahead of her.

The woman looked around at the gathering night as she rode. Her liquid black eyes were large and framed by arched brows—stern power and keen wits at odds with demure beauty. Whether for the power or the beauty there, most men did not look past the honey-brown tresses curling around her pert white face, and even queens lusted after her beauty—one at least did, of a certainty. Yet as she rode along, her large eyes held no pride, only sadness. In the spring, wildfires had raged across all these lands, leaving behind legions of charred and leafless spars instead of the lush green beauty she recalled. Such fond memories were all that was left of Halangorn Forest now.

As dusk came down on the dusty road, a wolf howled somewhere away to the north. The call was answered from near at hand, but the lone rider showed no fear. Her calm would have raised the eyebrows of the hardened knights who dared ride this road only in large, well-armed patrols—and their wary surprise would not have ended there. The lady rode easily, a long cloak swirling around her, time and again flapping around her hips and hampering her sword arm. Only a fool would allow such a thing—but this tall, lean lady rode the perilous road without even a sword at her hip. A patrol of knights would have judged her either a madwoman or a sorceress and reached for their blades accordingly. They'd not have been wrong.

She was Myrjala 'Darkeyes,' as the silvern sigil on her cloak proclaimed. Myrjala was feared for her wild ways as much as for the might of her magic, but though all folk feared her, many farmers and townsfolk loved her. Proud lords in castles did not; she'd been known to hurl down cruel barons and plundering knights like a vengeful whirlwind, leaving blazing bodies in dark warning to others. In some places she was most unwelcome.

As night's full gloom fell on the road, Myrjala slowed her

horse, twisted in her saddle, and did off her cloak. She spoke a single soft word, and the cloth twisted in her hands, changing from its usual dark green to a russet hue. The silver mage-sigil slithered and writhed like an angry snake and became a pair of entwined golden trumpets.

The transformation did not end with the cloak. Myrjala's long curls darkened and shrank about her shoulders—shoulders suddenly alive and broadening with roiling humps of muscle. The hands that donned the cloak again had become hairy and stubby fingered. They plucked a scabbarded blade out from the pack behind the saddle and belted it on. Thus armed, the man in the saddle arranged his cloak so its newly shaped herald badge could be clearly seen, listened to the wolf howl again—closer now—and calmly urged his mount forward at a trot, over one last hill. Ahead lay a castle where a spy dined this night—a spy for the evil wizards bent on seizing the Stag Throne of Athalantar. That realm lay not far off to the east. The man in the saddle stroked his elegant beard and spurred his horse onward. Where the most feared sorceress in these lands might be met with arrows and ready blades, a lord herald was always welcome. Yet magic was the best blade against a wizard's spy.

The guards were lighting the lamps over the gate as the herald's horse clottered over the wooden drawbridge. The badge on his cloak and tabard were recognized, and he was greeted with quiet courtesy by the gate guards. A bell tolled once within, and the knight of the gate bade him hasten in to the evening feast.

"Be welcome in Morlin Castle, if ye come in peace."

The herald bowed his head in the usual silent response.

" 'Tis a long way from Tavaray, Lord Herald; ye must know hunger," the knight added less formally, helping him down from his mount. The herald took a few slow steps, awkward with saddle stiffness, and smiled thinly.

Startling dark eyes rose to meet those of the knight. "Oh, I've come much farther than that," the herald said softly, nodded a wordless farewell, and strode away into the castle. He walked like a man who knew his way—and welcome—well.

The knight watched him go, face expressionless in puzzlement. An armsman nearby leaned close and murmured, "No spurs . . . and no esquires or armsmen. What manner of herald is this?"

The knight of the gate shrugged. "If he lost them on the road or there's some other tale of interest, we'll know it soon enough. See to his horse." He turned, then stiffened in fresh surprise. The herald's horse was standing near and watching him, for all the world as if it were listening to their talk. It nodded and took a half step to bring its reins smoothly to the armsman's hand. The men exchanged wary glances before the armsman led it away.

The knight watched them for a moment before shrugging and striding back to the mouth of the gate. There'd be much talk on watch later, whatever befell. Out in the night nearby, a wolf howled again. One of the horses snorted and stamped nervously.

Then a window in the castle above flickered with sudden light—*magical* light from a battle spell, and the battle was joined. There was a terrific commotion within, scattering plates and overturned tables, shrieks of serving maids and roars of flame. Next moment, these sounds were joined by the shouts of the knights in the courtyard below.

That had been no herald, and from the sound and smell of it, others within the castle were not what they seemed, either. The knight gritted his teeth and clenched his sword, starting for the keep. If Morlin fell to these wicked spell-slingers, would the Stag King fall next? And if all Athalantar fell, there would be years upon years of sorcerous tyranny. Aye, there would be ruin and misery ahead. . . . And who could ever rise to oppose these mage-lords?

PART I
BRIGAND

One

DRAGON FIRE—AND DOOM

Dragons? Splendid things, lad—so long as ye look upon them only in tapestries, or in the masks worn at revels, or from about three realms off. . . .

Astragarl Hornwood, Mage of Elembar
said to an apprentice
Year of the Tusk

The sun beat down bright and hot on the rock pile that crowned the high pasture. Far below, the village, cloaked in trees, lay under a blue-green haze of mist—magic mist, some said, conjured by the mist-mages of the Fair Folk, whose magic worked both good and ill. The ill things were spoken of more often, of course, for many folk in Heldon did not love elves.

Elminster was not one of them. He hoped to meet the elves someday—really meet, that is—to touch smooth skin and pointed ears, to converse with them. These woods had once been theirs, and they yet knew the secret places where beasts laired and suchlike. He'd like to know all that, someday, when he was a man and could walk where he pleased.

El sighed, shifted into a more comfortable position against his favorite rock, and from habit glanced at the falling slopes of the meadow to be sure his sheep were safe. They were.

Not for the first time, the bony, beak-nosed youth peered south, squinting. Brushing unruly jet-black hair aside with one slim hand, he kept his fingers raised to shade his piercing blue-gray eyes, trying vainly to see the turrets of far-off, splendid Athalgard, in the heart of Hastarl, by the river. As always, he could see the faint bluish haze that marked the nearest curve of the Delimbiyr, but no more. Father told him often that the castle was much too far off to be seen from here—and, from time to time, added that the fair span of distance between it and their village was a good thing.

Elminster longed to know what that meant, but this was one of the many things his father would not speak of. When asked, he settled his oft-smiling lips into a stony line, and his level gray eyes would meet Elminster's own with a sharper look than usual

. . . but no words ever emerged. El hated secrets—at least those he didn't know. He'd learn all the secrets someday, somehow. Someday, too, he'd see the castle the minstrels said was so splendid . . . mayhap even walk its battlements . . . aye. . . :

A breeze ghosted gently over the meadow, bending the weed heads briefly. It was the Year of Flaming Forests, in the month of Eleasias, a few days short of Eleint. Already the nights were turning very cold. After six seasons of minding sheep on the high meadow, El knew it'd not be long before leaves were blowing about, and the Fading would truly begin.

The shepherd-lad sighed and shrugged his worn, patched leather jerkin closer about him. It had once belonged to a forester. Under a patch on the back, it still bore a ragged, dark-stained hole where an arrow—an elfin arrow, some said—had taken the man's life. Elminster wore the old jack—scabbard buckles, tears from long-gone lord's badges, and worn edges from past adventures—for all the dash its history made him feel. Sometimes, though, he wished it fit him a little better.

A shadow fell over the meadow, and he looked up. From behind him came a sharp, rippling roar of wind he'd never heard before. He spun around, his shoulder against the rock, and sprang up for a better view. He needn't have bothered. The sky above the meadow was filled with two huge, batlike wings—and between them, a dark red scaled bulk larger than a house! Long-taloned claws hung beneath a belly that rose into a long, long neck, which ended in a head that housed two cruel eyes and a wide-gaping jaw lined with jagged teeth as long as Elminster was tall! Trailing back far behind, over the hill, a tail switched and swung. . . .

A dragon! Elminster forgot to gulp. He just stared.

Vast and terrible, it swept toward him, slowing ponderously with wings spread to catch the air, looming against the blue northern sky. And there was a man on its back!

"Dragon at the gate," Elminster whispered the oath unthinkingly, as that gigantic head tilted a little, and he found himself gazing full into the old, wise, and cruel eyes of the great wyrm.

Deep they were, and unblinking; pools of dark evil into which he plunged, sinking, sinking. . . .

The dragon's claws bit deeply into the rock pile with a shriek of riven stone and a spray of sparks. It reared up twice as high as the tallest tower in the village, and those great wings flapped once. In their deafening thunderclap Elminster was flung helplessly back and away, head over heels down the slope as sheep tumbled and bleated their terror around him. He landed hard, rolling painfully on one shoulder. He should run, should—

"Swords!" He spat the strongest oath he knew as he felt his frantic run being dragged to a halt by something unseen. A trembling, quivering boiling arose in his veins—magic! He felt himself turning, being pulled slowly around to face the dragon. Elminster had always hoped to see magic at work up close, but instead of the wild excitement he'd expected, El found he didn't like the feel of magic at all. Anger and fear awoke in him as his head was forced up. No, did not like it at all.

The dragon had folded its wings, and now sat atop the rock pile like a vulture—a vulture as tall as a keep, with a long tail that curled half around the western slope of the meadow. Elminster gulped; his mouth was suddenly dry. The man had dismounted and stood on a sloping rock beside the dragon, an imperious hand raised to point at Elminster.

Elminster felt his gaze dragged—that horrible, helpless feeling in his body again, the cruel control of another's will moving his own limbs—to meet the man's eyes. Looking into the eyes of the dragon had been terrible but somehow splendid. This was worse. These eyes were cold and promised pain and death . . . perhaps more. El tasted the cold tang of rising fear.

There was cruel amusement in the man's almond eyes. El forced himself to look a little down and aside, and saw the dusky skin around those deadly eyes, and coppery curls, and a winking pendant on the man's hairless breast. Under it were markings on the man's skin, half-hidden by his robe of darkest green. He wore rings, too, of gold and some shining blue metal, and soft boots finer than any El had ever seen. The faint blue glow of magic—something Father had said only Elminster could see, and must never speak of—clung to the pendant, the rings, the robes, and the markings on the man's breast, as well as to what looked like the ends of smoothed wooden sticks, protruding from high slits on the outside of the man's boots. That rare glow rippled more brightly around the man's outstretched arm . . . but Elminster didn't need any other secret sign to know that this was a wizard.

"What is the name of the village below?" The question was cold, quick.

"Heldon." The name left Elminster's lips before he could think. He felt spittle flooding his mouth, and with it a hint of blood.

"Is its lord there now?"

Elminster struggled, but found himself saying, "A-Aye."

The wizard's eyes narrowed. "Name him." He raised his

hand, and the blue glow flared brighter.

Elminster felt a sudden eagerness to tell this rude stranger everything—*everything*. Cold fear coiled inside him. "Elthryn, Lord." He felt his lips trembling.

"Describe him."

"He's tall, Lord, and slim. He smiles often, and always has a kind w—"

"What hue is his hair?" the wizard snapped.

"B-Brown, Lord, with gray at the sides and in his beard. He's—"

The wizard made a sharp gesture, and Elminster felt his limbs moving by themselves. He tried to fight against them, whimpering, but already he was wheeling about and running. He pounded hard through the grass, helpless against the driving magic, stumbling in haste, charging down the grassy slope to where the meadow ended—in a sheer drop into the ravine.

As he churned along through the weeds and tall grass, El clung to a small victory; at least he'd not told the wizard that Elthryn was his father.

Small victory, indeed. The cliff-edge seemed to leap at him; the wind of his breathless run roared past his ears. The rolling countryside of Athalantar, below, looked beautiful in the mists.

Headlong, Elminster rushed over the edge—and felt the terrible trembling compulsion leave him. As the rocks rushed up to meet him, he struggled against fear and fury, trying to save his life.

Sometimes, he could move things with his mind. Sometimes—please, gods, let it be now!

The ravine was narrow, the rocks very near. Only last month a lamb had fallen in, and the life had been smashed from it long before its broken, loll-limbed body had settled at the bottom. Elminster bit his lip. And then the white glow he was seeking rose and stole over his sight, veiling his view of rushing rocks. He clawed at the air with desperate fingers and twisted sideways as if he'd grown wings for an instant.

Then he was crashing through a thornbush, skin burning as it was slashed open a dozen times. He struck earth and stone, then something springy—a vine?—and was flung away, falling again.

"Uhhh!" Onto rocks this time, hard. The world spun. El gasped for breath he could not find, and the white haze rose around his eyes.

Gods and goddesses preserve . . .

The haze rose and then receded—and then, from above,

came a horrible snapping sound.

Something dark and wet fell past him, to the rocks unseen in the gloom below. El shook his head to clear it and peered around. Fresh blood dappled the rocks close by. The sunlight overhead dimmed; Elminster froze, head to one side, and tried to look dead. His arms and ribs and one hip throbbed and ached . . . but he'd been able to move them all. Would the wizard or the dragon come down to make sure he was dead?

The dragon wheeled over the meadow, one limb of a sheep dangling from its jaws, and passed out of his view. When its next languid circle brought it back over the ravine, two sheep were struggling in its mouth. The crunching sounds began again as it passed out of sight.

Elminster shuddered, feeling sick and empty. He clung to the rock as if its hard, solid strength could tell him what to do now. Then the rippling roar of the dragon's wings rose again. El lay as still as possible, head still twisted awkwardly. Letting his mouth fall open, he stared steadily off into the cloudless sky.

The wizard in his high saddle gave the huddled boy a keen look as the dragon rushed past, and then leaned forward and shouted something Elminster couldn't catch, which echoed and hissed in the mouth of the ravine. The dragon's powerful shoulders surged in response, and it rose slightly—only to drop out of sight in a dive so swift that the raw sound of its rushing wings rose to a shrill scream. A dive toward Heldon.

El found his feet, wincing and staggering, and stumbled along the ravine to its end, hissing as every movement made him ache. There was a place he'd climbed before . . . his fingers bled as they scraped over sharp rocks. A terrible fear was rising inside him, almost choking him.

At last he reached the grassy edge of the meadow, rolled onto it, gasping, and looked down on Heldon. Then Elminster found he still had breath enough to scream.

*   *   *   *   *   *

A woman shrieked outside. A moment later, the incessant din of hammering from the smithy came to a sudden, ragged stop. Frowning, Elthryn Aumar rose from the farm tallies in haste, scattering clay tiles. He sighed at his own clumsiness as he snatched his blade down from the wall and strode out into the street, tearing the steel free of the scabbard as he went. Tallies that wouldn't balance all morning, and now this . . . what was it *now?*

The Lion Sword, oldest treasure of Athalantar, shone its proud flame as he came out into the sunlight. Strong magics slumbered in the old blade, and as always, it felt solid in Elthryn's hand, hungry for blood. It flashed as he looked quickly about. Folk were shrieking and running wildly south down the street, faces white in sheer terror. Elthryn had to duck out of the way of a woman so fat that he was astonished she could run at all—one of Tesla's seamstresses—and turned to look north at the dark bulk of the High Forest. The street was full of his neighbors, running south down the road, past him. Some were weeping as they came. A haze—smoke—was in the air whence they'd come.

Brigands? Orcs? Something out of the woods?

He ran up the road, the enchanted blade that was his proudest possession naked in his hand. The sharp reek of burning came to him. A sick fear was already rising in his throat when he rounded the butcher's shop and behind it found the fire.

His own cottage was an inferno of leaping flame. Perhaps she'd been out—but no . . . no . . .

"Amrythale," he whispered. Sudden tears blinded him, and he wiped at them with his sleeve. Somewhere in all that roaring were her bones.

He knew some folk had whispered that a common forester's lass must have used witchery to find a bridal bed with one of the most respected princes of Athalantar—but Elthryn had loved her. And she him. He gazed in horror at her pyre, and in his memory saw her smiling face. As the tears rolled down his cheeks, the prince felt a black rage build inside him.

"Who has done this thing?" he roared. His shout echoed back from the now-empty shops and houses of Heldon, but was answered only by crackling flames . . . and then by a roar so loud and deep that the shops and houses around trembled, and the very cobbles of the street shifted under his boots. Amid the dust that curled up from them, the prince looked up and saw it, aloft, wheeling with contemptuous laziness over the trees: an elder red dragon of great size, its scales dark as dried blood. A man rode it, a man in robes who held a wand ready, a man Elthryn did not know but a wizard without a doubt, and that could mean only one thing: the cruel hand of his eldest brother Belaur was finally about to close on him.

Elthryn had been his father's favorite, and Belaur had always hated him for it. The king had given Elthryn the Lion Sword—it was all he had left of his father, now. It had served him often and well . . . but it was a legacy, not a miracle-spell. As he heard the

wizard laugh and lean out to hurl lightning down at some villager fleeing over the back fields, Prince Elthryn looked up into
the sky and saw his own death there, wheeling on proud wings.

He raised the Lion Sword to his lips, kissed it, and summoned
the lean, serious face of his son to mind: beak-nosed and surrounded by an unruly mane of jet-black hair. Elminster, with all
his loneliness, seriousness, and homeliness, and with his secret,
the mind-powers the gods gave few folk in Faerun. Perhaps the
gods had something special in mind for him. Clinging to that
last, slim hope, Elthryn clutched the sword and spoke through
tears.

"Live, my son," he whispered. "Live to avenge thy mother . . .
and restore honor to the Stag Throne. Hear me!"

* * * * *

Panting his slithering way down a tree-clad slope, still a long
way above the village, Elminster stiffened and fetched up
breathless against a tree, his eyes blazing. The ghostly whisper
of his father's voice was clear in his ears; he was calling on a
power of his enchanted sword that El had seen him use only
once, when his mother had been lost in a snow squall. He knew
what those words meant. His father was about to die.

"I'm coming, Father!" he shouted at the unhearing trees
around. "I'm coming!" And he stumbled on, recklessly leaping
deadfalls and crashing through thickets, gasping for breath,
knowing he'd be too late. . . .

* * * * *

Grimly, Elthryn Aumar set his feet firmly on the road, raised
his sword, and prepared to die as a prince should. The dragon
swept past, ignoring the lone man with the sword as its rider
pointed two wands and calmly struck down the fleeing folk of
Heldon with hurled lightning and bolts of magical death. As he
swept over the prince, the wizard carelessly aimed one wand at
the lone swordsman below.

There was a flash of white light, and then the whole world
seemed to be dancing and crawling. Lightning crackled and
coiled around Elthryn, but he felt no pain; the blade in his hands
drew the magic into itself in angrily crawling arcs of white fire
until it was all gone.

The prince saw the wizard turn in his saddle and frown back
at him. Holding the Lion Sword high so that the mage could see

it, hoping he could lure the wizard down to seize it—and knowing that hope vain—Elthryn lifted his head to curse the man, speaking the slow, heavy words he'd been taught so long ago.

The wizard made a gesture—and then his mouth fell open in surprise: the curse had shattered whatever spell he'd cast at Elthryn. As the dragon swept on, he aimed his other wand at the prince. Bolts of force leapt from it—and were swept into the enchanted blade, which sang and glowed with their fury, thrumming in Elthryn's hands. Spells it could stop . . . but not dragon fire. The prince knew he had only a few breaths of life left.

"O Mystra, let my boy escape this," he prayed as the dragon turned in the air with slow might and swept down on him, "and let him have the sense to flee far." Then he had no time left for prayers.

Bright dragon fire roared around Elthryn Aumar, and as he snarled defiance and swung his blade at the raging flames, he was overwhelmed and swept away. . . .

* * * * *

Elminster burst out onto the village street by the miller's house, now only a smoking heap of shattered timbers and tumbled stones. A single hand, blackened by fire that had breathed death through the house and swept on, protruded from under the collapsed chimney, clutching vainly at nothing.

Elminster looked down at it, swallowed, and hurried on around the heap of ruin. After only a few paces, however, his running steps faltered, and he stood staring. There was no need for haste; every building in Heldon was smashed flat or in flames. Thick smoke hid the lower end of the village from him, and small fires blazed here and there, where trees or woodpiles had caught fire. His home was only a blackened area and drifting ashes; beyond, the butcher's shop had fallen into the street, a mass of half-burnt timbers and smashed belongings. The dragon had gone; Elminster was alone with the dead.

Grimly, Elminster searched the village. He found corpses, tumbled or fried among the ruins of their homes, but not a soul that yet lived. Of his mother and father there was no sign . . . but he knew they'd not have fled. It was only when he turned, sick at heart, toward the meadow—where else could he go?—that he stepped on something amid the ashes that lay thick on the road: the half-melted hilt of the Lion Sword.

He took it up in hands that trembled. All but a few fingers of the blade were burnt away, and most of the proud gold; blue magic coursed no longer about this remnant. Yet he knew the feel of the worn hilt. El clutched it to his breast, and the world suddenly wavered.

Tears fell from his sightless eyes for a long time as he knelt among the ashes in the street and the patient sun moved across the sky. At some point he must have fallen senseless, for he roused at the creeping touch of cold to feel hard cobbles under his cheek.

Sitting up, he found dusk upon the ruin of Heldon, and full night coming down from the High Forest. His numb hands tingled as he fumbled with the sword hilt. Elminster got to his feet slowly, looking around at what was left of his home. Somewhere nearby, a wolf called and was answered. Elminster looked at the useless weapon he held, and he shivered. It was time to be gone from this place, before the wolves came down to feed.

Slowly he raised the riven Lion Sword to the sky. For an instant it caught the last feeble glow of sunset, and Elminster stared hard at it and muttered, "I shall slay that wizard, and avenge ye all—or die in the trying. Hear me . . . Mother, Father. This I *swear*."

A wolf howled in reply. Elminster bared his teeth in its direction, shook the ruined hilt at it, and started the long run back up to the meadow.

As he went, Selune rose serenely over the dying fires of Heldon, bathing the ruins in bright, bone-white moonlight. Elminster did not look back.

*   *   *   *   *

He awoke suddenly, in the close darkness of a cavern he'd hidden in once when playing seek-the-ogre with other lads. The hilt of the Lion Sword lay, hard and unyielding, beneath him. Elminster remained still, listening. Someone had said something, very nearby.

"No sign of a raid . . . no one sworded," came the sudden grave words, loud and close. Elminster tensed, lying still and peering into the darkness.

"I suppose all the huts caught fire by themselves, then," another, deeper man's voice said sarcastically. "And the rest fell over just because they were tired of standing up, eh?"

"Enough, Bellard. Everyone's dead, aye—but there's no sword work, not an arrow to be seen. Wolves have been at some of the bodies, but not a one's been rummaged. I found a gold ring on one lady's hand that shone at me clear down the street."

"What kills with fire, then—an' knocks down cottages?"

"Dragons," said another voice, lower still, and grim.

"Dragons? And we saw it not?" The sarcastic voice rose almost jestingly.

"More'n one thing befalls up an' down the Delimbiyr that ye see not, Bellard. What else could it be? A mage, aye—but what mage has spells enough to scorch houses an' haystacks an' odd patches of meadow, as well as every stone-built building in the place?" There was a brief silence, and the voice went on. "Well, if ye think of any other good answer, speak. Until then, if ye've sense, we'll raid only at dawn, before we can be well seen from the air—an' not stray far from the forest, for cover."

"Nay! I'll not sit here like some old woman while others pick over all the coins and good, only to be left fighting with wolves over the refuse."

"Go then, Bellard. I stay here."

"Aye—with the sheep."

"Indeed. That way there may be something for you to eat—besides cooked villager—when you're done . . . or were you going to herd them all down there an' watch over them as you pick through the rubble?"

There was a disgusted snort, and someone else laughed. "Helm's right, as usual, Bel. Now belt up; let's go. He'll probably have some cooked for us by nightfall, if you speak to him as a lover would instead of always wagging the sharp-tongue . . . what say, Helm?"

The grim voice answered, "No promises. If I think something's lurking that might be drawn by a smoke-plume, the meat'll be cold. If any of ye sees a good cauldron there—big and stout, mind—have the sense to bring it back, will ye? Then I can boil enough food for us to eat all at once."

"And your helm'll smell less like beans for a while, eh?"

"That, too. Forget not, now."

"I'll not waste my hands on a pot," Bellard said sullenly, "if there's coins or good blades to be had."

"No, no, helmhead—carry thy loot in the pot, see? Then ye can bring that much more, nay?"

There were chuckles. "He's got ye there, Bel."

"Again."

"Aye, let's be off." Then there came the sounds of scrambling and scuffling; stones turned and rolled by the mouth of the cave, and then clattered and were still. Silence fell.

Elminster waited for a long time, but heard only the wind. They must have all gone. Carefully he rose, stretched his stiff arms and legs, and crept forward in the darkness, around the corner—and almost onto the point of a sword. The man at the other end of it said calmly, "An' who might ye be, lad? Run from the village down there?" He wore tattered leather armor, rusty gauntlets, a dented, scratched helm, and a heavy, stubbly beard. This close, Elminster could smell the stench of an unwashed man in armor, the stink of oil and wood smoke.

"Those are my sheep, Helm," he said calmly. "Leave them be."

"Thine? Who be ye herding them for, with all down there dead?"

Elminster met the man's level gaze and was ashamed when sudden tears welled up in his own eyes. He sprang back, wiping at his eyes, and drew the Lion Sword out of the breast of his jerkin.

The man regarded him with what might have been pity and said, "Put that away, boy. I've no interest in crossing blades with ye, even if ye had proper steel to wield. Ye had folk down"—he pointed with a sideways tilt of his head, never taking his eyes from Elminster—"in Heldon?"

"Aye," El managed to say, voice trembling only a little.

"Where will ye go now?"

Elminster shrugged. "I was going to stay here," he said bitterly, "and eat sheep."

Helm's eyes met the young, angry gaze calmly. "A change of plans must needs be in order, then. Shall I save ye one to get ye started?"

Sudden rage rose up inside Elminster at that. "Thief!" he snarled, backing away. "Thief!"

The man shrugged. "I've been called worse."

Elminster found his hands were trembling; he thrust them and the ruined sword back into the front of his jerkin. Helm stood across the only way out. If there were a rock large enough . . .

"You'd not be so calm if there were knights of Athalantar near! They kill brigands, you know," Elminster said, biting off his words as he'd heard his father do when angry, putting a bark of authority in his tone.

The response astonished him. There was a sudden scuffling of boots on rock, and the man had him by the throat, one worn old gauntlet bunching up the jerkin under Elminster's nose. "I *am* a knight of Athalantar, boy—sworn to the Stag King himself, gods and goddesses watch over him. If there weren't so gods-cursed many wizards down in Hastarl, kinging it over the lot of us with the hired brigands they call 'loyal armsmen,' I'd be riding a realm at peace—an' doubtless ye'd still have a home, an' thy folks an' neighbors'd be alive!"

The old gray eyes burned with an anger equal to Elminster's own. El swallowed but looked steadily into them.

"If ye're a true knight," he said, "then let go."

Warily, with a little push that left them both apart, the man did so. "Right, then, boy—why?"

Elminster dragged out the sword hilt again and held it up. "Recognize ye this?" he said, voice wavering.

Helm squinted at it, shook his head—and then froze. "The Lion Sword," he said roughly. "It should be in Uthgrael's tomb. How came you by it, boy?" He held out his hand for it.

Elminster shook his head and thrust the ruined stub of blade back into his jerkin. " 'Tis mine—it was my father's, and . . ." he fought down a tightness of unshed tears in his throat, and went on ". . . and I think he died wielding it, yestereve."

He and Helm stared into each other's eyes for a long moment, and then El asked curiously, "Who's this Uthgrael? Why would he be buried with my father's sword?"

Helm was staring at him as if he had three heads, and a crown on each one. "I'll answer that, lad, if ye'll tell me thy father's name first." He leaned forward, eyes suddenly dark and intent.

Elminster drew himself up proudly and said, "My father is— was—Elthryn Aumar. Everyone called him the uncrowned lord of Heldon."

Helm let out his breath in a ragged gasp. "Don't—don't tell *anyone* that, lad," he said quickly. "D'ye hear?"

"Why?" Elminster said, eyes narrowing. "I know my father was someone important, and he—" His voice broke, but he snarled at his own weakness and went on "—he was killed by a wizard with two wands, who rode on the back of a dragon. A dark red dragon." His eyes became bleak. "I shall never forget what they look like." He drew out what was left of the Lion Sword again, made a thrusting motion with it, and added fiercely, "One day . . ."

He was startled to see the dirty knight grin—not a sneering grin, but a smile of delight.

"What?" El demanded, suddenly embarrassed. He thrust the blade out of sight again. "What amuses ye so?"

"Lad, lad," the man said gently, "sit down here." He sheathed his own sword and pointed at a rock not far away. Elminster eyed him warily, and the man sighed, sat down himself, and un-clipped a stoppered trail-flask of chased metal from his belt. He held it out. "Will ye drink?"

Elminster eyed it. He was very thirsty, he realized suddenly. He took a step nearer. "If ye give me some answers," he said, "and promise not to slay me."

Helm regarded him almost with respect and said, "Ye have my word on it—the word of Helm Stoneblade, knight of the Stag Throne." He cleared his throat and said, "An' answers I'll give, too, if ye'll favor me with just one more." He leaned forward. "What is thy name?"

"Elminster Aumar, son of Elthryn."

"Only son?"

"Enough," Elminster said, taking the flask. "Ye've had your one answer; give me mine."

The man grinned again. "Please, Lord Prince? Just one answer more?"

Elminster stared at him. "D'ye mock me? 'Lord Prince'?"

Helm shook his head. "No, lad—Prince Elminster. I pray ye, I must know. Have ye brothers? Sisters?"

Elminster shook his head. "None, alive or dead."

"Thy mother?"

Elminster spread his hands. "Did ye find anyone alive down there?" he asked, suddenly angry again. "I'd like my answers now, Sir Knight." He took a long, deliberate drink from the flask.

His nose and throat exploded in bubbling fire. Elminster choked and gasped. His knees hit the stony ground, hard; through swimming eyes he saw Helm lean swiftly forward to rescue him—and the flask. Strong hands helped him to his seat and gently shook him.

"Firewine not to thy liking, lad? All right now?"

Elminster managed a nod, head bowed. Helm roughly patted him on the arm and said, "Well enough. Seems thy parents thought it safest to tell ye nothing. I agree with them."

Elminster's head came up in anger—but through swimming eyes he saw Helm holding up one gauntleted hand in the gesture that meant "halt."

"Yet I gave my word . . . an' you are a prince of Athalantar. A knight keeps his promises, however rashly made."

"So, speak," Elminster said.

"How much d'ye know of thy parents? Thy lineage?"

Elminster shrugged. "Nothing," he said bitterly, "beyond the names of my parents. My mother was Amrythale Goldsheaf; her father was a forester. My father was proud of this sword—it had magic—and was glad that we couldn't see Athalgard from Heldon. That's all."

Helm rolled his eyes, sighed, and said, "Well, then. Sit an' learn. If ye'd live, keep what I tell thee to thyself. Wizards hunt folk of thy blood in Athalantar, these days."

"Aye," Elminster told him bitterly, "I know."

Helm sighed. "I—my forgiveness, Prince. I forgot." He spread gauntleted hands as if to clear away underbrush before him, and said, "This realm, Athalantar, is called the Kingdom of the Stag after one man: Uthgrael Aumar, the Stag King; a mighty warrior—an' thy grandsire."

Elminster nodded. "That much, I suspected from all thy 'prince' talk. Why then am I not in rich robes right now in some high chamber of Athalgard?"

Helm give him that grin of delight again and chuckled. "Ye are as quick—an' as iron of nerves—as he was, lad." He reached an arm behind him, found a battered canvas pack, and rummaged in it as he went on. "The best answer to that is to tell things as they befell. Uthgrael was my lord, lad, and the greatest swordsman I've ever seen." His voice sank to a whisper, all traces of his smile gone. "He died in the Year of Frosts, going up against orcs near Jander. Many of us died that wolfwinter—an' the spine of Athalantar went with us."

Helm found what he was looking for: a half-loaf of hard, gray bread. He held it out wordlessly. Elminster took it, nodded his thanks, and gestured for the knight to say on. That brought the ghost of a smile to Helm's lips.

"Uthgrael was old an' ready to die; after Queen Syndrel went to her grave, he fell to grimness an' waited for a chance to fall in battle; I saw it in his eyes more than once. The orc-chieftain who cut him down left the realm in the hands of his seven sons. There were no daughters."

Helm stared into the depths of the cavern, seeing other times and places—and faces Elminster did not know. "Five princes were ruled by ambition, an' were ruthless, cruel men, all. One of these, Felodar, was interested in gold above all else an' traveled far in its pursuit—to hot Calimshan and beyond, lad, where he still is, for all I know—but the others all stayed in Athalantar."

The knight scratched himself for a moment, eyes still far away, and added, "There were two sons more. One was too young an' timid to be a threat to anyone. The other—thy father, Elthryn—was calm an' just, an' preferred the life of a farmer to the intrigue of the court. He retired here an' married a commoner. We thought that signified his renunciation of the crown. So, I fear, did he."

Helm sighed, met Elminster's intent gaze, and went on. "The

other princes fought for control of the realm. Folk as afar from
here as Elembar, on the coast, call them 'The Warring Princes of
Athalantar.' There're even songs about them. The winner, thus
far, has been the eldest son, Belaur."

The knight leaned forward suddenly to grip Elminster's
arms. "Ye must hear me in this," he said urgently. "Belaur bested
his brothers—but his victory has cost him, an' all of us, the
realm. He bought the services of mages from all over Faerun to
win him the Stag Throne. He sits on it today—but his wits are so
clouded by drink an' by their magic that he doesn't even know he
barks only when they kick him: his magelords are the true
rulers of Athalantar. Even the beggars in Hastarl know it."

"How many of these wizards are there? What are their
names?" Elminster asked quietly.

Helm released him and sat back, shaking his head. "I know
not—an' I doubt any folk in Athalantar do, below swordcaptains
of the Stag, except perhaps the house servants of Athalgard." He
cast a keen look at Elminster. "Sworn to avenge thy parents,
Prince?"

Elminster nodded.

"Wait," the knight told him bluntly. "Wait until ye're older,
an've gathered coins enough to buy mages of thy own. Ye'll need
them—unless ye want to spend the rest of your days as a purple
frog swimming in some palace perfume-bowl for the amusement
of some minor apprentice of the magelords. Though it took all of
them to do it, an' they had to split apart Wyrm Tower stone by
stone, they slew old Shandrath—as powerful an archmage as
ye'll find in all the lands of men—two summers back." He sighed.
"An' those they couldn't smash with spells, they slew with blades
or poison, Theskyn the court mage, for one. He was the oldest an'
most trusted of Uthgrael's friends."

"I will avenge them all," Elminster said quietly. "Before I die,
Athalantar will be free of these magelords—every last one, if I
have to tear them apart with my bare hands. This I swear."

Helm shook his head. "No, Prince, swear no great oaths. Men
who swear oaths are doomed to die by them. One thing hunts
and hounds them—an' so, they waste and stunt their lives."

Elminster regarded him darkly. "A wizard took my mother
and father—and all my friends, and the other folk I knew. It is
my life, to spend how I will."

Helm's face split in that delighted grin again. He shook his
head. "Ye're a fool, Prince—a prudent man'd foot it out of Athalantar and never look back, nor breathe a word of his past, his
family, or the Lion Sword to a soul . . . mayhap to live a long an'

happy life somewhere else." He leaned forward to clasp Elminster's forearm. "But ye could not do that an' still be an Aumar, prince of Athalantar. So ye will die in the trying." He shook his head again. "At least listen to me, then—an' wait until ye have a chance before letting anyone else in all Faerun know ye live . . . or ye'll not give one of the magelords more than a few minutes of cruel sport."

"They know of me?"

Helm gave him a pitying look. "Ye are a lamb to the ways of court, indeed. The wizard ye saw over Heldon doubtless had orders to eliminate Prince Elthryn an' all his blood before the son they knew he'd sired could grow old and well-trained enough to have royal ambitions of his own."

There was a little silence as the knight watched the youth grow pale. When the lad spoke again, however, Helm got another surprise.

"Sir Helm," Elminster said calmly, "Tell me the names of the magelords and ye can have my sheep."

Helm guffawed. "In faith, lad, I know them not—an' the others I run with'll have thy sheep whate'er befalls. I will give thee the names of thy uncles; ye'll need to know them."

Elminster's eyes flickered. "So tell."

"The eldest—thy chief enemy—is Belaur. A big, bellowing bully of a man, for all he's seen but nine-and-twenty winters. Cruel in the hunt and on the field, but the best trained to arms of all the princes. He's shorter of wits than he thinks he is, an' was Uthgrael's favorite until he showed his cruel ways an', o'er and o'er again, his short temper. He proclaimed himself king six summers ago, but many folk up and down the Delimbiyr don't recognize his title. They know what befell."

Elminster nodded. "And the second son?"

" 'Tis thought he's dead. Elthaun was a soft-tongued womanizer whose every third word was false. All the realm knew him for a master of intrigue, but he fled Hastarl a step ahead of Belaur's armsmen. The word is, some of the magelords found him in Calimshan later that year, hiding in a cellar in some city—an' used spells to make his death long and lingering."

"The third." Elminster was marking them off on his fingers; Helm grinned at that.

"Cauln was killed before Belaur claimed the throne. He was a sneaking, suspicious sort an' always liked watching wizards hurl fire an' the like. He fancied himself a wizard—an' was tricked into a spell-duel by a mage commonly thought to be hired for the purpose by Elthaun. The mage turned Cauln into a snake—fitting—an' then burst him apart from within with a spell I've never recognized or heard named. Then the first magelords Belaur had brought in struck him down in turn, 'for the safety of the realm.' I recall them proclaiming 'Death for treason!' in the streets of Hastarl when the news was cried."

Helm shook his head. "Then came your father. He was always quiet an' insisted on fairness among nobles and common folk. The people loved him for that, but there was little respect for him at court. He retired to Heldon early on, an' most folk in Hastarl forgot him. I never knew Uthgrael thought highly of him—but that sword ye bear proves he did."

"Four princes, thus far," Elminster said, nodding as if to nail them down in memory. "The others?"

Helm counted on his own grubby fingers. "Othglas was next—a fat man full of jolly jests, who stuffed himself at feasts every night he could. He was stouter than a barrel an' could barely wheeze his way around on two feet. He liked to poison those who displeased him an' made quite a push through the ranks of those at court, downing foes an' any who so much as spoke a word aloud against him, and advancing his own supporters."

Elminster stared at him, frowning. "Ye make my uncles seem like a lot of villains."

Helm looked steadily back at him. "That was the common judgment up an' down the Delimbiyr, aye. I but report to ye what they did; if ye come to the same judgment as most folk did, doubtless the gods will agree with ye."

He scratched himself again, took a pull from his flask, and added, "When Belaur took the throne, his pet mages made it clear they knew what Othglas was up to an' threatened to put him to death before all the court for it. So he fled to Dalniir an' joined the Huntsmen, who worship Malar. I doubt the Beastlord has ever had so fat a priest before—or since."

"Does he still live?"

Helm shook his head. "Most of Athalantar knows what befell; the magelords made sure we all heard. They turned him into a boar during a hunt, an' he was slain by his own underpriests."

Elminster shuddered despite himself, but all he said was, "The next prince?"

"Felodar—the one who went off to Calimshan. Gold and gems are his love; he left the realm before Uthgrael died, seeking them. Wherever he went, he fostered trade betwixt there and here, pleasing the king very much—an' bringing Athalantar what little name an' wealth it has in Faerun beyond the Delimbiyr valley today. I think the king'd have been less pleased if he'd known Felodar was raking in gold coins as fast as he could close his hands on them . . . trading in slaves, drugs, an' dark magic. He's still doing that, as far as I know, at least chin-deep in the intrigues of Calimshan." Helm chuckled suddenly. "He's even hired mages an' sent them here to work spells against Belaur's magelords."

"Not one to turn thy back on, for even a quick breath?" Elminster asked wryly, and Helm grinned and nodded.

"Last, there's Nrymm, the youngest. A timid, frail, sullen little brat, as I recall. He was brought up by women of the court after the queen's death, an' may never have stepped outside the gates of Athalgard in his life. He disappeared about four summers ago."

"Dead?"

Helm shrugged. "That, or held captive somewhere by the magelords so they have another blood heir of Uthgrael in their power should anything happen to Belaur."

Elminster reached for the flask; Helm handed it over. The youth drank carefully, sneezed once, and handed it back. He licked his lips, and said, "Ye don't make it sound a noble thing to be a prince of Athalantar."

Helm shrugged. "It's for every prince, himself, to make it a noble thing; a duty most princes these days seem to forget."

Elminster looked down at the Lion Sword, which had somehow found its way into his hands again. "What should I do now?"

Helm shrugged. "Go west, to the Horn Hills, and run with the outlaws there. Learn how to live hard, an' use a blade—an' kill. Your revenge, lad, isn't catching one mage in a privy an' running a sword up his backside—the gods have set ye up against far too many princes an' wizards an' hired lickspittle armsmen for that. Even if they all lined up and presented their behinds, your arm'd grow tired before the job was done."

He sighed and added, "Ye spoke truth when ye said it'll be your life's work. Ye have to be less the dreamy boy an' more the knight, an' somehow keep well clear of magelords until ye've learned how to stay alive more'n one battle, when the armsmen of Athalantar come looking to kill ye. Most of 'em aren't much in a fight—but right now, neither are ye. Go to the hills and offer your blade to the outlaws at least two winters. In the cities, everything is under the hand—an' the taint—of wizards. Evil rules, and good men must needs be outlaws—or corpses—if they're to stay good. So be ye an outlaw an' learn to be a good one." He did not quite smile as he added, "If ye survive, travel Faerun until ye find a weapon sharp enough to slay Neldryn—and then come back, and do it."

"Slay who?"

"Neldryn Hawklyn—probably the most powerful of the mage-lords."

Elminster eyed him with sudden fire in his blue-gray eyes. "Ye said ye knew no names of magelords! Is this what a knight of Athalantar calls 'truth'?"

Helm spat aside, into the darkness. "Truth?" He leaned forward. "Just what is 'truth,' boy?"

Elminster frowned. "It is what it is," he said icily. "I know of no hidden meanings."

"Truth," Helm said, "is a weapon. Remember that."

Silence hung between them for a long moment, and then Elminster said, "Right, I've learned thy clever lesson. Tell me then, O wise knight: how much else of all ye've said can I trust? About my father and my uncles?"

Helm hid a smile. When this lad's voice grew quiet, it betokened danger. No bluster about this one. He deserved a fair answer, well enough. The knight said simply, "All of it. As best I know. If ye're still hungry for names to work revenge on, add these to thy tally: Magelords Seldinor Stormcloak and Kadeln Olothstar—but I'd not know the faces of any of the three if I bumped noses with them in a brothel bathing pool."

Elminster regarded the unshaven, stinking man steadily. "Ye are not what I expected a knight of Athalantar to be."

Helm met his gaze squarely. "Ye thought to see shining armor, Prince? Astride a white horse as tall as a cottage? Courtly manners? Noble sacrifices? Not in this world, lad—not since the Queen of the Hunt died."

"Who?"

Helm sighed and looked away. "I forget ye know naught of your own realm. Queen Syndrel Hornweather; your granddam, Uthgrael's queen, an' mistress of all his stag hunts." He looked into the darkness, and added softly, "She was the most beautiful lady I've ever seen."

Elminster got up abruptly. "My thanks for this, Helm Stoneblade. I must be on my way before any of thy fellow wolves return from plundering Heldon. If the gods smile, we shall meet again."

Helm looked up at him. "I hope so, lad. I hope so—an' let it be when Athalantar is free of magelords again, an' my 'fellow wolves,' the true knights of Athalantar, can ride again."

He held out his hands. The flask was in one, and the bread in the other.

"Go west, to the Horn Hills," he said roughly, "an' take care not to be seen. Move at dusk an' dawn, and keep to fields and forest. 'Ware armsmen at patrol. Out there, they slay first, an' ask thy corpse its business after. Never forget: the blades the wizards hire are not knights; today's armsmen of Athalantar have no honor." He spat to one side thoughtfully and added, "If ye meet with outlaws, tell them Helm sent ye, an' ye're to be trusted."

Elminster took the bread and the flask. Their eyes met, and he nodded his thanks.

"Remember," Helm said, "tell no one thy true name—an' don't ask fool questions about princes or magelords, either. Be someone else 'til 'tis time."

Elminster nodded. "Have my trust, Sir Knight, and my thanks." He turned with all the gravity of his twelve winters and strode away to the mouth of the cavern.

The knight came after, grinning. Then he said, "Wait, lad— take my sword; ye'll need it. Best ye keep that hilt of thine out of sight."

The boy stopped and turned, trying not to show his excitement. A blade of his own! "What will ye use?" Elminster asked, taking the heavy, plain sword that the knight's dirty hands put into his. Buckles clinked and leather flapped, and a scabbard followed it.

Helm shrugged. "I'll loot me another. I'm supposed to serve any prince of the realm with my sword, so . . ."

Elminster smiled suddenly and swung the sword through the air, holding it with both hands. It felt reassuringly deadly; with it in his hands, he was powerful. He thrust at an imaginary foe, and the point of the blade lifted a little.

Helm gave him a fierce grin. "Aye—take it, and go!"

Elminster took a few steps out into the meadow . . . and then spun around and grinned back at the knight. Then he turned again to the sunlit meadow, the scabbarded blade cradled carefully in his hands, and ran.

Helm took a dagger from his belt and a stone from the floor, shook his head, and went out to kill sheep, wondering when he'd hear of the lad's death. Still, the first duty of a knight is to make the realm shine in the dreams of small boys—or where else will the knights of tomorrow arise, and what will become of the realm?

At that thought, his smile faded. What will become of Athalantar, indeed?

Two

WOLVES IN WINTER

Know that the purpose of families, in the eyes of the Morninglord at least, is to make each generation a little better than the one before: stronger, perhaps, or wiser; richer, or more capable. Some folk manage one of these aims; the best and the most fortunate manage more than one. That is the task of parents. The task of a ruler is to make, or keep, a realm that allows most of its subjects to see better in their striving, down the generations, than a single improvement.

Thorndar Erlin, High Priest of Lathander
Teachings of the Morning's Glory
Year of the Fallen Fury

He was huddled in the icy white heart of a swirling snowstorm, in the Hammer of Winter, that cruel month when men and sheep alike were found frozen hard and the winds howled and shrieked through the Horn Hills night and day, blowing snows in blinding clouds across the barren highlands. It was the Year of the Loremasters, though Elminster cared not a whit. All he cared about was that it was another cold season, his fourth since Heldon burned—and he was growing very weary of them.

A hand clapped him on one thick-clad shoulder. He patted it in reply. Sargeth had the keenest eyes of them all; his touch meant he'd spotted the patrol through the curtain of driving snow. El watched him reach the other way to pass on another warning. The six outlaws, bundled up in layers upon layers of stolen and corpse-stripped cloth until they looked like the fat and shuffling rag golems of fireside fear-tales, kicked their way out of the warmth of their snowbank, fumbled to draw blades with hands clad in thick-bound rags, and waddled down into the cleft.

Wind struck hard as they came down into the narrow space between the rocks, howling billowing snow around and past them. Engarl struggled to keep his feet as the wind tugged at the long lance he bore. He'd taken it from an armsman who'd needed it no more—Engarl had brought him down with a carefully slung stone before the leaves had started to fall.

The outlaws chose their spots, flopped down to kneel in the snows, and dug in. Snow streamed around and past them, and as they settled into stillness, it cloaked them in concealing whiteness, making them mere lumps and billows of snow in the storm.

"Gods *damn* all wizards!" The voice, borne by the winds, seemed startlingly close.

So did the reply. "None o' that. Ye know better than such talk."

"*I* might. My frozen feet don't. They'd much prefer to be next to a crackling fire, back in—"

"*All* of our feet'd rather be there. They will be, gods willing, soon enough. Swording outlaws'll warm ye, if ye're sharp-eyed enough to find any. Now belt up!"

"Perhaps," Elminster commented calmly, knowing the wind would sweep his words behind him, away from the armsmen, "the gods have other plans."

He could just hear an answering chuckle from off to his left: Sargeth. A moment more . . . Then he heard a sharp query, crunching snow, and the high whinny of a startled horse. The brothers had attacked. Arghel struck first, and then Baerold gave the call—from behind, if he could get there.

It came, a roar as much like the triumph-call of a wolf as Baerold could make it. Horses reared, cried out, and bucked in the deep snows on all sides. The patrol was on top of them.

Elminster rose up out of the snow like a vengeful ghost, sword drawn. To lie still could mean being ridden over and trampled. He saw a flicker of light through the whirling whiteness, as the nearest armsman drew steel.

A moment later, Engarl's awkwardly bobbing lance took the armsman in the throat. He choked, sobbed wetly around blood as the horse under him plunged on, and then he fell, head flopping, taking the lance with him. Elminster wasted no time on the dying man; another armsman off to the right in the swirling storm was trying to spur past him through the cleft.

El ran through the slithery snow as fast as he could, the way the outlaws had shown him, rocking comically from side to side to keep from slipping in the light drifts. All of the outlaws looked like drunken bears when they ran in deep snow. As slow as he was, the horse was even slower; its hooves were slipping in the potholes that marked the trail here, and it danced and stamped for footing, nearly tossing its rider.

The armsman saw Elminster and leaned forward to hack the outlaw. Elminster ducked back, let the blade sing past, and charged in at the man's leg, clawing with one hand as he blocked a return of the man's blade with the edge of his own.

The overbalanced man in armor howled in rising despair, waved his free arm wildly in a vain attempt to find a handhold in empty air—and crashed heavily from his saddle, bouncing in the snow at Elminster's feet. El drove his blade into the man's neck while the spray of snow still shielded the man's face, shuddered as the man spasmed under his steel, and then flopped back into the snow, limp. Four years ago he'd discovered he had no love of killing . . . and it hadn't grown much easier since.

Yet it was slay or be slain out here in the outlaw-haunted hills; Elminster sprang away from the man, glancing about in the confusion of swirling snows and muffled tumult of churning hooves.

There was a grunt, a roar of pain, and the heavy thudding of body and armor striking snow-cloaked ground off to the left, followed by a wail that ended abruptly. Elminster shuddered again, but kept his blade up warily. This was when outlaws who'd grown tired of their fellows sometimes decided to make a mistake, under the cloak of the storming snow, and bring down someone who was not an armsman of Athalantar.

El expected no such treachery from his companions . . . but only the gods knew the hearts of men. Like most in the Horn Hills—those who revered Helm Stoneblade and hated the magelords, at least—this band made no war on common folk. Not wanting to bring down the wrath of the wizards on farmers whose stable-straw sometimes served as warm beds and whose frozen and forgotten pot roots could be dug up by men near starvation, the outlaws avoided their neighbors out here in the hills. Even so, they had learned never to trust them. The armsmen of Athalantar paid fifty pieces of gold per head to folk who'd guide them to outlaws. More than one outlaw had been taken by trusting overmuch.

The cold lesson was to trust nothing that lived, from birds and foxes whose alarmed flight could draw the eyes of patrols, to peddlers who might go after the gold and speak of fires or watching men they'd seen deep in the hills where outlaws were known to lurk.

Sargeth strode up through the endless fall of snow, which drifted straight down now as there came a sudden lull in the winds. He was grinning through the cloud of vapor that curled about his mouth. "All dead, El: a dozen armsmen . . . and one of them was carrying a full pack of food!"

Elminster, called Eladar among the outlaws, grunted. "No mages?"

Sargeth chuckled and laid a hand on El's arm. He left bloody marks—the gore of some armsman now lying still in the snows. "Patience," he said. "If it's wizards you want to kill, let us slay enough armsmen—and by all the gods, the mages will come."

Elminster nodded. "Anything else?" Around them, the wind screamed with fresh strength, and it was hard to see through the driven snow.

"One horse hurt. We'll butcher it and wrap it in their cloaks here. Haste, now; the wolves are as hungry as we. Engarl's found a dozen daggers or more—and at least one good helm. Baerold's collecting boots, as usual. Go you and help Nind with the cutting."

Elminster sniffed. "Blood work, as always."

Sargeth laughed and clapped him on the back. "We all have to do it to live. Look upon it as preparing yerself several good feasts, and try not to gnaw on too much raw meat as you usually do . . . unless you *like* icing yer backside in the snow and feeling kitten weak, that is."

Elminster grunted and headed through the snow where Sargeth pointed. A happy shout jerked his head around. It was Baerold, leading back a snorting horse by the reins. Good; it could drag their spoils some way before they would have to kill it to end the trail its hooves would leave.

Around them, the whistle of the wind began to die, and with it the snowfall faltered. Curses came from all around; the outlaws knew they'd have to work fast indeed if it turned cold and clear—for even the weak wizards posted to the keeps out here had magic that could find them from afar when the weather was clear.

By the favor of the gods, another squall came in soon after they left the cleft; even someone already tracking them wouldn't be able to follow. The outlaws struggled on, following Sargeth and Baerold, who knew every slope of the hills here even in blinding snows. When they came to the deep spring that never froze, a place they knew the wizards watched by magic, from afar, Baerold spoke a few soothing words to the horse—and then swung his forester's axe with brutal strength, and leapt clear of its kicking hooves as it fell.

The outlaws left the steaming remnants of the carcass for the wolves to find. Then they rolled in deep drifts to clean off the worst of the gore and went on. North into the driving storm, up ravines narrow and dark, to Wind Cavern, where icy breezes moaned endlessly into a lightless cleft. Each man in turn bent and ducked through the narrow opening, by memory crossed the uneven cave beyond, and found the faint glowstone rock that marked the mouth of the next passage. They walked into the hollow dark until they saw the faint light ahead of another glowstone. Sargeth tapped the wall of the passage slowly and deliberately six times, paused, and then tapped once more. There came an answering tap, and Sargeth took two steps and turned into an unseen side passage. The outlaws followed him into the narrow tunnel. It smelled of earth and damp stone, and descended steeply beneath the Horn Hills.

Light grew somewhere ahead, ale-hued faint light from a cavernful of luminous fungi. As they came out into it, Sargeth said his name calmly to the darkness beyond, and the men who stood there set down their crossbows and replied. "All back safe?"

"All safe—and with meat to roast," Sargeth said triumphantly.

"Horse," a second voice asked sourly, "or chopped armsman?"

They exchanged chuckles before proceeding down another passage, through a cavern where daggers of rock jutted from floor and ceiling like the frozen jaws of some great monster, to a shaft in which vivid red light glowed. A stout ladder led down the hole into a large cavern always wreathed in steam. The light and the vapor came from rocky clefts at its far end, where folk sat huddled in blankets or lay snoring. With each step, the dank air grew warmer until the weary warriors stood beside the scalding waters of the hot spring and welcoming hands reached up to pat or clasp theirs. They were home, in the place proudly called Lawless Castle.

It was a good place, furnished with heaped blankets and old cloaks. Dwarves had shown it to Helm Stoneblade long ago, and from time to time the outlaws still found firewood, prepared torches, or cases of quarrels left in the deeper side-passages, next to the privies the outlaws used. The wrinkled old outlaw woman Mauri had told El once that they'd never seen the dwarves, "But they want us here. The Stout Folk like anything that weakens the wizards, for they see their doom in men growing overstrong. . . . We already outbreed them like rabbits, an' if ever we o'ermatch elven magic, they'll be staring at their graves. . . ."

Now she looked up through her warts and bristles at the arriving band, grinned toothlessly at them, and said, "Food, valiant warriors?"

"Aye," Engarl joked, "and when we've feasted, we'll give ye some to replace it." He chuckled at his jest, but the dozen or so ragged outlaws awake around them only snorted sourly in reply;

they'd no food left but four shriveled potatoes Mauri had kept safe in the filthy folds of her gargantuan bosom for the last two days, and had taken to chewing on the bitter glow-fungi to still aching stomachs while they waited for one of the bands to bring back meat.

Now they hustled to get a fire going and drag out the cooking frame of rusting sword blades woven together in a rough square. The band stamped the last snows from their boots and unwrapped their bloody bundles. Mauri leaned forward, slapping outlaw hands away to see what had been brought to her table.

Sargeth's band was the best; all of them knew that. El, the worst blade in it but the fastest on his feet, was glad to be a part of it and kept silent when his fellows fought or blustered. They were too cold and exhausted most of the winters to afford dispute among themselves. Once a wizard had found Wind Cavern and died in a hail of crossbow quarrels—but otherwise, Elminster had seen the hated mages of Athalantar little in the passing years; the outlaws struck at patrols of armsmen so often that the magelings had stopped riding with them.

A smiling, red-bearded rogue they all knew as Javal blew to make the fire catch and said with satisfaction, "We caught another two coming from Daera's earlier this night."

"That'd best be enough for a time," Sargeth grunted in reply as he and his companions shed gauntlets, headgear, and the heaviest of the furs and scraps of scavenged leather they wore, "or they'll think her night-comfort lasses are working with us an' burn them out, or lie ready with a mage to work our own trap on us."

Javal's smile went away. He made a face and nodded slowly. "Ye see the right road as usual, Sar."

Sargeth merely grunted and held his hands to the growing warmth of the kindling fire. Armsmen from Heldreth's Horn, the outermost fortress of Athalantar, had gone out to buy the favors of village lasses for as long as the keep had stood. A dozen summers back, some maids had converted an old farm into a house of pleasure and sold their guests wildflower wine besides; the outlaws had slain more than a few armsmen riding home from there drunken and alone. "Aye, 'tis best we leave the lustlorn alone for a time, an' catch 'em again in spring."

* * * * *

"What, and leave them to slay and pillage until spring? How many more warriors can you afford to lose?"

The wizard's voice was cold—colder than the chill battlements where they stood, looking out over the ice-cloaked waters of the Unicorn Run. The swordmaster of Sarn Torel spread strong, hairy hands and said helplessly, "None, Lord Mage. That's why I dare send no more—every man who rides west out of here's going to his death and knows it. They're *that* close to open defiance now . . . and I've the law to keep in the streets here, too. If caravan-merchants and peddlers are fool enough to go from realm to realm in the deep snows, let 'em look to their own hides, I say—and leave the bandits to freeze in the Hills without our swords to entertain 'em."

The wizard's gaze then was even colder than his voice had been.

The swordmaster quailed inwardly and firmly took hold of the stone merlon in front of him to keep from stepping back a pace or two and showing his fear. He dropped his own gaze to the frozen moss clinging to cracks and chips in the stone and wished he were somewhere else. Somewhere warmer, where they'd never heard of wizards.

"I do not recall the king asking for your view of your duties—though I've no doubt he'll be most interested to find how . . . creatively . . . they cleave from his own," came the mage's voice, silken-soft now.

The swordmaster forced himself to turn and stare into dark eyes that glittered with malice. " 'Tis *your* wish then, Lord Mage," he asked, stressing the word just enough that the wizard would know that the swordmaster thought the king a wiser warrior than all his strutting magelords, and would have no such view of his swordmaster's prudence, "that I send more armsmen to patrol from the Horn?"

The wizard hesitated, then as softly as before, asked, "Let me know *your* wish, Swordmaster. Perhaps we can come to some agreement."

The swordmaster took a deep breath and held those dark, deadly eyes with his own. "Send to the Horn a cutter full of mages, apprentices even, providing that one mage of experience commands them. Twenty armsmen—all I dare spare—ride with them to the Horn, and from there act as necessary to hunt these outlaws with magic and destroy them."

They stared at each other for a long, chill moment, and then, slowly, Magelord Kadeln Olothstar smiled—thinly, but the swordmaster had wondered if the man knew how. "A stout plan, indeed, Swordmaster. I *knew* we could agree on something this day." He looked north over the snow-clad farms across the river for a moment, then added, "I hope a suitable sledge can be speedily found rather than one that comes not or must be built and finds us still preparing come spring."

The swordmaster pointed down over the battlements with one gauntleted hand. "See the logs there by the mill? One of those cutters beneath 'em can be free by tonight, and a pair of the huts we use to cover the wells lashed atop it before morn."

The wizard smiled softly, a snake contemplating prey that cannot escape. "Then in the morn they'll set out. You shall have twelve mages, Swordmaster—one of them Magelord Landorl Valadarm."

The warrior nodded, wondering privately whether Landorl was a fumbling dolt or someone who had simply earned Kadeln's displeasure. He hoped for the latter. Then this Landorl might at least be useful if the gods-cursed outlaws attacked the cutter.

The two men smiled tightly at each other, there on the battlements, and then both turned their backs deliberately to show they dared to and strode slowly away with a show of casual unconcern. Their every step told the world they were strong men, free of all fear.

The battlements of Sarn Torel stood still and silent, unimpressed, as they would stand when both men were long in their graves. It takes a lot to impress a castle wall.

* * * * *

Elminster was happily blowing on scorched fingers, licking the last scraps of horseflesh from them, when one of the watchers burst into the cavern and gasped out, "Patrol! Found the way in—killed Aghelyn, an' prob'ly more. Some o' them ran straight back to tell where we lair!"

All over the cavern men swore and scrambled to their feet, shouting. Sargeth cut through the din with a bellow. "Crossbows and blades; all but Mauri. The lads and the wounded, stand guard in the glowcavern—all others with me, *now!*"

As they ran through the darkness, swearing and ringing their weapons off the unseen stone in their haste, Sargeth added, "Brerest! Eladar! Try to get clear of the fight here and go after those who're running back to the wizards—you're the fastest afoot of all here old enough to swing a real blade. I need those armsmen *all* dead—or *we* will be."

"Aye," Elminster and Brerest panted, and went through the mouth of Wind Cavern in a roll. The quarrel that sought their lives hissed past and struck the rock within easy reach of Sar-

geth's head. The second one missed entirely—but Elminster
came to a stop behind a snow-cloaked boulder in time to see the
third take Sargeth in the eye, and drive him back like a crumpled bag of bones, to slide down the rock wall, twitching.

Elminster laid his drawn dagger beside him in the snow,
snatched up the old, mended crossbow that had fallen from Sargeth's hands, and cranked at it for all he was worth. The windlass clattered loudly, but outlaws were rushing past and firing
their own bows now, and shouts told him that some of their bolts
were finding their marks.

Loaded at last. "Tempus aid my aim," Elminster murmured,
scratching his finger on his dagger tip until blood came to seal
the prayer to the war god. Then he laid the ready bow down,
whipped off the helm he wore, and waved it on one side of the
boulder.

A quarrel hissed past. Elminster scooped up the bow and was
around the boulder in an instant. As he'd expected, the armsman was standing to watch his target die—so Elminster had a
clear shot at his face, past a knot of howling, hacking outlaws
and coolly slaying armsmen.

El aimed carefully—and missed. Cursing, he leapt back—but
Brerest came past him with a loaded crossbow of his own, set
himself, and fired carefully.

The armsman had started to turn away, seeking cover. His
face sprouted a quarrel, his head spun around, and he staggered
back and fell.

Elminster threw down his bow, snatched up his dagger, and
sprinted through the snow, dodging desperately fighting men.
He was still a few hard-running paces short of the first rock
large enough to shelter behind when an armsman rose from behind the second rock, ready crossbow in hand, to aim into the
fray in front of the cavern. Seeing Elminster, he swung his
weapon around hurriedly. There was no way he could miss.

Elminster skidded to a desperate stop, then changed direction and dived into the nearest snowbank. He landed hard in a
flurry of snow, slid across unseen smooth rock, and flipped over,
expecting to feel the thump of death striking home at any moment.

It didn't come. El wiped snow from his face and looked up.

Brerest or one of the other outlaws had been lucky. The armsman was curled over the top of his rock, barehanded and groaning, a shaft through his shoulder.

"Thankee, Tempus," Elminster said with feeling, took two
running steps, and flung himself right over the top of the first

boulder, heels first, to crash down on whomever might be there.

The armsman was on his knees, struggling with a jammed windlass; Elminster's landing smashed him to the ground like a rag doll, and El dragged his dagger across the man's throat a breath later. "For Elthryn, prince of Athalantar!" he whispered, and found himself blinking back sudden tears as his father's face came to mind.

Not *now,* he told himself desperately, and ran on toward the next boulder. The wounded man saw him and struggled to get aside, groaning. Elminster drove his dagger home and snarled, "For Amrythale, his princess!" Then he ducked down, scooped up the man's loaded bow from where it had fallen—and looked up in time to fire it into another armsman, who had just risen from cover with a spear in his hand. Ahead, another armsman took an outlaw quarrel in the hand, screamed, and fell back behind his rock, sobbing.

The clash of arms back by the cavern had ceased. El risked a look back and saw only dead men. They lay in bloody heaps in front of the cavern . . . and just a few paces away lay Brerest, both hands clutching forever at a quarrel that stood out of his heart.

Gods! Sargeth and Brerest both . . . and everyone, if those armsmen got word back to the wizards. How many armsmen were there? Four dead, for sure, Elminster thought as he ran forward, crouching low, plus all those by the cavern. The hail of quarrels hissing up and down the ravine had ceased—was everyone dead?

No, the sobbing armsman and perhaps two more lay ahead, somewhere in these rocks. There had to be at least two patrols here, and they'd not have sent more than three from each patrol—perhaps only three in all—to report to the wizards. To have any hope of catching them, he had to find the horses these'd come on, and . . . of course! Some of the missing armsmen, two at least, were holding the horses below.

Elminster crawled around the boulder, keeping low, and took four daggers and a spear from the two dead men. An outlaw quarrel hissed out of the cavern and almost took him from behind; he sighed and crawled on in the snow.

He had almost reached the sobbing armsman when another rose from behind a rock to aim carefully at the cavern mouth. Elminster cast the spear; it was in the air before the man caught sight of him.

The armsman didn't have time to change his aim. His bow hurled a quarrel harmlessly down the ravine as the spear took

him in the breast, plucking him away from his rock, and flung
him back to crash down on his shoulders in the snow, bouncing
and arching in agony.

Elminster's charge took him onto the armsman's bloody
chest, and he stabbed down again with his bloody dagger. "For
Elthryn, prince of Athalantar!" he snarled as he dealt death,
and the warrior under his knees managed a startled look before
all light fled from behind his eyes.

Elminster flung himself aside in a roll. Quarrels and spears
from both ends of the ravine crossed in the air above the dead
warrior where he'd been kneeling. Scrabbling in the snow, Elminster slew the man who was still clutching his bleeding hand.
"For my mother, Amrythale!"

Panting, he took up the man's bow and ducked behind a rock
to catch his breath and ready the weapon. His boots bristled
with spare daggers now, and the bow was soon loaded. He
crouched low, cradled it in his arms, and came around the last
rock with his finger on the trigger.

No one was there. Elminster stood frozen for a moment, and
then knelt down. Another outlaw quarrel hummed past to fall
into the empty snows below the ravine. El watched it go, and
then looked up. He could climb the shoulder of the ravine and
from above see where the armsmen had gone; the snow had
stopped falling and the wind had died, leaving the hills around
white and smooth with fresh-fallen snow.

Everyone could see him as he climbed, too, aye—but then,
Tyche put a little hazard into everyone's life.

Elminster sighed as he plucked the quarrel from its groove
and slid it down into one of his boots. He left the bow cocked as
he slung it across his back by the carry-strap and scrambled up
the slope.

He'd not climbed more than his own height before a quarrel
tore into the snow a handspan away from his head. El snatched
at it, kicked himself free of the snowy rocks and frozen grass,
and slid back down the slope, feigning lifelessness. The quarrel
came with him as he crashed on his face in the snow, trying to
keep his bow unbroken.

Tears blinded him for a moment, but his nose didn't seem
broken. He blinked them away and spat out snow while he slid
the bow free. It was unbroken; he loaded it, emitting a drawn-
out rattling groan to cover the sounds he made.

An armsman with a second crossbow ready rose out of a
snowy thicket nearby, looking for the man he'd hit. He and Elminster saw each other at the same instant. Both fired. And

both missed. Elminster found his feet as the quarrel sang past him—would he *forever* be running around this ravine, panting and slipping?—snatched daggers from his boots, and ran toward the thicket, blades flashing in both fists. He was afraid the warrior had a third bow cocked and ready. . . .

He was right. The armsman rose again with a triumphant smile on his face—and Elminster flung a dagger at him. The man's smile tightened in fear, and he fired in haste.

The quarrel leapt at Elminster, who flung himself desperately over backward. As he fell, his knife met the quarrel with a clang and a spark. The dagger spun wildly away, and the quarrel burned past Elminster, ripping open his chin and thrusting his head around.

El roared in pain and fell on his knees, hearing the crunching of the armsman's boots behind him as the warrior came running. Elminster turned, shaking his head to clear it and growling at the pain. The man was scant paces away, sword raised to slay, when El flung the dagger in his other hand into the man's face.

It clanged harmlessly off the nose guard of the armsman's helm, but the man's swing missed the diving youth, the sword striking the snowy ground and the rocks beneath. The warrior roared and fell heavily on top of Elminster's left hand.

Elminster screamed. Gods, the *pain!* The man rolled about atop his hand, kicking at the snow to get a grip with his boots. Elminster sobbed, and the world turned green and yellow and swam fuzzily. He grabbed at his belt with his free hand. Nothing there. The man grunted; Elminster felt the hot breath of the armsman turning to face him and bring his blade down. His weight drove the hidden bulk of the Lion Sword, on its thong, bruisingly into Elminster's chest.

Desperate, Elminster tore at the throat of his jerkin. His fingers found the hilt of the sword. Over long nights in his first winter in the hills, he'd sharpened the broken stub of the blade until it had a keen, raw edge and point—but beyond the quillons, the weapon wasn't even as long as his hand. Its puny length saved him now. As the armsman's face glared into his, inches away, and his elbow swept his sword up for a gutting thrust, Elminster thrust the Lion Sword up and into his eye.

"For Elthryn, prince of Athalantar!" he hissed—and as the hot rush of blood drenched him, found himself sinking into red, wet darkness. . . .

* * * * *

He was floating somewhere dark and still. Whispers rose and fell around him, half-heard through a slow, rhythmic thudding. . . . Elminster felt the pain of his hand and an answering ache all around. In his head? Yes, and the white glow was rising and pulsing, now—the one he saw when he gathered his mind. The glow grew, and the pain lessened.

Ah, *thus!* Elminster *pushed* with his mind, and the white radiance faded. He felt a little tired, but the pain receded . . . he pushed again, and again felt weaker, but now the pain was almost gone.

So. He could push pain aside. Could he truly heal himself? Elminster bent his will . . . and suddenly all his aches and hurts returned, and he could feel cold, hard ground beneath his shoulders, and the wet stickiness of sweat all over. From the place of whispers, he swam up, up, and burst out into the light. . . .

The sky was blue and cloudless overhead. Elminster lay on his back on snowy rocks, stiff, cold, and aching. Gingerly, he rolled to one side and looked around. No sign of anyone or any movement—good, because his head swam and pounded and he had to duck down again to catch his breath. The darkness again rushed up to claim him . . . and it felt so good, his head so heavy. . . .

* * * * *

A little later, he rolled over. Snow vultures flapped heavily into the air, circled over the ravine, and squalled complaints at him.

The last armsman lay dead beside him, the Lion Sword in his face. Elminster winced at the sight, but put his hand to the blade, turned his head away, and pulled it free. Wiping it in the snow, he squinted at the dimming sky—steel-gray now, with the last light of day ebbing behind full clouds—and got up. He had a task to finish if he wanted to live.

He felt weak and a little numb. Down the ravine in the open space in front of the Wind Cavern, eight or more armsmen and more than twice that many outlaws lay dead, quarrels protruding from most of the still forms. The vultures were circling overhead, and wolves would be here soon. Hopefully they'd find enough to feed on without entering the caves, where the weak would guard until armsmen came to hack them down. He'd have to slay more armsmen to prevent that . . . and he was getting sick of killing. El grinned weakly as he went down the ravine, averting his eyes from the sprawled dead he passed. Some brave outlaw warrior he was!

At the mouth of the ravine was a large trampled area trailing off into tracks of horses coming and leaving. The armsmen must have given their fellows up for dead. Elminster's shoulders sagged. He couldn't outrun horses in this deep snow. He and the other survivors were doomed . . . unless he gathered all the bows and blades he could, took them to the last outlaws waiting in the darkness, and made the caves a death-trap for the armsmen. Still, some would survive to identify the lair for later forays, and besides, what if they began by hurling a fire-spell into the caves? No.

Elminster flopped down onto a boulder to think. His sudden descent saved his life; a crossbow quarrel hummed just over his head to vanish into a snowbank close by. The youngest prince of Athalantar—perhaps the *last* prince of Athalantar—dived hastily off his boulder into the snow, face first, and floundered about in the chilly stuff until he was huddled behind the rock. He peered up whence the bolt had come.

Sure enough. High on the shoulder of the ridge, overlooking the ravine, was one armsman. They'd left one behind to pin the outlaws in their lair—or track them if they burst out in numbers. Of course—that was why so many of the outlaws wore crossbow quarrels!

Elminster sighed. Some crafty woods-warrior *he* was. Well, this armsman's horse would be somewhere just below him, around the other side of the ridge. If he could get to it and ride out of bowshot, in time . . .

Aye, and frogs might fly, too . . . Elminster frowned and tried to recall where the crossbows had fallen. That last armsman, who'd almost slain him . . . yes! He'd had three bows, and dropped them all after firing—in that thicket, there! El sighed once, and then started to crawl on his belly in the snow. A quarrel hissed past him again—close, but hopefully there'd be no time for a second shot.

"Tempus and Tyche aid me; I feel the need of both of ye," Elminster muttered, hurrying in the cold powdery snow. And then he was in the thicket, crouching low as a third crossbow bolt rattled snow off the trunks around him, cracked against a sapling, and fell broken into the snow somewhere off to the left. How different battle was from what the traveling minstrels sang about!

That thought brought him to the first and second bows, lying in deep snow. They were wet—but if the gods smiled would still fire true until they dried; they'd doubtless twist a bit then. A belt-box and the scattered quarrels it had held were strewn beside the bows.

Elminster calmly worked the dead man's windlass. From the ridge above, he could hear the faint clatter of the living armsman's own bow-winch. The third bow lay fallen a few paces in front of the thicket; Elminster didn't dare go out to get it. When both bows were loaded and full-ready, Elminster started to worm his way sideways in the thicket.

A quarrel dusted snow from a tree back where he'd been. Elminster grinned tightly and stepped forward for a good look. The armsman had just bobbed down to get his second bow. El set down one of his own and raised the other, aimed at where the man had sunk out of view.

The moment he saw movement there, he fired.

Tyche was with him. The man rose right into the path of the quarrel; Elminster heard his startled gasp, saw him throw his hands up, and watched the man's crossbow crash and cartwheel down the snow-clad slope into the ravine. A moment later, thudding heavily, the body of the armsman followed it.

Elminster unloaded his second bow, fired it empty to leave its workings loose, then snatched up all three bows and the belt-box of quarrels and hurried around the ridge.

There was the horse—alone and unguarded, thank the gods! In a few breaths, Elminster had tied his gear to a seemingly endless collection of saddle-straps and thongs, and was in the saddle, urging the patrol-mount to follow the armsmen's trail. It went willingly enough, but slipped and slid in the snow in something a little faster than a trot and a lot slower than a gallop. The tracks ahead were clear and easy to follow so Elminster kicked his heels at the horse's flanks and urged it on. He had to get to Heldreth's Horn before any wizard there caught sight of him by some sort of scrying-spell and dealt death from afar.

Soon he was riding hard, the crossbows bouncing bruisingly at his back, and the mist of his breath streaming back behind him into the darkening air. Night was coming down fast over the hills. He had to succeed; the lives of the outlaws trapped back at Lawless Castle depended on it.

As he rode, he smiled at a sudden memory: his father's careful lessons on the duty of every man and maid in the kingdom, from farmer to king. If Elthryn had dwelt longer on the duties of king and prince than on those of a farmer or miller, Elminster had thought this only right—the duties were so much grander, the power mightier, the responsibilities heavier than those of all others. He'd not for a moment suspected that he was a prince or would become one when Elthryn died. He recalled clearly his father's words: "A king's first duty is to his subjects. Their lives are in his hands, and he must always look to their brightest, surest future in what he does. All depend on him—and all are lost if he neglects his duties, or governs by whim or wilful heart. Obedience is his due, aye, but he must earn loyalty. Some kings never learn this. And what are princes but young wilful lads learning to be kings?"

"What indeed, Father?" Elminster asked the wind of his passing as he rode hard for the Horn. The wind did not deign to reply.

Three

ALL TOO MUCH DEATH IN THE SNOWS

If in winter ye walk
When snow is deep
Beware when ye talk—
For afar echoes creep.

Old Sword Coast Snow-Rune

Tyche, at least, had heard his prayers. As Elminster rode
down a dusky valley along the clear trail the armsmen had left,
he caught sight of them gathered below, building fires—and the
trails in the snow made it clear they'd met with and joined another patrol instead of going down to the keep . . . which was still
a good ride away. Night would find them very soon, deep in the
hills, and they'd halted to make camp.

"Thankee, Tyche," El told the wind wryly, as he pulled his
weary mount to a halt. All his foes were gathered together and
would soon halt within his reach.

As with all the gifts of Lady Luck, this one was double-edged.
All he had to do was kill the five armsmen who'd fled from Lawless Castle—*and* all the others they'd met with down there. For
a fleeting moment, he wished he were some great mage to send
swift death screaming down upon the gathered camp below—or
to ride a dragon down to rake, burn, and scatter.

Elminster shivered at that memory of Heldon and touched
the Lion Sword where it rode on its thong inside his jerkin.
"Prince Elminster is a *warrior*," he told the wind with grand dignity—and then chuckled. More soberly, he added, "He kills a
man to warm up, helps cut up his horse and eat it, and then goes
out into a battle and slaughters eight more. As if that's not
enough, he's now about to sweep down alone on a score or more
ready-armed armsmen. What else could he be but a warrior?"

"A fool, of course," a cold voice answered from very near. Elminster whirled around in his saddle. A dark-robed man was
standing watching him—standing on empty air, booted feet well
above the unbroken snow.

El's hand stabbed to his belt, found one of the salvaged daggers he'd thrust there, and hurled it. It spun end over end, flashing as it caught the light of the newly kindled campfires below, and plunged straight through the man to bury itself deep in the snows beyond.

Only half the man's mouth smiled. "This is but a spell-image, fool," he said coldly. "You come riding hard, following the trail to our camp—who are you and why come you here?"

Elminster frowned, feigning ignorance as his thoughts raced. "Have I reached Athalantar yet?" He eyed the mage and added, "I seek a magelord, to pass on a message. Are ye such a one?"

"Unfortunately for you, I am," the man replied, "*Prince* Elminster. Oh, yes, I heard your proud little speech. You are Elthryn's son, then, the one we've been seeking."

Elminster sat very still, thinking. Could a wizard send a spell through his image? A cold inner voice answered: Why not?

Best keep moving, in case . . . He urged the horse with his knees until it trotted ahead, then turned it, circling. "That is the name I have taken to bring doom down on a certain magelord," he said, passing the image. It turned in the air and watched him in easy silence. Hmmm . . .

"Other magelords," Elminster added darkly, "have plans of their own."

The watching wizard laughed. "Well, of *course* they do, boastful boy—always have had. See me shiver at your sinister words? Do you dance and play cards, too?"

Elminster felt himself flush with anger. To ride so hard only to be taunted by a wizard from afar while armsmen no doubt rode out to encircle him and bring him down at leisure . . . He spurred away from the wizard, flinging only the calm reply, "Yes, of *course* I do," over his shoulder as he went.

He rode hard back the way he'd come but turned up the nearest easy slope to gain a height to look back. The wizard's image hadn't moved—but as he watched, it winked out and was gone, leaving behind only the circle of beaten snow where he'd ridden around it. Aye, there, below—two bands of mounted armsmen were setting out, riding hard in different directions to curve about and ring him in with swords and bows.

Full night was falling, but the stars were bright overhead, and Selune would rise all too soon. How far could that wizard see him?

Two plans sprang to mind: somehow ride wide around them all on his weary mount and sweep down on the camp, hoping to find the wizard and take him with quarrels before he could loose a spell. That's what a bard or teller-of-tales would expect him to do, to be sure. It sounded the work of a reckless fool even to his own ears.

The other plot was to get into the path of one band, dig into the snow with all his bows ready, and let his horse run free. If one band of armsmen followed it—he'd have time, perhaps, to take those coming toward him down with his bows, somehow get one of their mounts, and *then* attack the camp. Then, somehow victorious over a wizard who knew he was coming, he'd set forth on the trail of the other armsmen and take them down one by one with quarrels . . . it sounded almost as wild.

He quoted a line of a ballad he'd once heard, "Princes rush in, shouldering fools aside, and find glory," and turned his horse to the right to intercept the band of armsmen he could see better. He thought he counted nine riders, no telling how many were in the other group.

His tired horse stumbled twice on the ride and nearly fell when they blundered into a pocket of deep, loose snow.

"Gently," El murmured to it, suddenly feeling his own aches and weariness in full. All he could do in his mind was numb the pain for a time, and—he touched his chin thoughtfully—stop bleeding. He was no invincible warrior.

So? This attack required a fool, not an invincible warrior . . . but then, riding away would be a fool's act, too, without even the comfort of standing up for the memory of his mother and father and for a day when wizards would not rule Athalantar, and the knights would ride again. . . .

"The knights *will* ride again," he told the wind; it whirled his words away unheard behind him as he came to a good place for the ambush he planned, a narrow gully on the lee slope of a snow-swept rise, and brought his horse to a halt.

Getting down stiffly—he'd not been on a horse much since Heldon burned, and his legs were reminding him of that all too sharply—El unslung his bows and took what he'd need. "Grant me luck," he told the wind, but as before, it made no reply. Taking a deep breath of the sharp air, he slapped the horse's rump and roared. The beast bolted, paused to look back, and then trotted off into the snow. Elminster was alone in the night.

Not for long, by the gods. Nine armsmen in full armor were riding this way, after his blood. Elminster knelt in the snow just below the crest of the rise and worked his windlass like a frenzied-wits.

By the time he had all three bows loaded and ready, he was gasping for breath and could hear the creak of leather and jangle of metal on the wind. The armsmen were coming down upon him. Lying in the snow, breath streaming back over his shoulder, he arranged the bows, planted four daggers in the snow for ready snatching, and waited.

His life hung on the hope that they'd not have bows ready themselves—and wouldn't see him in time. Elminster shook his head at his own recklessness and found his mouth suddenly dry. Well, whatever befell, it wouldn't be long now.

There was a sudden thunder of hooves, shouts, and the clash of arms. What could be—? And suddenly Elminster had no time for speculation as an armsman burst into view, galloping hard, crouched low over the neck of his horse. The prince of Athalantar raised his bow carefully, steadied it, and fired.

The horse plunged on, rearing and giving a high grunt of alarm as it saw the steep descending slope. With no time to veer or slow, it felt the man on its back fall sideways, hard, pulling on its reins. It reared, fighting the reins that were tugging its head around. Its hooves skidded in the snow, and it crashed atop its rider. Together they slid down the hill. The horse sprang up and pranced away, shaking its head as if to clear it. The man lay still in the trampled snow.

No more horsemen rode into view, and from over the brow of the snow-clad rise came the shouts and steely skirl of battle. Elminster frowned in puzzlement, and then took up his daggers, thrusting them back into his belt. Holding his second bow ready, he advanced cautiously until he could see over the crest.

Mounted men were circling and hacking at each other in the nightgloom atop the hill. One group was clad in motley garb, the odds and ends of half a hundred mismatched armors it seemed, and where by all the gods had they come from? The other group were armsmen, outnumbered more than two to one and fast losing. As Elminster watched, one soldier of Athalantar broke free of the fray, spurring his horse desperately, and set off across the hills at a gallop.

The prince of Athalantar set his feet in the snow, raised his bow, and fired. The quarrel passed over the armsman's shoulder, and fleeing warrior galloped on. Elminster cursed and ran back for his third bow. Scooping it up, he sprinted along the edge of the hill. The distant armsman was smaller now, but coming into clear view as his horse climbed the unbroken snow of the next slope. Elminster aimed carefully, fired—and saw his quarrel speed true.

The armsman threw up his arms, tried to clutch at his back with both hands, and fell out of his saddle. The horse went on without him.

"I didn't *think* we had any bowmen with us, this night!"

Elminster turned in delighted recognition at that cheery voice. "Helm!"

The leather-jawed knight wore the same tattered leather armor, rusty gauntlets, dented helm, and stubbly beard El remembered—and probably, by the smell of him, hadn't taken them off or washed any part of him since that day on the meadow above Heldon. He rode a mean-looking black horse that was as scarred as its rider, and the long, curved sword in his fist was nicked and shining darkly with fresh blood.

"How came you here?" Elminster asked, grinning with the sudden hope that he might not die this night after all.

The knight of Athalantar leaned forward in his saddle. "We've just come from Lawless Castle," he said with raised brows. "Quite a few good men lying dead back there, but Mauri couldn't find Eladar among them."

"When I ran out of armsmen to kill, I came here," Elminster replied gravely. "They'd found the castle, and I had to slay the rest before they had a chance to report it. They went to a camp—those fires, there—and there's another band of armsmen, probably larger than this one, over there somewhere." He pointed into the night. "They were circling to take me."

Helm bellowed, "Onthrar! *To me!*" over his shoulder, and then said, "Join us, then, an' we'll ride 'em down together. There're empty saddles in plenty to spare!"

Elminster shook his head. "My business lies yonder," he said, pointing with a nod of his head toward the unseen camp. "With wizards."

Helm's fierce grin faded. "Are ye ready yet?" he asked quietly. "*Really*, lad?"

Elminster spread his hands, crossbow in one. "There's one down there, at least, who knows who I am and what I look like."

Helm frowned and nodded, urged his mount forward, and clapped Elminster on the shoulder. "Then I hope to see ye alive again, Prince." As his horse circled, he asked, "Would a wild outlaw charge into camp be any help?"

El shook his head. "Nay, Helm—just ride down those armsmen. If ye get every last one of them, Lawless Castle may be safe for a winter or two yet—so long as all outlaws have the sense to abandon it this summer. When the snows are gone, the wizards'll be sure to scour these hills with all the spells and swords they can muster."

Helm nodded. "Wise talk. Let us meet again among the living." He raised his blade in salute—Elminster lifted his bow in response—and spurred away as the snow began to fall again.

Soft flakes drifted down endlessly. Elminster ate a handful of snow to get a drink, recovered his bows and readied them, and set out over the hills toward the camp. He walked in a wide curve to the right, hoping to come on it from the other side . . . though with spells, couldn't wizards see in all directions?

Well, no doubt they run out of magic the same way armsmen run out of quarrels. He'd just have to count on their not scrying for a lone boy on foot in the snows. If he saw this night through, El reflected, he'd owe the gods much, indeed. . . .

* * * * *

Tripods of halberds held the flickering storm-lanterns high. Snow whirled endlessly down into their bright radiance where, at the heart of the camp, the wizard Caladar Thearyn frowned down at a sphere of glowing light that hung in the air before him. Though the night was cold, sweat beaded his brow from the effort of keeping the sphere in existence—and in a breath or two, he'd have to hold it together while he cast another spell into it . . . a spell of many leaping lightnings that, if he managed the casting, would burst forth from the distant sphere linked to this one, a sphere bobbing like a pale ghost over the snow-clad hills not far away, just in front of the hard-riding outlaw band.

The magelord muttered the incantation that would link the two spells and felt the power rising within him. He spread his hands in exultation and noted without looking the awed faces and hasty retreat of his bodyguards.

He almost grinned as he began calling up the lightnings. Two intricate gestures, a grand flourish, and the speaking of a single word. Now for the taking up of the pins, then a rub of the rod of crystal with the fur, and last, the crowning incantation. . . . His hand swept down.

The crossbow bolt intended for his heart struck him in the shoulder, numbing his arm and spinning him around. The sphere collapsed in a crackling burst of lightnings that drowned out the magelord's startled scream of pain. The wizard sank down, clutching at his shoulder as another quarrel hissed past him. An armsman flung himself headlong in the well-trodden snow to avoid it, and his fellows drew their blades and ran toward the source of the quarrels.

Coolly, Elminster watched them come, his last bow raised. There, as he suspected . . . out of a tent came another robed man; not much older than he was but with a wand in his hand, looking around for the source of all the commotion. Carefully Elminster put his last ready quarrel in the man's throat. Then he dropped his bow, unbuckled the bulky belt-box of quarrels and let it fall, and drew his own steel.

Angry armsmen were rushing to meet him. Elminster charged them, a sword in one hand and a dagger in the other. The first man tried to beat his blade aside and run him through, but Elminster locked their blades together, pushed until they were face to face, steel shrieking in their ears, and drove his dagger into one of the man's eyes.

Shoving the convulsing corpse away, the prince ran on toward the next man, shouting, "For Athalantar!" This armsman stepped to the left, yelling to a companion to head to the right and close. El flung a dagger at the second man's face. Helm was right; some of these warriors weren't much good. This one threw up both gauntleted hands to shield his face, and Elminster's low thrust left him groaning over the blade in his guts. As El tugged his steel free, the next armsman approached warily. Elminster bent, plucked a dagger from the belt of the feebly moving man he'd just felled, and ran to one side. The surviving foe was still circling when Elminster sped away, back toward the camp.

A man in gleaming armor met him just inside the circle of light, a halberd in his hands. Elminster ran for the blade, batted it aside with his own, and stabbed. The armor turned his point aside, but then he was past, charging right into a tripod of halberds. They toppled, and the lantern they held shattered and set a tent ablaze with a sudden roar.

Men shouted. In the intense, leaping light, El saw the magelord stagger away, the quarrel still in his shoulder, but men with gleaming swords were running toward him, between him and the wizard.

Elminster snarled and turned sharply to the right, dodging between tents and away from the light. He blundered right into a man coming out of one tent and stabbed frantically; the surprised armsman toppled onto the canvas without a sound. Wearily, Elminster headed out into the night. If he could circle back to his bows, and . . . but armsmen were close behind him and running hard. Well, at least there were no bowmen in camp, or he'd be dead already.

Elminster hurried over a hill and dropped down out of sight of the raging flames that now marked the camp. Looking back, he could see two men following. He slowed to a walk, and began his wide circle. Let them draw nearer, and save him the breath. Panting, he topped another ridge and saw men gathered below, and horses; Helm's band. Some of them looked up and started toward him with swords drawn, but Helm saw him and waved. "Eladar! Done?"

"One wizard dead, but the other just wounded," El managed to gasp. "Half . . . the camp . . . is after me, too."

Helm grinned. "We were resting our horses—and looting armsmen. Some o' them were wearing armor much too good for 'em. Change yer mind about that charge?"

El nodded wearily. "Seems . . . a better idea . . . now," he said, breathing heavily.

Helm grinned, turned and gave quick orders, and then pointed out a horse. "Take ye that one, Eladar, and follow me."

Leaving four outlaws behind with the loot and extra horses, the ragged knights of Athalantar rode along the way Elminster had come. One had scrounged a short horse bow; as they crested the hill, he drew and loosed, shoulders rolling smoothly, and one of the armsmen who'd been following Elminster clutched at his throat and fell over in the snow, kicking.

The others turned and fled. With a whoop one of the knights broke into a gallop, waving his sword as he urged his horse on, riding an armsman down and chopping another with his blade. The man fell and did not rise.

"Ye seem to bring us luck," Helm shouted as they rode. "Care to lead us to break down the walls of Hastarl?"

Elminster shook his head. "I grow tired of death, Helm," he shouted back, "and I fear the better ye do, the more the wizards'll hurl this way come spring. A few dead outlander merchants are one thing; entire patrols of armsmen slaughtered is another. They dare not let it go unpunished, or folk all o'er the realm will know, and remember, and get ideas."

Helm nodded. "All the same, it feels good to hit out an' really do some damage to these wolves. Ah, ye did quite a job!" He delightedly pointed ahead at the blazing tents. "Hope ye left the food tents alone!"

Elminster could only chuckle as they galloped in among the running, shouting defenders. The knights hacked armsmen as their horses reared, trampled the wounded and the fleeing—and the camp soon grew quiet.

Helm shouted for order. "Let us have watchguards there an' there an' there, in pairs an' in the saddle, well out beyond the light. The rest of ye: six to a tent, an' report back what ye find. *No* destroying stuff, mind. If ye find a live wizard or someone else to fight, call it out!"

The knights bent willingly to work. There were glad shouts when the kitchen tent was found to have several full metal sledges of meat, potatoes, and keg beer. Grim-faced knights also brought Helm some spellbooks and scrolls, but of the wounded wizard there was no sign, and there was no man who served magelords left alive in the camp.

"Right . . . we stay here this night," Helm said. "Picket all the horses ye can find, and let's make a feast and eat. In the morn we'll take all we can, scuttle back to the castle, and rig these tents in the ravine by Wind Cavern, as shelter for the horses. Then, all pray to Auril and Talos for fresh snows to cover our tracks!"

There was a general roar of approval, and Helm leaned close to Elminster and said, "Ye wanted to leave the hills, lad—an' I can't help but think ye've read the wizards aright. I need these books an' other mage-stuff hidden, an' I was thinking of that cavern in the meadow above Heldon. There's loose stones enough to wall 'em in, there—ye know where . . . an' ye can hunt deer and the like until summer, when I'll come looking for ye again. If armsmen sniff about, go into the High Forest an' hide there; they never dare go very far in."

He scratched his chin. "Ye'll never carry the brawn to be a horse-warrior, lad, an' I'd say ye've done better than most at learning to shoot quarrels an' swing swords an' shiver in caves as an outlaw. . . . P'raps the alleys and crowds of Hastarl'll do ye better as a place to hide, now—an' be closer to magelords who aren't alert for yer blood, to learn what ye can of 'em before ye decide ye must strike out." The knight turned keen eyes on the young prince. "What say?"

Elminster nodded slowly. "Aye . . . good plan," he murmured.

Helm grinned, clapped him on the shoulder, and then caught him, as Elminster sagged over sideways into the snow, the world spinning in a sudden green and yellow haze again. . . . The darkness of utter exhaustion rushed up to claim him, and El felt himself swept away. . . .

* * * * *

"Damned soft ride, these armsmen have," Helm commented briskly the next morning as they sat eating smoked beef and hard bread spread with garlic butter. Groans and satisfied belches from all around them told them that most of the long-hungry knights had gorged themselves. Snores from among empty casks betrayed how certain others had spent the dark hours.

Elminster nodded.

Helm looked at him sharply. "What's on yer mind, lad?"

"If I never have to kill a man again, 'twill be too soon," Elminster said quietly, looking around at bloodstains in the trampled snow.

The knight nodded. "I could see it in yer eyes last night." He grinned suddenly and added, "Yet ye took care of more trained and ready warriors yestereve than many men manage to slay in a long career of soldiering."

Elminster waved a hand. "I'm trying to forget it."

"Sorry, lad. Feeling up to the trip afoot, or would ye rather ride? The one's easier—as long as ye can find hay enough for the horse, an' they eat like proper pigs, mind. But they'll draw eyes yer way in a hurry, especially when ye cross the Run in Upshyn. Try to do that with a few wagons an' look like ye're part of the group, howe'er ye go. If anyone sees the spellbooks and scrolls ye're carrying, 'twill mean yer death." The knight scratched at his beard and went on. "The other way, though, is slow and hard, even if ye can keep warm—an' mind; to get feet wet is death in this weather. . . ."

"I'll walk," Elminster said. "I'll take a bow and as much food as I can stagger along with, as well . . . no armor, so long as I can get good gloves and a better scabbard."

Helm grinned. "A legion of dead armsmen will graciously provide."

Elminster could not manage to return the grin. He'd killed more than a few of them, men who should be riding proudly for Athalantar right now—free from the orders of wizards. It all came back to the magelords.

"They are the ones who have to die," he whispered to himself, "for Athalantar to live."

Helm nodded. "Nice phrase, that: 'They must die, for Athalantar to live!' A good battle-cry; think I'll use it."

Elminster smiled. "Just be sure the folk hearing it know who the 'they' is."

Helm gave back a twisted smile. "That's a problem many have had, down the years."

* * * * *

The fox that had followed him for the last few miles took a final look at Elminster, its dark eyes glistening, and then scampered away through frozen ferns. El listened to its retreat, wondering if the fox were a magelord spy, but somehow knowing it was not. When the creature was long gone, he moved on as quietly as he could through the trees, around the back of the inn paddock.

Seek the feed hatch by the haystack, Helm had said, and there was the hay, against the back wall of the stables. The structure kept out most of the snow by means of a long sagging roof on pillars that had only a nodding acquaintance with the word "straight." Just as Helm had described it: the back way into Woodsedge Inn.

Elminster moved closer, hoping there were no dogs awake to sound an alarm. None yet. Elminster silently thanked the gods as he crept over the low gate on the inn side of the paddock, slipped around the haystack, and found the hatch. Only its own weight held it shut; he didn't even have to put down his sword to open it and climb in.

When he'd drawn the hatch closed behind him, the stable was very still, and warmer than the night outside. A horse shifted and kicked idly against the side of its stall. Elminster studied the stable and noted one stall filled with shovels, rakes, buckets, and hanging coils of lead-rein, another with straw. Sheathing his blade and taking down a long-tined fork, El probed carefully into it, but there was nothing solid beneath to wake or snarl, so he lifted the wooden pin and went in.

It was the work of but a few breaths to burrow into the straw. He settled himself so he was hidden from view and shielded against the cold by a thick blanket of hay. Relaxing, Elminster called on his will to take himself down to the floating place of whispers . . . to sink down amid white radiance, and sleep. . . .

* * * * *

Straw rustled and scratched his hands as he lurched up out of it. Elminster's eyes flew open. He was *rising* up through the straw—flying! His head struck a beam overhead, hard.

"My apologies, Prince," came a cold, familiar voice. "I fear I've wakened you." Elminster felt himself being turned in the air to hang in emptiness facing the wizard, who stood in the corridor between the stalls, smiling darkly. The blue glow of magic pulsed brightly around the man's hands and encircled a pendant at his throat.

Anger rose in Elminster as he tried to grab the Lion Sword but found his arms wouldn't move. He was at the mercy of this magelord! He tried to speak and found he could. "Who are ye?" he asked slowly.

The mage sketched an elaborate bow and said pleasantly, "Caladar Thearyn, at your service." Elminster felt himself being pulled forward in the air and at the same time saw a long-tined pitchfork rising from where it leaned against the side of the stall and turning one of its sharp points toward his left eye. Slowly, lazily, it drifted nearer.

Elminster stared past it at the wizard, fighting down an urge to swallow. "There is little of fairness in thy fighting, mage," he said coldly.

The wizard laughed. "*How* old are you, Prince—sixteen winters? And you still expect to find this world a fair place? Well, you *are* a dolt." He sneered. "You fancy yourself a warrior and fight with sharpened pieces of metal . . . well, then: I am a mage, and do *my* fighting with spells. Where's the unfairness in that?"

The blue radiance of magic began to pulse strongly about the magelord's hands, and the fork drifted closer. Elminster's throat was unbearably dry now; he swallowed despite himself.

The wizard laughed. "Not so brave now, are we? Tell me, Prince of Athalantar, how much are you willing to do for me, to be allowed to live?"

"Live? Why won't ye kill me, wizard? I know ye want to," Elminster said, with more stern bravado than he felt.

"Other magelords," the wizard quoted his own words mockingly, "have plans of their own." He laughed coldly. "As a prince of Athalantar, you have great value. If anything happens to Belaur—or it becomes *necessary* that something should happen to him—it would be very handy to have my own pet princeling hidden away, for use in the . . . unpleasantness that would ensue." The fork drifted a little nearer. "Of course, blindness won't hamper you when I transform you into . . . a turtle, perhaps, or a slug. Even better, a maggot! You can feed on the gore of your friends the outlaws when we slay them. If we can't catch any, of course, you'll go hungry. . . ."

The mage's taunting voice trailed off into cold laughter. Elminster found himself drenched with sudden sweat as cold fear wormed its way up into his throat. He hung in the air, trembling and helpless, and closed his eyes.

An instant later, he felt them being forced open—and turned in their sockets until he was staring helplessly at the wizard. He found he couldn't speak any longer or make any sound short of the whistle of his breath.

"No screaming, now," the wizard said pleasantly. "We don't want you rousing the good folk of the inn—but I want to see your face when the fork goes in." Elminster could only stare in horror at the tine of the fork, looming closer, closer. . . .

Behind the wizard, a side door swung silently open, and a

stout man with a curling mustache leaned into the room, a heavy axe raised. He brought it down hard. There was a meaty thud, and the wizard's head lolled sideways as it was split. Blood flew—and Elminster and the fork both fell abruptly to the floor.

He was up in an instant, the Lion Sword in his hand, hurrying—

"*Back,* my prince!" the man roared, throwing out one huge hand to ward him away. "He may have spells linked to his death!"

The man himself took a pace back and watched the body narrowly, the bloody axe ready on his shoulder. Elminster watched, too, and saw the faint blue glows faded from everything except the mage's pendant. Then, slowly, he walked out of the stall. "That pendant is magical," he said quietly, "but I can see nothing else. My thanks."

The man bowed. "An honor, if you are what the magelord called you."

"I am," Elminster replied. "I am Elminster, son of Elthryn, who is dead. Helm Stoneblade said I could trust you . . . if you are the one called Broarn."

The man bowed again. "I am. Be welcome in my inn—though I must warn you, lord, that six armsmen sleep under this roof tonight, and at least one merchant who tells all he sees to magelings."

"This stable is palace enough," Elminster said with a smile. "I've run from wizards and armsmen across half the Horn Hills, to here . . . and was beginning to wonder where in the world I could be free of them."

"There *is* no place to hide from strong magic," Broarn said soberly. " 'Tis why men hold these lands now, and not the Fair Folk."

"I thought elven magic o'ermatched that of men," Elminster said curiously.

"If elven mages wielded it together, aye—but elves have little taste for war, and spend much of their time feuding with each other. Most of them are also . . . we would call it idle; they trouble themselves more about having a good time and less about doing things." The innkeeper reached back through the door he'd come in by, produced a blanket, and tossed it over the side of a stall.

"Human wizards know less," Broarn went on, stepping into the unseen passage beyond the door and reappearing with a covered serving platter and an old, battered tankard as large as Elminster's head, "but're always trying to find old spells or create new ones. Elven mages only smile, say they already know all they need to—or if they're arrogant, say they know everything there is to know—and do nothing."

Elminster saw a nearby stool and sat down. "Tell me more," he said. "Please. What that mage said about my simple ways is true enough. I would hear more of the way of the world, hereabouts."

Broarn smiled and passed him the tray and the tankard. His smile broadened as Elminster lifted the lid, saw cold fowl, and dug in eagerly. "Ah, but you have the wits to know that, lord, where most don't. Here in Athalantar, there's little to say: the magelords have this land by the throat and don't mean to shift their grip. Yet for all their airs, they couldn't hold a magic apprenticeship at some places in the southlands."

Elminster looked up with his mouth full but his eyebrows raised. The innkeeper nodded. "Aye, the lands down there have always been rich, and crowded—fair crawling with folk. The greatest realm is Calimshan; the place those dusky-skinned merchants with their heads wrapped, who come here all bundled up in furs in spring and fall, come from."

"I've never seen them," Elminster said quietly.

The innkeeper scratched at his mustache. "You *have* been hidden away, lad. Well, to tell the tale short, there's a huge lawless land north of Calimshan, all forests and rivers, where their nobles always go to hunt game—or went, that is. An archmage—that's a wizard stronger by far than these magelords—" Broarn paused to spit thoughtfully on the dead wizard at his feet "—set himself up there and now rules most of it. The Calishar, it used to be called; I know not if he's renamed it, as he seems bent on changing all else. The Mad Mage, they call him, because he chases his whims so fiercely, and doesn't care about what he destroys in the doing; Ilhundyl's his name. Since he claimed the land, all the folk as didn't want to be turned into frogs and falcons have moved on—north, most of them."

Elminster sighed. "It sounds as if there's nowhere in all the world at peace from mages."

Broarn smiled. "It feels that way, my lord, it does. If you must hide from the magelords, go up the Unicorn Run, deep into the High Forest. They fear the Fair Folk will rise against them there, and they're right on that . . . the elves fear to lose more land to the axes of Athalantar and will fight for every tree. If you need to hide only from armsmen, Wyrm Wood right behind us here will do—they fear dragons. The mages know better; they slew the last dragon hereabout—and took its hoard—some twenty winters gone, but can't get us simple folk to believe that."

Elminster smiled. "And if I want to stand and fight? How can I best a wizard?"

Broarn spread his large and hairy hands. "Learn—or hire—stronger magic."

El shook his head. "How would ye trust anyone stronger in magic than magelords? What's to stop them from just taking the throne themselves after they've slain these wizards?"

The innkeeper nodded and gave Elminster a nod of approval. "A point, aye. Well, the other way is much slower and less sure."

Elminster leaned forward on the stool, and swept his hand up in a beckoning wave. "So tell."

"Work from within, as a rat gnaws away in the pantry."

"How does a man become a rat?"

"Steal. Be a thief in the back streets and the low taverns and the markets of Hastarl, close to the wizards' backsides, and wait and watch and learn. Warriors have to stand tall and wave blades . . . and be seen and slain by any mageling that points a wand their way, and outlaws must needs come out to seize food all too often. You've probably seen enough of the wilderlands of your realm to satisfy your curiosity. 'Tis time to learn the ways of the city, of thieving. It prepares one for ruling, some say." He lifted a corner of his mouth at his own jest. "Besides, a warrior's way is no more nor less safe than being a thief; any man can be overcome if caught alone—as you learned tonight—and if you wait long enough . . ."

El grinned like a wolf over dinner, rose, and took hold of the magelord's legs. "Have ye a shovel?"

Broarn returned the look. "Aye, and a nice warm manure pile to dig with it, Prince." They clasped each other's arms, as one warrior to another.

* * * * *

"At least get some more food into you before you move on," Broarn grunted, handing a tray into the end stall.

Elminster took it; steam and a delicious smell were rising together from a bowl on the tray. "Nay," he said, "I should be—" And then his stomach growled so loudly that he and the innkeeper both laughed.

"Mind you take that pendant with you when you go, and hide it somewhere else," Broarn said sternly. "I don't want magelords tracing it here, digging it up from whatever clever hidingplace you've chosen, and then trying to gently 'question' me with their spells."

"It will leave with me," Elminster promised. "It's under a stone on the road outside right now, where a road-thief might have left it."

"Well enough," said Broarn, "so I—" He broke off and held up a hand to bid Elminster to silence.

Then the innkeeper bent his head to the hatch at the back of the stables, listening intently. After a moment, he slid his hand back through the side door. It reappeared clutching the old axe, raised and ready.

Elminster drew the broken Lion Sword and sank down in the stall, holding up a large armload of straw to conceal himself, though betraying steam rose idly from the tray.

The hatch opened in well-oiled silence. Broarn stood calmly just inside it and broke into a smile at about the time a familiar voice said, "Waiting up for me, dearest? Wert expecting me?"

"In with you, Helm, while there's still some warmth in my stables," the innkeeper growled in reply, stepping back.

"I brought friends," the knight said as he stepped into the room, looking dirtier than ever. He scowled as Elminster rose in his stall, straw in his hair and sword in hand.

"Is *this* how far ye've got? I thought ye'd be well across the river by now," he said.

Elminster shook his head, losing his grin fast. "The magelord who escaped us at the camp found me here somehow—probably he can trace the spellbook—and nearly slew me. Broarn cut him down with that axe."

Helm turned to regard the innkeeper with new respect. "A slayer of magelords, now." He circled Broarn as if viewing a lady in a bold new gown, then nodded approvingly. " 'Tis a most exclusive brotherhood, ye know . . . besides the lad here an' meself, its only members are the dead, an' a few living magelords. Why, th—"

"Helm," Broarn broke in bluntly, "why are you here? I've armsmen in the house, as you should know."

As they'd been talking, knight after outlaw knight had slipped in through the hatch, crowding into the end stalls. So many of them wore armor scavenged from the soldiery of Athalantar that it looked as if a dozen or more rather scruffy armsmen stood in the stable now.

"There is a matter of some small urgency, aye," Helm said more soberly. "Which is why Mauri's shivering in a sledge outside, with another twenty-odd brave blades."

"They took Lawless Castle?" The innkeeper sounded shocked.

"Nay. We fled from it before they could trap us there. The

magelords sent a large band of armsmen out of Sarn Torel, guarding over a dozen mages. They've slain twenty or more wildswords we know of and tortured at least one with spells—they know where the castle is, by now, and are heading straight for it."

"So you brought them here. My thanks, Helm," Broarn said bitterly and sketched a courtly bow.

"They'll have no way of knowing we did any more than steal a horse or two," Helm said firmly. "We're leaving very soon, now that ye—and the lad, here, a country boy called Eladar, by the way, if he hasn't told ye—" The two men exchanged a fleeting, level look "—know the tidings. Eladar was right, we've been too good at killing armsmen an' now they're determined to slay the lot o' us. The wizards daren't let such defiance succeed or soon the whole realm will be up in arms. We must run. Any suggestions, wise innkeeper?"

Broarn snorted. "Run to the Calishar and get Ilhundyl to teach you to be master mages so you can come back and fight these magelords . . . get a friendly mage to hide all of you as frogs before the magelords can find you and do it swifter . . . go to the depths of the elven realms and get them to hide you somehow . . . call on the gods for miracles . . . I believe that about covers it."

"There's one other place," Elminster said quietly.

The silence of utter astonishment fell on both Helm and Broarn. They turned as one to look at the lad in the scorched leather jerkin, standing alone in his stall. He'd slid his sword into hiding and picked up the bowl of turkey soup Broarn had brought him. As they watched, he calmly took a spoonful, smiled, dipped his spoon into the bowl again, drew forth another spoonful, and blew on it to cool it.

"I'll *slay* ye, lad, if ye don't stop playing the fool," Helm growled, taking a step toward him.

"That's more or less what the magelord said to me," Elminster remarked mildly, "and look ye what befell him."

Helplessly, Helm started to laugh, and that set Broarn and the other outlaws off into roars of mirth while Elminster assumed an air of innocence over his bowl and ladled several spoonfuls into his mouth, fearing chances to do so later would be few.

"All right, lad," Broarn managed when he had breath enough, "give. Where to hide?"

"Among a lot of folk that wizards dare not slay or upset too many of, or they'll have no realm left. In Hastarl itself," Elminster said.

Helm—and alot of the outlaw knights behind him—stared at

the youth with open mouths, aghast.

"But ye'll attack the first mage ye see when ye step inside the gates, and we'll all perish right then!" the battered knight protested.

Elminster shook his head. "Nay," he said. "Watching sheep taught me patience . . . and hunting wizards is teaching me guile."

"Ye're crazed," one of the other outlaws muttered.

"Aye," another agreed.

"Wait a bit," still another protested. "The more I think on it, the better it seems."

"Ye want death at yer elbow every day, whene'er ye go out?"

"I've got that *now* . . . an' if I go to Hastarl like the lad says, I might get me a warm house to sleep in o' winters."

Then they were all talking, arguing earnestly, until Broarn hissed, "You will be *quiet!*" to knight after knight, waving his axe under their noses for emphasis. When he had silence, the fat innkeeper said, "If you make that sort of noise, I'll have armsmen up from their beds and in here to see what fun they're missing. Anyone want that?"

He let silence stretch for a moment or two, and then went on quietly, "Some of you will want to remain in the hills or flee to other lands, but some may want to go with the lad here to Hastarl. Whatever you decide, do it well back in the woods; I want all of you away from here before dawn. Helm, bring Mauri and the home-stuffs she's got in by the back door. She stays here. Don't let anyone help you who can't move quietly. Now out, all of you—and may the luck of the gods cloak you and keep you!"

* * * * *

The meeting was breaking up; the time to strike was now. This deed would surely win him a rank among the magelords! No more apprenticeship to fat old Harskur . . . and real power at last!

Saphardin Olen rose from the cold hillside, letting his eavesdropping spell fade away. He raised the wands in his hands, aiming at the hatch—best to strike now, before any of them left the place.

"Die, fools!" he said with a smile, and then pitched forward like a felled tree as a stone the size of a war helm smashed into the back of his head.

As the blood-spattered rock settled smoothly into the snow, the two fallen wands rose by themselves and glided in a gentle arc through the trees to the next knoll, where a tall, lean woman stood watching them come with large, dark eyes.

Her face was bone white, and her hair a curling honey-brown. At one glance, a farmer would have bowed to her as a lady. She put out a hand to take the wands as they glided up to her, and her dark green cloak swirled about her, as if moved by unseen hands. Silvern threads on its shoulders were worked in a mage-sigil of linked circles.

The sorceress watched the outlaws stride into the woods, and waved a hand. Her body faded, rippled, and became just another of the shifting shadows here in the winter-stripped trees—cloaked and unseen, save for her large, liquid black eyes.

They blinked once as they watched Elminster hug Helm in farewell before heading south, alone.

"The soul is strong in you, Prince of Athalantar," their owner said quietly. "Live, then, and let us see what you can do."

PART II
BURGLAR

Four

THEY COME OUT AT NIGHT

Thieves? Ah, such an ugly word . . . think of them instead as kings-in-training. Ye seem upset, even disputatious. Well, then, look upon them as the most honest sort of merchant.

> The character Oglar the Thieflord
> in the anonymous play ***Shards and Swords***
> Year of the Screeching Vole

It was just one more in an endless string of hot, damp days in the early summer of the Year of the Black Flame. Folk in Hastarl had taken to lying more or less unclad on the flat stretches of their rooftops and their balconies after sunset, hoping for a breeze to blow over their skin and bring them some fleeting moments of comfort.

This was good for both pleasure and business—the predictable pleasure, and one business in particular.

"Ah," Farl said softly, leaning forward to peer out of the slit window. "The show of flesh beginneth again, so it doth."

"When ye've finished drooling down the stonework," the slim, beak-nosed youth behind him said dryly, "do ye hold the line while I go down."

"That'll be about dawn, I'd say," was the reply.

"Aye, then, hold the line now and look later." Elminster cast a glance over the head of his fellow thief and squinted professionally. "Ah, yes, quite a tattoo there . . . though how the man sees it, with the curve of his belly between his eyes and where it is, only the gods can know."

Farl chuckled. "Think of what it must have felt like, getting it, too." He winced with an exaggerated flourish, and added, "But you're supposed to be looking at the maids, El, not at the men!"

"Ah, I've *got* to learn to tell the difference. It gets me into more trouble," Elminster replied serenely. Then what he'd been waiting for befell: a large bank of clouds drifted across the moon. Without another word, he slipped through the narrow window, one hand on the rope harness, and was gone.

Farl settled the smooth leather rope slide securely on the sill, and with surprising strength slowed the line gliding through it to a gentle, continuous movement until a sharp jerk told him to stop. He thrust a dagger into one of the holes in the wheel from which the rope unwound, then looked out the window.

Directly under him, in the empty air beneath the outthrust upper room of the tower, Elminster calmly hung suspended outside the window of the room below. One of his hands—the hand wearing a wrapping coated with sticky honeycake—was on the tower wall; El was keeping himself to one side of the window, out of the view of the room's occupants. He peered in for what seemed a very long time before raising his hand in a signal, not looking up.

Farl passed the reachers down on their own lines.

Hanging there in the quickening night breeze, Elminster took hold of them: two long, thin wooden sticks with wrist-braces at one end, like crutches, and sticky balls of precious stirge glue on their other ends. A hooked and pad-ended side-prong jutted from one stick.

El delicately used that prong to swing the shutters fully back—and then withdrew the reachers and waited patiently. No sound came from within, and after several long breaths, he reached out again. One stick slid in until its leather sleeve caught the sill. He balanced its weight there, and then slid it onward through its sleeve, probing delicately inside the room. When he drew it out, a gem gleamed on the sticky end. He backed the stick until he could slide his hand up to its tip, let it dangle from its line while he thrust the gem into the tube-bag of stout canvas he wore around his neck, and then reached into the room with the stick again, slowly . . . smoothly . . . silently.

Thrice more the sticks appeared, were emptied of precious cargo, and returned to the room. Farl saw the youth below wipe sweating hands on dark, dusty leather breeches, and then lean forward again. He held this breath, knowing what *that* gesture meant: Eladar the Dark was about to try something especially reckless. Farl mouthed a silent prayer to Mask, Lord of All Thieves.

Elminster reached into the bedchamber once more. His sticks slid over the bare, slumbering body of the young merchant's wife, only inches above the soft curves of her flesh—and paused over her throat. She wore a dark ribbon there . . . and below it, a pectoral of linked emeralds, topped by a spider of black wire whose body was a single huge ruby.

Elminster watched the jewelry rise and fall, ever so slightly, with her slow and even breathing. If it was like others he'd seen, the spider could be unclasped to be worn alone as a cloak-pin.

If . . . a touch, just so—a wiggle to be sure it was caught . . . and
now so was he (This had to work, or he'd be left with a stick twice
as long as a man stuck to the breast of a naked woman who'd not
stay asleep for very long) . . . and a little lift, up and back, *so*.
Don't brush her nose with it, now . . . with infinite care and patience El brought the reachers back out of the window.

When he dropped the jewels into the bag and jerked the rope
for Farl to pull him up, he felt that the spider was still warm
from her breathing. Elminster smelled the musky scent clinging
to it, sighed soundlessly, and wondered fleetingly what women
were like. . . .

*   *   *   *   *

"With those, we can live like idle rich blades for five tendays,
at least," Farl said, eyes shining in the dim light of their hovel
hideaway.

"Aye," Elminster said, "and get noticed in three evenings.
Just who d'ye think we think we can sell that spider to in *this*
city? We'll have to wait for a discreet merchant—who's got something to hide an' knows we know it—leaving the city, and sell it
to him then. Nay; we sell the ring with the emerald this night,
before word gets out; no marks there to say it's hers for certain.
Then we lie low—back to hanging around the Black Boots waiting for hire as dockhands and errand-runners."

Farl stared at him for a moment, mouth open to protest, but
then closed it in a smile and nodded. "You've the right of it as
usual, Eladar. You've the cunning of an alley cat, to be sure."

Elminster shrugged. "I'm still alive, if that's what ye mean.
Let's go discover some place that serves drink to young blades
with dry throats and loose purses."

Farl laughed, slid the bag back into the hollow stone block,
clambered up the ragged stones of the crumbling chimney, and
shoved the block the full length of his arm back into the dark,
hollow space between floor and ceiling. Withdrawing his arm
from the splinter-edged hole, he replaced the dead, dangling,
half-eaten rat they used to deter searchers, and slid back down
the chimney to the floor.

Around them, the gloomy back room of the shut-up cobbler's
shop stank from its occasional use as a toilet by cats, dogs,
drunks, and stray street folk. The cobbler had died of black-
tongue fever early in the spring, and sane folk made no plans to
disturb the place until at least a season had passed. Then it
would be smoked to clear disease-vapors and torn down; by then,

Farl and Elminster planned to have a new and better loot-cache among the ornamental roof-spires of the proud houses near Hastarl's north wall. They had their eyes on a tall residence whose roof sported crouching, snarling sculpted gargoyles; if one could be beheaded and hollowed out without anyone in the grand house beneath noticing, they'd have an ideal place. Aye, 'if.'

The two youths nodded to each other, knowing their silent thoughts had skulked along the same alley. Farl peered out the watch hole and after a moment waved Elminster on. He stepped unconcernedly out into the narrow, dark passage outside, and slipped away. Farl followed, dagger drawn—just in case. It was a full breath later before any of the rats dared come out into the open to get at the moldy slab of cheese the young thieves had thoughtfully left behind.

* * * * *

The Kissing Wench was a loud, crowded press of goodfolk— ribaldry and slapping and pinching, pursuit of a night's lust, roared jests and tossed coins, and reckless chase of wine-soaked oblivion. Farl and Eladar took their tankards to their favorite dark corner, just off the bar, where they could see who came in but be seen only by the night-sighted and the determined.

Their spot was occupied already, of course, by ladies whose names they knew well despite a persistent lack of the coinage necessary for more intimate acquaintance. The hour was too early for business to be brisk, so the evening-lasses were sipping from glasses in their hands and rubbing scent into the backs of their knees and the crooks of their elbows, and there was still room to sit down on the benches.

"Game for an early kiss and cuddle?" Ashanda asked disinterestedly, examining her nails. She knew what their reply would be before it came. Nothing from the one with the unruly black hair and the beaky nose, and from Farl—

"Nay. We just like to watch." He leered at her over his tankard.

She gave him a mock coquettish look, batting her eyes and putting two delicate fingers to her mouth in a shocked expression, and then replied, "An' most of 'em want a cheering audience, so that's aright. Just be sure to give way when we need the space on the benches, or it's my blade-toe you'll be feeling!"

They'd seen her put her dagger-tipped boot into the shins of many a man, and once into the gut of a sailor who didn't know his own cruel strength; he'd ended up screaming his guts out—

literally—on the tavern floor. Both thieves nodded hastily as the other girls tittered.

Farl gave one of them a wink, and she leaned forward to pat his knee. The movement made her low-cut silken bodice slide, smooth and cool, across Elminster's arm. He hastily transferred his tankard out of the way, feeling a stirring in him.

Budaera saw his swift movement and turned her head to smile up at him. Her scent—something of roses, not so strong as some of the reeks the ladies used—wafted to his nostrils. Elminster shivered.

"Anytime you have the coins, love," she breathed huskily. Elminster managed to get the back of his hand over his nose in time. Then his sneeze slopped beer down the side of his tankard, and nearly knocked her sideways to the floor.

Hoots and roars filled the corner. Budaera gave him a glare, and then softened it to an expression of sorrow when she saw that his distress and his stammered apology were genuine. She patted his knee and said, "There, there. 'Tis all a matter of improving your technique—and that, I can teach you."

"If ye can afford her lessons," another girl cackled, and there were chuckles all around. El wiped his streaming eyes on the back of his sleeve and nodded thanks to Budaera, but she was already turning away to ask another girl where that coppery nail daub had come from, and how much it had cost.

Farl ran his fingers through the hair above his ear and drew his hand down to stare in delight at a silver coin in his fingers, as if he'd never seen it before. "Look at *this*," he said to Eladar. "Mayhap there's another!"

There was. He held them up in triumph, and said, "I'm ready, Budaera, an' I'm willing, an' I see you're free of guests at the m—"

"For two silver bits," she said in a flat, cold tone, "that's the way I'm staying, 'my love.'" The laughter of the girls galed around them; men with tall frosted flagons in hand drifted nearer to see what merriment was afoot . . . or abench.

Farl looked crestfallen. "I don't think there's anything more back there, but I didn't comb my hair this morn. . . . " His look changed to hopeful, and he ran his hands through his hair again, then shook his head.

"Nay." One of the girls made a sound of mock sorrow, but he held up his hand. "Wait a bit, wait a bit—I've not checked all me hair, now have I?" Farl leered again and reached inside his dark shirt to scratch at his armpit. His fingers worked lustily, and then paused. Farl frowned, drew out an imaginary—at least, so

Elminster hoped—pinch of lice, and examined them critically. Then he pretended to eat them, licked his fingers daintily, and when he was done darted his hand into his shirt again, trying the other armpit.

Almost immediately his eyes grew round and wondering. Slowly he drew out—a gold coin! He sniffed at it, drew back in mock disgust, and then held it up with a laugh of triumph. "See you?"

"Now that," Budaera purred, leaning forward again, "is worth more than a sneeze. Have you another?"

Farl looked hurt. "Just how dirty d'you think my armpits are, anyway?"

Tinkling, genuine laughter surrounded them; the ladies were amused. El watched impassively, only a corner of his mouth crooked upward, as Budaera leaned forward until her darting tongue almost brushed Farl's ear, and breathed, "For just two silver bits more, I might be persuaded to make a pauper's exception . . . just this once. . . ."

"For just two silver bits more," Farl said with elaborate dignity, "I might be compelled to accept your generous offer, good lady. Now, if someone in this august company would be so good as to lend me the trifling sum of—ah, two silver bits?"

There were snorts and lazily rude gestures from the benches beside him. Elminster held out a hand; when he turned it over, two silver coins were stuck to his palm.

Rather dubiously, Farl bent and plucked them free, one after another. Elminster had used only a trifling touch of gum on each; by the time Farl presented them to Budaera with a flourish, they were quite clean.

Budaera beckoned for the gold first. When she had it, she reached into her own armpit and made the coin disappear into the little scented safe pouch most of the ladies wore there. Then she took the pieces of silver, spun them briefly in the air in expert fingers, held up the last one, and kissed it, eyes on Farl's. "We have a deal, then, my lord of love."

She leaned forward, eyes suddenly full of mystery, and like a silent and watchful snake Elminster slid out from his seat beside Farl to give them room. Budaera purred wordless thanks to him as she moved her lithe body into the vacated space, and set to work.

Elminster stepped away, shaking his tankard in little circular movements to feel what little was left at the bottom of it—and froze. A slim finger was stroking him, ever so softly. He looked down—and caught his breath.

They called Shandathe "the Shadow" for the silence of her entrances and exits. More than once, El and Farl had agreed she must be an accomplished thief, or if she wasn't, was as accomplished at skulking as the best of them. Her large, dark eyes looked up past his belt buckle at Elminster—and he felt the need to swallow, his throat suddenly dry.

"Coins to lend, Eladar the Dark? Have ye—coins to spend?" Her voice was husky, her eyes hungry. . . .

Elminster made a helpless little sound of need deep in his throat and dipped his hand to his sleeve, whose cuff was stuffed with gold pieces. "One or two," he managed, in a voice that was not quite steady.

Her eyes danced. "One or two, my lord? I'm sure I heard ye say three or four . . . aye, four gold. One for each of the delights I'll give thee." She licked his hand, the lightest of velvet touches in his palm. Elminster trembled.

Then he was shoved rudely aside. Whirling, he found himself looking into the cold grin of a burly bodyguard in livery. The man held up spiked gauntlets in warning, and El saw another bodyguard beyond him. Between them, in his own little ring of light provided by a small oil-lamp held above him on a curving pole by a weary servant, stood a short, pouty-looking man in flame-orange silks. His reddish hair fell in well-oiled ringlets to stain the silken shoulders of his open-fronted shirt. On his hairless chest was a lump of gold as large as a man's fist: a lion's head frozen in an endless, silent snarl, as it hung on a heavy gold chain. Rings of many gems and metals glittered and flashed on his fingers—two and three baubles to each digit, El noted with disgust, and all of it real.

He exchanged glances with Farl over Budaera's shocked face, and then the man thrust his codpiece, adorned with an openwork ivory and gold sheath that made it look like the figurehead of a very decadent Calishite pleasure-barge, right into Shandathe's face.

"Too busy, my little lass?" he drawled, and snapped his fingers. The servant with the lamp put a purse in them, and the man lazily spilled a dozen or so gold pieces down the front of Shandathe's gown. "Or have you time enough for a real man . . . with real gold to spend?"

"How many years does my lord want to spend with me?" Shandathe breathed in reply, lifting her hands in welcome. The man grinned tightly, and gestured to his bodyguards. They reached out brutal spiked hands to clear the corner, ignoring the sudden, shrill protests of the other ladies.

One laid hold of Budaera's ankle, and hauled her off Farl to a hard landing on the floor. She squealed in pain, and anger rode high in Farl's face as he rose from the bench.

"Just who in Hastarl do you think *you* are?" he addressed the perfumed man. The bodyguard reached a menacing hand toward him, and Farl snapped his own fingers like the man's master had done, and as if by a spell a dagger gleamed in them. He waved it warningly at the bodyguard's eyes, and the man hesitated.

"Jansibal is my name," came arrogant tones that obviously expected the name to awe everyone within hearing. "Jansibal Otharr."

Farl shrugged. "Heard of any testers of cheap scent by that name, El?" he asked. Elminster waved a dagger of his own under the nose of the bodyguard who'd shoved him, and slipped out from under the man's gauntleted hands.

"No," he said calmly, "but one rat looks quite the same as another." That did bring little gasps and indrawn hisses of breath from around, and a little silence fell. The dandy's face turned dark with anger, and his fingers tightened in Shandathe's hair as she knelt in front of him. Then a sick, lopsided, sneering smile slid onto Jansibal's face, and Elminster felt a little chill inside. This man meant their deaths, here and now. The bodyguards drifted nearer.

"This sounds like the sort of insult that a man of honor"—the loud, new voice that had broken in from behind them dropped little commas around that last word, and Jansibal paled in recognition and fresh anger—"can answer only with a formal duel, not a distressing brawl that will cost him at least two body-guards."

Jansibal and his men spun around—to find another dandy, as well-garbed as the first, eyeing them with dancing amusement in his eyes. He, too, wore silks, with crawling dragons embroidered on his puffed sleeves. A flagon was in his hand—and to either side of him stood men in matching livery, slim swords in their hands. The needlelike blades were aimed at the crotches of Jansibal's bodyguards. A hush spread across the dark taproom, and men craned their necks to watch.

"Fair even, Jansibal," the newcomer said calmly, rubbing at the thin beginnings of a moustache with the lip of his flagon. "Laryssa spurn you again? Dlaedra insufficiently impressed with your—ah, rampant glory?"

Jansibal snarled. "Get gone, Thelorn! You can't strut in the safety of your sire's shadow forever!"

"His shadow stretches longer than your father's, Janz. My

men and I but stopped for a drink . . . but the appalling stench drew us to this corner to see what had died. You really must stop wearing that stuff, Janz; some chambermaid's likely to empty a pisspot out a window to try and wash your stink away!"

"Your yapping tongue carries you ever closer to a waiting grave, Selemban!" Jansibal spat. "Now begone, or I'll have one of my men spoil that pretty face of yours with a few shards of glass!"

"I love thee too, Jansibal. Which of your two men is it to be? My *six* would dearly love to know." From behind him, another pair of men in livery glided forward, blades raised and glittering in the little dangling lamp that a trembling servant still held aloft on its pole.

"I'll not fight a duel with all these blades of yours around," Jansibal said, drawing himself up. "I know your liking for convenient 'accidents.'"

"While you grandly slash at someone with that blade you've dipped in sleep-venom? Aren't you tired of such deceits, Janz? Doesn't using them remind you, every even', that you're a worm? Or is it so much part of your lovely nature that you don't even notice?"

"Shut your lying mouth," Jansibal snarled, "or—"

"Or you'll get away with your little trick, yes? And stab all these lads and lasses around to work off your little rage, no doubt. And what would you be doing with them once they were asleep? Robbing them, of course—you have such *expensive* habits, Janz—but perhaps a little idle butchering . . . or worse? I've noticed the ladies raising their rates down your street, Janz. . . ."

Jansibal snarled wordlessly and charged forward. There was a flash of light and a spray of scattering sparks as the blades of the two nearest bodyguards met some invisible shield of magic around the charging dandy—and then Jansibal came to a sudden halt as Thelorn Selemban, moving without apparent haste, drew a blade and pointed it at Jansibal's nose. Tiny white lightnings spiraled along the steel as its own enchantment cut through Jansibal's shield. Around the two nobles, their bodyguards surged forward, blades out and up.

"Hold, men of Otharr and Selemban, in the name of the king!" came a sudden deep bellow from behind them all, in the direction of the bar. The liveried men halted as their masters stiffened—and the crowd around parted as if before a drawn sword.

A man with a short-trimmed, graying beard came into view, a

tankard in his hand. "Swordmaster Adarbron," he identified himself flatly. "I'll report any deaths or bloodletting here to the magelords when I see them this night. . . . And I'll also let them know if either of you disobey me, my lords. Now order your men out of this place, and back to your homes—now!"

He stood hard-eyed, and the two dandies saw men drift up to stand at his back. Off-duty armsmen, to be sure, faces not quite masking their glee. If the dandies defied the swordmaster, the soldiers would do their level best to 'accidentally' slay or maim them both—and none of their bodyguards would leave the tavern alive.

"My men have had enough to drink anyway," Thelorn said easily, but a vein was working near his jaw. He did not look in Otharr's direction as he said almost gently to the men around him, "You may go. I shall follow after I drink to the health of this excellent and dedicated officer—whose word I utterly support, for the honor of Athalantar."

"For the honor of Athalantar," half a hundred men muttered in reply, waving their flagons and tankards halfheartedly. Unimpressed, the swordmaster watched the men go. Then, ignoring Thelorn Selemban's smile, he shot a cold look at Jansibal Otharr, and said, "My lord?"

Sullenly, without a reply, Jansibal waved a hand at his men. Then he turned back to the Shadow, who still knelt fearfully in the alcove, and said coldly, "My lords, I was occupied before Selemban took it upon himself to interrupt. If you'll excuse me—?"

"Through there," Elminster murmured, pointing, "is rather more private. I'm sure the folk who were sitting here before thy enthusiastic men shoved them aside would like to resume what they were doing before *thy* interruption, too, my lord."

The dandy snarled at him, promised death again in his eyes, but the swordmaster said firmly, "Take the young man's advice, Otharr. He but tries to rescue your family name . . . and remind you of a few simple basics of courtesy."

Otharr did not look around, but his shoulders stiffened, and he turned without a word, fingers firmly wound in Shandathe's hair so that she gave a little shriek and then hurried along on her knees to avoid being dragged.

Elminster took a step forward, but the noble had already halted to fling the curtain wide. "A light in here," he ordered curtly. The young alcove-lass unhooded a slow-wick lamp and blew it into brightness before slipping hurriedly away.

The curtained pleasure-alcove normally cost six gold falcons—but before the fury of the noble and the watchful gaze of

the swordmaster, the young girl did not tarry to try for the price
. . . and the bodyguards who stood to defend her and her demand
kept to the walls and held their silence. Jansibal Otharr surveyed the cushioned, draperied bed that almost filled the niche,
nodded in satisfaction, and curtly waved Shandathe to the bed.
The curtains fell into place behind them with an angry switch.

Farl reached up the wall with a slow, stealthy hand and
dimmed the lamp there by pinching down its wick. He caught
the eyes of a lady across the benches, and she did the same, dimming that side of the taproom into darkness again.

The swordmaster turned away, keeping Thelorn Selemban
carefully at his side. They went back to the bar together.

Farl and El exchanged glances. Farl sketched the swell of an
imaginary bosom with one hand, pointed at the curtain, and
then jerked his thumb at himself. El blinked slowly, once, and
then pointed toward the jakes and touched his own chest. Farl
nodded, and El set out across the room to where he could relieve
himself. If there was going to be creeping about or fighting, he'd
best be more at ease.

Had it been like this before the magelords came to Hastarl?
Shouldering and slipping his way through drunken revelers into
the dimly lit privy area, El wondered what the Wench had been
like when his grandfather sat on the Stag Throne. Were all men
of power as cruel as the two nobles who'd almost begun a battle
here? And just how were they more honorable—or more villain-
ous—than Farl and Eladar the Dark, two young and impudent
rooftop thieves?

Just who stands better in the eyes of the gods—a magelord, a
dandified noble, or a thief? What's the choice between the lot of
them? The first two have more influence to do ill, and the thief is
at least honest or open about what he does . . . hmm . . . perhaps
these would not be safe questions to ask a priest or sage in Hastarl. The foul-smelling trough in front of him had no ready answers either, and he'd best get back out there before Farl did
something reckless. If they were going to have all the armsmen
in the city out looking for them, he wanted to know about it . . .

When he returned along the far wall, Farl was sitting beside
the curtain. He caught El's eye and then slipped smoothly behind it, keeping low. El took his seat, noted that the couple beside him were well beyond noticing what anyone else was doing,
and followed.

The two friends lay still, side by side and unseen on the dark
carpeted floor, as the gasps in the dimly lit alcove grew louder
and more urgent. Farl crawled slowly forward as the amorous

sounds built to a height, and reached up silently to lift the glass of wine—complimentary with hire of the alcove, its surface thick with settled dust—from its usual spot. Deftly he tossed its contents over the lamp-wick.

The alcove was plunged into sudden, hissing darkness. Elminster rose from the carpet like a vengeful, striking snake and plunged one hand over the dandy's mouth from behind, reaching to stifle the man into slumber with the other.

Farl's hands were already over the Shadow's mouth. She jerked and burbled under him, fighting for breath enough to scream, but her eyes widened when she recognized the man atop her and she stopped struggling. Elminster saw one of her slim hands cease its clawing, and reach up to stroke Farl's shoulder. Then he had no time left to spare for looking at anyone except the noble under him.

Jansibal was oiled and perfumed, slippery under Elminster's hands. He'd never known the hard hours and harsh battle that the youth from Heldon had felt—but he was shorter and heavier, and fury lent him strength. He threw himself sideways, dragging Elminster with him, and tried to bite the fingers that were smothering him.

Elminster drew back one arm, dagger-hilt foremost, and slugged the noble hard on the jaw. Jansibal's head snapped around, spittle and blood flying together. The dandy gave a little grunt, shook his head—and toppled over sideways on the bed, knocked senseless. One open eye stared up unseeing at Elminster; satisfied, El spun to look behind them and be sure no one had noticed the sudden dousing of the light behind the curtain, or heard the brief, unloving sounds. The hubbub of folk drinking continued unabated—and sudden soft sounds from beside him proclaimed that Farl was taking full advantage of the noble's generous payment to Shandathe. The gold coins lay on the floor around, freed when Otharr had torn open her bodice; El ignored them to bend closer over the entwined couple, and delicately free a single distinctive earring from where the Shadow's hair curled around her ear.

Shandathe freed her lips from Farl's long enough to whisper a sharp, *"What—?"*

Elminster put a finger to his lips and murmured, "To lure the other one; ye'll see it again, I promise."

Holding it cupped carefully in his hand, he slipped around the curtain again and made his way unhurriedly across the taproom. As he'd hoped, the swordmaster and Thelorn stood side by side at the bar.

"You'll appreciate," the officer was saying wearily, "that sons of magelords *must* set an example that makes the people feel they're close and among them, not aloof. Magic, and those who wield it, are feared enough; if the kingdom is ever to be strong, th—"

He broke off as Elminster glided up between them, displayed the earring, and murmured, "Cry pardon for the interruption, my lords, but I am sent on a mission of love. The lady Lord Otharr was so anxious to make the acquaintance of confesses herself somewhat disappointed by his . . . ah, brief performance, and hopeful that another man of importance—such as yourself, my lord—would be made of rather sterner stuff. She bade me be sure to tell ye that she found thy tongue and bearing *most* impressive, and would know both better."

Thelorn looked up at Elminster and grinned suddenly; the swordmaster shook his head, rolled his eyes, and turned away. The young noble's eyes went across the room to the curtain. Elminster nodded and strode toward it, Thelorn following through the way that the youth cleared.

When they reached the curtain, El ducked a look around it and held it a little aside; Thelorn peered in.

A heap of clothing and bed-draperies lay close by; beyond them, a single flickering stub of candle glimmered in the navel of the lady who lay bare to his sight on the bed. A silk half-mask hooded her face, and she was smiling through the swirl of long hair that lay across her mouth as she lounged with her arms clasped behind her head. "Come in, and be at ease," she murmured, "my lord."

Thelorn's smile widened, and he stepped forward. As the curtain fell into place behind them both, Elminster moved with the noble, raised his trusty dagger hilt, and clubbed down, leaping a little off the floor to put his strength behind the blow.

Thelorn fell forward onto the end of the bed like a chopped sapling; Farl exploded from his concealment under heaped pillows to pull Shandathe's feet away before he crashed down atop them.

Farl and El grinned at each other, working swiftly. Rings that might carry spells they dared not take, and Shandathe was due her coins; they tossed them to her as she swiftly dressed, and were rewarded with an enthusiastic kiss each. She was as beautiful as El had thought she'd be; well, some other night, perhaps.

They quickly stripped Selemban's clothes away, dragged the senseless Jansibal out from under the heap of draperies, and arranged the two naked lordlings in an embrace on the bed for others to find. Supporting the Shadow between them as if she were faint, arms around her shoulders, they helped her out through the taproom, to the alley door by the jakes.

A hopeful slug-and-snatcher glided out from a dark angle of walls, saw Farl's warning gaze and El's dagger gleaming ready, and drew back again. Without a word the trio turned north, toward old Hannibur's.

The grizzled old baker lived alone over his shop. His weathered face, wooden foot, acerbic tongue, and natural stinginess made him unattractive to the ladies of Hastarl. Most days, he tossed drying, unbought bread-ends, and sometimes even whole loaves, out his back door to the hopeful and hungry urchins who played there. Tonight his snores rumbled faintly out into the alley through the closed shutters of his bedchamber.

"Where are we going, m'lords?" Shandathe was still amused at the jest—and grateful for the extra gold—but her voice held a note of alarm. She'd heard some things about her two young escorts.

"We must hide you before those beasts awaken and send their bodyguards out to collect what you neglected to give them—and your hide along with it," Farl said in her ear, embracing her.

"Aye, but where?" the Shadow asked, putting her arms around him. Farl pointed up at the window from which the snoring was coming.

Shandathe stared at him. "Are you *crazed?*" she hissed in sudden anger. "If you think I'm g—"

Farl's hands glided to just the right places as he pressed his lips to hers. She struggled angrily for a moment, managing to utter some angry-sounding murmurs . . . and then went limp. Farl promptly passed her to Elminster. "Here," he said brightly.

He turned away and hastily erected a pyramid of crates from the baker's litter of shipping-refuse. Elminster stared at him and then down at the girl in his arms. She was soft and beautiful—if heavy—and was stirring already; in a breath or two, she'd return to her senses . . . and if El knew anything about the Shadow, she'd be *very* angry. He looked around gingerly for a place to put her.

" 'Tis Hannibur's lucky night," Farl said with a smile, as he swarmed back down the swiftly erected pyramid. Above, the shutters now hung open, and the snores roared out unmuted down the alley. He pointed at Elminster and at Shandathe, and then up at the window again.

"To be sure," El murmured in reply, mounting the crates with the limp Shadow heavy on his back. Her delicate scent played at his nostrils, and he added under his breath, "Luckier than me, I'll warrant."

Then he was climbing carefully through the window, Farl steadying Shandathe's limbs to prevent a fall or noise. She stirred as they crossed the bare board floor to Hannibur's bed.

They drew back the patched woollen covers and laid her carefully beside the sleeping baker. Then they both turned away to stifle rising mirth: the old man wore a daringly cut, frilly wanton wench's robe. Hairy vein-mottled flesh and bony knees protruded from the sheer silk.

El bit his lip and staggered to the window, shoulders shaking silently. Farl mastered himself sooner, and delicately drew aside two sets of garments; their owners stirred. Softly he stroked two bodies, and raced on catlike feet for the window. El was already halfway down the crates, outside.

The two thieves giggled at each other as they hauled out the bottom crates. Everything above tumbled and fell, creating a din that ought to cut through even Hannibur's snores, and they raced away around a corner.

Pausing for breath in a courtyard half Hastarl away, Farl said, "Whew! A good even's work. Pity I hadn't time to empty my tankard before that hippopotamus-ass pushed his way in on you."

Elminster grinned and handed him Shandathe's earring. Farl smiled down at it. "Well, at least we got some pay for all our thoughtful work."

El's own grin widened as he dropped three heavy links of gold chain into Farl's other hand. "Twisted it open and shortened the thing by a few links," he said innocently. "He was wearing his lion too low for the full effect, anyway."

Farl burst into delighted laughter, and they clung together, chuckling, until Farl caught sight of a nearby signboard. "Let's go hoist a tankard," he puffed.

"What?" Elminster's blue-gray eyes danced dangerously. "Again?"

* * * * *

Three times Selune had risen over the high towers of Athalgard since that night, and talk of the two young and very friendly sons of magelords was all over the city. The bodyguards of both were prowling through every tavern and beanpot dining room in the poorer parts of Hastarl, obviously looking for a certain hawk-nosed, black-haired youth and his clever-tongued friend . . . so Eladar and Farl had judged it prudent to take a brief vacation until the searchers grew careless enough for accidents to happen to them—or until some street thief too desperate to be wise tried to rob one of them, and their search was diverted to new targets.

Lying exposed to the gaze and bows of bored guards on the battlements of Athalgard made both the friends uneasy, so they had taken to chatting, relaxing, and plotting in the seclusion of the old walled burial-ground at the other end of the city: an overgrown, disused place where the cracked and leaning stone vaults of wealthy families crumbled into rubble amid stunted trees that burst up through them, and spread concealing branches in all directions.

Proud names and thieves successful enough to buy wealth and station all came here in the end . . . all their boasts and plots and gold coins bought them no more than crumbling gravestones, inscribed with lies about their greatness and good character. Scant comfort, El thought, to the moldering bones beneath.

In the tranquil shade of the tomb-trees, the two friends lay atop the sloping roof of Ansildabar's Last Rest, knowing but not caring that the bones of the once-famous explorer lay gnawed and exposed in the pillaged tomb beneath, and passed a wineskin back and forth as they watched the shadows cast by the lowering sun creep across leaning tombs and collapsed mausoleums, heralding dusk.

"I've been thinking," Farl said suddenly, holding out his hand for the skin.

"Usually a bad sign," Elminster agreed affably, handing it over.

"Hah-ha," Farl replied, "between wild orgies, I mean."

"Ah, I'd been wondering what those momentary pauses were," Elminster said, extending his hand for the skin. Farl, who hadn't yet drunk, gave him a hurt look and a 'stay' gesture, and then drank deeply. Sighing with satisfaction, he wiped his mouth and held it out.

"D'you recall how much Budaera was asking me for pleasure together?"

Elminster grinned. "Aye. A low price—just for thee."

Farl nodded. "Exactly. Gold pieces hand over fist, these maids make . . . 'twould be easy, I'm thinking, to find out where some of 'em hide their loot—and help ourselves while they were sleeping, or out 'busy' at the taverns and rich merchants' clubs."

"Nay," El said firmly, "count me out of such plots. Fleece such sheep an' ye'll do it alone."

Farl looked at him. "Right, consider the plot abandoned. Now tell me why."

Elminster set his jaw. "I'll not steal from those who barely have enough coins for food, let alone taxes or saving."

"Principles?" Farl rescued the nearly empty wineskin.

"I've always had 'em. Ye know that." El waved away the skin, and Farl happily drained it.

"I thought ye wanted to slay all the wizards in Athalantar."

Elminster nodded. "All the magelords. Aye, I've sworn that oath—and slow, iron-careful, I've set about fulfilling it," he replied, staring out over the river, where a pole barge had just come into view in the distance, heading downstream toward the docks. "Yet sometimes I wonder what else I should do—what more life should be."

"Roast boar feasts every night," Farl said. "So much coin to buy them that I'll never have to feel the bite of a knife or hide in rotting dung while armsmen poke into it with their halberds."

"Nothing more?" El asked. "Nothing—higher?"

"What's the point?" Farl asked with a touch of scorn. "There're priests enough all over Faerun to worry about things like that—and my empty stomach never tires of telling me what *I* should be tending to." Satisfied that the very last drop of wine had fallen into his open mouth, he lowered the skin, rolled it, and thrust it through his belt. Then he looked across at his friend.

Eladar the Dark was frowning at him. "What gods should I worship?"

Farl shrugged, taken aback, and spread his hands. "A man must find that out for himself—or should. Only fools obey the nearest priest."

Amusement came into the blue-gray eyes locked on his. "What do priests do, then?"

Farl shrugged. "A lot of chanting and angry shouting and sticking swords into people who worship other gods."

In the same quiet, serious voice, El asked, "What use are faiths, then?"

Farl shrugged wildly, adopting a crazed, 'Who can know?' expression, but El's serious eyes stayed on him, and after a silence Farl said slowly, "Folk always have to believe there's something better, somewhere, than what they have right now—and that they just *might* get it. And they like to belong, to be part of a group, and feel superior to outlanders. It's why folk join clubs, and companies, and fellowships."

Eladar looked at him. "And go out and stick swords in each

other in dark alleys—and then feel superior about it?"

Farl grinned. "Exactly." He watched the pole barge scrape to a stop against a distant dock, and said casually, "If we're going to be facing death together many nights longer, it'd probably be a good thing if I knew this code of yours. I know you prefer shop-guarding, dockwork, and errand- and package-running to thieving, but who wouldn't?"

"Crazed-wits out looking for thrills," El said dryly.

Farl laughed. "Leave me out of it for a breath or two, and tell."

Elminster thought for a moment. "I won't slay innocent folk . . . and I don't like stealing from anyone except rich merchants who are grasping, unpleasant, or openly dishonest. Oh, and wizards of course."

"You really hate them, don't you?"

Elminster shrugged. "I—I've contempt for those who hide behind magic and lord it over the rest of us because someone taught them to read, or the gods gave them the power to wield magic, or something. They should be using the Art to help us all, not keep folk down and lord it over them."

"If you were Belaur right now," Farl said softly, "what in the name of the gods could you do but obey the wizards?"

El shrugged. "The king may be trapped, and he may not be. He never shows himself for us unwashed to get to know him—ye know, the subjects he's supposed to be serving—so how can I tell?"

"You said once your parents were killed by a dragon-riding wizard," Farl said.

Elminster looked at him sharply. "Did I?"

"You were drunk. I—not long after we met—I had to know if I could trust you, so I got you drunk. That night at the Ring of Blades, you wouldn't say anything else except 'outlaw' and 'kill magelords.' You kept repeating that."

Elminster stared steadily at the shattered crown of a nearby vault. "Every man needs an obsession," he said. He turned his head. "What's thine?"

Farl shrugged his shoulders. "Excitement. If I'm not in danger or doing high, hidden, and important deeds, I'm not alive."

Elminster nodded, remembering.

It had been a cold, blustery day, muddy slush ankle-deep in the streets of Hastarl. Newly arrived and wandering wide-eyed, El turned down a blind alley only to find, when he spun about, that he was facing a line of hard-eyed, grinning men blocking his way. A balding, burly giant in worn leathers stood at their head, a padded stick in one hand and a canvas sack big enough to enclose Elminster's head—for that was its purpose—in the other. They stalked down the alley toward him.

El backed away, fingering the Lion Sword and wondering if he could fight so many hardened men in such a confined space and hope to win.

He took a stand in a corner, blade out, but they didn't slow their steady, menacing advance. The bald man raised his stick, obviously planning to strike aside the lad's sword while the others wrestled him down, but before he could, a calm voice broke in from overhead.

"I wouldn't do that if I were you, Shildo. He's Hawklyn's meat already, marked and in use; see how bedazed he is?—and you know what Hawklyn does to blades who meddle."

The bald man looked up, face ugly. "And who's going to say we did it?"

The slim youth crouching on the windowsill, hand crossbow sliding gently back and forth to menace one bravo after another, smiled and said, "That's already been done, bald-pate. Two breaths ago Antaerl flew off to report. He left me to dissuade you because he recalls an old debt he owes you—and what happened the *last* time a snatch band took the wrong man. Wasn't pleasant, was it, Shildo? Recall what Undarl said he'd do to you if you made another unfortunate mistake? *I* remember."

Snarling, the bald man spun around and stalked off, breaking the line of bravos and waving at them to accompany him.

When the alley was empty, Elminster looked up and said, "Thankee for a rescue. My life is thine, Sir—?"

"Farl's the name, an' no 'sir' am I. I'm proud of that, mind." Farl explained that 'meat' was the name given to bumpkins, slaves, and other unfortunates used by magelords for experiments that slew, twisted, transformed, or left them mind-slaves. The wandering, obviously bewildered Elminster had looked like a prime snatch candidate, or a mind-slave already in thrall. "That's what I persuaded him you were," he said warningly.

"Thankee, I think," El replied wryly. "Why did that make a difference?"

"I intimated you were the property of the most powerful magelord. Shildo serves a rival whose power isn't great enough for open challenges yet. Shildo's under *very* strict orders not to provoke anything just now." He shifted on the snowy ledge and added, "Want to put away that blade? We could go somewhere warmer I know of, where they'll overcharge us for some hot turtle soup and burned toast . . . if you'll pay."

"Gladly," Elminster said, "if ye'll tell me where I can find a bed in this city, an' tell me what not to do."

"I'll do that," the laughing youth replied, jumping lightly down. "You need to learn, and I like to talk. Better; you look like you need a friend, and I find myself in short supply of them right now, too . . . hey?"

"Lead on," Elminster said.

He'd learned much that day, and in the days since then—but not where Farl had come from. The merry thief seemed part of Hastarl, as if he'd always been there and the city echoed his moods and manner. The two had taken a liking to each other and stolen more than their own weights in gold and gems through a slow spring and much of a long, hot summer.

Musing about this damp city of the magelords around him, Elminster found himself back on the sloping stone of the tomb roof, in the ebbing heat of a long, lazy summer day. He turned to look into his friend's face. "More than once, ye've said ye knew I came from Heldon."

Farl nodded. "The way you speak: up-country, for sure, and east. More—the winter when Undarl joined the magelords, talk went around the city that he'd impressed the others into accepting him in by riding a dragon he could command. At Lord Hawklyn's bidding he went to the village of Heldon to slay a man and wife there—and to show them what he could do, he had it tear the place stone from stone, an' burn all, even dogs running away across the fields."

"Undarl," Elminster repeated softly.

Farl saw that his friend's hands were clenched, white, and trembling. He nodded. "If it makes you feel better, El, I understand how you feel."

The eyes that Elminster turned on him blazed like a fire of blue steel, but his voice came with terrible softness as he asked, "Oh? How?"

"The magelords killed my mother," Farl said calmly.

Elminster looked at him, the fire dying. "What befell thy father then?"

Farl shrugged. "Oh, he's very well indeed."

Elminster looked a silent question, and Farl smiled a little sadly. "In fact, he's probably up in that tower there right now—and if Tyche frowns on us, he'll have magic up that enables him to hear us when I use his name."

Elminster looked up at the tower and said, "Could he strike us with a spell from there?"

Farl shrugged. "Who knows what wizards have learned to do? But I doubt it, or certain men'd be falling on their faces all over

Hastarl. Besides, the magelords I know could never resist taunting their foes before smiting them down, face-to-face."

"Then use his name," Elminster said deliberately, "and mayhap he'll come down where I can reach him."

"After I do," Farl replied softly. "After I'm done tearing his tongue out by the roots and breaking all his fingers to stop his spells—then I'll let you have some fun. He shouldn't die in any great haste."

"So who is he?"

Farl lifted one side of his mouth in a mirthless smile. "Lord Hawklyn, master magelord. Mage Royal of Athalantar, to you." He turned his head to watch a fleetwing whirl from one broken pillar to another. "I was illegitimate. Hawklyn had my mother— a lady of the court, loved by many, they say—killed when he learned of my birth."

"Why d'ye still live—outside yon tower?"

Farl stared into the past, not seeing the tombs ahead of him. "His men slaughtered a baby—but the wrong one; some other poor brat. I was stolen by a woman my mother had befriended . . . a lady of the evening."

Elminster raised his brows. "Yet ye proposed stealing from those same night maids?"

Farl shrugged. "One of them strangled my foster-mother for a few coins; I've never found out who, but almost certainly one of the girls in the Wench on"—his voice mockingly assumed the pedantic tones of a sage relating a tale of awesome importance— "the night when two magelords' sons revealed their love to all Hastarl."

"Oh, gods," Elminster said quietly, "and I've felt sorry for meself a time or two. Farl, ye—"

"Can tell you to belt up and not say whatever tearful mush you were about to spout," Farl said serenely. "When the feebleness brought on by my advancing dotage requires sympathy from thee, Eladar Mage-Killer, I shall not keep thee unapprised of the fact."

His grandiose tones brought forth a chuckle from Elminster, who asked, "What's it to be now, then?"

Farl grinned and, in one smooth movement, rolled to his feet. "Rest time's over. Back to the wars. So you won't let me take advantage of ladies of the evening or innocent folk—well, that's not a hard bind. There can't be more than two or three of the latter in all Hastarl—an' we've hit the wizards and the high-and-mighty families overmuch. If we roost too often on the same perch, 'tis traps we'll find waiting, not piles of coins ready for the taking. This leaves us with two targets: temples—"

"Nay," Elminster said firmly. "No meddling with the affairs of gods. I'd rather not spend the rest of a short and unhappy life with most of Those Who Hear All furious with me—to say nothing of their priesthoods."

Farl grinned. "I expected that. Well, then, there's but one field we've not touched: rich merchants."

He held up a hand to forestall Elminster's coming protest about plundering hardworking shopkeepers and said quickly, "I mean those who lend coins and invest in back rooms and behind secure doors, working secretly in groups to keep prices high and arrange accidents for competitors . . . ever notice how few companies own the barges that actually land here? And the warehouses? Hmmm? We've got to learn how these folk operate, because if we're ever to retire from plucking things out of the pockets of lesser folk—and no one's fingers stay nimble forever, you know—we'll have to join the folk who sit idle and let their coins work for them."

Elminster was frowning thoughtfully. "A hidden world, masked by what most see in the streets."

"Just as our world—the realm of thieves—is hidden," Farl added.

"Right," El said with enthusiasm. "That's our battlefield, then. What now? How to begin?"

"This night," Farl said, "by handsomely bribing a man who owes me an old favor, I plan to attend a dinner I'd never be allowed in to. He'd be serving wine there, but I'll be doing it in his place, and listening to what I should not hear. If I'm right, I'll hear plans and agreements for quite a bit of quiet trade into and out of the city for the rest of the season." He frowned. "There's one problem. You can't come. There's no way you can get close enough to hear anything without being caught; these folk have guards everywhere. I've no excuse for getting you into the place, either."

Elminster nodded. "So I go elsewhere. An evening of idleness, or have ye any suggestions?"

Farl nodded slowly. "Aye, but there's great danger. There's a certain house I've had my eye on for four summers now; 'tis home to three free-spending merchants who deal in exchanging goods and lending coins but never seem to lift a finger to do any real work. They're probably part of this chain of investors. Can you skulk about the place without being seen? We need to know where doors, and approaches, and important rooms and the like are—and if you can overhear anything interesting while they dine. . . ."

El nodded. "Lead me to the place. Just so long as ye don't expect any great tales when we meet on the morrow. I think it's only in minstrels' tales that folk sit around explaining things they already know for eavesdroppers to understand."

Farl nodded. "Just slip in, see where things are, try to find out if there's anything of import befalling—and get you gone again, as quietly as the thing can be done. I want no dead heroes in this partnership; it's too hard to find trustworthy partners."

"Ye prefer live cowards, eh?" Elminster asked as they dropped lightly down from the roof of the tomb and set off through the rubble and tangled plants toward the bough they'd come in by.

Farl stopped him. "Seriously, El—I've never found such fearlessness and honesty in anyone. To find it in one who also has endurance and dexterity . . . I've only one regret."

"Which is?" Elminster was blushing furiously.

"You're not a pretty lass."

Elminster replied with a rude noise, and they both chuckled and clambered up the tree that would afford them exit.

"I see only one worry ahead," Farl added. "Hastarl grows rich under the wizards, and thieves are coming in. Gangs. As they grow larger, you and I will have to join or start one of our own to survive. Besides, we'll need more hands than these four if we're to tackle these back room investors."

"And thy worry?"

"Betrayal."

That word hung in somber silence between them as they leapt down from the crumbling wall into a garbage-choked alley, and watched the rats run. Elminster said softly, "I've found something precious in thee, too, Farl."

"A friend prettier than yourself?"

"A friend, aye. Loyalty, and trust, too—more precious by far than all the gold we've taken together."

"Pretty speech. I've remembered another regret, too," Farl added gravely. "I couldn't be there in the room to see Shandathe and old Hannibur waking up and seeing each other!"

They convulsed in shared laughter. "I have noted," Elminster added a few helpless breaths later as they went on down the street, "word of *that* meeting has *not* spread across Hastarl."

"A pity, indeed," Farl replied. They threw their arms around each other's shoulders and strode down the slippery cobbles, the conquest of all Hastarl bright ahead of them.

Five

TO CHAIN A MAGE

*To chain a mage? Why, the promise of power and knowing secrets
('magic,' if you will), greed, and love—the things that chain all
men . . . and some of the more foolish women, too.*

Athaeal of Evermeet
Musings Of A Witch-Queen In Exile
Year of the Black Flame

The smell wafting up through the high windows was wonderful. In spite of himself, Elminster's stomach growled. He clung to
the stone sill, frozen in an awkward head-down pose, and hoped
no one would hear.

The feast below was a merry one; glass tinkled and men
laughed, short barks of merriment punctuating the general
murmur of jests and earnest talk. He was still too distant to hear
what was being said. El finished the knot and tugged on it; firm.
Aye, then, into the hands of the gods . . .

He waited for a burst of laughter and, when it came, slid
down the thin cord to the balcony below. For the entire journey
he was clearly visible to anyone at the board below who bothered
to look up; he was sweating hard as his boots touched the balcony floor, and he could sink thankfully down into a sitting position behind the parapet, completely concealed from those at
table. No outcry came. After a moment, he relaxed enough to
peer carefully around. The balcony was dark and disused; he
tried not to stir up dust that might force a sneeze or leave betraying marks behind.

Elminster then bent his attention to the chatter below—and
within a few words was sitting frozen in fear and rising excitement. His hand went unbidden to his breast, where the Lion
Sword was hidden.

"I've heard some sly whispers, Havilyn, that you doubt our
powers," a cold and proud voice said, words falling into a sudden,
tense silence, "that we are meant to scare the common folk into
obedience to the Stag Throne and are not real wizards, daring to
set foot outside our realm . . . that our spells may be showy, but
would avail little against thieves and the night-work of competi-

tors, leaving our shared investments unprotected."

"I've said no such thing."

"Perhaps not, but your tone now tells me that you believe it. Nay, put your blade away. I intend no harm to you this night. 'Twould be churlish to strike down a man in his own house—and the act of a fool to destroy a good ally and wealthy supporter. All I'd like you to do is watch a little demonstration."

"What sort of magic do you plan to spin, Hawklyn?" Havilyn's tone was wary. "I warn you that some here are not as protected by amulets and shields as I am—and have less reason to love you than I do. It would not be wise to make a man reach for a weapon at this table."

"I have no great violence in mind. I merely wish to reveal the efficacy of my magic by casting for you a spell I've recently perfected, which can compel any mortal whose name and likeness I know into my presence."

"Any mortal?"

"Any living mortal. Yet before you name some old foe you'd like to get your hands on, I want to show you the true power of the magic we wield here in Hastarl . . . the magic you've belittled as mere tricks and flame-balls to cow the common folk."

There was a strange, high ringing and clanking sound. "Behold this chain," came the cold voice of Neldryn Hawklyn, Mage Royal of Athalantar. "Set it down and withdraw; my thanks." There was a glassy shifting sound and then the receding tread of soft and hasty feet.

The clink of moving glass came again, and reflections of flame suddenly danced on the wall above Elminster. He peered at them narrowly and saw that a transparent chain was rising by itself from the floor, rising and coiling upward to hang in the air and turn slowly in a great spiral.

The cold voice of Hawklyn spoke again. "This is the Crystal Chain of Binding, wrought in Netheril long ages ago. Elves, dwarves, and men all searched for it and failed and thought it lost forever. I found it; behold the chain that can imprison any mage—and prevent his use of any magic. Beautiful, is it not?"

There were murmurs of response, and then the mightiest of the magelords continued. "Who is the mightiest mage in all Faerun, Havilyn?"

"You want me to say you, I suppose . . . in truth, I know not—you're the expert in matters magical, not me . . . this Mad Mage we hear about, I guess. . . ."

"Nay, think greater than that. Recall you nothing of the teachings of Mystra?"

"*Her?* You plan a chain a *goddess?*"

"Nay; a mortal, I said, and it's a mortal I have in mind."

"Stop all this grand questioning and tell us," a sour voice said. "There's a time for cleverness and a time for plain talk—and I think we've fast reached the latter."

"Do you doubt my power?"

"Nay, Magelord, I believe you have magic to spare. I told you to stop lording it over us with arrogant word-games and behave more like a great mage and less like a boy trying to impress with his brilliance."

These words ended in a sudden cry of disgust, and a murmur followed. Elminster risked a quick glance above the parapet to peer down, and as quickly ducked back below it again. He'd seen a man sitting at the table gaping in horror at his plate—and on it had been a human head, staring unseeing at him.

"Behold the head of the last man who tried to steal from your warehouse, beheaded by a spell-blade I conjured. There, 'tis gone now. By all means enjoy the rest of your dinner, Nalith; it was only an illusion."

"I think you should tell us plainly, too, Hawklyn," said another, older voice. "Enough games."

"Well enough," the mage royal replied. "Watch, then, and keep silent."

There was a brief muttering, a flash of light, and a high-pitched sound like the jangle of clashing crystal or tiny ankle bells.

"Tell everyone who you are." There was cold triumph in Hawklyn's voice.

"I am called the Magister," came a new voice, calm but quavering with age. There were gasps from around the table, and Elminster could not restrain himself. This was the wizard who wore the mantle of Mystra's power. The greatest mage of all. He *had* to see. Slowly and cautiously he raised his head to peer over the parapet and froze, chilled by a sudden thought: if the magelords controlled the most powerful magic in all Faerun, how could he ever hope to defeat them?

Below stretched the long, gleaming feast table. All the men seated around it were staring at a thin, bearded and robed man who stood upright in an area of radiance a little way down the hall. The hitherto empty spiral of chain was now revolving slowly around him. Little lightnings leapt and played among its coils as it turned, fed by the radiance around the Magister.

"Do you know where you are?" the mage royal asked coldly.

"This room, I know not—some grand house, surely. In Hastarl, in the Realm of the Stag."

"And what is it that binds you?" Magelord Hawklyn leaned forward as he spoke those eager words. Lamplight caught gem-adorned ward-runes on his dark robes, and they flashed as he moved, drawing eyes to him. He looked lean and dangerous as he spread long-fingered hands before him on the table and half rose to challenge the wizard in the grip of the chain.

The Magister looked at the chain with mild curiosity, rather like a man surveying sale-goods after idly entering a shop with an unspectacular facade. He reached out to touch it, ignoring the sudden lightnings that spat and crackled, blinding-white, around his wrinkled hand, tapped it thoughtfully, and said, "It appears to be the Crystal Chain of Binding, forged long ago in Netheril, and thought to be lost. Is it that, or some new chain of thy devising?"

"*I* shall ask the questions," Neldryn Hawklyn commanded grandly, "and you will give answer—or I'll use this crossbow, and Faerun will have a new Magister." As he spoke, a cocked and loaded crossbow floated into view from behind a curtained door. Startled looks sped between the merchants sitting around the table.

"Oh," the old man said mildly, "is this a challenge, then?"

"Not unless you defy me. Consider it a threat hanging over you. Obey or perish—the same alternatives any king gives his subjects."

"You must live in rather more barbaric lands than I am used to," the Magister said in a dry voice. "Can it be, Neldryn Hawklyn, you have reshaped Athalantar into a tyranny of mages? I have heard things of you and your fellow magelords . . . and they were not good things."

"I don't doubt it," Hawklyn sneered. "Now hold your tongue 'til I bid you speak—or a new Magister will speak, in your stead."

"Do you then seek to control when and how the Magister speaks?" The old man's tone seemed almost sad.

"I do." The crossbow drifted nearer, rising menacingly to hang above the table, aimed at the old man's face.

"Mystra forbids that," the Magister said quietly, "and so I have no choice left. I must answer your challenge."

His body suddenly boiled into billowing vapors, faded, and was gone. The chains hung around emptiness for a moment, and then crashed to the floor.

The crossbow jerked as it fired—but the quarrel sped through emptiness, leaping across the room to strike a hanging shield and rebound. It cracked against the stone wall in a corner, fell, and flew no more.

"Let all that is hidden be *revealed!*" Mage Royal Hawklyn thundered, standing with his arms raised. Then he recoiled; the old man melted out of the air right in front of his face, sitting calmly on nothing in the air just above the table.

Half a dozen spells lashed out as alarmed wizards saw a clear chance to slay. Amid the leaping magic, terrified merchants upset chairs in their haste to bolt from the table. Food sprayed into the air as ravening flame, bolts of lightning, and mist-shedding beams of coldness cut the air, meeting in hissing chaos where the old man—had been. He was gone, instants before deadly magic struck . . . if he'd ever been there at all.

"Those who live by the slaying spell," the Magister said mildly from the balcony—Elminster whirled and gaped in terror as the man in robes suddenly appeared beside him—"must expect, in the end, to die by it."

He raised his wrinkled hands. From each finger a ruby ray of light stabbed out across the room. Solid things they touched boiled silently away. El gulped as he saw legs standing with no body left above them—and beyond, a sobbing wizard crash to the floor as his frantically running feet were suddenly gone from under him. Amid the screams and crashes the rays slowly faded, leaving only spreading flames behind, where they'd scorched wood or singed tapestries.

The rays were still dying away as men all over the room started to rise into the air—whole or in remains, floating slowly straight up, regardless of their struggles or frantic spellcastings. Glass tinkled and sang as the chain also rose into the air, gliding and coiling like a gigantic snake.

From somewhere nearby, Hawklyn snarled an incantation in a high, frightened voice. The old man ignored him.

The rising men came to a smooth halt at the same height as the balcony, and the chain wove its way among them, gleaming in the light of the fires below.

There was a flash and a roar. Elminster dived for his life as Hawklyn's spell smashed half the balcony into a splintered ruin of paneling and shattered stone. Desperately the young thief clawed his way along a stone floor that was crumbling and collapsing under and behind him.

With a shudder and then a gathering roar, most of the tiles of the broken balcony floor slid down to the stones of the feasting-hall amid a cloud of dust. The rubble piled up in a heap around a lone, leaning pillar that had supported that end of the balcony moments before. Sprawled on the surviving remnant of the balcony, Elminster turned in haste to see the Magister unconcernedly standing on empty air, surrounded by a ring of helpless, floating, frightened men.

"Is *that* the best you can do, Hawklyn?" The old man shook his head. "You had no business even thinking you could ever grow mighty enough to challenge me, with such feeble powers . . . and dull wits driving them." He sighed. Elminster saw the crystal chain had wrapped itself around the neck of one floating man.

The man's head was turned with slow, terrible, unseen force, until he hung helplessly staring into the old man's eyes. "So you are a magelord, Maulygh . . . of long service, I see, and you fancy yourself too cunning to appear openly ambitious. Yet you desire to rule over all and await any chance to smite down these others, and take the throne for yourself. And you have plans; your reign would not be gentle."

The Magister waved a hand in dismissal, and the crystal links around the wizard's neck burst apart in tinkling shards. Maulygh's headless body jerked once and then hung limp and dripping. The shortened chain glided on to the next man.

"Only a merchant, eh? Othyl Naerimmin, a panderer, smuggler, and dealer in scents and beer." The quavering voice seemed almost hopeful, but when it came again, it was a low, bitter tone of disappointment. "You arrange poisonings." The coil of the chain burst again, leaving another hanging body behind.

Someone wailed in terror, almost drowning out the frantic mutterings of several spellcastings. The Magister ignored it all as he watched the chain wind its deadly way on through the air. One man—a fat merchant, gasping and staring in horror, was spared. He floated gently down to the floor, fell when the magic released him, and then scrambled up, whimpering, and fled from the hall.

The next man was another mage, who spat defiance and went to his death raging. When he was headless, pulses of purple radiance flared around the body. The Magister studied them. "An interesting web of contingencies—don't you think, Hawklyn?"

The mage royal spat a word that echoed and rolled around the hall, and there was a sudden burst of flame. Elminster shrank back into the corner and hid his face, feeling a sudden wash of heat. Then it was gone, and amid the creaking of cooling stone and the rush of tortured air, they heard the old man sigh.

"Fireballs . . . always fireballs. Can't the young cast anything else?"

The Magister stood unharmed on empty air, watching the chain—much shortened now, its surface cracked and blackened from fire—move to the next man. He proved to be dead already, of fright or self-spell or a stray glass shard, and the chain drifted on.

Twice more it burst, and then another merchant was spared. He fled sobbing, leaving only the mage royal of Athalantar hanging alive before the Magister. Hawklyn looked right and left at the headless things in the air around him and snarled in fear.

"I must confess that killing you will bring me satisfaction," the old man said. "Yet I'd be more pleased still if you renounced all claims to this realm here and now and agreed to serve Mystra under my direction."

Hawklyn cursed, and with trembling hands tried to shape one last spell. The Magister listened politely and then shook his head, ignoring the shadowy taloned beast that appeared in the air before him.

Its cruel claws passed right through the old man, and then faded away as the last links of the Chain of Binding burst. Blood spattered on the stone floor far below.

Leaving the corpses hanging in grisly array, the Magister turned to regard the youth crouched watching in the surviving corner of the balcony. There was a dangerous glint in his eyes as they met Elminster's awed gaze. "Are you a magelord, boy, or a servant of this house?"

"Neither." Tearing his gaze free with an effort, Elminster leapt from the balcony, landing hard on the blood-spattered stones below. The old man's eyes narrowed, and he lifted a finger. A wall of flames sprang up in a ring around the thief, who spun around, the sharpened stub of an old war-sword suddenly in his hand.

Fear lent Elminster anger; his voice trembled with both as he faced the old man standing on air above him. "Can ye not see I'm no wild-spells wizard? Are ye no better than these cruel mages who rule Athalantar?" He waved his blade at the roaring flames around him. "Or are all who wield magic so twisted by its power that they become tyrants who delight in maiming, destroying, and spreading fear among honest folk?"

"Are you not—with these?" the Magister asked, spreading his hand to indicate the bodies hanging silently around him.

"*With* them?" Elminster spat. "I fight them whenever I dare—and hope one day to destroy them all so men can walk Athalantar free and happy again!" His face twisted at a sudden thought. "I sound a bit like a high minstrel, don't I?" he added, more quietly.

The Magister regarded him thoughtfully. "That's not a bad way to think," he said quietly, "if you survive the dangers of talking the same way." A sudden smile lit his face, and Elminster found himself smiling back.

Unseen by them both, down the hall, a pair of eyes appeared amid swirling points of light, in the flames flickering around the canted wreckage of the collapsed feast-table. They watched the boy and the floating mage, and looked thoughtful.

"Can ye really see all that men are, and think?" Elminster asked, awkwardly blurting out the question.

"No," the Magister replied simply. His old brown eyes looked down into unflinching blue-gray ones as he made the crackling wall of flames die away to nothing.

Elminster looked once to see what had befallen, but made no move to flee. Standing on the rubble-strewn, blood-spattered floor, he looked back up at the old wizard. "Are ye going to blast me or let me go?"

"I have no interest in destroying honest folk—and very little at all in the affairs of those who have no magic. I see you have mage-sight, lad . . . why don't you try your hand at sorcery?"

Elminster gave him a dark look. His voice was scornful as he said, "I've no interest in such things, or in becoming the sort of man who wields magic. Whenever I look upon mages, I see snakes who use their spells to make folk fear them—like a whip to drive others to obey. Hard, arrogant men who can take a life, or—" he raised hard eyes to look at the destruction all around; the eyes watching from the flames shrank down to avoid notice—"destroy a hall in a few breaths, and not care what they've done, so long as their whims are satisfied. Leave me out of the ranks of wizards, lord."

Then, staring up at the old man's calm face, Elminster knew sudden fear. His words had been harsh, and the Magister was a mage like any other. The mild old eyes, though, seemed to hold . . . approval?

"Those who don't love hurling power make the best mages," the Magister replied. His eyes seemed suddenly to bore deep into Elminster's soul like seeking, darting things, and sadness was in his voice again as he added, "And those who live by stealing almost always rob themselves of their own lives, in the end."

"The taking gives me no pleasure," Elminster retorted. "I do it to have enough to eat—and to strike against the magelords where and when I can."

The Magister nodded. "That's why ye might listen," he said. "I'd not have wasted my breath otherwise."

Elminster stared up at him thoughtfully—and then stiffened as he heard the sudden, approaching thunder of running, booted

feet echoing in the passages nearby. That sound could mean only
one thing: armsmen of Athalantar.

"Save thyself!" he snapped, without stopping to think what a
ridiculous warning that was to the mightiest archmage in all the
world, and darted toward the nearest archway that did not ring
with footfalls.

He was still three running strides short of it when men with
halberds and crossbows burst into the room, but the puffing
merchant with them stabbed a finger up at the floating mage
and bellowed, "There!"

By the time the volley of quarrels and hastily conjured flames
had torn through suddenly empty air, both the running boy and
the eyes in the licking flames that played about the ruin of Havilyn's once-grand table had vanished. A breath later, the floating
corpses suddenly fell from the air, striking the stone floor with
wet, heavy thuds. White-faced armsmen drew back, calling
aloud on Tempus to defend them and Tyche to aid them.

Elminster took one door out of the kitchen, found himself in a
dead-end cluster of pantries, and raced frantically back to the
kitchen's other, smaller door, offering his own quieter prayer to
Tyche that it not be another pantry—when he heard Havilyn's
furious voice snarl, "Find that boy! He's no part of my house-
hold!"

Cursing aloud, Elminster snatched open the door. Yes, this
was the way the terrified cooks had fled. He took the stairs two
at time until at a bend in the stair several halberds crashed
down together in front of him, striking sparks. Snarling armsmen struggled to tear them free of the stair-rails and wrestle
them around to stab downward—but El had already seen a third
armsman lumbering along the passage above with a ready crossbow. He leapt back down the stairs in a single bound, landed
hard on his haunches, and sprang sideways into an evil-smelling
alcove.

A breath later, a crossbow quarrel cracked off the wall nearby
and rattled down into the kitchens. A second quarrel followed,
speeding deep into the throat of the foremost armsman racing
up the stairs.

Elminster didn't spare the time to watch the man gurgle and
fall; he was looking around the dark alcove for the scullery door.
There! Wrenching it open, he skidded across the noisome room,
through a maze of sloped boards where meat was washed and
buckets where food scraps were thrown, hoping the house was
old enough to have . . . *yes!*

El seized the pull-ring and hauled up the trapdoor of the

refuse-pit. He could hear the waters of the Run rushing past in the darkness below as he slid feetfirst down to join them.

The drop was farther than he'd thought it would be, and the waters numbingly cold. El's heels struck a mucky bottom for a moment, and he twisted to one side to come up off to one side of the door above.

Trying to ignore the unseen slimy lumps floating in the water with him, he came up gasping for breath, in time to hear a quarrel crack off the hatch somewhere above and behind him, followed by the shout, "The sewers! He's gone below!"

Elminster swam with the rushing river, trying not to make noise. He didn't trust the avid armsmen not to come down after him or lower torches and try their archery along the river tunnel. The chill of the waters crept into him as they carried him around a corner and away.

It seemed the first chance he'd had in a long while to collect his wits. The mage royal and at least three other magelords had been swept away in a single night—but the hand of Elminster had done nothing to them. He hadn't even a bite of supper or a spare coin from the house to show for his efforts.

"Elminster gives thee thanks, Tyche," he murmured into the rushing darkness. He'd managed to hang on to his head in that chamber of death; he supposed that was something . . . something even mighty wizards hadn't managed! Prudence stifled the whoop of exultation that suddenly rose within him—but it warmed him as he was swept out of the darkness into the blue, lamplit dimness of evening beneath the docks. He turned his head to look up at the dark spires of Athalgard and grinned his defiance at them.

The feeling lasted until he'd clambered out of the water onto a disused dock and started the cold, dripping walk home. If he'd been Farl, he'd have taken his knowledge of who'd died in that chamber to swoop down on a hand's-worth of houses this very night and seize riches their owners would never claim before relatives or lesser vultures knew man or treasure was missing, and be safely gone into the night.

"But I'm not Farl," Elminster told the night, "and not even all that good a thief—what I am is a good runner."

To prove it, he outran the armsman who came around a corner just then, halberd in hand, who with a startled shout recognized the youth he'd almost spitted in a stairway in Havilyn's house not twenty breaths ago. Their pounding pursuit took them along a winding street lined with the walled gardens of the wealthy. As they ran under overhanging trees, a dark shadow reached down from one of them and struck the armsmen hard and accurately in the face with a cobblestone.

The man pitched to the cobbles with a clatter, and Farl dropped lightly down into the road, calling, "Eladar!"

Elminster turned at the top of the road and looked back. His friend stood with hands on hips, shaking his head.

"Can't leave you alone for an evening, I see," Farl said as El puffed his way back down the street.

As he came up, his friend was kneeling on the guard's neck, expertly feeling for purses, spare daggers, medallions, and other items of interest. "Something important's happened," Farl said, not looking up. "Havilyn came running in, all out of breath, and said something to Fentarn—and we were all ordered out of the house, and the armsmen after us to be sure we were turned out into the street—while the lot of them ran somewhere—*ran*, El, I tell you . . . I didn't know any high-and-mighty merchants *remembered* how to run. . . ."

"I was where the important thing happened," Elminster said quietly. "That's why this one was chasing me."

Farl looked up at him, eyes alight. "Tell," was all he said.

"Later," Elminster replied. "Let me describe the dead first, and once ye've named them, we can visit whichever unsuspecting incipient houses of grief bid fair to have the heaviest loot lying around for the taking."

Farl grinned fiercely. "Suppose we do just that, O prince of thieves." In his excitement and the effort of lifting the guard's body, he did not see Elminster stiffen at the word 'prince.'

* * * * *

"We're fair out of room in there," Farl said in satisfaction when they were safely away from the boarded-up shop where their takings were cached. "Now let's go somewhere where we can talk and not be seen."

"The burial ground again?"

"Fair enough—once we make sure it's free of lovers."

They did so, and Elminster told Farl the tale. His friend shook his head at El's description of the Magister. "I thought he was just a legend," he protested.

"Nay," El said quietly, "he was frightening—ah, but it was magnificent, the way he ignored their best spells, and calmly judged each and struck them down. The *power!*"

Farl cast a sidelong glance at his friend. Elminster was staring up at the moon, eyes bright. "To have that much power, someday," he murmured, "and never have to run from an armsman again!"

"I thought you hated wizards."

"I-I do . . . magelords, at least. There's something about see-ing spells hurled, though, that—"

"Fascinates, eh? I've felt that." Farl nodded in the moonlight. "You'll get over it once you've tried to fire a wand or speak a spell over and over again and nothing happens. You learn to admire it from a distance and keep well clear—or be swiftly slain. Gods-bedamned wizards." He yawned. "Well, a good night's work. . . . Let's get some slumber under Selune—or we'll be snoring some-where when full day comes again."

"Here?"

"Nay—two of those dead, at least, have family vaults right here—and what if their servants, sent to clean up the tombs and the brush for a burial, are fearful enough of walking dead to de-mand an escort of armsmen? Nay, we need to find a roof else-where."

A sudden thought came to Elminster, and he grinned. "Han-nibur's?"

Farl grinned back. "His snores'd wake a corpse."

"Exactly." They laughed and hastened back through the dark streets and alleys of the city, avoiding aroused bands of arms-men who were tramping aimlessly about in the night, looking for a running youth in dark leathers and an old mage strolling along in the air—and no doubt inwardly hoping they'd find nei-ther.

As the half-light that heralds dawn stole down the river and into Hastarl, El and Farl settled down on Hannibur's roof, won-dering at the silence from below. "What's become of his snoring?" El murmured, and Farl shrugged his own puzzlement in reply.

Then they heard the small sound from below that meant Hannibur had slid open the eye-panel on his back door. They ex-changed raised eyebrows and bent to look down into the alley—in time to see Shandathe Llaerin, called "the Shadow" for her smoothly silent ways, and perhaps the most beautiful woman in all Hastarl, come lightly up the alley to Hannibur's back door. They heard her say softly, "I'm here at last, love."

"At last," the baker rumbled as he drew the door warily open. "I thought ye'd never come. Come to the bed ye belong in, now."

Elminster and Farl exchanged delighted glances, and clasped hands with fierce joy in the night. Then, all thoughts of sleep gone, they settled down to listen to what befell in the room below.

And were fast asleep within seven breaths.

* * * * *

The hot sun woke the two exhausted, filthy thieves sometime late in the morning . . . and once they were awake, the smell of fresh-baked rolls and loaves wafting up from Hannibur's shop made sure they stayed that way.

Stomachs growling, the two thieves peered carefully down at the bedroom below. They could just see Shandathe's elbow as she slept the day peacefully away.

"Don't seem right, that she should sleep when we can't," Farl complained, rubbing his eyes.

"Let her sleep," Elminster replied. "She's doubtless earned it. Come." They climbed carefully down the crumbling back sills and cross-beams of the shop next door and went off to the silver-bit baths—only to find folk lined up.

"Whence this sudden urge for cleanliness, goodsir?" Farl asked a sausage vendor they knew by sight.

He frowned at them. "Haven't ye heard? The mage royal and a dozen other mages were killed last night! The dirge-walk begins at highsun."

"Killed? Just who could manage to slay the mage royal?"

"Ah." The sausage seller leaned close confidentially, pretending not to see the eight or so folk who crowded or leaned out of the line to listen. "There's some who says it was a mage they awakened from sleeping in a tomb all these years since the fall of Netheril!"

"Nay," a woman standing near put in, " 'Twas—"

"And there's some," the sausage seller went on, raising his voice to ride over her, "what says it was a poor wretch they caught an' were going to eat, *alive,* so they say, for some foul magic—but when they sat down at the table, he turned into a dragon, and burned 'em all! Others say 'twas a beholder, or a mind flayer, or summat worse!"

"Nay, nay," the woman said, pushing in, "that's not it at all—"

"But meself," the sausage-vendor said, elbowing her back and raising his voice again, so that it echoed back off the stone wall across the alley, "I think the first tale I heard is the true one: their wickedness was punished by a visit from Mystra *herself!*"

"Yes! That's it! 'Twas just that as happened, I tell thee!" The woman was hopping up and down in her excitement now; her capacious bosom heaved and rolled like tied bundles on the docks in high winds. "The mage royal thought he had a spell that would bring her to heel like a dog so he could use her power to destroy all wizards but ours and conquer all the lands from here to the

Great Sea beyond Elembar! But he was wrong, and she—"

"She turned them all to boars, thrust spits up their behinds, and seared 'em in the hearth fires!" The gleeful voice belonged to a man nearby who stank of fish.

"Nay! I heard she plucked off all their heads—and *ate* 'em!" an old woman said proudly, as if King Belaur personally had told her.

"Ah, get gone wi' ye. Why'd she do that, eh?" The man next to her stepped on her foot, hard.

She hopped in pain, shaking her finger under his nose. "Just you wait, clever-nose! Jus' you wait an' see—if they has carved wooden 'eads when they're borne past us, or their heads covered wi' the burial cloaks, then I'm right! An' there's some folk in Hastarl as'll tell you Berdeece Hettir's *never* wrong! Jus' you wait!"

Farl and Elminster had been trading amused looks, but at this Farl smiled and said out of the side of his mouth, changing his voice so that it sounded gruff and distant: "I suppose as thou wouldn't put *money* on it, hey?"

In an instant, the alley was a bedlam of shouting, red-faced Hastarl folk holding up fingers to indicate their wagers.

"Wait a bit, wait a bit," Elminster said—and silence fell: Eladar the Dark *never* talked. "It always distresses me to see ye wager," he said, looking around earnestly, "because after, there's so much hard talk and people furious at those who didn't pay. So if ye must wager—and ye know *I* don't throw my coins about thus—I'll write down thy claims, and all can be settled fair, after."

There was much talk . . . and then a growing agreement that this was a good idea. Elminster tore the sleeve from the rotten shirt he was wearing, got some ink from the street-scribe in trade for a quill that he'd stolen out of a window a tenday ago, and was still carrying in his boot, and set to work, scratching out sums with a rough-pointed needle.

In the rush, none of the folk noticed Farl met several heavy wagers, standing always for the headless side. Elminster worked his way along the line to its head, dodged inside to continue wagering, hung the scribbled sleeve on a high nail, and plunged headlong and fully clothed into the old wine-press tub that served as the bath. The water was already gray with filth, and Elminster came out again just as fast, pursued by the furious proprietor. They dodged around the rinse-pump while Farl worked the handle, dousing them both with rather cleaner water—and then Elminster thrust four silver bits into the man's hand, leapt to retrieve the wager sleeve, and scampered out again.

"Gods *blast* thee! 'Tis a gold piece a head this day!" the man bellowed after them.

El spun around, disgusted, and tossed a handful of silver bits in the bath-keeper's direction. "He's a worse thief than we've *ever* been," he muttered to Farl as they headed for a good place to hide the sleeve. It seemed fitting that the folk of Hastarl were willing to pay good gold to see the backs forever of the mage royal and a good handful of magelords besides.

"Or a better," Farl agreed. Word of what had befallen was all over the city; folk talked of nothing else around them as they walked—and something of the air of a festival hung over the city. El shook his head at the open laughter, even among the patrols of armsmen. "Well, of *course* they're happy," Farl explained to his wondering partner. "It's not every night that some helpful young thief—even if he does prefer to give all the credit to some mysterious mage who conveniently came out of thin air and just as helpfully vanished back into it again—downs the most hated and feared man in all Athalantar and many of his fellow mages . . . not to mention a bunch of men that shopkeepers in this city owe a lot of coins to. Wouldn't you be, in their place?"

"They just haven't thought about which cruel magelord will step forward to proclaim himself mage royal, and make them even more fearful than before," Elminster replied darkly.

The wide streets along the route of the dirge-walk were filling already; folk who owned finery (and bath facilities of their own to prepare for its wearing) were pushing for the best positions—unaware of the flood of less polite and poorer neighbors who would shortly be charging in to seize the vantage points they wanted, regardless of who thought they owned it already. In most such processions, a good score of folk ended up crushed under the wheels of the carts, shoved forward by the press of leaning, shouting common folk.

"Are you thinking of what houses may be standing empty this good day, groaning with the weight of coins for the taking, while all Hastarl turns out to watch corpses paraded by?" Farl asked lightly.

"Nay," Elminster said. "I was thinking of switching the bucket that bath-keeper sits on for another—taking the one he's filling up with coins right now, and in its place leaving a bucket of—"

"Dung?" Farl grinned. "Too risky, though, by far—half the folk in line'd see us."

"Ye think they don't know what we do for a living, Farl? Even ye can't be that much the idiot!" Elminster replied.

Farl drew himself up with an air of injured dignity. " 'Tis not that, goodsir—'tis that we have a reputation to maintain. Everyone may know that we take, aye—but none should ever see us doing the taking. It shouldst be magic, d'you see? Like those wizards you're so fond of."

El gave him a look. "Let's go take things," he said, and they strolled off to arm themselves for the workday ahead.

* * * * *

One house topped the list of places to loot, and they hastened hence, wearing livery that was not their own but that served to conceal carry-bags strapped to their backs and bellies and to hide the handfuls of daggers they both carried.

They dropped over the back wall into a pleasant garden, crossed it like two hungry shadows, and swarmed up a climbing thornflower to a balcony. A servant was asleep in the sun in the room beyond, seizing a prize opportunity while his master was out of the house.

"This is *too* easy," Farl said as they sped up the stairs to a gilded door. He thrust his dagger into the carved snarling lion in its center and waited while the spring-loaded darts flashed away harmlessly down the stairs. "Don't these fools realize that the shops that sell 'em thief-traps are always run by thieves?"

He dug his blade into one of the lion's eyes, and the cut-glass eye popped out of its setting to dangle from the end of a cloth ribbon. Finding the wire in the opening behind the eye, Farl cut it and swung the door open. El looked back down the stairs as they went in, but the house was silent.

The bedchamber was a vision of red and deep pinkish tapestries, cushions, and couches. "I feel as if I'm in someone's stomach," Farl muttered as they crossed this sea of red.

"Or wading around in an open wound," Elminster agreed, striding up to a silver jewel-coffer.

As he reached for it, a hard-thrown dart flashed past his fingers. Farl spun, dagger in hand—to stare into the eyes of two women and a man who were climbing swiftly in through a window. They were all clad in matching black leathers, and bore a sigil on their breasts: a crossed moon and dagger.

"This loot belongs to the Moonclaws," said one woman in a steely whisper, her eyes hard.

"Ah, no," Farl replied disgustedly, hurling his dagger. "Gangs!"

His blade spun through the air to plunge through the hand of the other woman, the hand that had been sweeping up with a dart in it. She screamed and fell to her knees.

Elminster hurled a dagger hilt-first into the man's face, tossed a cushion after it, and then sudden rage took hold of him. He leapt forward to plant a kick so hard in the man's gut that he groaned aloud as his toes struck the armor plate there—but its wearer was driven headlong back out the window to fall screaming to the garden below, a garrote waving uselessly in his hands.

"So noisy . . . so unprofessional," Farl murmured, snatching up the jewel-coffer. The wounded woman was fleeing for the rope at the window she'd come in by, sobbing from the pain and shaking blood all over the red carpets. "Hey—that's one of my good blades!" he complained as the other woman leapt at him, hurling one dagger and raising another.

Farl ducked and swept the coffer up; her blade struck it and shot into the ceiling, where it struck a roof-beam and stood quivering. The woman tried to reach over the coffer and slash his face, but Farl simply stepped around her, keeping the coffer between them, his head low and out of reach, and shoved her away with its end. She slipped on the carpet, and he brought the coffer down hard on her head. She collapsed soundlessly, and Elminster gently laid her unconscious companion atop of her, handing Farl his blade.

Farl examined its bloody tip and wiped it on the woman. "Dead?"

Elminster shook his head. "Just asleep; too hurt to defend herself." They knelt together over the gem-coffer, scooping and snatching in real haste, until Farl said, "Enough! Use their rope—let's begone!"

They paused to check the firmness of the gang's grapnel, and then hastily clambered down, Farl first. The male thief lay sprawled senseless on the turf, with a shocked-looking servant gazing down at him. Seeing the rope dance and jerk, he stared up at them. Then he screamed and ran, and from the window above them, the two thieves heard an angry shout.

"Gods be-*damned!* Let's hope they've no crossbows!" Farl snarled, slipping down the rope as his hands burned.

Then suddenly, sickeningly, the rope was no longer attached, and they were falling. There was a thud and a grunt from below as Farl landed. El tensed at the thought he might soon land atop his partner, but Farl was already up and sprinting out of the way. Elminster tried to relax as the turf swiftly rushed up to meet him.

The landing was hard. He got up, wincing; his right foot hurt,

and beside him lay the man he'd kicked, mouth open and face
white. A sick feeling rose in him, but as he scrambled to his feet,
he saw the man's hand move feebly, grasping for a windowsill
that wasn't there. Elminster and Farl sprinted together across
the garden and scrabbled hastily up and over the wall. They
dropped into the street outside and began strolling nonchalantly
toward the nearest cross-street, but a heavy clothyard shaft
hummed low over the wall and struck the high wooden gate of
the house across from them.

Farl stared up at it. "By the gods, a proper archer! Let's begone!"

So it was at an undignified run that the two fetched up, puffing, behind the boarded-up shop to lose loot and gear. Then Farl
smote his forehead. "Gangs!" he hissed. "They've always someone to spare, must've set a watcher!" He turned and ran back the
way they'd come, motioning to Elminster to hurry on down the
alley.

Elminster continued to flee, moving purposefully but not running, looking around warily from time to time. He'd gone two
streets farther when Farl dropped down from a nearby rooftop,
puffing, and said, "Right . . . let's dump all of this and buy some
of Hannibur's hot buttered rolls! We've earned an early evenfeast!"

"The watcher?" Elminster asked.

"I threw a blade at him an' missed by half a league—but he
was so startled he fell over backward off his roof—and split his
head open on the edge of a wagon, below. He'll be watching nothing, forevermore." Elminster shuddered.

Farl shook his head and looked gloomy. "What'd I warn you?
Gangs! There goes the high tone of Hastarl!"

Six

SQUALOR AMONG THIEVES

*There is one sort of a city that's worse than one where thieves rule
the night streets: the sort where thieves form the government, and
rule night and day.*

Urkitbaeran of Calimport
The Book of Black Tidings
Year of the Shattered Skulls

The best Calishite silks rarely made the long and perilous
way up the pirate-infested and storm-racked coast of the Great
Sea in numbers enough that Elembar, Uthtower, and Yarlith did
not drink them all in—leaving some for the long, arduous pole-
barge journey up the Delimbiyr. It was rarer still for the merchants who owned such barges to stop in tiny, provincial
Hastarl, where homespun was the favored wear and a good
sword-scabbard was more admired than an elegantly cut jerkin.
It was rarer yet for the shining, ornamented purple-and-emerald
Tashtan weaves from the fabled Cities of the Seabreeze farther
south to accompany the silks. Crowds at the docks were heavy.
Some of the fat, strutting cloth merchants didn't even bother to
climb the streets to the tall, narrow shops of the master tailors,
but sold all their wares on the docks.

Farl and Elminster thought themselves subtle indeed not to
try for a single thread of that first exciting landing. When a second followed, they left it alone, too, and watched from afar as an
unfortunate grab-artist of the Moonclaws was caught stealing
silks, whipped skinless, and hanged from the city wall.

The master tailors had no guild because the magelords did
not hold with guilds. They did, however, meet earnestly over
wine and roast boar in the Dancing Dryad feasting house and
come to a business agreement of mutual advantage. A lass who
served them at table and collected rather too many pinches for
her liking told Farl and Elminster (in return for four gold coins)
what had been decided. 'Twas money well spent, Farl judged. Elminster, as was his wont, said nothing.

And so this moonless night found them on the roof of a warehouse overlooking a certain dock, waiting for the creak of oars

and surreptitious shining of unshuttered lanterns that would mark the arrival of the private shipment to the master tailors, including (it was rumored) cloth-of-gold and amber buttons.

It was a crisp, breezy night, the first heralding of leaf-fall to come and another cold damp winter, but wrapped in their dark cloaks, they hadn't time to grow stiff and cold before the flashes of lamplight were seen glimmering over the dark waters below.

The two thieves waited in patient silence for their victims-to-be to helpfully load the wagons, four in all and heavy-laden, then slid silently down from their perch, avoiding the lumbering hire-guards who clustered around the lead wagon. It was the work of but a moment to hurl a stone over into the heap of rusted metal pans in the alley behind the confectioners' shop, and while heads and blades were turned that way, to slip up into the fourth wagon from the other side of the street. Then they'd have a breath or six to sort before another diversion became necessary to cover their leaving.

It was about the time of the fourth breath that they heard a startled oath from somewhere nearby, the scream of a wounded horse, and the skirl of steel. "Competition?" El breathed into his friend's ear, and Farl nodded.

"Our diversion," he murmured, "provided by the Moonclaws, no doubt. Wait a bit, now—that horse means they've got at least one bow with them. Let the fight get well underway before we go out."

The fight obliged, and the two companions hastened to finish sorting and stowing their loot for carrying.When they were done, they drew their daggers and unlatched the back doors of the wagon to peer cautiously out into the night.

A face with a blade held ready beside it was glaring up at them. Farl leapt high to avoid the man's thrust, landed with both feet atop the blade, and jumped down on the sword-wielder's arm, burying his dagger in that face before the man even had time to cry out.

As El jumped to the cobbles beside them, staggering under the weight of their booty, Farl tugged his dagger free and hurled it into the night, which seemed to be full of running men and drawn swords. It struck the brow of a hireguard, who cursed, clutched at the streaming blood, and ran.

Farl scooped up the long sword that had fallen from the shattered arm of his first victim and hissed, "Come *on,* out o' this!"

They ran to the right, toward one of the rising side streets where folk dwelt who were too respectable to live in hovels but not rich enough to have walls around their homes. Daggers flashed and spun in the night on all sides, but the Moonclaws hadn't a decent blade-tosser among them. It seemed the guards had been inept, or spineless, or paid off: the fight was over. All the other folk yet alive in the street were Moonclaws.

Farl and El didn't waste breath on curses. They dodged from side to side erratically to discourage the Moonclaws' archer and plunged along the street, puffing for breath. The expected humming of a seeking arrow came to their ears accompanied by a startled curse from close behind them. The arrow wobbled past them strangely; Farl frowned at it and looked back. A Moonclaws man who'd been pursuing them was stumbling and rubbing at his shoulder.

"Dare they . . . shoot again?" El gasped. "With . . . their own folk . . ."

"Hasn't stopped 'em yet," Farl puffed. "Keep dodging!"

The next arrow came as they reached the top of the street and turned aside to duck along an alley, crouching low. The humming grew louder, and they both dived to the cobbles. The arrow whipped low over them, and cracked into some shutters across the way just as a patrol of armsmen shouldered out of the alley, halberds held high. The patrol-captain peered down in the dimness at the two men sprawled in front of him and snapped, "Get that light up here! Something befalls! Swords ou—"

The Moonclaws had a second archer, it seemed. His shaft hit home with a solid thump—and the captain gurgled, spun around, and plunged to the cobbles, strangling on the long, dark shaft through his throat.

Farl and El rolled to their feet while startled armsmen were still wrestling their halberds down, and ran down the alley past the patrol, hooking the feet out from under the only armsman who tried to block their path.

As the soldier crashed to the cobbles, Farl swarmed up a draper's outside wooden staircase, with El close behind. The roof was an easy leap up from the rail, but slippery with puddles of rainwater. The next roof was thatch, and they burrowed thankfully into its far slope to catch their breaths.

They looked at each other in the darkness, panting. "There's naught for it," Farl said a few frantic breaths later, "but to form our own gang."

"Tyche aid us," El murmured.

Farl looked at him. "Don't you mean Mask, Lord of Thieves?"

"Nay," Elminster replied. "I was praying that this 'gang' does not end our friendship . . . or our lives."

Farl was a silent for a long time. Then Elminster heard him murmur, "Oh, Lady Tyche, hear me. . . ."

* * * * *

"Ah, Naneetha! Those velvet hands . . ." Farl was laughing—and then he stopped. "That's it! We'll call ourselves the 'Velvet Hands'!"

Groans and laughter rang round the tiny room. It was dusty and stank of decades of salted fish—but the owner of the warehouse was dead, and the two broken-down carts they'd carefully jammed together in the mouth of the alley made it unlikely any patrols would get close enough to hear them. Over a dozen folk were in the room, keeping a wary distance apart, with careful eyes on each other and their hands close to their weapons.

Farl eyed them all, and sighed. "I know none of you are delighted at this idea . . . but everyone here knows it's band together or be slain—or leave Hastarl to try our luck elsewhere . . . in strange places where we'll be marked as suspicious outlanders an' find a local gang of thieves waiting to sink knives into us."

"Why not join the Moonclaws?" Klaern rasped. He was one of the Blaenbar brothers, who lounged together by a window where they could give a signal to someone outside.

"On what terms?" he asked reasonably. "Every time Eladar or I have crossed paths with 'em, they've tried to put their blades into us before a word was exchanged. We'd start out on the fringes, all of us, untrusted and expendable."

"More than that," Elminster put in, drawing startled looks from all over the room. "I've wondered at all those leathers an' matching badges they wear. Expensive, that—an' right from the outset, before they'd taken two coins to rub together. Good weapons, too. Does that remind all of ye of anything? A private bodyguard, belike? An army in Hastarl that strikes at thieves—us—whenever they see us. That sounds like the work of someone in the hire of a magelord, or the king, or someone rich and important. What better way to rid the city of thieves and arrange 'accidents' for thy rivals but than to put thine own band on the streets?"

There were thoughtful nods all around the room now. "Now *that*," fat old Chaslarla said, scratching herself, "makes more sense o' the mess than I've heard since I first saw 'em. An' it explains why some armsmen seem to look the other way when they strike out—under orders, belike."

"Aye," young Rhegaer said, idly turning a little knife in his fingers as he perched atop a barrel taller than he was. As usual, he was very dirty . . . but then, so was the barrel, and a peering eye might have missed him, but for the flash and turn of the little blade.

"Well, I think it's so much smart lies and fancy-castles talk," Klaern snarled, "an' I'll not listen to more of it. Ye're fools, all of ye, if ye listen to these two dreamers. What have they but smart tongues?" He strode out of his corner to stare around the room, and like a silent wave rolling in his wake his two brothers came to stand at his back in a solid, threatening wall of flesh. "If there's to be a band to rival the Moonclaws, *I'll* lead it. 'Velvet Hands,' indeed! While these two perfumed dancing lads are strutting an' crowing, my brothers 'n' me can make ye rich . . . guaranteed."

"Oh?" A very deep voice rumbled out from one dark corner. "And just how, Blaenbar, are ye going to manage to make me trust *thee?* After watching thy bullying and blustering in the alleys these past three summers, all I know of ye is that I'd best never turn my back—or thy blade'll be in, right sharp."

Klaern sneered. "Jhardin, everyone in Hastarl knows ye're as strong as an ox—but anyone might give ye a good run in a race of wits. What can ye know of planning, or—"

"More than some folk," Jhardin growled. "Where I come from, 'planning' always means some clever jack is going to try to trick me."

"Why don't ye go back there, then?"

"Enough, Klaern," Farl said with cold scorn. "Trust is something the rest of us can never have when you're near, that's for certain. You'd best leave."

The red-maned man turned on him. "Afraid ye'll lose mastery of this little band of Pawing Hands, eh? Well, let's just see . . . who speaks for ye, here?"

Elminster stepped a silent pace forward.

"Yes, yes, we know yer pretty boy does . . . as well as anything else ye ask him to."

Amid his coarse laughter, Jhardin lumbered forward a pace, eyes hard. Rhegaer leapt lightly down from his barrel, and Chaslarla wheezed forward too.

Klaern looked around. "Tassabra?"

The lithe figure in the deepest shadows shifted slightly and said in a low, musical voice, "Sorry, Klaern. I side with Farl, too."

"Fah! Gods frown upon all of ye fools!" Klaern spat on the floor, turned, and strode grandly out, his silent brothers Korlar and Othkyn backing watchfully away to guard his going.

"I thought he was thy lover," another man murmured from the shadows.

"Take care, Larrin!" Tassabra's voice was testy. "That rutting boar my lover? Nay, he was but a plaything."

Jhardin looked to Farl, who nodded. The huge man walked out of the room, moving with surprising, silent lightness. Klaern might well have less time left in life than he realized. Farl stepped forward. "Are we agreed, then? Do the Velvet Hands fare forth in Hastarl from this night on?"

"Aye," came the rough voice of one-eyed Tarth. "I'll follow your orders."

"And I," Chaslarla said, wheezing forward, "so long as ye turn not into one of those cold-hearts who thinks himself the true ruler of his city an' sends us out to stab armsmen and magelords all the night through."

There was a general rumble of agreement. Farl grinned and bowed. "We have agreement, then. As our first work together, let's get out of here with blades ready, and as I bid—in case the Moonclaws are waiting for us with bows, or've told a patrol when and where to expect us."

"Can I have first blood?" Rhegaer asked eagerly.

Behind him, they heard Tassabra's low laugh. "Just be sure it's not yours," she said. The darkness covered the look he gave her . . . but they could all feel it. There were chuckles in the night as they went down the stairs together.

* * * * *

All Hastarl knew the noble Athalantan families Glarmeir and Trumpettower had been joined that same night in a true love-match. Peeryst Trumpettower had worn a high-plumed hat and cloth-of-gold doublet specially crafted for the occasion, with his usual bell-trimmed hose and best curl-tip shoes. Strapping on his father's lightest sword, he proudly paraded his lady to the shrines of Sune, Lathander, Helm, and Tyche before the hand-fasting was completed under the sword of Tyr.

The father of the bride had gifted the happy pair with a statue of the rearing Stag of Athalantar (the beast, not the dead king) that had been sculpted from a single gigantic diamond, and was worth more than some large castles. The servant who carried it around all day on a glass-domed platter thought it might well have been heavier than some castles, too. Under a heavy guard, this eminently practical gift had been installed in the bridal bedchamber at the foot of the bed, where, as old Darrigo Trumpettower had put it with a wink and a leer, " 'Twould be in a fine position to watch!"

Nanue Glarmeir had worn an exquisite sky-blue gown crafted by the elves of far-off Shantel Othreier; her mother had proudly announced it had cost a thousand pieces of gold. Now it lay crumpled on the floor like so much discarded wrapping—which is precisely what the squeakily excited Peeryst thought it was—as the newly wedded couple toasted each other with sparkling moonbubble wine, and turned to raise their glasses to Selune, that she might smile down upon the bridal bed. The first pale rays of her radiance had peeked in the window far enough to touch the statue of the stag with moonlight, where it stood rampant and watchful on its own table at the foot of the bed.

Neither man nor wife noticed the deft pair of black-gloved hands reach up from under the bed and take away the gem-headed hairpins Nanue had just drawn out to let her hair cascade unbound down her elegant back (to Peeryst's breathless delight). Both newlyweds, however, did notice the sudden appearance of a pair of booted feet that blotted out the moon and then crashed through the fine glass of the largest arched bedchamber window, followed by their owner: a woman clad in tight-fitting black leathers with a badge on her breast, who wore a black half-mask.

The shapely intruder smiled at them sweetly as she drew a needle-thin blade from one boot and approached the stag. In all this excitement, none of the three heard an exasperated sigh from under the bed.

"Scream just once," she warned softly, "and I'll slide this into you."

Having been handed the idea, Nanue screamed—just once. Piercingly, too; shards of glass fell from the window-frame with a tinkling clatter.

The woman's face darkened into a snarl, and she ran across the room, poniard raised to stab. Seemingly by itself, a footstool beside the bed leapt up from the floor to catch her in the face; she reeled, lost her dagger, and fell heavily sideways into a wardrobe—which promptly toppled, slowly and grandly, over on top of her.

Nanue and Peeryst both boldly seized the initiative, shrieking in unison.

* * * * *

Downstairs, befurred and bejeweled elders of both families heard the mighty crash and the screams. They raised knowing eyes and grins toward the ceiling and then toasted each other.

"Ah, yes," Darrigo Trumpettower said, leering over his glass at a Glarmeir lass almost half his age and blowing his bristling mustache out of his wine with a practiced puff. "I remember well my wedding night—the first one, at least; I was sober for that one. 'Twas back in the Year of the Gorgon Moon, as I recall. . . ."

* * * * *

A dark figure rose up from beneath the bed, crept across the room, and ducked behind a lounge onto which Peeryst had grandly tossed his boots, one after the other, not so long ago. The intruder was safely out of sight before the next two thieves in leathers burst in through the other two windows, raining fresh glass onto the thick fur rugs. Peeryst and Nanue clutched each other, naked but not noticing anymore, and howled in fear, clawing at each other's backs in a frantic attempt to get going elsewhere—anywhere!

The two fresh arrivals wore the same masks and tight leathers with breast-badges as the first one had. One was a woman, the other a man, and both were looking wildly about the room.

"Where's she gone, then?"

"*Hush,* Minter—you'll rouse the house."

"*Don't* use my name, gods damn thy tongue!"

They drew daggers from their boots and approached the terrified couple on the bed—who screamed and tried to burrow under the fur-trimmed silk sheets.

"Hold, damn ye!" Minter reached for a fleeing foot, missed, and got hold of an ankle. He pulled. A vainly struggling Peeryst clawed at the sheets and managed to drag them off his wife, who knelt on the bed and screamed again, piercingly. Across the room, a glass figurine shattered, causing the black-gloved hand that had been reaching up from behind the lounge for it to withdraw, with a hasty curse.

Peeryst Trumpettower was hauled from the bed to bounce and then sprawl on the carpet at Minter's feet, gibbering in fear.

Minter flipped him over, reflecting briefly on how ridiculous other naked men look, and snarled, "Where'd she go?" He waved his dagger under the man's nose for effect.

"Wh-Who?" Peeryst shrieked.

Minter pointed with his blade at the whirlwind that was his partner Isparla, who was plucking gem-coffers and silken underthings from the floor and tables around, and tossing them all onto one of the sheets on the floor. As they watched, she scooped up the stag, grunted in surprise under its weight, staggered off-balance, slipped on the carpet, and fell on both elbows atop the piled loot. She moaned in pain—and the stag in her grasp slipped free and thumped down sideways onto one of her hands. She grunted again, louder.

"Another like her, who came in before us!" Minter growled, indicating his partner.

"U-Under the wardrobe," Peeryst panted, pointing. "It fell on her."

Minter turned and saw a ribbon of dark blood running from under the wardrobe, which was as large—and probably as heavy—as a long-haul wagon. He shuddered. He kept on shuddering, all the way to the floor, as a figure rose from under the bed and brought a perfume-bottle down on his head.

Isparla clambered to her feet, saw the figure with the shards of the perfume bottle in his hand, obligingly spat, "Velvets! *Again!*" and threw her dagger. The figure obediently dived back behind the bed, and the dagger flashed harmlessly across the room. A titanic sneeze came from behind the bed.

Nanue screamed again—and the woman in black leathers slapped her across the face, backhanded, as she leapt past, grabbing for the elusive sneezing figure. She tripped over the stag in her haste, hopped, and moaned in pain. The stag thumped over onto its other side, and a shard of diamond broke off it.

The mysterious person behind the bed was curled up and shaking in the throes of uncontrollable sneezing, but managed to drive the broken perfume bottle into the Moonclaws woman's face, which she had just stuck around behind the bed. Isparla recoiled, rearing up on the bed, and Nanue slapped her back, hard.

Her masked head whipped around. She snarled, leaned forward, and there was a meaty smack as her face met the brass chamberpot that Peeryst's shaking hands had just swept upward.

Isparla collapsed silently across the bed. Nanue, kneeling beside her, saw blood flowing from the masked woman's mouth onto the silken sheets, and helpfully screamed again.

Peeryst saw what he'd done, threw the chamberpot down in horror—there was a sharp crack as it struck the stag and then a hollow metallic gonging when it skipped across the room and rolled to a stop—and fled across the room, howling. A dark figure burst up from behind the lounge and sprinted to intercept him.

Peeryst was two running paces from the safety of the bedchamber door when the figure caught up with him. They crashed into the door together; it boomed, burst open from the impact, and was instantly smashed shut again by their falling bodies.

* * * * *

Downstairs, the befurred and bejeweled elders of both families heard the crash, raised their eyebrows at each other, and poured another toast.

"Well," Janatha Glarmeir said brightly, staring around as color rose prettily into her cheeks, "they certainly seem to be . . . hitting it off, don't they?"

"*Hitting* sounds like it would be about right," Darrigo Trumpettower agreed with a guffaw, leering at her. "I remember my second wife was like that. . . ."

* * * * *

Elminster rose from atop Peeryst's unconscious form, made sure the door was bolted this time, and hurried to where Farl, eyes still streaming from the perfume, was staggering away from the bed.

"We've got to get out of here," he muttered, shaking Farl.

"Damned Moonclaws," his partner snarled. "Grab *something* to make all this worthwhile."

"I have," El said, "now let's *begone!*"

His words rose into an excited shout as a new pair of leather-clad figures swung in the window, using yet more silken lines.

They landed running, blades out. Elminster swept up a small glass-topped table, spilling figurines in all directions, and hurled it hard.

His target ducked, and the table sailed harmlessly out the window—just as one of the figurines landed, hard, on his foot.

Elminster hopped in pain, roaring. The grinning Moonclaws man closed in on him, raising a gleaming blade, as the other one dived to grab the nude, shrieking woman on the bed.

* * * * *

The table fell through the night to explode in shards of glass and twisted spars of brass on the cobbles far below. Some of them clattered on the windows of the feasting-hall and the parlor. The befurred and bejeweled elders of both families turned at the sound, and more eyebrows were raised.

"They wouldn't be *fighting*, would they?" Janatha Glarmeir said anxiously, fanning herself to conceal her burning cheeks. "It certainly seems *lively*."

"Nay," Darrigo Trumpettower roared, "that's just . . . what

d'they ca—oh, aye, 'foreplay;' y'know, the fun 'n' games before-
hand . . . great big room up there to chase each other around in
. . ." He sighed, looking up at the ceiling. Obligingly, it shook
under another sharp, booming crash, and a cloud of dust drifted
down. "Wish I were younger and Peeryst was calling for
help. . . ."

Promptly there came a faint, quavering cry. "Help!"

"Well," Darrigo said in delight, "if the lad ain't the very
shinin' image of his old uncle, indeed! Where're those stairs?
Hope I can remember how to do the deed, after all these
years. . . ."

* * * * *

Elminster danced backward, wincing. The Moonclaws man
lunged at him, blade flashing, and then grunted in surprise as
Farl reached out and wrapped himself around the man's leg. The
Moonclaws thief toppled like a felled tree, and Farl stabbed him
in the throat before he'd even stopped bouncing. The stag statue,
cracked and somewhat smaller now, spun away from under the
man's sprawled body.

Elminster saw what Farl had done, turned his head away,
and promptly emptied his dinner all over a blue-dyed fur rug
from Calimshan.

"Well, that's *one* rug we won't be taking back with us," Farl
called merrily as he sprinted across the room to where the last
Moonclaws woman was struggling with the sobbing bride. Just
as he got there, the thief managed to get her hands on Nanue's
face and throat, and looked up.

Farl didn't slow. He planted a firm fist in her mask as he ran
past.

She hadn't even hit the carpet when he leapt out the window,
one of the swing-lines hissing through his gloved hands as he
slid down in haste.

Elminster snatched up a hand-sized jewel-coffer to add to the
hairpins he'd stowed in his boots, thrust it down the front of his
shirt to free his hands for climbing, and ran after Farl. Screaming, Nanue ran the other way, toward the door where her husband lay senseless.

Elminster tripped over the stag, cursed, and ended his flight
to the windows in a helpless roll. The statue slid away across
slick tiles exposed when rugs were rucked up in the battle, and
caromed off a wall, spitting pieces of itself in all directions.

El fetched up against the windowsill in an untidy heap—un-

seen by the Moonclaws man who swung grandly in the window at
that moment and stepped right over the thieving prince. His eyes
fixed on the statue, gliding to a gleaming stop in the moonlight.

"Aha! A king's ransom—mine!" the thief bellowed, hurling a
dagger out of habit at the nude woman fleeing across the chamber. The flashing fang struck an upright mirror, which pivoted
on its pintles, overbalanced, and came crashing down at Nanue.
She shrieked and leapt desperately backward, skidding helplessly on the rugs. The mirror crashed down beside it and shattered, shards bouncing on the tiles; Nanue rolled away blindly to
escape them, and overturned an ornamental table crowded with
scent-bottles. The reek that arose was incredible; it even made
the thief, gloved hand about to close on what was left of the stag,
recoil.

This sudden movement sent him skidding on a fragment broken off the statue, and he sat down hard, jarring a portrait down
off the wall. Roaruld Trumpettower, Scourge of Stirges—depicted holding a glass of blood aloft in one hand and a wrung-
out, limp-winged stirge in the other—landed with a crash that
shook the room, hopped forward as the frame shivered, and
smashed down atop the thief. The stag spun away again, still
growing smaller.

Nanue sobbed at the overpowering smell as she wallowed in
glass shards and spilled perfume; she was drenched with half a
hundred secret oils and glowing daubs, and the tiles were so
slippery she couldn't find footing. At length, weeping with frustration—and at the smell—she started to crawl toward the nearest rug. It was the one Elminster had recently decorated. Nanue
recoiled from it, selected another as her goal, and crawled in that
direction, weeping with fresh energy.

Elminster shook his head in disbelief at the scene of devasta-
tion in the room, caught hold of the rope, and was gone into the
night. Behind him there was a sharp tearing sound as a gloved
hand holding a dagger punched up through the heart of Roaruld
Trumpettower, cutting a hole in the massive portrait so that its
masked Moonclaws owner could emerge and look wildly around
the room for—there!

The stag lay in a serene pool of moonlight near the bed,
starred now with many cracks. The thief hastened to scoop it up.
"Mine at last!"

"Nay," responded a cold voice from the window. " 'Tis *mine!*"

A dagger was flung, but missed, coming to quivering rest in a
wooden wall-carving with a solid thunk.

The first thief sneered as he scooped up the stag—then, realizing the other Moonclaws man couldn't see his expression through the mask, made a rude gesture with the statue. The second thief snarled in rage and threw another dagger. It flashed across the room and passed just in front of Nanue's nose. The crawling bride hastily changed course again, scuttling back across the tiles toward safety behind the lounge.

The thief with the statue strode toward the window. "Keep back!" he warned, waving his dagger.

The second thief scooped up one of the fallen gem-coffers and calmly flung it at the head of the first thief. It hit home and burst open, spilling a glistening rain of gems to the floor. The first thief joined them in the general cascade, the stag flying up from his hand.

End over end it spun through the air—toward the window.

"No!" The second thief lunged desperately after it, slipping and sliding on the bouncing gems. His gloved hands stretched, reaching, reaching—and into the very tips of his straining fingers the proud stag fell.

He clung to it in gloating triumph, skidding across the floor with the momentum of his desperate run. "Hah! I have it! My precious! Oh, my precious stag!"

And then the gems under his boots slid him hard into the low windowsill, and he kicked helplessly, toppled, and with a shriek fell out into the night, wailing, and was gone.

Nanue saw the thief disappear, shivered, and came carefully to her feet, turning again toward the door. She must get *out*—

Another pair of thieves in black leathers swung in through the windows. "Oh, *dungheaps!*" Nanue wailed, and started yet another desperate dash for the door.

The thieves looked around at the wreckage and carnage and swore horribly. One bounded forward into the room, swept up the masked woman from the bed, threw her over his shoulder, and made straight for the window again. The other sprinted down the room after Nanue to snatch her for a ransom.

She screamed, and was slipping on rugs, trying not to crash into the door in her haste and fall on the crumpled Peeryst, when something heavy hit the door from the other side. The bolt twisted and jammed, and Nanue slid helplessly into the wall. Snarled curses echoed through the door from the passage beyond, and then it shook under another thunderous blow. Nanue scrambled aside, shrieking at the thief who grabbed for her kicking legs.

The door splintered then and flew inward, hurling the thief a good distance away across the furs. He rolled to his feet, and two

daggers gleamed as he drew them. The Moonclaws thief saluted
the nude woman with them, and advanced menacingly. Nanue
screamed again.

Darrigo Trumpettower looked around the ruined bedchamber
in bewilderment. At his feet lay his nephew and right beside
him, his terrified bride on her knees, shrieking as she crawled
toward Darrigo.

Darrigo looked up again, mustache bristling. An intruder in
black leathers was coming at him in a run, daggers gleaming in
both hands. There wasn't even time to leer down at Nanue—
who, he couldn't help noticing, looked like a fine wife indeed. He
looked up at the onrushing thief again and drew a deep breath.
'Twas time to uphold the honor of the Trumpettowers!

With a roar, Darrigo Trumpettower charged across the room.
The thief swept his daggers up to stab—but the old man took
one in the arm without flinching, and smashed home a bone-
shattering blow to the thief's jaw. Still roaring, he snatched at
the reeling man's throat before he could fall, picked the thief up
by the neck the same way he carried turkeys in to be cooked at
home, and strode across the room, streaming blood.

Straight to the shattered windows he went, lifted the thief,
and hurled him out into the empty darkness. He listened for the
thud from the cobbles far below, nodded in satisfaction when it
came, and went back for another thief.

Nanue decided it was safe to faint now. As the second thief
sailed out into the night, the blushing bride sank gracefully
down on Peeryst's chest, and knew no more. . . .

* * * * *

Word was all over the city by midmorn how the old, blustering warrior Darrigo Trumpettower had fought a dozen thieves in
the bridal bedchamber of his nephew while the unhearing lovers
had calmly consummated their match, and how he (Darrigo)
hurled every one of the Moonclaws in uniform out the high windows, to their deaths in the courtyard of Trumpettower House.

Farl and El raised eyebrows and tankards of strong ale to the
news. "It sounds as though one of them rescued Isparla and got
out again," Farl said, sipping.

"How many does that leave?" Elminster asked quietly.

Farl shrugged. "Who knows? The gods and the Moonclaws,
alone. But they lost Waera, Minter, Annathe, Obaerig, for certain, and probably Irtil, too. Let's say we're a lot more even after
last night—though they did blunder in on a perfectly good grab

job and lose us all but the little stuff."

"One of the hairpins broke, too," Elminster reminded him.

"Aye, but we have both pieces; little loss there," Farl said. "Now, if we—"

He broke off, frowned, and bent his head to listen to an excited whisper at a table nearby, laying a hand on El's arm to bid for silence. Elminster, who'd been holding his peace, continued to do so.

"Aye, magic! Doubtless hidden away by King Uthgrael, years agone!" One man was saying, leaning forward almost into his friend's face to avoid being overheard. "In a secret chamber somewheres in the castle, they say!"

Farl and Elminster leaned forward to listen carefully. A moment later, the need to do so passed: a minstrel came in, bounded up onto the nearest table, and cried the tale at the top of his young, excited voice.

In truth, it was a tale straight out of the legends minstrels kept shining: a chest of magical ioun stones had been found in the castle—hidden away years before, probably by (or on the orders of) King Uthgrael. The magelords are, and remain, in heated disagreement about who shall have them, and how they'll be used. By decree of King Belaur himself, the stones—glowing and floating about by themselves, giving off faint chimings and musical sounds like harp-chords from time to time—are on display, guarded by the officers and senior armsmen of Athalgard, in a certain audience chamber no wizards are allowed to approach, until a decision is made. As they left the tavern, the excited minstrel was declaiming in ringing tones that he'd seen the stones himself, and that this was all *true!*

Farl smiled. "You know we *have* to go for those stones."

Elminster shook his head. "Ye couldn't turn thy back on them and still be Farl, Master of the Velvet Hands," he said dryly.

Farl chuckled.

"This time," Elminster told him firmly, "ye should wait, let the Moonclaws spring the trap—and go in only if ye can see a safe, clear way to do so."

"Trap?"

"Don't ye smell the hands of calculating wizards in this wondrous tale? I do."

After a moment, Farl nodded. Their eyes met.

"Why did you say 'ye'?" Farl asked quietly.

"I am done with thieving," Elminster said slowly. "If ye go after these wonderful magical stones, ye must do it alone. I'll be leaving Hastarl after I do one thing more."

Farl stood frozen, eyes very dark. "Why?"

"Robbing and slaying hurts folk I have no quarrel with and brings revenge no closer to the magelords. You saw the stag statue; the grasping hands of thieving only take what's precious and make it battered and broken and worthless. I've learned as much as the street can teach and have had enough." Elminster stared into Farl's stunned eyes and added, "Seasons slip away— and the things I've not done eat at me. I must leave."

"I knew it was coming," Farl admitted, his face going very red. "It's the scruples that assured it. But this 'one thing more'— 'twouldn't be a betrayal, would it?"

Elminster shook his head and spoke slowly and deliberately. "I've never had a friend as close and as true as Farl, son of Hawklyn."

Suddenly their arms were around each other in a tight embrace. They stood in the alley and wept, pounding each other on backs and shoulders.

After a time, Farl said, "Ah, El—what'm I to do without you?"

"Take up with Tassabra," Elminster said, and added with a gleam in his eye, "Ye can show her appreciation in a more satisfying way than ye can with me."

They stepped back from each other—and then, slowly, both grinned.

"So we part," Farl said, shaking his head. "Half our wealth is yours."

Elminster shrugged. "I'll take only what I need, for the road."

Farl sighed. "So it's loot for me—and killing magelords for you."

"Mayhap," Elminster said softly, "if the gods are kind."

PART III
PRIEST

Seven

THE ONE TRUE SPELL

In ancient days, sorcerers sought to learn the One True Spell that would give them power over all the world and understanding of all magic. Some said they'd found it, but such men were usually dismissed as crazed.

I saw one of these "crazed" mages myself. He could ignore spells cast at him as if they did not exist, or work any magic himself by silent thought alone. I did not think he was mad—but at peace, driven by urges and vices no longer. He told me the One True Spell was a woman, that her name was Mystra—and that her kisses were wonderful.

Halivon Tharnstar, Avowed of Mystra
Tales Told To A Blind Wizard
Year of the Wyvern

The night was warm and still. Elminster took a deep breath and counted out most of what Farl had insisted he take. He owed a debt . . . and besides, the other matter he meant to see to this night would probably kill him. Then it would be too late to pay any debts.

When he was done, he was looking at a heap of coins—a hundred regals, bright in the moonlight. In the sun, come morn, they'd blaze their true gold color . . . but he'd probably not be around to see them, one way or another.

Elminster shrugged. At least his life was his own again, and he was free to pursue any folly he desired. So, of course, he reflected wryly, here he was, bent on one last thiefly act. He slung the coins together in the sack—tight, so they'd not clink—and set off over the rooftops in search of a certain bedchamber.

The shutters were open to let in any breezes that might drift by, to cool a sleeping bridal couple whose furnishings failed by far to match those of the Trumpettowers. Elminster had been delighted to hear of their betrothal, even if it would cost him most of the coins he'd worked for. He stole in over the sill like a purposeful shadow and grinned down at them.

The bridal garter was exquisite, a little thing of lace and silken ribbon. Impishly, Elminster reached down and stroked it.

Take it, as a trophy? But no—he was a thief no more.

Shandathe stirred as she felt the light touch high on her thigh. Yet deep in dreams, she stretched out a hand to the familiar warm and hairy bulk of Hannibur, snoring as deep as any drunken tavern-singer could. As Elminster smoothed her new bridal garter back into place where Hannibur had tied it on her hip, she smiled but didn't awaken.

Elminster noted other gifts, too: a stout cudgel and a new apron lying on the carpet on Hannibur's side of the bed . . . and the hilt of a dagger protruding, like a winking eye, from beneath Shandathe's pillow.

He laid his bridal gift carefully between them. It was a tight fit between the smooth flank and the hairy one, and it took all his thiefly skills to avoid a clink and rattle as he slid the coins into a smooth sweep of gleaming gold from end to end of the bed. When he'd crammed in all the regals he dared, there were still over a dozen left. He laid the last of his belated bridal gift gently on Shandathe's belly, and left hastily as the touch of cold metal made her stir in earnest.

* * * * *

Selune was riding high in the deep blue sky over Hastarl as Elminster stood on a rooftop, looking across the empty, silent street at the crumbling front of the disused temple of Mystra.

The place was dark and decaying, and from where he stood Elminster could see the massive lock on the door. The magelords, it seemed, didn't want anyone in Hastarl worshiping the Mistress of All Magic but themselves—and they could do that in the safety and privacy of their own tower inside Athalgard. Yet they hadn't dared desecrate Mystra's temple.

Perhaps their power was rooted in it, and striking here could shake their mastery of sorcery and their grip on the realm. Perhaps he could force Mystra's hand, just as she had forced his when she let his parents be slain. Or perhaps, Elminster admitted to himself as he stared at the temple, he was just weary of doing nothing that mattered, wasting days on rooftops, looking for a chance to steal this bauble or that. Wizards might not dare desecrate Mystra's temple, but Elminster would. Tonight. The world—or at least Athalantar—would be a much better place without any magic at all.

Destroying one temple, though, could hardly hope to do that. But perhaps it might bring down Mystra's curse on the city, so no wizards could work magic within its walls. Or perhaps the temple held some item of magic he could use against the wizards. Or perhaps it just held his death. Any result would be welcome.

Elminster eyed the shabby, peeling paint and the motionless stone bat-things adorning both front corners of the roof. They clutched the tops of the temple's front pillars with many claws, and their beaks hung open hungrily. They did not glow under his mage-sight—but perhaps the magical gargoyles minstrels sang of didn't glow. . . . The only magic he could see was lower down, and visible to all. Faintly glowing letters over the doors spelled out the words "I Am the One True Spell."

Elminster shook his head, sighed, and began the climb down from the rooftop. Revenge, it seemed, was a demanding business.

He could see no spells on the lock, and it surrendered easily to his metal probes; Farl had taught him well. Elminster looked up and down the silent street one last time, and then eased the door open, stood for a few breaths in its shadow to let his eyes adjust to the darkness, and slipped inside, dagger ready.

Dust and empty darkness. Elminster peered in all directions, but there didn't seem to be any furnishings in the temple of Mystra, only stone pillars. Cautiously he stepped sideways until he was well away from the door—traps were usually right in front of doors—and stepped forward.

Something was not right about this place. Oh, aye, he'd expected to feel watched, his skin creeping with the singing tension of slumbering spells waiting all around him . . . and that was here, all right. There was something else, though, som—

Of course: a place this big and empty should echo back the sounds he made. Yet there were no echoes. Elminster opened a belt pouch, took one of the dried peas every thief carries to scatter and make pursuers trip, and cast it ahead of him into the darkness.

He did not hear it land. El swallowed and took a cautious step forward. He was in an entry hall, separated from a great open chamber beyond by a row of massive, smooth-curved stone pillars . . . featureless cylinders, as far as he could tell. Nothing moved in the thick blankets of dust over the floor. El cast a last look back at the door he'd drawn closed, and then walked into the darkness.

The great chamber was circular and reached up high overhead to unseen heights—it must go clear to the roof Elminster had looked at outside. There was a circular stone altar in the center of the room and balconies—three tiers of them—curving all around the vast open space. The chamber was dark, empty, and silent.

And that was it. Nothing here to desecrate. No acolytes.

The door behind him suddenly clattered open, and as men with torches came in, Elminster ran toward the back of the temple, seeking pillars to hide behind. Many men; armsmen, at least two patrols, with spears in their hands.

"Spread out," said a cold voice, "and search. No one dares enter a temple of Mystra just on a lark."

The speaker strode forward, lifted a hand, and sketched some sort of salute or respectful gesture toward the altar. Then he said calmly, "We shall have light," and at his words, though he cast no spell, the very stones around Elminster began to glow.

All of the stone in the temple began to shine until a soft, pearly-white radiance filled the room, revealing the young thief for everyone to see. In this case, 'everyone' was more than a score of armsmen, advancing across the chamber with grim faces and ready spears. The man who'd spoken stood in their midst and said, "Just a thief. Hold weapons."

"What if he runs, lord?"

The robed man smiled and said, "My magic will force him to walk where I want him to, and nowhere else."

He gestured, and Elminster felt a sudden tugging at his limbs . . . a tingling, numbing trembling akin to what he'd felt on that terrible day in the meadow above Heldon, long ago. His body was no longer his own; he found himself turning, sick despair rising inside, and walking toward the men.

No, toward the altar. A bare circular block of stone, with not even a rune to grace it. The armsmen raised their spears and ringed him in as he came.

"The law holds that those who desecrate temples be put to death," an old armsman growled, "on the spot."

"Indeed," the robed man said, and smiled again. "I, however, shall choose that spot. When this fool's on the altar, you may throw your spears at will. Fresh blood on Mystra's altar will allow me to work a magic I've long wanted to try."

Elminster strode steadily on toward the altar, raging inwardly. He had been a fool to come here. This was it, then. His death, and an end to his futile fight against the magelords. Sorry, Father . . . Mother. . . . Elminster broke into a run and charged the altar, hoping he might somehow break free and knowing he could do nothing else. At least he could die trying to do *something*.

The wizard merely smiled and crooked one finger. Elminster's rush became a smooth trot until he stood in front of the altar. The mage turned him about again, until they stood facing each other.

Then the wizard bowed. "Greetings, thief. I am Lord Ildru, magelord of Athalantar. You may speak. Who are you?"

Elminster found that he could move his jaws. "As you said, Magelord," he responded coldly, "a thief."

The wizard raised an eyebrow. "Why came you here, this night?"

"To speak with Mystra," Elminster said, surprising himself.

Ildru's eyes narrowed. "Why? Are you a mage?"

"No," Elminster spat, "I am proud to say. I came to get Mystra's aid to cast down magelords like you—or curse her if she refused."

The wizard's brows shot up again. "And just what made you think Mystra would aid you?"

Elminster swallowed and found he couldn't shrug. Or move anything except his mouth. "The gods exist," he said slowly, "and their power is real. I have need of that power."

"Oh? The traditional way," the wizard said pleasantly, "is to study—long and hard, for most of a lifetime—and abase oneself as an apprentice, and risk life in trying spells one doesn't understand or in devising one's own new magics. What colossal arrogance, to think Mystra would just give you something when you asked for it!"

"The colossal arrogance in Athalantar," Elminster said softly, "is held by magelords. Your hold on this land is so tight that no other men in it have the luxury of colossal arrogance."

There was a murmur, somewhere among the ring of armsmen. Ildru glared around, and abrupt silence returned. Then the wizard sighed theatrically. "I weary of your bitter words. Be still, unless you want to plead."

Elminster felt himself being forced backward, to clamber up onto the altar.

"No spears yet," the magelord ordered. "I must work a spell first, to learn if this youth is all clever words and deluded dreams . . . or if he holds some secrets yet."

The wizard raised his hands, cast a spell, and then peered narrowly at Elminster, frowning.

"No magic," he said as if to himself, "and yet you have some link to sorcery, some minor ability to shape . . . I've not seen such before." He stepped forward. "What are your powers?"

"I have no magic," Elminster spat. "I abhor magic, and all that is done with it."

"If I freed you and studied what is within you to see where your aptitude lies, would you be loyal to the Stag Throne?"

"Forever!"

The mage's eyes narrowed at that proud, quick answer, and

he added, "And to the magelords of Athalantar?"

"Never!" Elminster's shout echoed around the room, and the mage sighed again, watching the raging youth struggle vainly to spring down from the altar. "Enough," he said in a bored voice. "Kill him."

He turned away, and Elminster saw a dozen armsmen—and probably more he couldn't see, behind him—raise their spears, heft them, and take a pace or two back for a good throw.

"Forgive me, Mother . . . Father," Elminster said, through trembling lips, "I—I tried to be a true prince!"

The magelord whirled about. "*What?*"

And then the spears were in the air, and Elminster glared into the wizard's eyes and hissed, "I curse thee, Ildru of the magelords, with my death and the—"

He broke off in confusion. He hadn't expected to get this far in his curse, and he could see the wizard had raised his hands to weave some spell, crying out, "Wait! Stop! No spears!"

He could also see the armsmen staring at him as if he were a dragon—a purple dragon with three heads and a maiden's body, at that!

And the spears . . . they hung in the air, motionless, surrounded by pearly radiance. Elminster found he could move, and whirled around. There were spears on all sides, aye, a deadly ring of points leaping in to transfix him, but they all hung motionless in the air, and by the look on the wizard's face, it was none of his doing.

Elminster flung himself flat before this strange magic faded away. His move brought his face down low against the altar top, in time to see two floating eyes fade away, and a flame leap up from the bare stone.

Armsmen shouted and backed away, and Elminster heard the magelord cry out in astonishment.

The flame climbed, crackling, and then from it, bolts of flame roared out, consuming the spears where they hung. The spears became spars of flame that curled slowly and faded into smoke.

Elminster watched, openmouthed. A golden radiance was stealing outward from the altar, now, washing over him. Armsmen shook in real fear and backed away. Elminster saw them turn and reach for blades and try to run, but they seemed to be shimmering and moving slowly, as if they were figures drifting in a dream. Slowly, and more slowly still the armsmen shifted as flames that did not burn them sprang up and surrounded their bodies. Then they stood still and silent, frozen and unseeing . . . frozen in flames.

Elminster spun around to look at the magelord. The wizard stood as still as the rest, golden flames flickering before his staring eyes. His mouth was open, and his hands raised in the gestures of a spell . . . but he moved not.

What had befallen?

The flame pulsed and twisted. Elminster whirled back to face its changing flickering, and it shaped itself into someone . . . someone tall and dark robed and shapely, who strolled calmly over to stand by the brazier. A human woman . . . a sorceress?

Eyes of molten gold met his, and little flames danced in them. "Hail, Elminster Aumar, prince of Athalantar."

Elminster took a pace back, shocked. No, he'd never seen this great lady before—or anyone so beautiful. He swallowed. "Who *are* ye?"

"One who has been watching you for years, hoping to see great things," came the reply.

Elminster swallowed again.

The lady's eyes held dark depths of mystery, and her voice had a musical lilt. She smiled and raised an empty hand—and suddenly, she held a metal scepter. Lights pulsed and winked down its length. Elminster had never seen anything of the like before, but it blazed with blue mage-fire in his gaze, and its very look shouted that it held power.

"With this," the lady said quietly, "you can destroy all your foes here at once. Merely will it and speak the word graven on the grip."

She released the scepter, which rose a little and then drifted smoothly through the air toward Elminster. He watched it come, eyes narrow, then snatched it out of the air. Silent power shuddered in his grasp. Elminster felt it crackle and roil around in him, and his face brightened. He raised it, turning to face the motionless armsmen, feeling a fierce exultation rising in him. The lady watched him. He stood still for a long moment, then carefully bent and set the scepter down on the stone floor at his feet.

"Nay," he said, lifting his eyes to meet hers, " 'twould not be right, to use magic against men who are helpless. That's just what I'm fighting against, Lady."

"Oh?" She raised her head to stare at him in sudden challenge. "Are you afraid of it?"

Elminster shrugged. "A little." He watched her steadily. "More afraid of what I'd do wrongly. Thy scepter burns with power; such magic could do much ill if used carelessly. I'd rather not see the Realms laid waste by mine own hand." He shook his head. "Wielding a little power can be . . . pleasure. No one should have too much."

"What is 'too much'?"

"For me, Lady, anything. I hate magic. A mage slew my parents, on a whim, it seems, or for an afternoon's entertainment. He destroyed a village in less time than it takes me to tell ye what befell. No man should be able to do that."

"Is magic, then, evil?"

"Yes," Elminster snapped, then looked upon her beauty and said, "or perhaps not—but its power twists men to indulge evil."

"Ah," she replied. "Is a sword evil?"

"Nay, Lady—but dangerous. Not all folk should have them to hand."

"Oh? Who is to stop tyrants—and magelords—then?"

Elminster frowned angrily. "Ye seek to trick me with clever words, Lady!"

"Nay," came the soft reply. "I seek to make you think before you offer your own clever words and quick, sure judgments. I ask again: is a sword evil?"

"Nay," Elminster said, "for a sword cannot think."

The lady nodded. "Is a plow evil?"

"Nay," Elminster replied, raising an eyebrow. "What mean ye?"

"If a blade is not evil, but may be used for evil, is not this scepter the same?"

Elminster frowned and shook his head slightly, but did not reply.

Those eyes of light held his steadily. "What if I offered this scepter to a wizard, an innocent apprentice in some other land, not a magelord? What would you say to that?"

Elminster felt anger rising in him. Was everyone who worked sorcery given to fencing with clever words? Why did they always toy with him, as if he were a child, or a beast to be slain or transformed with but a passing thought? "I would say against it, Lady. No one should use such a thing without knowing first *how* to use it—and knowing its work well enough to realize what changes it will work in Faerun."

"Sober words for one so young. Most youths, and most mages, are so full of whim and pride that they'll dare anything."

Her words calmed him a little. At least she listened and did not dismiss him out of hand. Who *was* she? Did Mystra bind wizards to guard every one of her temples?

Elminster shook his head again. "I am a thief, Lady, in a city ruled by cruel wizards. Whim and pride are luxuries only rich

fools can afford. If I want to indulge in them, I must needs do it
by night, in bedchambers or on rooftops." He smiled thinly.
"Thieves—and indeed farmers, beggars, and folk who own only a
small shop or hand-trade, methinks—must keep themselves
under rather more control by day, or soon perish."

"What would you do," the sorceress asked curiously, eyes very
bright, "if you could work magic and became a wizard as strong
as those who dwell here?"

"I'd use my spells to drive all the wizards out of Athalantar so
folk could be free. I'd set a few other things right, too, and then
renounce magic forever."

"For you hate magic," the lady said softly. "What if you did not
and someone gave you the power, and told you that it must be
used, that you *must* be a wizard? What then?"

"I'd try to be a good one," Elminster replied, shrugging again.
Did temple wizards just *talk* to every intruder all the night
through? Still, it felt good to speak openly at last to someone who
listened and seemed to understand but not judge.

"Would you make yourself king?"

Elminster shook his head. "I'd not be a good one," he said. "I
have not the patience." He smiled suddenly and added, "Yet if I
found a man or a maid who'd wear the crown well, I'd stand behind him or her. That, I think, is the true work of a wizard—to
make life in the lands he dwells in good for all who dwell there."

Her smile, then, was dazzling. Elminster felt sudden power
in the air around him. His hair crackled, and his skin tingled.
"Will you kneel to me?" the sorceress asked, striding nearer.

Elminster swallowed, mouth suddenly dry. She was very
beautiful, and yet somehow terrifying, her eyes and hair alight
with power like flame waiting to burst forth. Trembling, Elminster held his ground and asked, "L-Lady, what is thy name? Who
are ye?"

"I am *Mystra*," came a voice that crashed around him like a
mighty wave smashing on rocks. Its echoes rolled around the
chamber. "*I* am the Lady of Might and the Mistress of Magic! I
am *Power Incarnate!* Wherever magic is worked, there am I—
from the cold poles of Toril to its hottest jungles, whatever the
hand or claw or will that works the sorcery! Behold me and fear
me! Yet behold me and love me—as all who deal with me in honesty do. This world is my domain. I *am* magic, mightiest among
all those men worship. I am the One True Spell at the heart of
all spells. There is no other."

Echoes rolled away. Elminster felt the very pillars of the
temple shaking around him. He wavered in awe, like a man

struggling in a high wind, but kept his feet. Silence fell, and their eyes met.

Golden flames burned in her gaze. Elminster felt as if he were burning inside; hot fire raced along his veins, pain rising in him like an angry red wave.

"Man," the goddess said, in an awful whisper, "do you defy me?"

Elminster shook his head. "I came here to curse thee or desecrate thy holy place or demand aid from thee, but now—no. I wish ye hadn't let the magelords slay my parents and ruin my realm, and I would . . . know why. But I have no wish to defy ye."

"What do you feel, instead?"

Elminster sighed. Somehow he'd felt he had to speak the truth since her first words to him, and it was still so. "I fear ye, and . . ." He was silent for a time, and then what might have been a smile touched his lips, and he went on. " . . . I think I could learn to love ye."

Mystra was very close to him now, and her eyes were dark pools of mystery. She smiled, and suddenly Elminster felt cool and refreshed, at ease.

"I let mages use spells freely so that all beings who use magic may escape tyranny. But from that freedom come such as the magelords in this land," she said. "If you would overthrow them, why not become a mage yourself? It is but a tool in your hand . . . and it seems to fit your hand better than many I have seen grasping at it."

Elminster took a pace back, lifting his hands in an unconscious warding gesture.

Mystra halted, eyes suddenly stern. "I ask again: will you kneel to me?"

Eyes locked on hers, he knelt slowly. "Lady, I confess I am awed," he said slowly, "but if I serve thee . . . I'd rather do it with my eyes open."

Mystra laughed, eyes sparkling. "Ah, but it is long since I've met such a one as you!"

Then her face was again solemn, and her voice low. "Extend your hand, freely and in trust, or go unharmed; choose."

Elminster extended his hand without hesitation. Mystra smiled and touched it. Fire consumed him, spun him down helplessly into nothing and beyond, and whirled him away into golden depths . . . as a thousand lightning bolts struck through his heart and roared back out of him as consuming flame. . . .

Elminster screamed, or tried to, as he was flung away into many-hued madness, a place of blinding light and blazing pain.

He roared, and when darkness rushed up to meet him, he plunged headlong into it, striking it as if it were a stone wall. Dashed against it, he was . . . gone. . . .

*   *   *   *   *

It was the cold, again, that awakened him. Elminster sat up, half expecting to see the burial-ground slumbering around him, and found instead the temple, still and dark. Power yet flowed in it, though, in a silent, invisible web of stirrings all around him, from the bare altar to the armsmen and the magelord who stood motionless all around the circular chancel.

Now he could feel magic as well as see it!

Awed, Elminster looked all around. He was naked; everything had been burned away to lie in ashes around him except for the Lion Sword, which lay beside him, unchanged from its ruined state. Taking it up with a smile—the Mistress of Magic knew his duty, too, it seemed—he got to his feet. The blue glow of magic was everywhere in this vast chamber, but brightest of all behind him. He turned and beheld the altar.

Mystra was gone, and her scepter with her, but as he looked, words flamed out brightly on the altar. He hurried forward to read them. "Teach thyself magic, and see the Realms. You will know when to come back to Athalantar. Worship me always with that keen mind and that lack of pride, and you will please me well. Serve me first by touching my altar."

As he finished reading, the words faded. When the altar was bare and dark again, he reached forward tentatively—paused in sudden, trembling fear—and then laid a hand firmly on the cold stone.

He thought he heard a faint chuckle, somewhere nearby . . . and then darkness claimed him again.

Eight

TO SERVE MYSTRA

*Did I ever tell thee how I first came to serve Mystra? No? Ye won't
believe a word of it naetheless. The way of the Lady seems strange
to most men—but then, most men are sane. Well, more or less.*

Sundral Morthyn
The Way of a Wizard
Year of Singing Shards

The world was drifting white mists. Elminster shook his
head to be free of them and heard a bird calling. A bird? In the
depths of the dark, empty temple? He shook his head again, and
realized with a start that his bare feet stood on moss and earth,
not cold stone. Where *was* he?

El found himself struggling now to break free of the mists . . .
clouds in his mind, not the world around. Shaking his head, he
heard bird calls again, and a soft rustling, a sound he remembered from long-ago Heldon: breezes blowing through leaves.

He was in a forest somewhere. As the last of the mists fell
away, El looked around and caught his breath. He stood in the
heart of a deep wood, with duskwoods and shadowtops and
blueleaf trees standing all crowded together around him, the
ground beneath them a dim and mushroom-studded place
stretching off into gloomy, rolling distances.

He stood in sunlight on a little knoll where several old giants
of the forest had toppled, leaving a clearing into which the sun
could reach. It was a small patch of sunlit moss where a large
flat stone lay, and beyond it, a tiny, crystal-clear pool. The Lion
Sword lay on the stone. Mystra's magic must have brought it
here with him.

Elminster bent forward to take it up. There was an unfamiliar swaying sensation at his chest as he knelt. Frowning, he
looked down and saw the breasts and the smooth curves of a
maid. Elminster stared down at himself in astonishment, and
ran a wondering hand over his body. It was solid and real . . . he
looked wildly around, but he was alone. Mystra had turned him
into a woman!

Clutching the reassuring, familiar hilt of the Lion Sword, El crawled forward across the rock until he could stare down into the placid waters of the pool. He studied his reflection there, seeing his own sharp nose and black hair, but a rather softer face, with a pert mouth—now frowning in consternation—a long neck and below it, a slim-hipped, rather bony woman. He was Elminster no more.

As he stared down, something seemed to grow in the depths of the pool . . . something blue-white and leaping—a flame.

El sat back. A flame was burning under the water, a flame with nothing to feed on! A flame that was rising, and becoming golden . . . Mystra!

He reached out an eager hand to touch the flame as it broke the surface, never thinking that it might destroy him until it was too late and his slim fingers were already feeling—coolness! A voice seemed to speak in his head. "Elminster becomes Elmara to see the world through the eyes of a woman. Learn how magic is a part of all things and a living force in itself, and pray to me by kindling flame. You will find a teacher in this forest." The flame faded and Elminster shivered. He knew that voice.

He looked down again in wonder. Now he was . . . "Elmara," she said aloud, and repeated it, her voice more musical than before.

She shook her head, suddenly recalling a night in Hastarl bought with stolen coins at Farl's urging. She remembered hot kisses and smooth, cool shoulders sliding soft and curved under his fingers, which wandered with tentative awe.

If he went into such a room now, he'd—she'd—be on the other end of the lovemaking. Hmmm.

So this was Mystra's first trick. Elmara twisted her lips wryly, shivered again, and then drew a deep breath. Elminster, the upstart prince whose failed battles had made him known to at least two magelords, was gone . . . at least for now, perhaps forever. His cause, she vowed, would never die, but end fulfilled. That might take years, though, and for now—

Elmara murmured, "So now what?" A breeze rustled the leaves again in answer.

Shrugging, she rose and walked all over the little knoll—noting that her stride was subtly different, shorter and swaying from side to side more—but there was nothing else to be found except moss and dead leaves. She was alone, and nude, the occasional twig sharp under her bare feet. What to do?

There was no food here, and no shelter. The sun already felt hot on her head and shoulders . . . she'd best get into the shade.

Mystra's voice had said she'd find a tutor in the forest, but she was reluctant to leave the pool, perhaps her only link to the goddess . . . but no. Mystra had said that El should pray to her by kindling flame, and there was not enough wood or leaves on this knoll to do that. Mystra had also said she'd *find* a tutor, and that implied she'd have to look for one.

Elmara sighed, juggled the Lion Sword thoughtfully, and squinted up at the sun. This forest looked like the High Forest above Heldon. If this was the High Forest, going south would bring her to its edge, and perhaps to food, if she couldn't find anything to eat among the trees, and to some idea of where exactly she was. The ground under the trees was dark and rolling, with sharp slopes and little gullies everywhere. If she left this knoll, she doubted she could ever find it again. That thought made her remember the pool, and she knelt and drank deeply, not knowing when next she'd see water.

Right, then. Time waited on no man—or woman, she reminded herself wryly, wondering how long it would take to get used to this. As she set off down into the trees, she did not look back, and so didn't see the pair of floating eyes that appeared above the pool, watched her go, and seemed to nod approvingly.

* * * * *

She'd walked all day, and her feet were cut to ribbons. She winced as she went and left a bloody trail. She'd have to get into a tree before dark, or some prowling forest cat or wolf would follow her trail. If it bit her throat, she'd be dead before she could wake.

Elmara looked around uneasily. The endless forest seemed dark and menacing now as the small glimpses of sunlight turned amber with sunset, and twilight came creeping . . . should she light a fire? It might attract beasts that could eat her, but yes. Only a little one, and let it die out before she slept. A flame to pray to Mystra. She'd do this every night, she vowed, beginning now.

She bent and gathered a dry tangle of twigs from under a large leaf and spread them on a nearby rock. Then she stopped in confusion. How could she make them burn? With a flint, aye, but she had no flint, nor steel.

A moment later, she smote her forehead and made a disgusted sound. Of course she did: the Lion Sword! She raised it, shaking her head at her slow wits, and rang it off the rock.

A spark jumped. Yes! This was the way. She set about belaboring the edge of the rock with the stoutest part of the blade, the unsharpened length just below the hilt, and pushed kindling in around where she struck, to catch any spark. The ringing sounds she made echoed a long way under the trees . . . and sparks jumped and winked where she didn't want them, disdaining her dry kindling.

Frustration and then anger rose in her . . . could she do *nothing* right? "I'm trying, Mystra," she snarled, "but—"

She broke off as the white glow arose at the back of her mind. Use her mind to call up fire? She'd never done more than nudge things a trifle, or slow falls a bit, or staunch bleeding . . . could she?

Well, why not try? She bent her gaze on the sword and summoned up the white fire within, building it with her anger until it blazed up and filled her mind. Then she brought the sword crashing down on the rock. A spark leapt up—and seemed to grow, expanding into a little ball of light before it arced back down and faded away.

El's eyes widened. She stared down where the spark had been, then shrugged and began the slow process of building the fire in her mind again. This time, the spark glowed white, expanded—and Elmara set her teeth and willed it to drift sideways and keep blazing . . . and it settled down into the kindling.

A curl of smoke drifted up. El watched and grinned in sudden exultation. She blew ever so gently at the kindling, and then shifted some twigs and a leaf so that they'd catch, if only the gods smiled—*yes!* A tiny flame rose, a tongue of faint amber that licked at the leaf and spread brown over it as it fed, growing higher.

El trembled, suddenly aware that a painful throbbing was beginning in her head, licked her lips, and said over the flame, "My thanks, great Mystra. I shall try to learn, and serve thee well."

The flame soared suddenly, almost burning her nose, and then winked out, gone as if it had never been. Elmara stared at where it wasn't, then sat back, holding her suddenly splitting head. No normal flame would behave that way; Mystra *must* have heard her.

She knelt there for a few breaths, hoping for some sign or word from the goddess, but there was nothing but darkness under the trees, and a faint whiff of woodsmoke. But then, why should she expect anything more? She'd never seen Mystra in all her life before last night . . . and there were other folk and other doings in Faerun besides Elminster of Athalantar.

Elmara, she corrected herself absently. What *did* gods spend their days at, anyway?

And then a booted foot came down softly on the ground she was staring at, treading firmly on the Lion Sword. She gasped and looked up. Proud eyes—elven eyes—stared down at her, and their gaze was not friendly. A hand was extended toward her, and there was a sudden glow of light from its palm. The bright radiance grew, stretching out straight down at her, until the tip of a sword of light was in front of her chin.

"Tell me," a light, high voice said calmly, "why I should let you live."

* * * * *

Delsaran sniffed suddenly and raised his head. "Fire!" The tree he'd been shaping fell back limply under his hands as his magic faltered. Quick anger turned the tips of his ears red. "Here, in the very heart of the old trees!"

"Yes," Baerithryn agreed, but laid a restraining hand on his friend's arm. "But a small one; tarry." He raised his other hand, sketched a circle in the air with two fingers, and spoke a soft word.

A moment later, an intent face appeared in the air between them, the face of a human woman. Delsaran hissed but said no more as they heard the woman speak: "My thanks, great Mystra. I shall try to learn, and serve thee well."

The flame soared then, and their spell-vision exploded into a tiny twinkling of blue sparks. Delsaran's jaw dropped. "The goddess heard her," he said in grudging disbelief.

Baerithryn nodded. "This must be the one the Lady said would come." He rose, a silent shadow in the gathering night-gloom, and said, "I shall guide her, as I promised. Leave us be . . . as you promised."

Delsaran nodded slowly. "The Lady grant us success"—his lips twisted wryly—"all three." Baerithryn laid a silent hand on his shoulder, then was gone.

Delsaran stared unseeing at the tree he'd been shaping, and then shook his head. Humans had slain his parents and their axes had felled the trees he'd first played in . . . why did the Lady have to send a human? Didn't she want the People to be guided in learning her service and true mastery of magic?

"I guess she thinks elves are wise enough to guide themselves," he said aloud, smiled almost wistfully, and got to his feet. Mystra had never spoken to *him*. He shrugged, set his

hand reassuringly on the tree for a moment, and then slipped
away into the night.

* * * * *

Elmara stared up at the sword. "There is no special reason,"
she said at last. "Mystra brought me here, and"—she gestured
down at herself, and a sudden blush stole across her face—
"changed me, thus. I mean no harm to you or to this place."

The elf regarded her gravely for a moment and said, "Yet
there is the will in you to do great harm to many folk."

El stared into his eyes and found her throat suddenly dry.
She swallowed and said, "I live to avenge my slain parents. My
foes are the magelords of Athalantar."

The elf stood silent, as still and dark as the trees around.
The sword of light did not waver. He seemed to be awaiting
more words.

Elmara shrugged. "To destroy them, I must master magic—
or find some way to destroy theirs. I . . . met with Mystra. She
said I'd find a tutor here. . . . Do ye know of a wizard or a priest
of Mystra in this wood?"

The sword vanished. Blinking in the sudden darkness, El
heard that light voice say simply, "Yes." Silence followed.

Afraid of being left alone in the night in this endless forest,
El asked quickly, "Will ye guide me to that person?" To her own
astonishment, her voice quavered.

"You have found 'that person,' " the elf replied with an un-
dertone that might have been satisfaction or quiet amusement.
"Give me your name."

"El-Elmara," she answered, and something made her add, "I
was Elminster until this morn."

The elf nodded. "Baerithryn," he replied. "I was Braer to the
last human who knew me."

"Who was that?" El asked, suddenly curious.

Those grave eyes flickered. "A lady mage . . . dead these
three hundred summers."

El looked down. "Oh."

"I'm not overfond of questions, you'll find," the elf added.
"Look and listen to learn. That is the elven way. You humans
have so much less time and always gabble questions and then
rush off to do things without waiting for, or truly understanding, the answers. I hope to curb that in you . . . just a little." He
leaned forward and added, "Now lie back."

El looked up at him, and then did so, wondering what would

come next. Unconsciously, she covered her breasts and loins
with her hands.

The elf seemed to smile. "I've seen maids before . . . and all of
you, already." He dropped silently into a crouch and said, "Give
me your foot."

El looked at him in wonder, and then raised her left foot. The
elf cupped it—his touch was feather-soft—and the pain slowly
ebbed away. El looked at him in wonder.

"The other," he said simply. She let her healed foot fall and
extended the other to him. Again the pain fled. "You've given
the forest blood," he said, "which satisfies a ritual some find unpleasant." His grip on her heel became stronger, and he made a
surprised sound and let her foot fall.

A moment later—he moved like soundless liquid, or a
smooth-flowing shadow—the elf was kneeling by her head.
"Allow me," he said, and added, "Lie still." Elmara felt his fingers touch her lightly over each eye, and linger there . . . and
slowly, very slowly, the ache in her head subsided, the pain
stealing away.

With it went all her weariness, and she was suddenly alert,
eager, and awake. "Wh—My thanks, sir—what did you do?"

"Several things. I used simple magic, what you'll need to
learn first. Then I winced at being called 'sir' and waited patiently to be called 'Braer' and seen as a person, not some sort of
magic-wielding monster." The words were lightly spoken beside
her ear, but Elmara felt her answer was very important.

She raised her head slowly, to find those eyes staring into
hers from only a finger's-length away. "Please forgive me, Braer.
Will ye be—my friend?" Impulsively, she leaned forward and
kissed the face she could barely see. The elf's eyes blinked into
hers as her lips touched—a sharp-boned nose.

Braer did not pull away. His lips did not meet hers, but a moment later Elmara felt soft fingers stroke the length of her chin.
"That's better, daughter of a prince. Now sleep."

El was falling down, down into a void of warm darkness before she even had time to wonder how Braer knew his—her—father had been a prince . . . perhaps, she managed to think, as
whispering mists rose in her mind, all Faerun knew it. . . .

* * * * *

"You began as all younglings do: awed by magic. Then you
learned to fear it, and hate those who wielded it. After a time,
you saw its usefulness as a weapon too powerful to ignore. Mas-

tering it or finding a shield against it then became a necessity."

Braer fell silent and leaned forward, watching intently as blue mage-fire danced at the tips of Elmara's fingers. He gestured, and obediently she made the fire move up and down each finger in turn, racing along her tingling skin.

"You wonder now why I waste so much of your brief life with a child's playing about with magic," Braer said flatly. "It's not to make you familiar with it. You are that, already. It's to make you love magic, for itself, not for what you can do with it."

"Why," Elmara asked in the elven manner, reflected fire dancing in her eyes as her gaze met his, "should a man or a maid love magic?"

Her teacher remained silent, as he did all too often for her liking. They looked into each other's eyes until finally she added, "I would think that leads to bent men who wall themselves up in little rooms and become crabbed and crazed, chasing some elusive spell or detail of magecraft, and wasting their lives away."

"In some, it does," Braer agreed. "But love of magic is more necessary for those who worship Mystra—priests of the goddess, if you will, though most see no difference between such folk and mages—than it is for wizards. One must love magic to properly revere magic."

Elmara frowned a little. There were a few gray hairs in her long, unruly black mane now; she'd studied magic for two winters through at Braer's side, praying to Mystra each night . . . without reply. Hastarl and her days as a thief seemed almost a dream to her now, but she could still remember the faces of the magelords she'd seen.

"Some folk worship out of fear. Is their respect any the less?"

The elf nodded. "It is," he said simply, "even if they do not know it." He rose, as smooth and silent as ever. "Now put away that fire and come and help me find evenfeast."

He strode away through the trees, knowing she'd follow. Elmara rose, smiled a little, and did so. They spent their days thus, talking while she practiced magic under his direction, and then foraging in the forest for food. Once the elf had shown her how to take the shape of a wolf, then bounded off to run down a stag, with her stumbling along behind. In all their days together, she'd never seen him do anything but guide her, though he left her side every nightfall and did not return until dawn. He always chose the spot where she slept, and her mage-sight told her he cast some sort of magical ring about her.

Braer never seemed tired, or dirty, or less than patient. His garb never changed, and there was never a day when he did not come to her. She saw no other elves, or anyone else . . . though he'd once confirmed they were somewhere in the High Forest, supposedly home to the greatest kingdom of elves in all Faerun.

On her first morning in the forest, he'd brought her a rough gown of animal hide, glossy high boots of unexpected quality, a thong for tying the Lion Sword around her neck (she kept it wrapped in a skin to avoid cutting her breast), and a trowel for digging her own privy-holes. To clean herself, she scrubbed with leaves and moss and washed in the little pools and rivulets that seemed to be everywhere in the endless forest. When she commented that one seemed to find water unexpectedly around every third or fourth hillock or gully, Braer had nodded and replied, "Like magic."

That memory came to Elmara suddenly. She looked ahead at the elf gliding among the trees like a silent shadow, and suddenly scrambled to catch up with him. As always when she hurried, twigs cracked and leaves rustled under her feet. Braer turned and frowned at her.

She matched his frown, and asked the question that had arisen in her. "Braer . . . why do elves love magic?"

For a fleeting moment, a grin of exultation washed across his face. Then it was gone, and his face held its usual expression of calm, open interest. Yet El knew she'd seen that look of delight, and her heart lifted. The elf's next words sent it soaring. "Ah . . . now you begin to think, and to ask the right questions. I can begin teaching you." He turned and walked on.

"*Begin* teaching me?" Elmara asked his back indignantly. "So just *what* have ye been doing these past two seasons?"

"Wasting much time," he told the trees ahead calmly, and her heart came crashing down.

Tears welled up in her, and burst forth. Elmara sank down on her knees and wept. She cried a long time, lonely and lost and feeling worthless, and when the tears were all gone she finally sat up wearily, and looked all around. She was alone.

"Braer!" she cried. "*Braer! Where are you?*" Her shout echoed back at her from the trees, but there came no reply. She sank down again, and whispered, "Mystra, aid me. Mystra . . . help me!"

It was growing dark. Elmara looked wildly in all directions. She was in a part of the forest they'd never walked in before. With sudden urgency she called forth mage-fire, and held up her blazing hand like a lantern. The trees around seemed to rustle and stir for a moment—but then a tense, watchful stillness fell.

"Braer," she said into the darkness. "*Please* . . . come back!"

A tree nearby wavered and bowed—and then stepped forward. It was Baerithryn, looking sad. "Forgive me, Elmara?"

Two running steps later, Elmara crashed into him and threw her arms around him, sobbing. "Where did ye go? Oh, Braer, what did I do?"

"I—am sorry, Lady. I did not mean my words as a judgment." The elf held her gently but firmly, rocking her slightly from side to side as if she were a small child to be soothed. With infinite tenderness, his hands stroked her long, tangled hair.

Elmara pulled her head back, tears bright on her cheeks. "But ye went *away!*"

"You seemed to need a time to grieve . . . a release," the elf said softly. "It seemed churlish to smother what you felt. More than that: sometimes, things must be faced and fought alone."

He took hold of her shoulders and gently pushed her away until they stood facing each other. Then he smiled and raised a hand—and it suddenly held a steaming bowl. A heavenly scent of cooked fowl swirled around them both. "Care to dine?"

Elmara laughed weakly and nodded. Braer whirled his other hand, and out of nowhere a silver goblet appeared in it. He handed it to her with a flourish. When El took it, Braer spun his hand grandly again, and this time two ornate forks and dining-knives appeared. He gestured for her to sit.

Elmara discovered she was ravenous. The forest bustards had been cooked in a mushroom sauce and were delicious—and the goblet proved to be full of the best mint wine, incredibly clear and heady. She devoured everything; Braer smiled and shook his head more than once as he watched.

When she was done, another flourish of the elf's hands produced a bowl of warmed vinegar-water and a fine linen cloth for Elmara to wash her face and hands with. As she wiped grease from her chin, she saw his grave expression had returned.

"I ask again, Elmara: do you forgive me? I have wronged you."

"Forgive—of course." El stretched forth her newly cleaned hand to squeeze one of his.

Braer looked down at her hand on his, and then back up at her. "I did to you what we of the forest consider a very bad thing: I misjudged you. I did not mean to upset you . . . nor make it worse by leaving you to your grief. Do you recall just what was said between us?"

Elmara stared at him. "Ye said ye'd wasted much time these past two seasons, and only now could begin to teach me."

Braer nodded. "What question did you ask, to make me say so?"

El wrinkled her brow, and then said slowly, "I asked you why elves love magic."

Braer nodded. "Yes." He waved a hand. All the dinner-things vanished, and a vivid ring of blue mage-fire raced into being around them. He settled himself cross-legged, and asked, "Do you feel up to talking the night through?"

El frowned. "Of course . . . why?"

"There are some things you should know . . . and at last are ready to hear."

Elmara met his grave eyes and leaned forward. "Speak, then," she whispered eagerly.

Braer smiled. "To answer one of your questions directly for once: we of the People love magic because we love life. Magic is the life energy of Faerun, lass, gathered in its raw form and used to power specific effects by those who know how. Elves—and the Stout Folk, too, deep in the rocks beneath us—live close to the land . . . part of it, linked to it—and in balance with it. We grow no more numerous than the land will bear and shape our lives to what the land will support. Forgive me, but humans are different."

Elmara nodded and waved at him to continue.

Braer met her eyes with his own and said steadily, "Like orcs, humans know best how to do four things: breed too rapidly; covet everything around them; destroy anything and everything that stands in the way of any of their desires; and dominate what they can't or won't bother to destroy."

Elmara stared at him. Her face had paled, but she nodded slowly and again gestured for him to continue.

"Harsh words, I know," said the elf gently, "but that is what your kin mean to us. Men seek to change Faerun around them to suit their own desires. When we—or anything else—stand in their way, they cut us down. Men are quick and clever—I'll give them that—and seem to stumble on new ideas and ways more often and more swiftly than any other people . . . but to us, and to the land, they are a creeping danger. A creeping rot that eats away at this forest and every other untouched part of the realm . . . and at us with it. You are the first of your race to be tolerated here in the depths of the wood for a very long time—and there are some among my folk who would rather you were safely dead, your flesh feeding the trees."

Elmara stared silently at him, face white and eyes very dark.

Braer smiled slightly, and added, "Death is a goal too few of your race strive for, but one more laudable than many they do pursue."

Elmara let out a long, shuddering breath, and asked, "Why then do you . . . tolerate me here?"

The elf reached out a hand slowly and tentatively, and as Elmara watched in wonder, he squeezed one of her hands just as she had done to him earlier. "Out of simple respect for the Lady, I undertook to guide you," he said, "and to turn you into ways that could do us the least damage, down the years, if the gods willed that you should live."

His smile broadened. "I've come to know you . . . and respect you. I know your life's tale, Elminster Aumar, prince of Athalantar. I know what you hope to do—and it would be mere prudence to aid one dedicated to fighting our most powerful and nearest foes, the magelords. Your character—especially your strength in setting aside your hatred of magic long enough to agree to serve the Lady and in clinging to sanity and dignity when she made you a woman without warning—have made my task more than a duty and prudence; you have made it a pleasure."

Elmara swallowed, feeling fresh tears well up and run down her cheeks. "Ye-ye are the kindest and most patient person I've ever known," she whispered. "Please forgive me, for my tears earlier."

Braer patted her hand. "The fault was mine. To answer the question that has just occurred to you: Mystra made you a maid both to hide you from the magelords and to make you able to feel the link between magic, the land, and life; women are able to feel it better than men. In the days ahead, I can show you how to feel and work with that link."

"Ye can read my thoughts?" Elmara cried, drawing back from him sharply. "Then why, by all the gods, didn't ye just *tell* me what I needed to know?"

Braer shook his head. "I can only read thoughts when they're charged with strong emotion, and when I'm very close by. More than that: few folk can truly learn by having every idle thought answered in an instant. They don't bother to think about or remember anything, but merely come to rely on the one answering them for all wisdom and direction."

Elmara frowned, nodding very slowly. "Aye," she said softly. "Ye're right."

Braer nodded. "I know. It's the curse of my race."

Elmara looked at him for a moment, and then whooped with laughter. After a few helpless breaths of mirth, she broke off at a sound she'd never heard before: a deep, dry sound . . . Baerithryn of the People was chuckling.

* * * * *

Dawn was stealing through the trees when Braer said, "Too tired to go on?"

Elmara was stiff with sitting and swayed with weariness, but she whispered fiercely, "No! I have to know! Say on!"

Braer inclined his head in salute, and said, "Know then: the High Forest is dying, little by little, year by year, under the axes of men and the spells of magelords. They know our power—and being insecure in their own, feel they can only win the safety of their realm by destroying us."

He waved one hand in a slow arc at the silent trees around them. "Our power is rooted in the shiftings of the seasons. It is drawn from the vitality and endurance of the land—and is not a thing of flashing battle spells and destruction. The magelords know this and how to force us to fight in ways and places where they know they can defeat us, so we often dare not fight them openly . . . and they know that, too. I've lost many friends who would not admit the magelords' power rivaled or overmatched our own."

Braer sighed and continued, "You, and others like you, we can aid in your own battles against them . . . and we will. So long as you respect the land and live with it, our ways lie together, and our battles shall, too. When you need aid against the magelords and call to us, we shall come. This we swear."

A moment later, half a dozen trees around them shifted and stepped forward, and his words were echoed by a fierce chorus. *"This we swear."*

Elmara stared around at all the solemn elven eyes, swallowed, and bowed her head. "And I, in turn, swear not to work against thee or the land. Show me how to do this, please."

The elves bowed in return and melted away again into the forest.

El swallowed. "Are they always here, as trees, around us?"

Braer smiled. "No. You happened to pause and weep in a special place."

El gave him a fierce expression, but it slid into a smile and a weary shake of her head. "I am honored . . . and understand your people enough, now, not to step wrongly with each stride." She yawned helplessly and added, "I think I'm more than ready to sleep now, too. Promise to show me—finally—some earth-shaking spells in the days ahead?"

Baerithryn smiled. "I promise." He reached out and stroked her cheek, and as his spell sent her instantly to sleep, caught her shoulder and lowered her tenderly to the mossy ground.

Then he settled down beside her and stroked her cheek again. In her little time left in the forest, he would keep careful watch over this weapon against the magelords. More than that: he would keep careful watch over this precious friend.

Nine

THE WAY OF A MAGE

The way of a mage is a dark and lonely one. This is why so many wizards fall early into the darkness of the grave—or later into the endless twilight of undeath. Such bright prospects are why the road to mastery of magecraft is always such a crowded one.

Jhalivar Thrunn
Trail Tales of the North
Year of the Sundered Shields

A flame was suddenly dancing above the rock, in air that had been empty a moment before. Elmara caught her breath. "Mystra?" she asked, and the flame seemed to brighten for a moment in response—but then it faded away into nothingness, and there was no other reply.

Elmara sighed and knelt beside the pool. "I hoped for something more."

"A little less pride, lass," Braer murmured, touching her elbow. " 'Tis more than most of my folk ever see of the Lady."

She looked at him curiously. "Just how many of the People worship Mystra?"

"Not many . . . we have our own gods, and most of us have always preferred to turn our back on the rest of the world and all its unpleasantnesses and keep to the old ways. The problem is that the rest of the world always seems to reach out and thrust blades into our backsides while we're trying to ignore it."

El grinned at his words, despite their tragic meaning. " 'Backsides'? I never thought to hear an elf say that."

Braer's mouth crooked. "I never thought to see a human hear an elf say it, if it comes to that. Do you still think of us as unearthly tall and thin noble creatures, gliding around above it all?"

"I—aye, I suppose I do."

The elf shook his head. "We have you fooled with the rest, then. We're as earthy and as untidy as the forest. We *are* the forest, lass. Try not to forget that as you walk out into the world of men."

" 'Walk out'?" Elmara frowned at him. "Why d'ye say that?"

"I can't help but read your thoughts, Lady. You've been happier here than ever before in your short life—but you know you've learned all you can here that'll make of yourself a better blade against the magelords . . . and you grow restless to move on."

He held up a hand as she made a small sound of protest, and went on. "Nay, lass; I can see it in you and hear it in you, and for you it is right. You can never be free, never be yourself, until your parents have been avenged and you've set Athalantar back to what you think it should be. You're driven by this, and it's a burden no one in Faerun can lift but you, by doing the deeds you've set yourself." He smiled wryly. "You didn't want to leave Farl, and now you don't want to leave me. Are you sure you shouldn't stay a woman the rest of your days?"

Elmara made a face and added softly, "I didn't know I had a choice."

"Not yet, perhaps, but you will . . . when you start to become a realm-shattering archmage. Thus far, you've become familiar with magic, and by the grace of Mystra call up and shape what slumbers in the land around. Did you truly think this prayer, now, and all the others each night, were wasted?"

"I—"

"You've begun to fear so, yes. I'm telling you differently," Braer said almost sternly and stood up in a single smooth movement. He reached down a hand to assist her to rise and added, "I'll miss you, but I won't be sad or angry; 'tis time for you to move on. You'll return when you must. My task hasn't been to teach you spells that'll blast magelords and their dragon steeds out of the sky, but to teach you familiarity with magic and wisdom in the use of it. I am a priest of Mystra, yes—but there's a priestess of Mystra greater far than I am. You must go to see her soon, outside the forest. Her temple is at Ladyhouse Falls, and she knows more of the ways of men . . . and of where you should go in the days ahead."

Elmara frowned. "I—ye are right, I do grow restless, but I don't want to leave."

The elf smiled. "Ah, but you do." Then his smile vanished, and he added, "And before you go, I'd like to see that revealment spell cast properly for once!"

Elmara sighed. "It's just a spell I've a little trouble with, one among—what is it?—two score and more?"

Braer raised eyebrows and hands together. " 'Just a spell'? Lass, lass. Nothing should ever be just a spell to you. *Revere* magic, remember? Else it's just a faster sword or longer lance to you—only a grubbing after more power than you can grasp by other means."

"It's *not* that to me!" Elmara protested, turning on him angrily. "Oh, before I came here, perhaps! Do you think I've learned nothing from you?"

"Easy, lass, easy. I'm not a magelord, remember?"

El stared at him for a moment, and then managed a laugh. "I did hold my temper and tongue better when I was a thief, didn't I?"

Braer shrugged. "You were a man, then, in a city of men—with a close friend to joke with—and you knew, every moment, that lack of iron control would mean death. Now you're a woman, attuned to the forest, feeling its flows of emotion and energy. Little things are more intense outside the crowded city, more raw, more engaging." He smiled and added, "I can't believe I've started babbling so much—and like a human sage, too!—since you've been here."

Elmara laughed. "I have done some good, then."

Braer flipped the tip of one of his ears back and forth with a finger, a gesture of mild derision among elves, and said, "I believe I mentioned a revealment spell?"

El rolled her eyes. "Didn't think I could lead ye into forgetting about it forever. . . ."

Braer gave her an imperious wave that she knew meant 'get on with it,' and folded his arms across his chest. Elmara assumed an apologetic little-lass smile for a moment, then turned to face the pool. Spreading her arms wide, she closed her eyes and whispered the prayer to Mystra, feeling the power within her surge up her arms and outward, expanding. . . . She opened her eyes, expecting to see the familiar blue glows of magic on the pool, perhaps on the rock where Mystra's flame had manifested, and when she swung around, here and there on Braer's body, where he wore or carried small tokens of magic.

"Ahhh!" Staggered, she stepped back, letting her hands fall. Everything was bright and blinding blue wherever she looked—was the whole world alive with magic?

"Yes," Braer replied calmly, reading her thoughts again. "At *last* you're able to see it. Now," he went on briskly, "you were still having a little trouble with casting a sphere of spells, were you not?"

She turned angry eyes on him, but recoiled again, astonished. The tall, dignified elf she knew stood watching her, but in the special sight the spell gave her was revealed ablaze with magic of great power, and the blue-white glow around him rose into the shadowy shape of a dragon. "Ye—ye're a dragon!"

"Sometimes," Braer shrugged, "I take that shape. But I'm truly an elf who's learned how to take on dragon shape . . . not the other way around. I'm the last reason the magelords did so much dragon hunting in Athalantar."

"The last reason?"

"The others," he said tightly, "are dead. They saw to it very efficiently."

"Oh," Elmara said quietly. "I'm sorry, Braer."

"Why?" he asked lightly. "You didn't do it—'tis the magelords who should be sorry . . . and I and my kin are counting on you to make them so, someday."

Elmara drew herself up. "I intend to. Soon."

The elf shook his head. "No, lass, not yet. You aren't ready . . . and a single archmage, no matter how mighty, can't hope to succeed against all the magelords and their servant creatures, if they whelm against you." He smiled and added, "And you haven't even learned to be an archmage yet. Set aside revenge for a time. 'Tis best savored when one waits a long time for it, anyway."

Elmara sighed. "I may die of old age with the magelords still lording it over Athalantar."

"I've read that fear in your mind often, since we first met," Braer replied, "and I know it will drive you until your death—or theirs. It's why you must leave the High Forest before it starts to feel like a cage around you."

Elmara took a deep breath, then nodded. "When should I go?"

Braer smiled. "As soon as I've conjured up crying-towels for us both. Elves hate long, sad farewells even more than humans do."

El tried to laugh, but sudden tears welled up and burst forth.

"You see?" Braer said lightly, stepping forward to embrace her. Elmara saw tears in his own eyes before they embraced fiercely.

* * * * *

The night was soft and still and deep blue overhead as El left the familiar shade of the forest and headed across the rolling hills toward distant Ladyhouse Falls. She felt suddenly naked, away from the sheltering trees, but fought down the urge to hurry. Folk in too much haste make excellent targets for outlaws with bows . . . and with no foe in sight and a heavy load of sausage, roast fowl, cheese, wine, and bread riding between her shoulder blades, she really had no need to hurry.

She struck the Hastarl road and almost immediately passed by the last marker cairn. It felt marvelous to set foot outside the Kingdom of the Stag for the first time in her life.

Elmara breathed deeply of the crisp air of fast-approaching leaf-fall, and looked at the land around as she went. She was wading through waist-deep brush, where the Great Fires had been set ten years agone to drive the elves out of all these lands and take them for men. But men huddled in ever-more-crowded cities and towns along the Delimbiyr, and summer by summer, the forest crept back to reclaim the hills. Soon the elves—more bitter and swifter with their arrows than they'd once been—would return, too.

Here shadowtops rose like a dark stand of halberds; there two hawks circled high in the clear air. She went on with joy in her step, and did not halt until it grew too dark to go on and the wolves began to howl.

* * * * *

She'd expected more than a few ragged stone cottages and a tumbledown barn—but the road ran on and up through the trees toward a distant roar of water; this must be Ladyhouse Falls.

The road narrowed to a deep-rutted cart trail and turned east. A little path led off it into the trees, along which came the sound of water. Elmara took the way it offered and came out in a field broken by a huge, fire-scarred sheet of rock, with the rushing river hard by, and a high-peaked hall in front of her.

Ivy was thick on its old stones, and its door was dark, but to Elmara's mage-sight it blazed blue, the heart of a web of radiant lines sweeping out across the fields and down the trail she had walked upon. That strand blinked beneath her feet; she stepped aside hastily and advanced thereafter by walking on the mosses beside the trail.

She almost fell over the old woman in dark robes who was kneeling in the dirt, planting small yellow-green things and covering them over deeply.

"I was wondering if you'd stride right through my bed without seeing me at all," she said without looking up, her voice sharp-edged but amused.

Elmara stared, and then swallowed, finding herself shy. "My—pardon, Lady. In truth, I saw thee not. I seek—"

"The glories of Mystra, I know." The wrinkled hands patted another plant into its resting-place—like so many tiny graves,

El thought suddenly—and the white-haired head came up. Elmara found herself looking into two clear eyes of green flame that seemed to thrust right through her like two emerald blades. "Why?"

El found herself bereft of words. She opened her mouth twice, and then the third time blurted out, "I—Mystra spoke to me. She said it'd been a long time since she'd met such a one as me. She asked me to kneel to her, and I did." Unable to meet that bright gaze longer, Elmara looked away.

"Aye, so they all say. I suppose she told thee to worship her well."

"She wrote that, aye. I—"

"What has life taught thee thus far, young maid?"

Elmara raised steady blue-gray eyes to meet that glittering green gaze. The old woman's eyes seemed even brighter than before, but she was determined to hold them with her own, and she did.

"I've learned how to hate, steal, grieve, and kill," she said. "I hope there's more to being a priestess of Mystra than that."

The wrinkled old mouth crooked. "For many, not much more. Let's see if we can do better with thee." She looked down at the bed in front of her and tapped thoughtfully at the loose earth.

"What must I do to begin?" Elmara asked, looking down at the dirt. There seemed to be nothing of interest there, but perhaps the priestess meant that she should tend plants, as Braer had wanted her to learn the ways of the woods. She looked around . . . hadn't there been a shovel thrust into the earth nearby?

As if the old woman could read her thoughts (as of course she doubtless could, El thought wryly) the priestess shook her head. "After all these years," she said, "I've learned how to do this right, lass. The last thing I need is eager but careless hands mucking in or a young, impatient tongue asking me questions morn and even through. Nay, get ye gone."

"Gone?"

"Go and walk the world, lass; Mystra doesn't gather toothless, chanting men or maids to kneel to stones carved in her seeming. All Faerun around us is Mystra's true temple."

She waved a bony hand. "Go and do as I bid, thus; and listen well, lass. Learn from mages, without yourself taking the title or spellhurling habits of a wizard. Spread word of the power of magic, its mysteries and lore; make folk you meet hunger to work magic themselves, and give those who seem most eager a taste of spellcasting, for no more payment than food and a place to sleep. Make maids and men into mages."

El frowned doubtfully. "How shall I know when I'm doing right—is there anything I should not do?"

The priestess shook her head. "Be guided by your own heart—but know that Mystra forbids nothing. Go and experience everything that can befall a man and a maid in Faerun. *Everything.*"

El frowned again. Slowly, she turned away.

That sharp voice came again. "Sit down and eat first, fool-head. Bitterness lends the weak-witted wings . . . always try to make a stop to eat into a time to think, and you'll think more in a season than most think in all their days."

Elmara smiled slightly, threw her cloak back, and sat, reaching for the shoulder sack Braer had given her.

The old woman shook her head again and snapped her fingers. Out of nowhere, a wooden platter of steaming greens appeared in front of El. Then a silver fork blinked into being above it and hung motionless in the air.

Reluctantly El reached out for it.

The old woman snorted. "Frightened of a little magic? A *fine* advocate of Mystra you'll be."

"I—have seen magic used to slay and destroy and rule through fear," Elmara said slowly. "Wherefore I'm wary of it." She took firm hold of the fork. "I did not choose to look upon Mystra—she came to me."

"Then be more grateful; some wizards dream of seeing her all their lives and die disappointed." The white-haired head bent to regard the dirt again. "If you hate or fear magic so much, why have you come here?"

Silence stretched. "To do a thing I am sworn to do," Elmara said finally, "I'll need strong magic . . . and to understand what it is I wield."

"Well, then . . . eat, and get you going. Mind you try some of that thinking I suggest."

"Thinking of—what?"

"That, I leave to you. Remember, Mystra forbids nothing."

"Think . . . of everything?"

" 'Twould be a welcome change."

* * * * *

The old woman watched until the young maid in the cloak was gone through the trees. Then she went on watching; a few trees were nothing to her.

Finally she turned and walked to the temple, growing as she

went, her shape shifting and rising until a tall and shapely lady in shimmering, iridescent robes strolled to the temple door. She turned once more to look where Elmara had gone. Her eyes were dark and yet golden, and little flames danced in them.

"Seen enough?" The voice from the darkness within the door was a deep rumble.

Mystra tossed her head; long, glossy hair slithered and danced. "This could be the one. His mind has the width, and his heart the depth."

The temple rippled, flowed, and shifted, even as she had done, and split, revealing itself as a bronze dragon rising away from around a much smaller, stone house.

The dragon stretched out gigantic wings with a creak and a sigh and inclined its head until one wise old eye regarded the goddess. Its voice was a purr so deep that the front of the stone house shivered. "As did all the others . . . those many, many others. Having the skill doesn't mean one must or will use it rightly, and take the true path."

"True," Mystra answered, a certain soft bitterness in her tone, and then she smiled and laid a hand on its scales. "My thanks, faithful friend. Until next we fly together."

As gently as if it were brushing her with a feather, the dragon stroked her cheek with one massive claw. Then it drew in its wings and melted, dwindling down into the form of a bent, wrinkled white-haired woman with bright green eyes. Without a backward glance, the priestess went into the temple, moving with the slow gait and bent back of age. Mystra sighed, turned away herself, and became a dazzling web of lights that whirled and spun, faster and faster—until she was gone.

* * * * *

The sack Braer had given her proved to hold over twenty silver coins at the bottom, wrapped in a scrap of hide. That was not so many that she could afford to hurl them away for a warm bed every night, at least before the deep snows came down on the world. Hedges and thickets were her bedchambers, but Elmara usually warmed herself of evenings at an inn with a hot meal and a seat as close to the hearth as she could manage. Lone young women walking the roads were few, but conjuring a little mage-fire and looking mysterious always kept any over-amorous local men at a distance.

This night found her in the latest house of raised flagons, somewhere in the Mlembryn lands. To all who would listen, she spun tales of the glory of magic, tales drawn from what Braer and Helm and the streets of Hastarl had told her. Sometimes these tales won her a few drinks, and on nights when the gods smiled, someone else would tell stories of sorcery to top her own, and thereby tell her more of what most folk thought of magic . . . and win her new marvels to tell on evenings to come.

She had hopes of that happening this night; two men, at least, were edging forward in their chairs, itching to unburden themselves of something, as she warmed to the height of her most splendid tale. ". . . And the last the king and all his court saw of the nine Royal Wizards, they were standing on thin air, facing each other in a circle, already higher than the tallest turret of the castle, and rising!" Elmara drew breath dramatically, looked around at her rapt audience, and went on.

"Lightnings danced ever faster between their hands, weaving a web so bright that it hurt the eyes to look upon it—but the last thing the king saw, ere they rose out of sight, was a dragon appearing in the midst of those lightnings, *fading in,* he said. . . .'"

And then a curtain across a booth in the back of the room parted, and Elmara knew she was in trouble. The eager men turned hurriedly away, and the room filled with a sudden tension centered on a splendidly dressed, curl-bearded man who was striding across the room toward her. Rings gleamed on his fingers, and anger shone in his eyes.

"You! Outlander!"

Elmara raised a mild eyebrow. "Goodman?"

" '*Lord,*' to you. I am Lord Mage Dunsteen, and I bid you take heed, wench!" The man drew himself up importantly, and Elmara knew that though he looked only at her, he was aware of everyone in the room. "The matters you so idly speak of are not fancies, but sorcery." The lord mage strutted grandly forward and said sharply, "Magic interests everyone with its power—but it is, and rightly, an art of secrets—secrets to be learned only by those fit to know them. If you are wise, you will cease your talk of sorcery at once."

At the end of his words, the room was very still, and into that silence, Elmara said quietly, "I was told to speak of magic, wherever I go."

"Oh? By whom?"

"A priestess of Mystra."

"And why," Lord Mage Dunsteen asked with silken derision, "would a priestess of Mystra waste three words on you?"

Color rose in Elmara's cheeks, but she answered as quietly as before, "She was expecting me."

"Oh? Who sent *you* out into Faerun to seek priestesses of the Holy Lady of Mysteries?"

"Mystra," Elmara said quietly.

"Oh, *Mystra*. Of course." The wizard scoffed openly. "I suppose she talked to you."

"She did."

"Oh? Then what did she look like?"

"Like eyes floating in flame, and then as a tall woman; dark robed and dark eyed."

Lord Mage Dunsteen addressed the ceiling. "Faerun is home to many mad folk, some so lost in their wits, I've heard, that they can delude even themselves."

Elmara set down her tankard. "Ye've used many proud, provoking words, Lord Mage, and they tell me ye think thyself a wizard of some . . . *local* importance."

The wizard stiffened, eyes flashing.

Elmara held up a staying hand. "I've heard many times in my life that wizards are seekers after truth. Well, then, so important a wizard as thyself should have spells enough to determine if I speak truly." She sat back in her chair and added, "Ye bade me speak no more of magic. Well, then, I bid ye: use thy spells to see my truth, and stay thy own talk of madness and wild lies."

The lord mage shrugged. "I'll not waste spells on a madwoman."

Elmara shrugged in turn, turned away, and said, "As I was saying, the last the king ever saw of his Royal Wizards, their lightnings were chaining a dragon they'd summoned, and it was spitting fire at them. . . ."

The lord mage glared at the young woman, but Elmara ignored him. The wizard cast angry glances around the room, but men carefully did not meet his eyes, and from where he wasn't glaring, there came chuckles.

After a moment, Lord Mage Dunsteen turned, robes swirling, and stalked back to his private booth. Elmara shrugged, and talked on.

* * * * *

The moon was bright, riding high above the few cold fingers of cloud that crept along above the trees. Elmara drew her cloak closer around herself—clear nights like this brought a frostchill—and hurried on. Before seeking the inn, she'd chosen a fern-choked hollow ahead to bed down in.

Far behind her, branches snapped. It wasn't the first such

sound she'd heard. Elmara paused to listen a moment, and then went on, moving a little faster.

She came to the hollow and darted across it, clambering up its far bank and turning to crouch among the bushes there. Then she did off her cloak and sack and waited. As she'd expected, the stalker was no excited young lad wanting to hear more of magic, but a certain lord mage, moving uncertainly now in the darkness.

Elmara decided to get this over with. "Fair even, Lord Mage," she said calmly, keeping low among the ferns.

The wizard paused, stepped back, and hissed some words.

A breath later, the night exploded in flames. Elmara dived aside as searing heat rolled over her. When she had her feet under her again and her breath back, she forced herself to say laconically, "A campfire would have been sufficient."

Then she tossed a rock to one side, and as it crashed down through the brush, leapt to her feet and ran in the other direction, around the edge of the hollow.

The mage's next fireball exploded well away from her. "*Die, dangerous fool!*"

Elmara pointed at the wizard, who stood clearly outlined by moonlight, and murmured the words of a prayer to Mystra. Her hand tingled, and the lord mage was abruptly hurled backward, crashing roughly through bushes.

"Gods spit on you, outlander!" the wizard cursed, clawing his painful way to his feet. Elmara heard cloth tearing, and another hissed curse.

"*I* don't hurl fire at women whose only offense is not cringing before me," Elmara said coldly. "Why are ye doing this?"

The lord mage stepped forward into the light again. Elmara raised her hands, waiting to ward off magic—but no spell came.

Dunsteen snarled in anger. El sighed and whispered a spell of her own. Blue-white light outlined the mage's head, and she saw his features twist and struggle as he found himself compelled to speak truthfully.

The string of fearful curses he was spitting became the words, "I don't want half the folk in Faerun to work magic! What price my powers *then*, eh?" Dunsteen's voice rose into a wordless shriek of fear.

"You live now only at my whim, wizard," Elmara told him, pretending a casualness she did not feel. If his fear would just keep him from weaving another fireball . . .

Swallowing her own rising fear, Elmara uttered another prayer to Mystra. When the tingling in her limbs told her its magic had taken effect, she strode off the lip of the hollow, walk-

ing on empty air to stand facing the wizard. She pointed down,
trembling with the effort to hold herself in midair. "I do not wish
to slay ye, Lord Mage. Mystra bade me bring more magic into
Faerun, not rob the Realms of the lives and skills of wizards."

The Lord Mage gulped and took a quick step back. He obviously thought less of his powers than he'd pretended to in the
tavern. "And so?"

"Go to thy home and trouble me no more," Elmara said in a
voice of doom, "and I shall not bring down the curse of Mystra on
thee."

That sounded good—and the priestess had told him to try
everything. If Mystra thought her words ill said . . . she'd doubtless say so soon enough.

The night remained still and silent—except for the sounds
made by Lord Mage Dunsteen, backing hurriedly away through
ferns and brambles.

"*Hold!*" Elmara put the ring of command into her words. She
felt herself sinking slowly toward the ground as she turned her
will back to her truth-compulsion spell.

Dunsteen froze as if someone had tugged on a leash about his
neck.

Elmara said to his moonlit back, "I was told to learn all I
could from the mages I met. Where would you suggest I go to
learn more about being a mage?"

The magic of her truth-compulsion glowed brightly around
the Lord Mage—but he did not turn, so Elmara did not see his
twisted smile. "Go see Ilhundyl, ruler of the Calishar, and ask
him that . . . and you shall have the best answer any living man
can give."

* * * * *

Most intruders wandered in the maze, calling helplessly until
Ilhundyl tired of their cries and had them brought to an audience chamber, or released the lions to feed. This young lass, however, strode through the illusory walls and around the portal
traps as if she could see them.

Ilhundyl leaned forward to peer out the window in sudden interest as Elmara strode out onto the broad pavement in front of
the Great Gate, peered narrowly up at it, and then walked without hesitation toward the hidden door, avoiding the golems and
the statues whose welcoming hands could spit lightnings at
those who stepped between them.

The Mad Mage valued his privacy, and his life . . . and not

many days passed without someone trying to deprive him of either. Thus his Castle of Sorcery was ringed by traps mechanical as well as magical. Now one of his long-fingered hands tapped idly on the table. He seized a slim brass hammer, lifted it, and rapped on a certain bell.

At his signal, unseen men sweated belowground, and the paving-stones suddenly opened up under the young woman, who obligingly plunged from view. Ilhundyl smiled tightly and turned to the tall, handsome servant who stood patiently awaiting his orders. Garadic obligingly glided forward. "Lord?"

"Go and see that one's body," he said, "and bring ba—"

"Lord." The servant's rapped word was urgent; Ilhundyl followed his gaze even before he could raise his arm to point. The wizard wheeled around in his chair.

The young intruder was walking on air, treading steadily forward on nothing, and rising up out of the yawning pit. Ilhundyl raised his eyebrows and leaned forward. "Garadic," he said decisively, "go down and bring that maid to me. Alive, if she can stay that way until you get there."

* * * * *

"A priestess of Mystra told me to learn about sorcery from mages . . . and a mage told me you were the best man alive to tell me what it is to work magic."

Ilhundyl smiled thinly. "Why do you want to learn magic—if you don't want to be a mage?"

"I must serve Mystra as best I can," Elmara said steadily, "even as she commanded me."

Ilhundyl nodded. "And so, Elmara, you seek mages to tell you the ways of sorcery, so you can better serve the Lady of Mysteries."

Elmara nodded.

Ilhundyl waved his hands, and darkness enshrouded the chamber, save for two globes of radiance that hung above the Mad Mage and the young intruder. They looked at each other, and when Ilhundyl spoke again, his voice echoed with tones of doom.

"Know then, O Elmara, that you must apprentice yourself to a mage, and once you learn to hurl fire and lightning, slip away without a word to anyone, travel far, and join an adventuring band. Then see the Realms, face danger, and use your spells in earnest."

The ruler of the Calishar leaned forward, voice thinning in

urgent precision. "When you can battle a lich spell for spell and prevail, seek out Ondil's Book of Spells and take it to the altar of Mystra on the island called Mystra's Dance. Surrender it to the goddess there."

His voice changed again, thundering once more. "Once you know you hold Ondil's tome in your hands, look no longer on its pages, nor seek to learn the spells therein, for that is the sacrifice Mystra demands! Go, now, and do this."

The light above the Mad Mage's high seat faded, leaving Elmara facing darkness. "My thanks," she said, and turned away. As she walked back down the great chamber, the globe of light moved with her. The light faded beyond the great bronze doors, which ground shut with their usual boom. When the echoes had died away Ilhundyl added quietly, "And once you've got me that book, go and get yourself killed, mageling."

Garadic's handsome features melted soundlessly into the fanged and scaled horror of his true face. The scaled minion stepped forward and asked curiously, "Why, master?"

The Mad Mage frowned. "I've never met anyone with so much latent power before. If she lives, she could grow in magic to master the Realms." He shrugged. "But she'll die."

Garadic took another step, his tail scraping along the floor. "And if she does not, master?"

Ilhundyl smiled and said, "You will see to it that she does."

PART IV
MAGUS

Ten

IN THE FLOATING TOWER

Great adventure? Hah! Frantic fear and scrabbling about in tombs or worse, spilling blood or trying to strike down things that can no longer bleed. If ye're a mage, it lasts only until some other wizard hurls a spell faster than thee. Speak to me not of "great adventure."

Theldaun "Firehurler" Ieirson
Teachings of an Angry Old Mage
Year of the Griffon

It was a cold, clear day in early Marpenoth, in the Year of Much Ale. The leaves on the trees all around were touched with gold and flame-orange as the Brave Blades reined in beneath the place they'd sought for so long.

Their destination hung dark and silent above them: the Floating Tower, the lifeless hold of the long-dead mage Ondil, hidden away in this bramble-choked ravine in the wilderlands somewhere well west of the Horn Hills.

Upright it stood, a lone, crumbling stone tower reaching into the bright sky . . . but as the tales had said, its base was a ruin of tumbled stones, and there was a stretch of empty air twelve men or so high between the ground and the dark, empty room of the tower's sixth level. Ondil's tower hung patiently in the air as it had for centuries, held up by an awesome sorcery.

The Blades looked up at it, and then looked away—except for the only woman among them, who stood with a wand raised warily, peering past her hawk nose at the silent, waiting keep hanging above her.

The Blades had come here by a long and perilous road. In a spider-haunted sorcerer's tomb of lost Thaeravel, said by some to be the land of mages from which Netheril sprang, they'd found writings that spoke of the mighty archwizard Ondil and his withdrawal in his later days into a spell-guarded tower to craft many new and powerful sorceries.

Then old Lhangaern of the Blades crafted a potion to make his limbs young again, drank it—and fell screaming into crumbling dust before their eyes . . . and they were without a mage.

The Brave Blades dared not take the road again without so much as a light-bringing incantation to aid them. So when a young woman came to their inn and spun tales of the wonders of magic—and proved she could work spells of a sort—they practically dragged this Elmara into their ranks.

She was not a pretty woman. Her fierce hawk nose and dark, serious gaze made many a man and most maids draw back from her, and she rode garbed as a warrior in boots and breeches, avoiding the robes and airs of most mages. None of the Blades felt inclined to lure her to bed, even if the threat of defensive spells weren't hanging around her. Her first demand was for time to study the spellbooks Lhangaern would never read again . . . and the second was for a chance to use them.

The Blades granted her that, riding out to make red war on a band of brigands who oppressed that land. In the crumbling old keep the defeated band used as their stronghold, Elmara found wands they could not use and books of spells they could not read, and bore these out in triumph.

All the next winter, as the howling winds piled up snow deep and cold outside, the Blades sat before fires, sharpened their swords, and told restless tales of what bright deeds they'd done and what brighter things they would do when summer came again. Apart from them, the young sorceress studied.

Her eyes grew deep-set and heavy-lidded, and her body ever more gaunt. She squinted as she went about and used few words, her wits distant and confused—for all the world as if the spells baffled her. Yet she could conjure fires in rooms that the winter had chilled and light for them all to see by without enduring the smoke of fires and candles or the work of chopping firewood.

The Blades learned to keep out of her way, for their every plan brought from her an earnest torrent of moral questions: "Should we slay such a man? Is it right?" or "But what has the dragon done to us? Would it not be more prudent to leave it in peace?"

Winter passed, and the Blades took to the road again—and fell afoul of the Bright Shields, an arrogant and widely known band of lawless adventurers. They fought in the streets of Baerlith, and the dreams of several Blades died there. Elmara pleaded with the two Bright Shields mages who stood against her not to fight, but to share their spells, "laying the glories of magic before all."

The two mages laughed their derision, and hurled slaying spells—but the wizard of the Blades was no longer there. She reappeared behind the two and struck them down with the hilt of a dagger she held. Then she wept when the other Blades, over her protests, cut their throats while they lay senseless. "But they could have taught me so much!" the maid wailed. "And where is the honor in slaying those who lie asleep?"

Yet at the end of that day, the Bright Shields were no more, and the Blades took coins, armor, horses, and all for their own. Their sorceress found herself the owner of boots and belts and rings and rods and more that glowed with the deep blue of enchantments. She couldn't wait to use them but dared not try to wield most of them—yet. The Blades might think her a sorceress, but she was a priestess of Mystra, with no better magecraft than an eager but untutored apprentice . . . and having seen their hot tempers, she did not reveal this truth.

And so it went as the long hot summer passed. The Blades rode from triumph to triumph, saddlebags bulging with coins, throwing what riches they couldn't carry liberally into the laps of willing ladies wherever they went—all but their dark and serious sorceress, who kept apart, spending her nights wrestling with spells rather than wenches.

Then came the day Tarthe found a merchant's account of a trip across the high hills north of Ong Wood, and of a vale where griffons flew out of a lone keep and drove his band away. They were collared griffons, their breasts bearing shields with the mark of Ondil of the Many Spells.

That excited moment of decision, when they had all leapt at the thought of plundering the Floating Tower, seemed long ago now as they tethered their horses in the shadow of its grim and silent bulk.

Tarthe turned to the fierce-eyed woman with the wand. The sun gleamed on the warrior's broad, armored shoulders and danced in his curling, reddish hair and beard. He looked like a lion among men, every inch the proud leader of a famous adventuring band.

"Well, mage?" Tarthe waved one gauntleted hand at the tower floating above them.

Elmara nodded in reply, stepped forward, and made the circling gesture that meant fall back to give her space for a spell. She tossed a long, heavy coil of rope to the turf between her feet.

Her hands dipped to one of the vials at her belt, flicked back its stopper, and tipped it, then deftly restoppered it while holding some of its powder in one cupped hand. A few gestures, a long murmured incantation as the powder was cast aloft, and some lightning-fast work with a strip of parchment—twisting it in the still-falling powder—and the coil of rope on the ground stirred. As the young mage stepped back, the rope rose from the ground like a snake, wavered, and then began to climb steadily, straight up.

Elmara watched it calmly. When the rope ceased to move, hanging motionless and upright in the air, she made a "keep back" gesture and went to the saddles for a second coil of rope. Wearing the coil about her shoulders, she climbed the first rope, slowly and clumsily, making several Blades shake their heads or grin with amusement, and came at last to the top of the rope. Curled around it by the crook of one elbow and the crossed grip of her booted feet, she calmly opened another vial, tapped a drop of something from it, and blew it from her palm while gesturing with the other hand.

Nothing seemed to occur—but when the sorceress stepped off the rope to stand on empty air, it was clear that an unseen platform hung there. It sank a trifle under her boots, but Elmara calmly laid the coil of rope on it and began her first spell over again.

When she was done, the second rope stretched straight up through the air, into the darkness of the riven, floorless chamber at the bottom of the hanging keep. The wizardess spared no breath on any words, but looked down at her fellow Blades as she traced a wide circle with her hands, showing them the limits of the platform. Then she turned, and without another look back, began her slow, awkward climb again.

Sudden lightnings flashed in the air around the wizard, and she slid hastily down the rope, hugging it in pain. She hung there a long time, motionless, while the anxious Blades called up to her. Though she made no reply, she seemed unhurt when at last she stretched forth her arms again and cast something that made the lightnings blaze and crackle, then fade away.

She climbed on, into the darkness of the lowest chamber. Just before disappearing into its gaping gloom, she turned on the rope and beckoned once.

"Right, Blades!" Tarthe was climbing swiftly up the rope while his eager bellow was still echoing around them.

The lean warrior beside the rope shrugged, spat on his hands, and followed. The hard-eyed priest of Tempus elbowed his way past the others in his haste to be next on the rope. The thieves and warriors shrugged and gave way, then calmly took their turns. So did the stout priest of Tyche, his mace dangling at his belt as he puffed and heaved his way up.

The youngest warrior checked his cocked and loaded crossbows again and sat down among the tethered horses. He

watched them calmly cropping all the grass and weeds they
could reach, and spat thoughtfully off into the dark hollows
below, whence came the faint tinkling of running water. More
than once he stared up at the ropes above him, straight as iron
rods, but his orders were clear. Which is more than many an
armsman can say, he thought, and settled down for a long wait.

* * * * *

"Look ye!" The rough whisper held awe and wonder aplenty;
even the veteran Blades had not seen the likes of this in their
adventures before. Time had touched the tower, but it seemed
enchantments held wind, cold, and damp at bay in some places.
At the end of a crumbling passage whose very roof-blocks fell at
his cautious tread, a Blade might step through a curtain of magical gloom into glory.

One room was carpeted in red velvet: a dancing-floor ringed
with sparkling hanging curtains crafted of gems threaded onto
fine wire. Another held smooth whitestone statues, perfectly life-
like in their size and detail and depicting beautiful human maidens with wings arching from their shoulders. Some were
speaking statues, who greeted all intruders with soft, sighing
voices, uttering poetry a thousand years dead.

*"Such shouldst be my only joy, to behold thee, but yet mine
eyes see the sun and the moon and cannot but compare them to
thee . . . and thou art the brightest ennobled star of my seeing. . . ."*

*"Look to find me no more, where silent towers stare down upon
the stars, trapped in still pools of dark water. . . ."*

*"What is this but the mist-dreams of bold faerie, wherein noth-
ing is as it seems and all that one can touch, and kiss, are but
dreams?"*

Marveling, the Blades stalked among them, careful to touch
nothing, as the endless, repetitious sighing of the unfeeling
voices echoed all around them. "Gods," even the unshakable
Tarthe was heard to mutter, "to see such beauty . . ."

"And not to be able to take it with us," one of the thieves murmured, voice deep with loss and longing. For once, the priests
felt as he did, or so their nods and awestruck gawking said, if
their mouths did not.

The room beyond the chamber of speaking statues was dark
but lit by a rainbow of tiny, glittering lights—sparks of many
hues that darted and soared about the chamber like schooling
fish, a riot of swirling emerald and gold and ruby that never
went out.

Lightning, they all thought, and hung back. Tarthe finally said, "Gralkyn . . . your foray, I fear."

One of the thieves sighed eloquently and set about the long process of divesting himself of every item of metal, from the dozen or so lockpicks behind his ears and elsewhere on his person to the small forest of blades tucked and slid into boots, under clothes, and into nearly every hollow in his slim, almost bony body. When he was done, he stood almost naked. He swallowed, once, said to Tarthe, "This is a very large thing you owe me," and strode forward on catlike feet into the midst of the lights.

They reacted immediately, darting away like frightened minnows and then circling about, faster and faster, until they rushed in on him from all sides with frightening speed, clung—the watching Blades saw Gralkyn wriggle, as if tickled by many unseen hands—and cloaked him in glittering lights.

He looked like an emperor robed all in gems, and stared down at himself in wonder for a time before he said, "Right. Well . . . who's next?"

The other thief, Ithym, came into the chamber hesitantly, but the lights did not move from around Gralkyn, and nothing else seemed to happen. Sighing out a tensely held breath of his own, Ithym glided over to his fellow thief and stretched out a hand toward the lights, but then drew it back. Gralkyn nodded at the wisdom of this.

Ithym went on into the far, dim regions of the room and moved about in soft silence for a time before returning far enough for them to see him trace a square in the air: there was a door beyond.

Tarthe took out his cloak, raked all Gralkyn's discarded metal in it, bundled it onto his shoulder, and strode into the room next, sword drawn. Instantly some of the lights drifted away from the thief in an inquisitive stream, heading for the tall warrior in full armor. The tensely watching Blades saw sudden sweat on Tarthe's forehead as he strode toward the second thief. The lights swirled around Tarthe as buzzing flies survey a walking man . . . and then returned slowly to Gralkyn.

The warrior shook his head in relief, and they heard him whisper hoarsely, "Now, Ithym—where's this door?"

A few scufflings later his voice floated back to them out of the gloom. "Hither, all! The way beyond looks clear!"

Cautiously, one by one, the other Blades hurried or edged past Gralkyn, until at last only the thief in his cloak of lights was left in the room. He walked calmly up to the door, peered through it, and saw the Blades standing anxiously in a little corridor that led into a large, dim, open space beyond. "Back, all of you!" Gralkyn said. "Get well away—right out of the passage! I'm coming through!"

The others obeyed, but waited at the far end of the hall, watching. Gralkyn sprinted toward the door, dived through it, and hit the stone floor hard. As he passed through the opening, the lights halted, as if held by an invisible wall, so he was stripped of all of them. After a moment, he got to his knees and crawled as fast as he could out of the passage. Only then did he look back, at a smooth wall of twinkling lights, solidly filling the doorway.

"Are ye . . . well?" The words were out of Elmara's mouth before she thought about the prudence of asking.

Gralkyn rubbed at his shoulders. "I . . . know not. Everything seems aright . . . now that the tingling's stopped." He was flexing thoughtful fingers when Ithym shrugged, drew a slim dagger from his belt, and flung it at the doorful of floating lights. There was a vicious crackle of tiny lightnings, so bright they all drew their heads back and grunted in pain, and the weapon was gone. There was nothing left to strike the floor. When they could see clearly again, the lights were still filling the doorway, forming a smooth, unbroken barrier.

Tarthe looked at it sourly. "Well," he said, "that's no way back as I'd care to try. So . . . forward."

They all turned and looked about. They stood on a balcony that curved slightly as if on the inside of a vast circle. The waist-high stone railing in front of them opened on to nothingness. Vast, open darkness. They peered along the walls, and could dimly see other balconies nearby—some higher, some lower . . . all of them empty.

Tarthe shrugged. "Well, mage?"

Elmara raised an eyebrow. "Do ye seek my counsel, or a spell?"

"Can you conjure a sphere of light and sail it out into this?" He waved an arm at the great darkness before them, being careful not to extend it beyond the rail.

Elmara nodded. "I can," she said quietly, "but should I? This has the feeling of—something waiting. A trap, belike, awaiting my spell to set it off."

Tarthe sighed. "We're in a wizard's tower! Of *course* there're hanging spells and traps all about . . . and of course we invite danger by working magic here! You think none of us realize that?"

Elmara shrugged. "I . . . strong magic is all about us in webs.

I know not what will befall if I disturb it. I want all of ye to be aware of this and be not unprepared to leap aside if . . . the worst comes down on us. So I ask ye again: should I?"

Tarthe exploded. "Why these endless questions about what is right and should you do thus or so? You've got the power—*use it!* When d'you ever hear other mages asking if hurling a spell is to the liking of those around?"

"Not often enough," one of the other warriors murmured, and Tarthe wheeled around to give him a flat glare.

The warrior shrugged and spread empty hands. "Eh, Tarthe," he protested, "I but speak my view of the world."

"Hmmph," Tarthe grunted. "Take care that someone does not alter your view of the world for you—forcefully, and mayhap working on what you view with, not what you see."

"Well enough," Elmara said, raising her hands. "I will give ye light. Be it on thy head, Tarthe, if the result be not pleasant. Stand ye back."

She took something small and glowing from a pouch at her belt, held it up, and muttered over it. It seemed to bubble and grow in her fingers, and she spread them to let it rise up and hang in front of her face, spinning, shaping itself into a sphere of pulsing, ever-growing light. Its flickering radiance gave the mage's sharp-nosed, intent face a brooding appearance.

When the sphere was as large as her head and hung bright and steady, Elmara bent her gaze on it. Obediently it moved away from her, gliding soundlessly through the air, out from the balcony into the darkness beyond. As it went, the darkness parted before it like a tattered curtain, showing them the true size of the vast chamber. Even before it reached the far wall of the great spherical room, other radiances not of Elmara's making appeared, here and there in the air before them, brightening and growing until the Blades could all see their surroundings. Balconies like their own lined the curving wall on all sides, save where darkness lingered above and below. The spherical space within was huge—much larger across than Ondil's tower was on the outside.

"Gods!" one of the warriors gasped.

The priest beside him murmured, "Holy Tyche, be with us."

Four spheres of hitherto dark, slowly brightening radiance floated in the center of the huge chamber. Three of these globes were as tall as two men, and one other, smaller globe hung between them.

The nearest globe held a motionless dragon, its vast bulk coiled up to fit within the radiance, its red scales clear to their gaze. It seemed asleep, yet its eyes were open. It looked strong,

healthy, proud—and waiting. The most distant globe held a being
they'd heard of in tales: a robed, manlike figure whose skin was a
glistening purple, whose eyes were featureless white orbs, and
whose mouth was a forest of squid tentacles. It, too, hung motionless in its radiance, standing upright in emptiness, its empty
hands having one finger less than their own. A mind flayer! The
third globe was partially hidden behind the dragon's bulk . . . but
the Blades could see enough to bring the cold, sword-biting taste
of fear strongly into all their mouths at last. The globe's dark oc-
cupant was a creature whose spherical body was inset with one
huge eye and a fanged mouth, and fringed with many snakelike
eyestalks: a beholder. Its dread kin were said to rule over many
small realms east of Calimshan, each eye tyrant treating all beings who dwelt or came into its territory as its slaves.

Elmara's gaze, however, was drawn to the fourth, smaller
globe. In its depths hung a large book held open by two disem-
bodied, skeletal human hands. When Elmara narrowed her eyes
against the bright blue glare—*everything* in this place was magical, making her mage-sight almost useless—she could see
bright webs linking the four globes and wavering between both
skeletal hands and the tome. They must be animated guardians,
those bones . . . as well as the three monsters.

"So do we turn away from our greatest challenge and live, or
go after that book and die gloriously?" Ithym's voice was wry.

"What use is a book?" one of the warriors replied with loud
fear.

"Aye," the other agreed. "Just what Faerun needs—more
deadly spells for mages to play with."

"How so?" Gralkyn put in. "Yon book might be prayers to a
god, or filled with writings that lead to treasure, or . . ."

The warrior Dlartarnan gave him a sour look. "I know a spellbook when I see one," he grunted.

"I did not ride all this way," Tarthe said crisply, "to turn back
now—if there is a way back that won't kill us all. I also have no
desire to ride back into that last inn empty-handed and have all
the tankard-drainers there think us a pack of cowards who did
nothing but ride out, eat a few rabbits in the wilderness, and
ride home again, our untested blades rusting in their sheaths."

"That's the spirit—" Ithym agreed, then added in a stage
whisper "—that'll get us all killed."

"Enough!" Elmara said. "We're here now and face two choices:
either we try to find another way onward, or we fight these
things, for be in no doubt: all of those globes are spell-linked to
the book, and those bone-hands, too."

"One death is imminent," the warrior Tharp said in his deep, seldom-heard voice. "The other we can look for later."

One of the priests held up his holy symbol. "Tyche bids the brave and true to chance glory," the Hand of Tyche said sharply.

"Tempus expects adventurers to embrace battle, not slip away when strong foes threaten," agreed the Sword of Tempus. The priests exchanged glances and grim grins as they readied weapons.

The thief Gralkyn sighed. "I knew riding with two battle-mad priests would bring us trouble, in depth and at speed."

"And disappointment came not to you," Tarthe said, "for which you gave much thanks. So you are now at peace, ready to speak of strategies against these globed beasts and not weasel words to try to get out of facing them!"

There was a little silence as the Blades smiled mirthlessly at each other or displayed looks of unconcern, all trying—in vain—to hide the fear in their eyes.

Elmara spoke into that quiet tension. "We are in the house of a mage, and as a worshiper of Mystra, I am closest among us to the mantle of wizardry. It is right that I make the first attack"—she swallowed, and they saw she was trembling with excitement and fear—"as I am the most likely of us to prevail against . . . what we face."

"What are ye, Elmara—the Magister in fool form, perhaps, or the Sorcerer Supreme of all Calimshan, out for a lark? Or are ye really just the soft-witted idiot ye sound to be?" Dlartarnan asked sourly.

"Hold hard, now," Tarthe said warningly. "This is no time for dispute!"

"When I'm dead," the warrior returned darkly, "it'll be just a blade-thrust or six too late for me to enjoy one last dispute. . . . I'd just as soon enjoy it *now*."

"Soft-witted idiot I may be," Elmara told him pleasantly, "but sit on thy fear long enough to think . . . and ye can't help but agree that however ill my efforts befall, they are still the best road we can set foot upon."

Several Blades protested at once—and then as one, their voices fell silent. Grim faces looked out at the globes, back at the trembling young mage, and then back at the globes again.

" 'Tis madness," Tarthe said at last, "but 'tis just as surely our best hope."

Troubled silence answered him; he raised his voice a little, and asked, "Does anyone here deny this? Or speak against it?"

In the hanging silence after these words, Ithym gave a little shake of his head. As if this had been a signal, the two priests shook their heads together—and one by one, the others followed, Dlartarnan last.

Elmara looked around. "We are agreed, then?" The Blades stared at her in silence until she added, "Well enough; I need every man here to have ready all the weapons he can hurl afar— but to loose *nothing* until I give word, whate'er befalls."

She waved them to one end of the balcony while she went to the other. "I must cast some spells," she said. "Someone keep an eye on those lights behind us and tell me if my work draws them hence."

She stamped and shuffled and murmured for a long time, casting powders into the air, drawing many small objects from various places in her clothing, and from sheaths beneath garments and in and about her well-worn boots.

In wary silence, the Blades watched the young mage trace small signs in the air; each glowed briefly and then faded as she traced the next. Radiances washed over the young mage and then were gone, and though her intent, earnest expression never changed, both she and her companions-at-arms noticed that with each new spell she worked, the four silent globes hanging so menacingly near pulsed and grew brighter. The lights in the doorway winked and drifted around each other, ever faster, but made no move to spill out into the passage.

At last El bent to her boots and drew forth six straight, smooth lengths of wood. She held two end-to-end so their slightly bulbous tips touched, deftly twisted and pushed, and they became one. In like manner she added length to length, until she held a knobbed staff as tall as she was.

She shook it as if half expecting pieces to fall off, but all held firm. Then she brandished it against an imaginary foe. Dlartarnan snorted; it looked like a toy.

Elmara leaned the toy staff against the balcony rail and came toward them, rubbing her hands thoughtfully. "I'm about ready," she said, casting a keen look at the waiting globes. Her hands trembled slightly.

"We gathered that," Ithym said.

Tarthe nodded, smiling thinly. "Mind telling us just what spells you've worked . . . *before* all the bloodletting begins?"

"I've not much time to chatter; the magics don't last overlong," Elmara replied, "but know ye all: I can fly, flames will harm me not—even dragonfire, though I doubt the mage who wrote the spell had ever faced it when he made his claim—and spells hurled my way will come back upon the sender."

"You can do all that?" Tharp's voice was thoughtful.

"Not every day," Elmara replied. "The spells are woven into a dwaeodem."

"How nice," Gralkyn said with light, lilting sarcasm. "That explains *everything* . . . now I can go to my deathbed content."

"The spells are linked in a shield about me," Elmara replied softly. "Its creation took the sacrifice of an enchanted item of power—and it drains the life from me, slowly but inescapably, more the longer I hold it."

"Then enough idle talk," Tarthe said sharply. "Lead us into battle, mage."

Elmara nodded, swallowed, ducked her head just as a helmed warrior does to pull down his visor before a charge—the warriors exchanged looks and smiled—caught up her staff, and scrambled up onto the balcony rail.

Then she leapt off into space—and plunged from view.

The Blades exchanged grim looks and leaned forward over the rail. Far below, Elmara was gliding, arms outstretched, across the chamber, tilting her body as if testing the air. Her flight pulled sharply upward a scant hand's-breadth in front of a balcony, and she began to soar toward them. Her face was white and set; they saw her swallow and begin to look green even as she released her staff and moved her hands in intricate passes and finger-linkings. The staff flew along beside her, mirroring her slight shifts of direction as Elmara rose up the far side of the chamber, working a spell. She seemed to cast it twice . . . and drifted to a halt facing them, arms spread above her head, two ghostly circles of radiance flickering about her hands. Then they saw but did not hear her mouth a word that made the chamber itself quiver—and the radiances rushed outward from her hands and vanished.

The four spheres in the center of the space began to move. The Blades watched, warily raising weapons as the globes of light glided around the chamber—and the beings within them stirred. As if awakened from a long sleep, they turned to look about. One of the Blades whispered a heartfelt curse. The thieves ducked low behind the balcony rail, peering at their crazed comrade hanging in the air, hands moving again as she cast yet another spell.

There was a soundless flash. The mind flayer had worked some spell of its own, seeking to break free of its globe, but the glowing magic had prevailed. The tentacled thing crouched down in seeming pain. Elmara frowned and gestured at it, and the mind flayer's prison of light scudded across the chamber, gathering speed as it spun toward the globe that held the dragon. The great wyrm was thrashing its tail, wriggling its shoulders, and roaring silently, trying to shatter the cramped confines of light about it. Its jaws flashed fire as it caught sight of the watching men on the balcony. Hatred glared in its gaze as it snarled at them.

Then the two globes rushed together, and the world shattered.

The Blades roared as a light brighter than they'd ever seen blasted into their eyes. They were staggering back even before the balcony shook beneath them, and they fell, blinded by the flash of the bursting globes. Only Asglyn, the Sword of Tempus, who'd expected spellfury of some sort and had closed his eyes in time, was able to see the mind flayer struggling in the dragon's jaws, hissing and burbling in futile spells before those teeth chomped down, once.

What remained of the purple body fell away in a dark rain of gore as the dragon opened its mouth and roared its rage. The third globe was already rushing in at the dragon, the beholder's eyestalks writhing as it prepared for the battle it knew would come.

Asglyn had a brief glimpse of Elmara, face a mask of sweat, jaw clenched in effort, driving the globe along the path she'd chosen. Then the priest shut his eyes tight, just before the flash of rending globes came again. It was followed by a second flash that lit his face with its heat. When Asglyn dared look, he saw the beholder wreathed in flames as the dragon beat its huge wings and raked at the eye tyrant with reaching claws. Stabbing rays of radiance leapt from the beholder's many eyes. The dragon's answering roars held a rising note of fear amid its fury.

Asglyn looked about him. Gralkyn was slumped almost against him, hands jammed to eyes as he knelt behind the rail. Tarthe was shaking his head, fighting to clear his vision.

"Up, Blades!" the priest hissed urgently, and then stiffened as the voice of Elmara sounded inside his head.

"Hurl everything that can pierce or slash at the tyrant's eyes, as soon as the gods make ye able!"

Asglyn hefted his heavy hammer, his favorite weapon borne through a hundred battles or more, and hurled it with all his might, end over end, in a careful, climbing arc, so that it might fall into the great central eye of the beholder. It spun through the air but he never saw if it struck home; he had turned to scramble about the balcony, shaking and slapping his dazed and groaning companions and hoping somehow they'd escape with their lives.

Elmara's next spell brought whirling blades into being from nothingness. They flashed and spun about the waving eyestalks of the beholder like so many fireflies. El saw more than one eye spurt gore or milky liquid and go dark before the madly spinning eye tyrant blasted the shards into drifting smoke with a ray that leapt on to stab at a certain young mage.

Leapt—and rebounded, slicing silently back into the roiling tangle of dragon wings and scaled shoulders and claws, and the darting, spinning, snarling eye tyrant. The dragon roared in pain, but El could see none harm the beholder.

The dragon spat fire again. As before, the gout of flames seemed to splash away over an invisible shield held in front the eye tyrant. Yet that shield was no barrier to the dragon's claws and tail. As Elmara watched, the tail slapped the beholder end-over-end across the chamber, its eyestalks curling and struggling vainly. It passed near the balcony where the Blades stood, and more than a few of them hurled daggers, darts, and blades just above and before it so it rushed helplessly into the stream of whirling steel. The monster squalled in pain and fury as it tumbled to a halt. What eyes it had left turned toward the nearby balcony.

Bright beams and flickering rays of feebler radiance flashed, and the Blades cried out and ran vainly about the balcony in terror. It shook and shuddered under them, and most of the rail was suddenly gone, melted away in the fury of the eye tyrant's attack.

Yet no searing spells tore into the men, though the crash and flicker of variegated lights was almost blinding. Magic spat and crawled all along the balcony before rebounding back at the struggling spherical monster; Elmara's last spell was doing its work.

Those Blades who could see well enough hurled more daggers, but in the fury of roiling magic around the balcony, most of these vanished in sparks and fragments or simply sighed into nothingness. Through the hail of blades, the furious dragon clapped its wings and rushed down at the beholder, seeking to slay the thing that had caused it such pain. As it came, it breathed fire again. The blackened eye tyrant rolled over in the streaming storm of flame so all its remaining eyestalks pointed straight at the great wyrm. Rays of magic leapt and thrust, and the oncoming dragon began to scream. The beholder rose a little to get out of the way as the dragon hurtled helplessly past. The wyrm crashed into the wall so hard that the Blades were hurled from their feet. The eye tyrant's eye-rays stabbed mercilessly at the thrashing dragon.

The beast seemed much smaller by the time it managed to flap free of the wall again, smoke rising from its body. Crushed balconies fell away in rubble as the dragon moved, its scream a raw and terrible sound of agony. Then its cries began to fade. The awestruck Blades saw bits of the dragon's straining body vanish as if it were just so much ice melting in the heart of a fire. It dwindled swiftly, lifeblood boiling away into nothing in the face of the cruel powers bent upon it. Beyond the fury of flashing magic, the Blades could see the floating figure of Elmara, arms waving in careful haste as she cast another spell.

When the dragon vanished in a last puff of dark scales and boiling blood, the beholder turned with menacing slowness toward the mage and rolled over so that the broad ray of its central eye could strike at her—the eye that drained all magic.

Caught in that spell-draining field, Elmara fell, arms waving. The watching men heard her sob in fear. The beholder swiftly rolled over again to bring its eyestalks to bear all at once on the sorceress, as it had done to the dragon. As the Blades on the balcony desperately hurled blades, shields, and even boots at it, they heard the cold, cruel thunder of its laughter.

Rays and beams flashed out again. Through that bright fury, the Blades saw Elmara raise one arm as if to lash the beholder with an invisible whip. The wand she held flared into sudden life.

The beholder shuddered under its attack and spun wildly about. The Blades ducked desperately as its rays sizzled across the balcony, but Elmara's barrier still held, and the rending magics rebounded back at the eye tyrant.

Tarthe and Asglyn stood shoulder to shoulder at what was left of the balcony rail, tense and helpless, all their weapons hurled and their foe beyond reach. Through narrowed eyes they saw Elmara draw a dagger from her belt and soar up at the beholder like a vengeful arrow. Eyestalks wriggled, and explosive light burst forth anew. The flying mage was thrown aside by the violent force, and the dagger in her fingers suddenly flared into flames.

She hurled it away, shaking her hand in pain, but in the same motion swept her hand into the front of her bodice. There was another dagger—no, the broken stub of an old sword—in Elmara's hand when she drew it forth. She tumbled in the air through a roiling area of intersecting rays and raced in toward the beholder.

Waiting spells burst into sudden life around the blade in her outstretched hand, coiling and flaring as Elmara struck home— and her tiny steel fang sank into a hard body-plate as if she were thrusting into so much hot stew.

The beholder shrieked like a terrified courtesan and hurled itself away from the sorceress. El was left tumbling alone in the air as the eye tyrant flew blindly into the nearest wall, snarling in pain.

Elmara snatched a wand from her belt and darted after it. Straight among the eyestalks she plunged to touch the thing's rolling body just above the hissing, snapping jaws. Then she kicked herself away and flew clear. Behind her, the beholder began to repeat its actions backward, rolling back to strike the wall again. Then it hurtled back to where Elmara had stabbed it.

It hung there a moment—and then rolled back at the wall again to crash and then roll away in an exact duplication of its previous movements. Fascinated, the watching Blades saw the monster's flight repeat, cycling through its squalling collision with the wall over and over again.

"How long will that go on?" Tarthe asked in wonder.

"The beholder is doomed to smash itself against the wall of the chamber over and over until its body falls apart," Asglyn said grimly. "That's not magic many wizards dare to use."

"I don't doubt it," Ithym put in from beside them. Then he gasped and pointed out into the center of the vast open chamber.

Elmara had retrieved her staff and flown into the heart of the last, smaller globe. One skeletal hand leapt at her eyes, but she smashed it aside. The second hand was already darting in at her from behind; they saw it dig bony digits into her neck as she whirled around, too late.

Elmara flung her staff away and spat the words of another spell, one hand flashing in intricate gestures. The skeletal hand was crawling its steady way around to her throat as she wove the spell—and the hand she'd hit away was flying at her face again, two smashed, bony fingers dangling uselessly.

Tarthe sighed in frustration. Elmara was struggling, a hand at her throat, jerking her head from side to side to keep the other bony claw from piercing her eyes. Her face darkened, but the Blades saw motes of light spring into being around her, growing brighter.

Then, without sound, both skeletal hands fell into dust, and the globe around them faded away entirely. As its magic failed, the Blades heard Elmara gasping for breath in the sudden silence—and the first winking lights drifted past their shoulders from the passage behind them.

The Blades drew aside in wary surprise. The many-hued lights that had cloaked Gralkyn emptied themselves from the doorway in a steady stream, drifting along the passage and out into the open center of the chamber, heading for their sorceress.

"Elmara—beware!" Tarthe called, his voice hoarse and cracked.

Elmara cast a look at him, saw the lights, and stared hard at them for a moment. Then she waved a dismissive hand and turned back to the floating book.

Across the chamber, the trapped beholder threw itself helplessly against the wall again and again, the wet thuds of its impacts marking a steady beat as Elmara bent to peer at the pages.

As her fingers touched the book, the moving lights suddenly rushed forward with a loud sigh. Elmara stiffened as they enveloped her.

The Blades saw the book drift out of her motionless hands and close smoothly. A band of shining metal crawled out of one end of the binding, darted smoothly around the tome, and tightened. There was a flash of light, and the book was bound shut.

The lights around the floating sorceress began to wink out, one by one, until they were all gone. Elmara shook herself, floating in midair, and smiled. She looked fresh, happy, and free of pain as she ran her finger along the metal band, tracing a runic inscription it bore. The Blades heard her gasp excitedly, "This is it! This is *it!* At *last!*"

The mage bound the book to her stomach with the length of climbing-cord she wore wound around her waist and retrieved what weapons she could find before she flew back to the balcony. Her companions eyed her with awe and new respect for a long moment before they stepped forward to reclaim their blades and embrace her sweat-soaked body in rough thanks.

"I hope it's worth all this," Dlartarnan said shortly, eyeing the tome and hefting the familiar weight of his sword. Then he turned away in disgust, striding back down the passage they'd taken to reach the chamber of balconies. "I hope this place holds something I can value as highly—a handful of gems, perhaps, or—"

His voice trailed away, and he lowered his sword in confusion. The room on the other side of the doorway now was not the dark room where they'd first found the lights, but a larger, brighter chamber they'd never seen before.

"More wizard tricks!" he snarled, whirling. "What do we do *now?*"

Tarthe shrugged. "Seek another balcony, perhaps. Ithym, look into yon room first—*without* putting yourself or anything else across the threshold—and tell us what you see."

The thief peered for long breaths, and then shrugged. "A tomb, I think it. That long block, there, is a stone casket, or I'm a dragon. There're at least two other doors I can see—and windows behind those screens . . . they must be: the light changes, like cloud-drifted sunlight, not like conjured light."

They stared at the oval silhouette-screens, and the draperies behind them, glowing, backlit. The room was still and empty of life or adornments. Waiting.

"Ondil's tomb," Tharp said in tones of slow doom.

"Aye, but a way out, if all else fails," Tarthe replied, voice calm, eyes darting all round. His gaze fell on Elmara, standing silent in their midst, and he shook his head slightly in disbelief. He'd seen it all happen, but he still wasn't sure he believed it. Perhaps some of those ridiculous tavern-tales old adventurers loved to tell were true, after all. . . .

"Let's try to get to another balcony," Gralkyn suggested. "I can reach at least four of them—more if El flies a rope to their rails."

"Aye, we must get out of here, now," Ithym said, "or no one at the inn will ever hear about our wizard destroying a beholder, a mind flayer, and a dragon—just to get something to read!"

As Gralkyn swung over the rail and dropped lightly onto the balcony below, the laughter from above him was a little wild.

Eleven

A BLUE FLAME

The most awesome thing a wizard can hope to see in a lifetime of hurling down towers, calling up fiends, and turning rivers into new beds? Why, the blue flame, lad. If ever ye see the blue flame, ye will have looked on the most awesome sight a mage can behold—and the most beautiful.

> Aumshar Urtrar, Master Mage
> said to an apprentice at Midsummer
> Year of the Weeping Moon

The cold hand of doom was tightening around the Brave Blades again. They could all feel it. They'd tried nine balconies now, and every door led somehow into the same silent tomb chamber. It lay across their paths like a waiting pit, patient and inescapable.

"Magic!" Dlartarnan spat, crouching down on a balcony and leaning on his drawn broadsword. "Always magic! Why don't the gods smile on a swung sword and a simple plan?"

"Mind, there!" Asglyn said sharply. "Tempus puts valor of the sword before all else, as well you know, and presuming to know better than any god, Dlar, is a fast leap into the grave!"

"Aye," the priest of Tyche agreed. "My Holy Lady looks well on those who complain little, but take advantage of what befalls and make their own good fortune!"

"Well enough," Dlartarnan grunted. "To please both your gods, I suppose I'd best lead the way into this tomb, and be the first to go down. That will make Tempus and Tyche *both* happy."

Without another word he rose from his haunches and strode into the tomb chamber beyond, his blade gleaming in his hand.

The other Blades exchanged glances and shrugs, and followed.

Dlartarnan was already across the chamber and at the nearest of its two closed doors, prying at the frame with his blade. "'Tis locked," he snarled, putting his weight behind his blade, "but if—"

There was a loud snapping sound. Blue fire burst from the door, racing briefly up and down the frame. Smoke rose from the blackened thing that had been Dlartarnan of Belanchor before it fell to the floor. The warrior's ashes rolled away in dark gray swirls as his bones bounced on the flagstones. The skull rolled over once and came to a stop grinning up at them reproachfully. They stared down at the remains, stunned.

"Tyche watch over his soul," the Hand of Tyche whispered, lips trembling. As if in answer, Dlartarnan's twisted, half-melted sword fell out of the door. With a cry like the sob of a young maiden, it struck the flagstones and shattered.

Elmara swayed, then fell to her knees and was sick. The comforting hand Ithym put on her shoulder trembled violently.

"Perhaps a spell to try to open the other one?" Gralkyn suggested, voice high.

Asglyn nodded. "I have a battleshatter that may serve," he said quietly, "Tempus willing."

He bent his head briefly in prayer, leveled one hand at the remaining door, and murmured a phrase under his breath.

There was a splintering crash. The door shook, but did not burst. Dust fell from the ceiling here and there, and a long, jagged crack split the flagstones with a sharp sound that smote their ears like a hammer. The Blades reeled back, staring, as the crack raced out from the base of the tomb toward the door. Asglyn was running away, face tight with fear, when sudden fire blazed up from his limbs.

"*Nooo!*" he cried, sprinting vainly across the chamber. "*Tempussss!*" Flames roared up to scorch the domed ceiling high overhead, and when they died away, the priest of Tempus was gone.

Into the shocked silence, Tarthe said, "Back—out of this place. That magic came from the tomb!"

Tharp was nearest the passage back to the balcony, so it was only a breath later that he plunged through the doorway—and froze in midstride, limbs trembling under the attack of some unseen force. The Blades watched in horror as the warrior's bones burst up out of his body in a grisly spray of blood and vanished near the ceiling. What was left collapsed in a boneless heap, blood raining down around it as Tharp's helm and armor rang on the floor.

The five remaining Blades looked at each other in horror. Elmara moaned and closed her eyes, face pale—but no less white than Tarthe's, as he reached out a reassuring arm to grip her shoulder. Othbar, the Hand of Tyche, swallowed and said, "Ondil slays us with spells spun from his tomb. Undeath and fell magic will take us all if we do not set our feet right."

Tarthe nodded, face sharp with fear. "What should we do?

You and Elmara know more of magic than the rest of us here."

"Dig our way out of the chamber?" Elmara asked faintly. "The doors and windows he must have covered with hanging spells that wait to slay us, but if he's not expected us to pry at the flagstones, he may have to rise from his rest to hurl spells at us."

"And when he rises, what then?" Gralkyn asked fearfully. Ithym nodded grimly, echoing the question.

"We strike with everything we have," Tarthe said, "both spell and blade."

"Let me cast a spell first," said Othbar. His face was very white and his voice shook. "If it works, Ondil will be bound into his tomb for a time, unable to work magic—and we can try to get out."

"To have him sending spells and beasts after us for the rest of our lives?" Ithym asked grimly.

Tarthe shrugged. "We'll have the chance to gather blades and spells enough to fight him if he does, where now he slaughters us at whim. Ready weapons, and I'll try these flagstones. Othbar, say out when you're ready."

The priest of Tyche fell to his knees in fervent prayer, bidding the Lady remember his long and faithful service. Then he pricked his palm with a belt knife, and caught the falling drops of blood in his other hand, intoning something they could not understand.

A moment later, he crumpled to the flagstones, arms flopping loosely. Gralkyn took an involuntary step forward—and then recoiled, as something ghost-white rose in wisps from the priest's body. It roiled in silence, growing taller and thinner—until a ghostly image of Othbar stood facing them. It pointed sternly at the four surviving Blades, and then at the windows. They watched in awe as Othbar's shade strode to the casket and laid its palms on the stone lid.

"What? Is he—?" Ithym was shaken.

Tarthe bent over the body. "Yes." When he straightened, the warrior's face looked older. "He knew the spell would cost him his life, I would guess, by what he said," Tarthe said, and his voice quavered. "Let's begone."

"By the windows?" Ithym asked, tears in his eyes as he looked back at the ghostly figure standing by the tomb.

"It's the way he pointed," Tarthe said heavily. "Ropes first."

The two thieves undid leather jerkins to reveal ropes wound many times around their bellies. Elmara took hold of one end of each rope, and the thieves spun around and around until the ropes lay in loose coils on the floor. Ithym caught up two ends and tied them together.

Then, gingerly, the two thieves approached a window, looking back over to be sure there was nothing visible that might spring at them. Ithym carried the coil of rope on his shoulder, and Gralkyn held one end of it in his hands as he approached the window.

He touched the end of the rope to the ornate wrought iron of the window screen, and then to the draperies beyond. Then he followed, gingerly, with one gloved hand. Nothing happened.

The oval window-screens depicted scenes of flying dragons, wizards standing atop rocky pinnacles, and rearing pegasi. With a shrug, Gralkyn chose the nearest one with a pegasus on it and swung the screen aside on its hinges. They made a slight squeal of protest, but nothing else befell. His blade parted the draperies beyond—to reveal bubble-pocked glass, and through it, a view of the sky and the wilderlands. Cautiously the thief probed the window opening with his blade, peering about for traps. Then he said, "These were not made to open. The glass is fixed in place."

"Break it, then," Ithym said.

Gralkyn shrugged, reversed his blade, and swung hard. The glass burst apart, shards flashing and tinkling everywhere.

Sudden motes of light shone in the air where the window had been, spiraling, slowly at first . . . and then faster. . . .

"Back!" Elmara shouted in sudden alarm. "Get ye back!"

The light of the activating spell flared before her words were half out—and a force of awesome power snatched both thieves out through the small opening, rope and all, smashing their limbs against the walls as they went, as if they were rag dolls being stuffed through a hole too small for them. Ithym had time for one despairing scream—long, raw, and falling—before hitting the rocks.

Tarthe drew a shuddering breath, shook his head, and turned to the young mage. "Just the two of us, now." He nodded at the book strapped to Elmara's chest. "Anything there that might help?"

"Ondil's magic sealed it. I would not like to try to break his spells here in his own keep—not while Othbar's sacrifice holds." Elmara looked at the silent and motionless image holding the coffin shut—and noted its flickering, fading extremities. She pointed. "Even now, the lich tries to break out of its coffin."

Tarthe's eyes went to the flickering hands of the image. "How long do we have?"

Elmara shrugged. "If I knew that, I'd be Ondil."

Tarthe waved his sword. "Don't jest about such things! How can I tell you haven't fallen under some spell or other and become Ondil's slave?"

Elmara stared at him, then slowly nodded. "Ye raise a wise concern."

Tarthe's eyes narrowed, and he drew a dagger, eyes fixed on the young sorceress. Then he turned and threw it back through the opening where Tharp had died. It spun into the passage beyond and was gone—unseen in the sudden flash and whirl of a hundred circling, clanging blades, darting about in the space that had been empty moments before.

"The magic continues," Tarthe said heavily. "Do we try to dig a way out in earnest?"

Elmara thought for a moment, and then shook her head. "Ondil is too strong—these magics can be broken only by destroying him."

"So we must fight him," Tarthe said grimly.

"Aye," Elmara replied, "and I must prepare ye before the fray."

"Oh?" Tarthe raised an eyebrow and his blade as the sorceress approached.

Elmara sighed and came to a halt well beyond his reach. "I can fly yet," she said gently. "If this tower stays aloft through Ondil's own magic, ye too must be able to take wing if we slay him—or ye will fall with the tower, and be crushed when it shatters below."

Tarthe swallowed, then nodded and put his blade on his shoulder. "Cast your spell, then," he said.

Elmara was barely done when sudden radiance flared behind her.

She spun around—in time to see Othbar's image vanish, along with the lid it had been holding down. She sighed again. "Ondil found a way," she murmured. Suddenly she nodded as if answering a question only she could hear, and her hands flashed in frantic haste, working a spell.

Tarthe looked uncertainly at her and risked a step forward, sword raised. Inside the stone casket lay a plain, dark wooden coffin, seemingly new—and on it, three small, thick books.

"Touch them not," Elmara said sharply, "unless ye are ready to kiss a lich!"

The warrior took a step back, blade up and ready. "I doubt I'll ever be ready for that," he said dryly. "Will you?"

"What must be, must be," the sorceress said curtly. "Stand back against yon wall now, as far off as ye can get."

Without looking to see if this direction had been obeyed, she stepped up to the casket and laid one hand firmly on a spellbook.

The dark wooden lid vanished. With inhuman speed, something tall, thin, and robed sprang up from where it had lain, the spellbooks tumbling down around it.

Icy hands clutched at Elmara, caught, and seared the living flesh in their grasp.

Instead of pulling back, Elmara leaned forward, smiled tightly into Ondil's shriveled face and said the last word of her spell. The lich found himself holding nothing—in the brief instant before the ceiling of the chamber smashed down atop him, burying the coffin.

The sorceress reappeared beside Tarthe, shoulders to the wall, eyes on the coffin. Dust and echoes rolled around them both as Elmara rubbed at her seared wrists and watched the stones of the central ceiling begin to rise up in a silent stream, back whence they'd come. Tarthe looked at her, then at the casket, and then back at the mage. His face wore a look of awe—but also, for the first time in quite a while, hope.

Something dusty and shattered rose up out of the casket when the stones were all gone, and it stood facing them, swaying. Slowly it lifted the slivered bones of one arm. Its skull was largely gone, but the jaw remained, chattering something as it fought to move its bent arm to point at them. A cold light burned in the one eyesocket that was whole. The jagged edges of the topless skull turned as the lich looked at Tarthe—and then Elmara whispered a word, and the ceiling came crashing down on it again.

Nothing rose out of the casket this time, and Elmara stepped cautiously forward to peer down into the open coffin.

In the bottom lay dust, smashed and splintered bones among the tatters of once-fine robes and the three spellbooks. Some of the bones shifted, trying to move. A ruined arm rose unsteadily up to point at Elmara—who coolly reached in, grabbed it, and pulled.

When she had the clutching, clawing arm free of the casket, she flung it down on the floor and stamped on it repeatedly until all the bones were shattered. Then she looked into the casket again, seeking other restive remains. Twice more she hauled out bones and stamped on them—and at the sight of her dancing on them, Tarthe broke into sudden shouts of laughter.

Elmara shook her head and reached into the coffin, touching the spellbooks and murmuring the words of one last spell. The books quietly disappeared.

Behind her, Tarthe's laughter ended abruptly. Elmara whirled around in time to see a smiling robed man thicken from a shadowy outline into full solidity above a winking curved thing of metal on the floor . . . Tharp's helm.

It was a cruel smile, and its owner turned to Elmara, who stiffened, recalling a face burned forever into her memories. The magelord who'd ridden the dragon and burned Heldon!

"Ah, yes, Elmara—or should I say Elminster Aumar, *Prince* of Athalantar? Tharp was my spy among the Brave Blades from the very beginning. Very useful you've been, too, finding all sorts of malcontents and hidden magic and gold. Yes, the magelords thank you in particular for the gold . . . one can never have enough, you know." He smiled as Tarthe's hurled dagger spun through him to clash and clatter against the far wall of the chamber.

An instant later, flames roared through the room. The blazing body of Tarthe Maermir, leader of the Brave Blades, was flung into the far wall, and Elmara heard the warrior's neck snap. The magelord looked down at the burning corpse and sneered. "You didn't think I'd be foolish enough to reveal where my true self stood? You did? Ah, well . . ."

Elmara's eyes narrowed, and she spoke a single word. The sound of a body heavily striking a wall came to her ears—and the magelord's image vanished.

A moment later, the man appeared nearby, slumped against the wall. He gazed coldly up at Elmara, who was stammering out a more powerful incantation, and said, "My thanks for destroying Ondil. I shall enjoy augmenting my magic with his. I am in your debt, mageling . . . and so it is my duty and pleasure to rid us of your annoying attacks, once and for all!" A ring on his finger winked once, and the world exploded in flames.

Hands still moving in the feeble, useless gestures of a broken spell, Elmara found herself hurled out the shattered window where the two thieves had gone, a coil of flames crackling and searing around her. She roared in pain, the flames clawing at her, and twisted about as she fell so as to appear helpless for as long as possible before she called on the powers of her still-working flight spell. The book strapped to her stomach seemed to ward off the flames, but her ears were full of the sizzle of her burning hair.

Below lay the shattered bodies of the two thieves, and a large blackened area where lumps still gave off smoke—all Briost had left of the youngest Blade and the horses he'd guarded. Scant feet above them, Elmara bent her will and darted away, soaring just above the ground, smoke trailing from her blackened clothes. She wept as she flew, but not from the growing pain of her burns.

* * * * *

The small open boat held a man and a woman. The old, grizzled man in the stern poled it steadily on through thick sunset mists.

He eyed the young, hawk-nosed woman who stood near the bow, and asked quietly, "Be going to the temple, young lady?"

Elmara nodded. Motes of light sparkled and swam continuously about the large bundle she held with both hands against her chest, veiling its true nature. The old man eyed it anyway, and then looked away and spat thoughtfully into the water.

"Have a care, lass," he said, resting his pole so the boat drifted. "Not many goes, but fewer comes back to the dock next morn. Some we never find at all, some we find only as heaps o' ashes or twisted bones, and others blind or just babbling at nothing, dawn 'til dusk."

The young, hawk-nosed maid turned and looked at him, face expressionless, for a long time. Then she lifted her shoulders, let them fall in a shrug, and said, "This is a thing I must do. I am bidden." She looked ahead into the mists and added quietly, "As are we all, too often, it seems."

The old man shrugged in his turn as the island of Mystra's Dance loomed up out of the scudding mists before them, a dark and silent bulk above the water.

They regarded it, growing larger as they approached. The old man turned the boat slightly. A few breaths later, his craft scraped gently along an old stone dock, and he said, "Mystra's Dance, young lady. Her altar stands atop the hill that's hidden, beyond the one above us. I'll return as we agreed. May Mystra smile upon ye."

Elmara bowed to him and stepped up onto the dock, leaving four gold regals in the old man's hand as she passed. The ferry man steadied his boat in silence, watching the young lady's determined stride as she climbed the hill. The full glory of the setting sun was past now, and purple dusk was coming down swiftly over the clear sky of Faerun.

Only when Elmara had disappeared over the crest of the bare summit did the boatman move. He turned away and leaned on his pole strongly. The boat pulled away from the dock, and the old, weathered face of its owner split in a sudden grin.

The grin widened horribly as the face above it slid down like rotten porridge. Fangs grew down to pierce the sliding flesh. The flesh dripped off a too-sharp chin and fell away to slop and spatter in the bottom of the boat, and the scaly, grinning face whispered, "Done, master." Garadic knew Ilhundyl was watching.

* * * * *

Elmara stopped in front of the altar: a plain, dark block of
stone standing alone atop the hill. The wind sighed past her. She
offered a heartfelt prayer to Mystra, and the wind seemed to die
away for a breath or two. When she was done, she unwrapped
Ondil's Book of Spells, its binding still bright around it, and
placed it reverently on the cold stone.

"Holy Lady of All Mysteries, please accept my gift," Elmara
mumbled, uncertain as to what she should say. She stood watching and waiting, prepared to stand vigil the night through if
need be.

A bare moment later, a chill ran down her spine. Two ghostly
hands, long-fingered and feminine, were rising up out of the
stone. They grasped the tome and began to descend again. Sudden, blinding radiance burst from the book, and there was a
high, clear singing sound.

Elmara winced and shaded her eyes. When she could see
again, the hands and the book were gone. The breezes blew
across the bare stone, just as it had been when she found it.

The young priestess stood before the altar for a long time,
feeling strangely empty, and weary—and yet at peace. There
would be time to choose a path ahead on the morrow . . . for now,
she was content just to stand. And remember.

The folk of Heldon and the outlaws in the ravine outside the
Castle, the Velvet Hands lying in the alley, the Brave Blades . . .
so many dead. Gone to meet the gods, leaving her alone
again. . . .

Lost in reverie, Elmara only gradually became aware of a
brightening glow from down the hill, behind the altar.

She stepped forward. The glow was coming from a slim female figure that stood twice as tall as she. The apparition was
gowned and regal and stood in the air well clear of the ground.
Her eyes were dark pools, and a smile fell across her face as she
raised her hand and beckoned. Then she turned and began to
walk away, striding on empty air down the hill. After a moment,
Elmara followed through the tugging breeze, down the wind-
blown slope, then around another hill, and on. They came out
onto a pebble beach on the far side of the isle from the dock, but
the glowing figure ahead walked on, straight into—no, above!—
the waves, striding out to sea.

Elmara slowed, eyeing the water's edge. Gray waves rolled
endlessly up onto the pebbles, and then sucked them back. The
water ahead was glowing where Mystra had walked above it.

Unbroken by the rolling waves, a shining path lay across the waters ahead of her. The goddess was growing distant now, still striding across the waves.

Gingerly, Elmara walked into the surf, and found her boots still dry. A fine mist covered her, but her feet did not plunge through the waters . . . she was walking on the waves! Emboldened, she began to hurry now, striding along in haste to catch up.

They were walking out to sea, leaving the island well behind. The breezes blew past, cool and steady, driving the sea to shore. Elmara hurried until her breath was coming in gasps, not quite daring to run on the moving waves . . . yet drew no closer to the glowing figure ahead.

El was just beginning to wonder where they were hurrying to when a cold, clear voice from just ahead of her said, "You have failed me."

Ahead, the glowing figure dimmed, fading quickly above the dark waves. Elmara started to run in earnest now, but the radiant waves in front of her grew darker and darker, until the path was gone, and the figure too—and she was suddenly walking on the water no more, but plunged into icy depths.

She rose, struggling, cold water crawling in her throat and nose as she coughed and thrashed . . . and a wave slapped her in the face. She spat out water and clawed her way around, so the next swell lifted her under the shoulders and carried her along.

Back toward the island, now only a dark spot on the running gray seas. She was alone in the chill waters, at night, far from land. . . .

* * * * *

In the breeze howling its way over the hilltop there came a sudden whirl of sparkling lights, rising up into a singing cloud of winking radiance. From its heart stepped a tall, dark-robed figure.

He strode to the bare stone block, looked down at it for a moment, and said coldly, "Rise!"

There was a sigh and a stirring from the stone in front of him, and wisps of pearly light began to stream from it, tugged by the quickening wind. The radiance swirled, thickened, and became a translucent figure—a woman who held a tome. She extended the book to the robed man, who stretched forth his hand in a quick gesture. Brief lightnings played around the book, and then died. Satisfied, the man took it.

The ghostly face leaned close. Its entreating whisper was almost a sob. "Now will ye let me rest, Mage Most Mighty?"

Ilhundyl nodded once. "For a time," he said curtly. "Now—go!"

The spirit's shadowy form wavered above the stone block, as if it were whipped in a gale, and her faint voice came again. "Who was the young mage, and what is her fate?"

"Death is her fate, and so she is nothing, of course," Ilhundyl said, and there was a clear edge of anger in his cold tones. "Go!"

The lich moaned and sank back into the stone; the last that could be seen of her before she faded utterly was a pair of spread, beseeching hands.

Ilhundyl ignored them, hefted the weighty book in his hands, and smiled coldly across the breezy night at the third hilltop, where only rubble remained of the shattered True Altar of Mystra. If he had learned one thing in all his years of spell work and ruthless advancement, it was that the Mistress of Magic valued magical might above all. Wherefore Ilhundyl proudly wore the "Mad Mage" title men whispered behind his back. Soon, soon he'd be the most powerful, the Magister over all Faerun—and then they'd be too busy screaming to whisper and work against him.

He stiffened, peering into the night. A blue flame was rising from the shattered stones on the other hilltop, flickering but growing ever brighter . . . and taller.

Ilhundyl's mouth was suddenly dry. A woman twice as tall as he stood looking across the empty air between them. A tall, regal lady of blue flame, her eyes dark and level as they met his.

Sudden fear rose to choke him. Ilhundyl muttered a hasty word and sketched a sign in the air, and the winking lights rose bright around him, bearing him away. . . .

* * * * *

Elmara groaned, coughed weakly, and opened her eyes. Dawn had come to Faerun again . . . and, it seemed, had found her still in it. She was lying half in water and half on sand, with the endless crash of the surf all around. Fingers of foaming water ran up the sand past her. El watched its flow, feeling weak and sick, and then tried to lift herself. Sand sucked at her, then she was on hands and knees . . . whole and unhurt, it seemed, just a little dizzy.

The beach was deserted. A cool, salty onshore breeze blew past her and made her shiver. She was naked except for the Lion Sword, still on its thong around her neck. Elmara sighed, and wobbled to her feet. There was no sign of houses or docks or fences . . . just stunted trees, rocks, and a tangle of grasses, old stumps, and bushes where the beach ended and the living things began.

She took a step forward, then froze. In the sand in front of her, someone had scratched one word: "Athalantar."

El looked down at the word in the sand, and then at her bare limbs, and shivered. She coughed, shook her head, lifted her chin, and strode away from the water, heading toward the rising sun.

* * * * *

In a place where guardian spells glowed night and day, deep in the Castle of Sorcery, a man settled down to read.

"Garadic," he said coldly, and sipped his drink.

The scaled minion reluctantly shuffled forward out of the shadows and gingerly opened Ondil's Book of Spells, where it lay on a lectern at the far end of the chamber from his master. Always-vigilant protective spells massed and swirled around the lectern, but no lightnings nor creeping death came. The revealed page was blank.

"Bring it," was the next cold command.

When the lectern stood before his high, padded chair, Ilhundyl set down the goblet of emerald wine and waved the scaled, shambling thing away. He turned the next page himself.

It was as blank and creamy as the flyleaf before it had been. He turned it back. So was the next . . . and the next . . . and the next . . . every one of the pages was blank! Ilhundyl's face froze, and a frown crept in around his eyes.

He spoke a word that made all the radiances in the room dim. The floor glowed briefly, and there came a grating sound, as a flagstone there moved back to reveal a hole. Very quickly, as if it had been waiting, a slyly questing tendril rose from unseen depths below. It touched the book delicately, almost caressingly, and then enfolded it—only to recoil, disappointed, and sink down again. That meant there were no hidden writings, nor portals or linkages to other spaces and other tomes. The book was empty.

Sudden rage seized Ilhundyl then. He rose from his seat in black anger, striding through portals that slid open and curtains that parted at his approach. His furious walk ended half the castle away, before a large sphere of sparkling crystal. It stood atop a black pedestal, alone in a small room of many lamps.

He glared into the depths of the sphere. Flames and flicker-

ings appeared and coiled there, fueled by his anger. Ilhundyl
stared into the crystal as the flames within it slowly grew,
reaching flickering talons up its curving sides, and suddenly he
was shouting. "I'll blast her bones! If she's drowned, I'll raise
her—and then smash her bones like hurled eggs, and make her
beg for release! *No* one tricks Ilhundyl! *No one!*"

He spat a word of summoning, and halfway across the Castle
of Sorcery, where he cowered in concealing shadows, the winged
and warty shape of Garadic rose hastily and flapped down the
swiftest ways to his master's side.

Ilhundyl glared into the crystal, summoning up the young,
hawk-nosed face from his memory. The fires swirled and
shifted, clearing, and he gathered himself to hurl a scything
blade of his will, to chop the young worm's legs off at the knees
and let her scream and crawl until Ilhundyl came—and gave
her *real* cause to scream and crawl!

But when the fires of the crystal spun into focus, the visage
looking calmly back at him was not the one Ilhundyl sought. He
gaped in astonishment.

The wrinkled, bearded face dropped its habitual expression
of mild curiosity to smile gently at him, nodded in greeting, and
said, "Fair day, Ilhundyl; gained a new spellbook, I see."

Ilhundyl spat at the Magister. The spittle hissed and smoked
as it struck the crystal. "The pages are blank—and you know it!"

The Magister smiled again, a trifle tightly. "Yes . . . but the
young mage who offered it to Mystra did not. You told her not to
look inside, and she obeyed you. Such honesty and trust is sadly
lacking in this world today—isn't it, Ilhundyl?"

The Mad Mage of the Calishar snarled and hurled a spell
into his crystal. The world inside the sphere flashed and rocked,
throwing back bright reflections from Ilhundyl's cheeks, but the
Magister only smiled a little more tightly—and then the Mad
Mage's spell came howling back at him, bursting out of the bobbing, chattering crystal to crash into Ilhundyl and then rage
about the chamber. Garadic flapped hastily aloft to avoid the
full force of the flaming points of force, only to be tumbled helplessly around the walls, scraping and squawking, by the force of
their flights.

"Temper, Ilhundyl, is the downfall of many a foolish young
mageling," the Magister said calmly.

Ilhundyl's scream of frustrated fury echoed around the
chamber—and then he turned, murder in his eyes, and hurled
rending fire. Garadic hadn't even time enough to finish his
squawk.

* * * * *

A minstrel was singing in the dimly lit taproom of the Unicorn's Horn as the young hawk-nosed woman stepped wearily inside. The roadside inn stood amid a cluster of sheep farms well west of Athalantar; to reach it, she'd walked all that day with nothing but brook water to drink and nothing at all to eat.

The innkeeper heard the traveler's stomach growl as she stalked past, and greeted her affably. "A table and some stew right off, goodwoman? With a roast and wine to follow, of course. . . ."

The young woman nodded, a smile almost rising to her grim lips. "A—quiet corner table, if ye would. Dark and private."

The innkeeper nodded. "I've many such . . . this way, along behind, here. . . ."

The traveler did smile this time and allowed herself to be led to a table. Her dark clothes were worn and nondescript, but by her manner, she'd known both book learning and gentle society, so the innkeeper didn't ask her for coins before service, but was astonished when the slim woman kicked off her boots with a contented sigh and spun a gold regal across the table.

"Let me know when that one needs company," she murmured, and the innkeeper happily assured her that all would be done as she directed.

* * * * *

The wine—a ruby-red dwarven vintage that burned all the way down—was good, the roast excellent, and the singing pleasant. The flagstone floor was cold, so Elmara put her boots back on, pulled her cloak around herself, and settled back against the wall, blowing out the single cup-candle on the table.

Cloaked in darkness, she relaxed, listening to the minstrel singing of she-dragons and brave lady knights rescuing young men who'd been chained out as sacrifices to them. It was good to be warm and full of food again, even if the morrow was sure to bring death and danger (hopefully someone else's, and not her own) as she reached Athalantar's borders.

Yet she would press on. Mystra expected it of her.

The mellow voice of the minstrel rose into words that made Elmara break off thinking about Mystra's disappointment in her, and lean forward to listen with her full attention. The ballad was one Elmara hadn't heard before; a hopeful song of praise to brave King Uthgrael of Athalantar. Listening to the warm words of re-

spect for the grandsire she'd never known, El found her eyes wet
with sudden tears. Then the mellow voice changed, thickening,
until it trailed off into a croak. Elmara peered through the shadows
toward the minstrel's stool beside the hearth, and stiffened.

The minstrel was clutching his throat, eyes staring in fear
as he convulsed on his stool. He was goggling at a man who'd
risen from his chair at a nearby table—a table of haughty, richly
robed men who were laughing at the minstrel's fate. The table in
their midst was a forest of already-emptied bottles, goblets, and
skins. Elmara saw wands at their belts, as well as daggers . . .
wizards.

"What're ye *doing?*" That sharp question came from a fat
merchant at another table.

The mage who stood with one outstretched hand slowly
clenching, choking the breath out of the minstrel, turned his
head to sneer, "We don't allow that dead man to be mentioned in
Athalantar."

"You're not *in* Athalantar!" a man at another table protested
as the minstrel gagged and gurgled helplessly.

The wizard shrugged as he stared coolly around the room.
"We are magelords of Athalantar, and all this land will soon be
part of our realm," he said flatly.

Elmara saw the innkeeper, emerging from the kitchens with
a steaming platter on his shoulder, come to a shocked halt as he
heard the magelord's words.

The wizard smiled silkily around the room. "Is anyone here
foolish enough to try to stop me?"

"Yes," Elmara said quietly from her corner, as she broke the
strangling spell. Her hands were already moving again as she
stepped aside into deeper shadows. The table of magelords—El
suspected they were in truth apprentices of little power, here to
escort a caravan or do some such lesser work—peered into the
darkness, trying to catch sight of her. Then her casting was done.
She strode forward, addressing the standing wizard. "Those who
wield powerful magic should never use it to bully those who have
none. D'ye agree?"

"You are mistaken," the magelord sneered, and raised his
hands to work another spell.

Elmara sighed and pointed. The wizard stiffened in midin-
cantation and clutched at his throat.

"Your own spell," Elmara informed the choking wizard pleasantly. "It seems quite effective . . . but then, perhaps I *am* mistaken."

Her words brought a roar of rage from six throats as the self-styled magelords erupted from their seats, snatching at wands and spilling bottles and flagons in their haste. Elmara watched glass topple and roll, smiled, and said the word that brought her waiting spell down upon them.

Wands were leveled and angry hands shaped gestures in the air. Words were spat and strange items flourished as the six able magelords bent malicious magic on their lone foe.

And nothing happened.

Elmara announced calmly to the room, "I can prevent these men from using their magic—for a time. I would enjoy a good spell battle, but I'd rather not destroy this inn doing it. If ye'd care to deal with them . . . ?"

There was a moment of shocked silence. Then chairs scraped back, and men reached for daggers—and the magelords fled. Or tried to. Outthrust boots tripped magelings not used to watching where they walked, and enthusiastic fists laid low apprentices not used to brawling with anything less than fireballs. One wizard's dagger slashed a merchant across the face, and the snarling man hauled out his own knife and made good use of it.

The crash of the mage's body going to the floor amid overturning chairs brought the room to silence again. Only the one magelord was dead; the rest lay senseless, strewn about amid the disarranged tables and chairs.

The innkeeper was the first to say what many of the diners were thinking. "That was all too easy—but who among us will live when their fellow mages come down on us for revenge?"

"Aye—they'll turn us all to snails and grind us under their boots!"

"They'll blow the inn apart with flame, and us in it!"

"Mayhap," Elmara said, "but only if some tongues here wag too freely." She calmly raised her hands and cast a spell, and then went about the room touching the wizards. Men backed out of her way in haste; it was easy to see they viewed wizards as swift and deadly trouble.

When she was done, she murmured a word, and suddenly, seven stones sat where the sprawled bodies had lain. Elmara made a gesture, and the rocks were gone, leaving only a small, dark pool of blood behind to mark that they'd ever been there.

The nearest merchant turned to Elmara. "You turned them to stones?"

"Aye," she said, and a sudden smile crossed her face. "Ye see— ye *can* get blood from stones." Amid a few uncertain chuckles, she turned to the minstrel. "Have ye breath enough to sing?"

The man nodded uncertainly. "Why?"

"If ye will, I'd like to hear the rest of the tale about King Uth-grael."

The minstrel bowed. "My pleasure, Lady—?"

"Elmara," Elmara told him. "Elmara Aumar—er, descendant of Elthryn of Heldon."

The minstrel looked at her as if Elmara had three heads and crowns on each one. "Heldon is ashes these nine winters past." El did not reply, and after a moment, the man asked curiously, "But tell me: where did you send the stones?"

Elmara shrugged. "A good way offshore near Mystra's Dance, where the water is deep. When my spell wears off and they regain their true forms, they'll have to swim to the surface to survive. I hope they have large and strong lungs."

Silence fell on the room at these words. The minstrel tried to break the mood by beginning the Ballad of the Stag again, but his voice was raw. After it broke the second time, he spread his hands and asked, "Can you wait, Lady Elmara, until the morrow?"

"Of course," El replied, taking a seat at the just-righted table where the wizards had been. "How are ye?"

"Alive, thanks to you," the minstrel said quietly. "May I pay for your dinner?"

"If ye allow me to buy all we drink," Elmara replied. After a moment, they both chuckled.

* * * * *

Elmara set down their third bottle, empty. She eyed it gravely, and asked, "Are any princes left alive?"

The minstrel shrugged. "Belaur, of course, though I've heard he styles himself 'king' now. I know of no others, but there could be, I suppose. It hardly matters now that the magelords rule openly, issuing decrees as if they were all kings. The only entertainment we have is watching them try to outwit each other. I don't go back often."

"How so?" Elmara stared at the last few swallows in her glass. Treacherous stuff.

"It's not a safe land for any who speak openly against the magelords—and that includes minstrels whose clever ballads may not be to the liking of any passing wizards or armsman."

The minstrel thoughtfully drained his own glass. "Athalantar doesn't see any visiting wizards, now, either . . . unless one has the power to defeat all the magelords, why go there? If any mage of power comes to Athalantar, the magelords'd doubtless see it as a threat to their rule and all rise up together against him!"

Elmara laughed quietly. "A prudent mage would go elsewhere, eh?"

The minstrel nodded. "And speedily." His eyes narrowed. "You wear a strange look, Lady. . . . Where will you go on the morrow?"

Elmara looked at him. Fire smoldered deep in eyes gone very dark, and the smile the mage gave the minstrel then had no mirth in it at all. "Athalantar, of course."

Twelve

HARD CHOICES, EASY DOOMS

Choosing what road to walk in life is a luxury given to few in Faerûn. Perhaps lack of practice is why so many who do have that choice make such a gods-cursed mess of it.

Galgarr Thormspur, Marshal of Maligh
A Warrior's Views
Year of the Blue Shield

The first sign of trouble was the empty road.

At this hour of a bright morning, the way to Narthil should have been crowded with groaning carts, snorting oxen pulling wagons along, any number of peddlers leading mules, laborers and pilgrims trudging along under the weight of their packs, and perhaps even a mounted messenger or two. Instead, Elmara had the road to herself as she topped the last rise and saw that her way was barred by a log swing-gate across the road. In all her days in Hastarl, there'd been no gates on the roads into Athalantar—or she'd surely have heard of it from the tired merchants who complained about every little thing on their journeys.

The guards lounging on benches behind the gate heaved themselves to their feet and picked up their halberds. Armsmen of Athalantar, or she was a magelord. They looked bored and brutal.

Elmara shifted her pack to better conceal the small spell-things she'd taken into her palm, and trudged up to the gate.

"Halt, woman," the swordcaptain of the guard said offhandedly. "Your name and trade?"

Elmara faced the officer across the gate and said politely, "The first is none of thy affair; as to the second, I work magic."

The armsmen drew back, their boredom gone in an instant. Halberds flashed as they came down over the gate to menace the lone woman. The swordcaptain's brows drew together in a frown that had made lesser men turn and run, but the stranger stood her ground.

"Mages who do not serve our king are not welcome here," said the swordcaptain. As he spoke, his men were moving steadily sideways around the ends of the gate, weapons at the ready, moving to encircle Elmara with steel.

El ignored them. "And what king might that be?"

"King Belaur, of course," the swordcaptain snapped, and Elmara felt the cold point of a halberd prodding her lower back.

"On your knees, *now*," the swordcaptain snapped, "and await our local lord mage, who will demand to know further of your business. Best you use a more respectful tongue with him than you did with us."

Elmara smiled tightly and raised one empty hand. She made a small gesture and replied, "Oh, I shall."

Behind him, the first gasps began, and the point probing at her spine was suddenly gone. All around, the guardsmen staggered, cried out or vomited, white-faced, and sank to their knees. One kept going, bonelessly, to the turf, his halberd dropping from loose, empty hands.

"What—what're you doing?" the swordcaptain gulped, face tightening in pain. "Magic—?"

"A small spell that makes ye feel what it is to have a sword sliding through your guts," the young, hawk-nosed maid said calmly. "But if it confuses thee . . ."

The swordcaptain felt a sudden twinge in his stomach, and in the same instant there was a flash in the air before him. He stared down—to see a shining steel blade standing forth from his belly, his own dark red blood running down the blade. He choked, clutched a vain hand to quell the wrenching, searing pain in his stomach—and then the sword and the pain both vanished.

The warrior stared down in astonishment at the unmarked leather over his belly. Then his eyes rose slowly, reluctantly, to meet those of the young woman, who smiled at him pleasantly and raised her other hand.

The guardcaptain paled, opened his mouth to say something, jaw quivering, and then fled, followed a moment later by the rest of the guard. Elmara watched them go, smiling a little, and then walked on along the road, toward the inn.

* * * * *

The sign above the door said Myrkiel's Rest, and merchants had told her it was the best (near the only) inn in Narthil. Elmara found it pleasant enough, and took a chair against a wall at the back of the room, where she could see who came in. She ordered a meal from the stout proprietress and asked if she could use a room for a few breaths, offering a regal if she could do it undisturbed.

The innkeeper's eyebrows rose, but without a word she took Elmara's coin and showed her a room with a door that could be barred. When Elmara returned to her seat, humming the verse "O for an iron guard!" her meal was waiting, hot butter-bread and rabbit stew.

It was good. She was most of the way through it when the front door of the Rest burst open, and armsmen with drawn swords pushed in. An angry-looking man in robes of red and silver strode in their midst.

"Ho, Asmartha!" the splendidly garbed man snapped. "Who is this outlaw you shelter?" With an imperious jerk of his head, he indicated the young woman sitting in the corner. The innkeeper turned angry eyes on Elmara, but the hawk-nosed maid was calmly licking the last sauce from a rabbit-bone, and paid no heed.

Motioning his armsmen to stay around him, the man in robes strode grandly toward Elmara's table. Other diners stared and hastily shifted their seats to be well out of the way—but close enough to see and hear all they could.

"A word with you, wench!"

Elmara raised her eyes, over another bone. She inspected it, set it aside, and selected another. "Ye may have several," she decreed calmly and went on eating. There were several sniggers and chuckles from around the tables—quelled by the cold and steady glare of the finely robed man as he turned on one boot heel to survey the room.

"I understand you style yourself a mage," he said coldly to the seated woman.

Elmara put down another bone. "No. I said I worked magic," she replied, not bothering to look up. After a few long breaths more, as she unconcernedly gnawed at a succession of bones, it became clear she had no intention of saying anything more.

"I'm speaking to you, wench!"

"I had noticed, aye," Elmara agreed. "Say on." She picked up another bone, decided it was too bare to suck on a second time, and put it down. "More beer, please," she called, leaning to look past the crowd of armsmen. There were more sounds of mirth from the watching diners.

"Raztan," the robed man said coldly, "run your blade into this arrogant whore."

Elmara yawned and leaned back in her chair, presenting an arched belly to Raztan, who did not fail to miss it, his steel sliding in so smoothly that he overbalanced and fell on his face in the young woman's bowl of stew. Everyone in the suddenly silent

room heard the point of the blade scrape the plastered wall behind the young woman. Elmara calmly pushed her plate and
bowl aside and selected a toothpick from the pewter holder before her.

"Sorcery!" one of the armsmen spat, and slashed Elmara
across the face. No blood spurted—and the blade swung freely
through the hawk-nosed face, as if it were only empty air. The
watchers gasped.

The robed man curled his lip. "I see you know the ironguard
spell," he said, unimpressed.

Elmara smiled up at him, nodded, and wiggled a finger. The
drawn swords around her twisted, sang, and became gray serpents. Horrified armsmen watched the fanged heads turn and
arch back to strike at the hands that wielded them! With one accord, the armsmen flung down their weapons and leapt back.
One man charged for the door, and his run became a thundering
rush of booted feet as his comrades joined him. All around the
guards, their blades, normal swords once more, clattered to the
floor.

The man in robes drew back, face pale. "We shall speak
again," he said, his haughty voice a trifle uncertain, "and when
we d—"

Elmara raised both her hands to trace an intricate pattern in
the air, and the man turned and strode hastily back across the
room, toward the door. Halfway there he halted, swaying, and
the watchers heard him snarl in fear and frustration. Sudden
sweat moistened his brow as he strained to move . . . but could
not advance another step. Elmara rose and walked around to
face the frozen man. Frightened eyes swiveled to watch her
come.

"Who rules here?" she asked.

The man snarled at her wordlessly.

Elmara raised an eyebrow and a hand at the same time.

"M-Mercy," the man gasped.

"There is no mercy for mages," Elmara told him quietly. "I've
learned that much." She turned away. "I ask again: who rules?"

"I—ah . . . we hold Narthil for King Belaur."

"Thank you, sir," Elmara murmured politely, and started
back to her seat.

The man in robes, suddenly released from magical restraint,
lurched and almost fell, took three quick steps toward the door,
and then spun around and snarled a spell, his dagger flashing
into his hand. The watching townsfolk gasped. The robed wizard's blade and all the discarded swords on the floor leapt up in

unison and hurtled through the air toward Elmara's back in a
deadly storm of steel. Without turning, El murmured a soft
word. The steel points so close to claiming her life swerved
away, flying back at the mage.

"*No!*" the robed wizard cried frantically, snatching at the
handle of the door. "Wha—"

The blades thudded home in a deadly rain, lifting the man's
body off his feet and carrying him past the door. He fell, kicked
once, and then lay still, the blades a shining forest in his back.

Elmara took up her cloak and pack. "Ye see? Mercy continues in short supply. Nor among mages, I've learned, is there
overmuch trust," she added and went out into the street.

Watching faces were pressed against the windows of the inn
as Elmara walked calmly out into the road and began to peer
into shop windows, as if she had coins to spare and a whim to
spend them. She had not been strolling long before there was
the sound of a horn from north up the road—from the small
stone pile of Narthil Keep. A sally port in the keep gate opened,
and the clatter of hooves was heard. An old man in a ceremonial
tabard rode out, two full-plated armsmen with lances behind
him. Elmara watched them turn toward her, saw no signs of
crossbows, shrugged, and turned away, heading back to the inn.

The street was rapidly filling with curious townsfolk. "Who
are ye, young lass?" asked one scar-nosed man.

"A friend . . . a traveling priestess of Mystra, from Athalantar," said Elmara.

"A magelord?" another man asked, sounding angry.

"A renegade magelord?" the woman beside him offered.

"No magelord at all, ever," Elmara replied, and turned to a
big-bosomed, weary-looking woman in apron and patched
skirts, who stood gaping at her as if she were a talking fish.
"How goes it here in Narthil, goodwoman?"

Taken aback by her words, she stammered for a trice, and
then said bitterly, "Bad, lass, since these Athalantan dogs came
and took the keep for their own. Since then, they've seized our
food and daughters an' all without so much as asking!"

"Aye!" several folk agreed.

"More cruel than most warriors?" Elmara asked, waving a
hand at the keep.

The woman shrugged. "Nae so much cruel, as . . . proud.
These young bucks'd not prance so free nor be so fast to smash
things and upset all, if they had to spend a tenday in my—or any
maid's!—place, cleaning up and setting to rights and mending!"

" 'Ware!" a man said warningly, and all around Elmara folk

drew back as the three horsemen came trotting up. The young woman stood calmly awaiting them.

At her unmoving stance, the old man in the tabard of purple adorned with silver moonflowers reined in his mount and said, "I am Aunsiber, lord steward of Narthil. Who are ye, who here work spells against lawful armsmen and mages of the realm?"

Elmara nodded in polite greeting. "One who would prefer to see wizards help folk, not rule them—who would prefer a king whose rule meant peace, stability, and help in harvesting, not taxes, ceaseless strife, and brutality."

Not surprisingly, there was a murmur of agreement from the watching townsfolk all around. The steward uneasily eyed the crowd, sidestepping his restless mount. His voice, when it came, was derisive. "A dream."

Elmara inclined her head. "As yet, 'tis—and not my only one."

The old man looked down from his high saddle and asked, "And your others, young dreamer?"

"Just one," Elmara replied mildly. "Revenge." She raised both her hands as if to cast a spell—and the old man's face paled. He jerked at his reins, wheeled his mount in a nervous flurry of snorts and hooves, and set off back to the keep at a gallop. There were some hoots and exultant yells from the crowd, but Elmara turned away without another word and went back into the inn.

"What'd she say?" one man was asking as she stepped through the door.

A woman sitting nearby leaned forward and said loudly, "Did ye not hear? *Revenge.*"

Then she saw Elmara was in the room and fell silent, a silence that suddenly hung tense and expectant over the whole room. El gave the woman a gentle smile and went to the bar. "Is that beer ready yet?" she asked calmly, and was pleased to hear at least one man behind her dare to chuckle aloud.

* * * * *

Briost was not having a good day. He burst out of his grand council chamber the moment the messenger had gone. The apprentice who'd been trying to eavesdrop by means of a just-perfected spell stiffened guiltily; his master's face was dark with anger.

"Go and practice hurling fireballs," Briost snapped, "or what spells you will. I'm called away on the king's business. Some mad traveling wizard's had the temerity to slay all of Seldinor's apprentices at an inn west of Narthil—and he's 'too busy' to avenge them. So *I'm* going to reap the idiot's head for the greater glory of the magelords!"

* * * * *

The hand that shook Elmara was soft but insistent. She came awake in the best bed in Myrkiel's Rest and peered at the woman bending over her. The innkeeper wore but a blanket, clutched about her. "Lass, lass," she hissed, hovering over El in the darkness, "ye'd best be gone from here right speedily, out into the woods. Word's come that armsmen are riding here to take thee!"

Elmara yawned, stretched, and said, "My thanks, fair lady. Would there be such a thing as hot cider about, and some sausage?"

The innkeeper stared at her. Then what might almost have been a smile flashed across her face as she turned and hurried out, bare feet flashing in the gloom.

* * * * *

The road fairly shook under their hooves in the gray gloom that comes before dawn. Sixty mounted knights of Athalantar, gleaming dark and deadly in their best battle armor, headed west, bent on battle. In their midst, the man whose helm bore the plumes of a commander turned his head to the man riding beside him.

"Suppose you tell me, mage," he ordered, "what urgent befalling brings us to ride through half the night."

"We go to work revenge, Prince," Magelord Eth snapped. "Is that good enough, or would you question my orders further?"

Prince Gartos appeared to consider the matter for a moment, and then said, "No—revenge is the best reason to make war."

There was a shout from ahead, and the horses broke stride. "Stay on the road, damn you!" Gartos ordered wearily, as the knights' mounts bunched up and snorted and tossed their heads all around him. The band of knights came to an uneasy halt.

"What?" he roared.

"The Narthil road-gate, Lord Prince—and no guard stands here."

Gartos snapped, "Helms on, all! Blades out!" and waved imperiously. The knights around him obeyed, and urged their mounts forward at speed. A breath later, they were thundering down into Narthil.

The gloom-shrouded road ahead was empty and in darkness; no lights glimmered in the houses and shops on either side. The foremost knights slowed their mounts, peering around uncertainly. The town looked asleep, but they'd all heard of knights tumbled from their mounts after riding into cords stretched stiff across streets. There were no cords . . . and no leaping arrows . . . and no one defying them at all. Unless . . .

A lone figure was trudging up the street toward them: a youngish, thin woman in nondescript garb, who held a steaming mug of cider in one hand. She halted calmly in their path and stood sipping and watching. They slowed to a trot and then, in a patter of hooves, swept up to and flowed around her.

Elmara found herself looking up into the hard eyes of a battle-worn warrior who wore magnificent armor and was flanked by a cold-eyed man in robes that bore no device, but somehow had "magelord" limned all over them.

"Fair morn," she offered them mildly, sipping cider. "Who are ye who come in arms to Narthil when honest folk are still abed?"

"*I'll* ask, and *you* will give swift answer," the warrior snapped, turning his mount to one side so he could lean down right over Elmara. "Who are *you?*"

"One who would see proud mages and cruel armsmen taken *down,*" El replied, and at the word 'down' her spell went off. Shards of shimmering force flashed out from her in all directions. Where they touched metal, it burst into crackling blue flames—and the man within the armor or holding the blade convulsed and toppled from his saddle.

For a brief instant, the world seemed full of bright light and rearing, crying horses, and then the terrified, riderless mounts were gone in a wild thunder of hooves, leaving Elmara facing just two riders, who sat white-faced in their saddles, a hastily raised protective spell glowing in the air around them.

"My turn," Elmara said, eyes glinting. "Who are ye?"

The warrior slowly and menacingly drew his sword, and Elmara saw magical runes flash and glow down its steely length. "Prince Gartos of Athalantar," he said proudly, "the man who'll slay thee, sorceress, as sure as the sun will rise in the sky o'er Narthil before long." As the warrior spoke, the hands of the silent magelord beside him were moving quickly—but in the next moment his eyes widened: Elmara had suddenly vanished.

Then Magelord Eth's mount was rearing and plunging, and there was a heavy weight behind him. He had just begun to turn when one hand slapped across his nose and mouth, bringing tears—and then another hand came up to punch him hard in the throat.

Gurgling, fighting for air, Magelord Eth reeled in his saddle, and felt something torn from his belt before the dark ground came up hard to hit him in the side of the head, and the Realms spun away from him, forever. . . .

Elmara leapt away from the horse even before the wizard toppled from the saddle; Gartos was very quick. He'd realized where El's magic had taken her, wheeled, and his blade was already cutting the air above the magelord's high-cantled saddle.

Elmara landed hard, jumped to one side to still the speed of her leap, and peered at the wand she'd snatched. Ah, *there!* Hooves were thudding toward her as Elmara looked up, pointed the wand, and carefully spoke the word that was scratched on its butt-end. Light pulsed and hissed away from the wand in a pair of bolts that swerved in the air to strike Prince Gartos full in the face. He threw back his head, snarled in pain, and slashed blindly with his blade as his horse galloped forward. Elmara leapt and rolled, and came up well to one side. She pointed the wand at the armored figure rushing past and spoke the word again.

Light flashed again and sped to its target. The gleaming armored arms jerked in pain. The warrior's sword spun away to the turf as his mount bucked under him and then galloped away, fleeing in earnest now. Elmara saw sleepy-eyed folk gaping at her out of their doorways as she dropped the wand to the road at her feet, pointed her hands at the horse, and spoke a few soft words.

The prince fell from his saddle, rolled over once with a mighty crash, and lay still. The horse sped on into the rising dawn.

El retrieved the wand, cast a quick look around for other foes, saw none, and stalked over to where the warrior lay. Gartos lay on his back, face dark with pain and fury.

"I have other questions, warrior," Elmara said. "What brings armsmen of Athalantar to Narthil?"

Gartos snarled angrily and wordlessly up at her. Elmara raised her eyebrow, and lifted her hands warningly to begin the gestures of a spell.

Gartos watched her fingers move, and rumbled, "S-Stay your spell. I was ordered to find the one who slew some magelings at the Unicorn's Horn, west of here . . . you?"

Elmara nodded. "I defeated them and sent them away; they may yet live. How is it that a prince of the realm gets ordered anywhere?"

The warrior's lips twisted wryly. "Even the king does the bidding of the elder magelords—and the king made me a prince."

"Why?"

The fallen man shrugged. "He trusted me . . . and needed to give me the right to command armsmen without having any young fool of a magelord strike down my orders or slay me out of spite."

Elmara nodded. "Who was the wizard with ye?"

"Magelord Eth—my watchdog, set by the magelords to make sure I don't do anything for Belaur that might work against them."

"Ye make Belaur seem a prisoner."

"He is," Gartos said simply, and Elmara saw his eyes dart aside, this way and that, looking for something.

"Tell me more of this Magelord Eth," Elmara said, taking a step forward and drawing the wand from her belt. It would be best to keep this warrior talking and give him no time to plot an attack.

Gartos shrugged again. "I know little; the magelords don't care to say much about themselves. He's called 'Stoneclaw;' he slew an umber hulk with his spells when he was young . . . but that's about all I . . . *Thaerin!*"

At the warrior's shout, magical radiance pulsed. Elmara turned hastily—in time to see the rune-carved blade flashing toward her, point first.

She leapt aside. The warrior snarled, "Osta! Indruu hathan *halarl!*" and the blade veered in the air, darting straight at Elmara.

She let go the wand and raised her hands desperately—and the blade cut right through them, searing aside her fingers to plunge deep into her. Elmara screamed. The dawn sky whirled around her as she staggered back, blood welling up, fought to speak, and fell back onto the turf, greater pain than she'd ever known hissing through her.

She heard a cold chuckle from Gartos as darkness rolled in, and fought with all her will to cling to something . . . anything . . . With her last breath she gasped, "Mystra, aid me . . ."

* * * * *

Prince Gartos struggled to his feet. He felt weak and sick inside and couldn't feel his feet at all . . . but they seemed to obey him. Grunting, he took a few unsteady steps and sat down, armor clanking. Narthil spun around him.

"Easy," he muttered, shaking his head. "Easy, now . . . " His men lay strewn along the road, with not a horse in sight. "Thaerin," he grunted, *"Aglos!"* Gartos extended his hand, watched the blade tug itself free of the dead woman and drift, dark and wet, to his waiting grasp. Young witch, who did she think she was to defy Athalantar's magelords? He fumbled at his gorget, got it aside, and grasped the amulet beneath, closing his eyes and trying to concentrate on the remembered face of Magelord Ithboltar. . . .

Firm fingers swept his aside. His eyes flew open, and he was staring up at the innkeeper's white, frightened face as she thrust a dagger into his throat and drew it firmly across. Blood sprayed. Prince Gartos struggled to swallow, could not, and tried to raise his blade. Its glowing runes dancing before his eyes, mocking him, were the last things he saw as he sank down into darkness. . . .

*   *   *   *   *

"Gartos will see that this sorceress dies," Briost said firmly, and a smile slowly crossed his face. "Eth will make sure he does."

"You're confident of Eth's abilities?" Undarl asked. The wizards seated around the table all looked down it to the high seat where the mage royal sat, in time to see his fire-red ring wink with sudden inner light.

Briost shrugged, wondering (not for the first time) just what powers slept in that ring. "He has proven himself able . . . and prudent . . . thus far."

"This was a testing, though, wasn't it?" Galath asked excitedly.

"Of course," Briost replied in a voice dry with patience. Why, he thought privately, did there always have to be one eager puppy at these meetings? Surely work could be found for such as Galath on these evenings—teaching him to unroll a scroll, perhaps, or put on his own robes so the hood was to the back and the tabard facing front? Anything would suffice, so long as it kept him far away. . . .

Galath leaned forward eagerly. "Has he reported in?"

Nasarn the Hooded snorted and looked coldly down the table. "If every mageling we set to a task did that, our ears'd be ringing with their babble every moment of the day—and all night, too!" With his unblinking stare, sharp nose, and dusty black robes, the old man resembled a vulture sitting and watching prey that would soon come its way.

Undarl nodded. "I'd not expect a magelord to waste magic on bothering his fellows just for idle chatter; a report should come only if something serious is amiss . . . if the intruding mage should prove to be a spy for another realm, for instance, or the leader of an invading army."

Galath flushed in embarrassment and looked away from the mage royal's calm face. Several of the other magelords let him see smiles of amusement on their faces as he looked swiftly and involuntarily up and down the table. Briost yawned openly as he smoothed one dark green sleeve of his robes and shifted into a more comfortable position in his chair. Alarashan, ever one to leap onto a popular cart, yawned too, and Galath's gaze fell to the table in front of him in misery.

"Your enthusiasm does you credit, Galath," Undarl Dragonrider added with a straight face. "If Eth asks us for aid or something befalls him, I assign you to act for us all in setting things to rights in Narthil."

Galath straightened with such swift and obvious pride, swelling visibly before their eyes, that more than one magelord at the table sputtered with swiftly repressed mirth. Briost rolled his eyes up to look at the ceiling and asked it silently if Galath knew how to open a spellbook, or if, presented with one, he'd peel it like a potato?

The stone vault overhead did not answer . . . but then, it had hung above this high chamber in Athalgard for almost a century, and had learned to be a patient ceiling.

* * * * *

The pain burned and roiled and threatened to sweep her away. In the darkening void, El clung grimly to the white light of her will. She must hold on, somehow. . . .

Pain surged as the enchanted blade shifted and then slid smoothly—oh, so smoothly, *in her own blood!*—out of her, leaving her feeling empty and . . . open. Violated. Faerun should not see her innards like this, hot blood rushing out of her into the sun . . . but she could do nothing, nothing at all to stop its flow. Her hands moved a bit, she thought, as she tried to clutch at her wound, but now the light and sounds around her were fading, and she was getting colder. Sinking, sinking into a void that was everywhere around her, scornful of her failing life-force . . . and as cold as ice.

Elmara gasped and tried to gather her will. The white radiance she'd always been able to summon flickered feebly before her, like a watchfire in the night. She thrust herself forward into it, enfolding it and clinging to it, until she was adrift in a white haze.

The pain was less, now. Someone seemed to be moving her, rolling her gently over . . . for a moment panic soared within her as the movement shook her hold on the radiance and it seemed to slip from under her. . . . El clawed at the void with her will until the white light surrounded her again.

Something—a voice?—echoed around her, eddying softly and crying afar like a trumpet, but she couldn't make out the words . . . if there were any. The void around seemed to grow darker, and El clung fiercely to her light. It seemed to grow in brightness, and from far away she heard that voice cry out in surprise and draw away, babbling in fear, or was it awe?

She was alone, adrift in a sea of light . . . and out of the pearly mists ahead something she knew swam up to embrace her. Dragonfire! Raging flames framing a street she knew well, and Elmara tried to cry out.

Prince Elthryn stood in the midst of blazing Heldon, the dancing flames gleaming on his mirror-polished black boots, and brandished the Lion Sword, whole and flashing back the flames. He turned, long hair swirling, and looked at Elmara. "Patience, my child."

Then smoke and flames swirled between them, and although she cried her father's name loud and desperately, she saw Elthryn no more, but instead a high hall of stone where cruel mages in rich robes bent over an ornate scrying-bowl held up by three winged maidens of glossy-polished gold. One was Undarl Dragonrider, the mage royal who'd destroyed Heldon. Another mage was passing his hand over the waters, waving his fingers angrily. "Where *is* he?" he snarled . . . and seemed for just an instant to see Elmara. His eyes narrowed, and then widened—but that chamber whirled and spun away into the void of light, and Elmara was suddenly staring into the eyes of Mystra, who stood in the air in front of her, smiling, her arms open to embrace.

Stumbling in haste, Elmara ran across unseen ground toward her. Tears welled up and burst forth. "Lady Mystra!" she sobbed. "Mystra!" The light around the goddess dimmed, and the smiling Lady of Mysteries was fading . . . fading. . . .

"*Mystra!*" El reached out desperately, tears blurring the darkening scene. She was falling . . . falling . . . into the void once more, chilled and whimpering, alone, her light gone.

She was dying. Elmara Aumar must be dead already, her spirit wandering until it fled and faded . . . but no! In the dark, floating distance El saw a tiny light sparkle and flare—and then rush toward her, bright and spinning. She cried out in wonder and fear as the blinding brightness leapt at her and flooded around her once more. Mystra's smile seemed to be all around her, too, warm and comforting, infinitely wise.

Through thinning mists Elmara saw another vision: she rose from her knees in prayer to Mystra and turned to a table where a large, ornately bound tome lay, surrounded by small items that she recognized as spell components. She sat, opened the spellbook, and began to study . . . mists roiled up, and when they cleared again, El saw herself casting a spell and then watching as a ball of flames burst into bright being in front of her. A fireball? That was a spell wizards commanded, not priestesses. . . .

The mists of light swirled and then parted again, revealing shapes of fire burning, endless and immobile, in emptiness. El stared at them. These fires were magic . . . and familiar. She stared at their coils and leaping tongues of fire . . . and—aye! These were the spells she'd memorized earlier, hanging in her own mind waiting to be released!

Yes, a warm and mighty voice said, echoing all round her, and added, *Watch.* One of the fires moved suddenly, writhing and twisting like a snake unfolding. It flared in sudden brilliance— too bright to watch, even as the voice said, *do thus, and behold!*

The fire flared up and was gone, leaving the white mists around a flickering amber. Elmara felt suddenly better, as if tension and pain had lessened . . . and at the same time, the weight in her mind eased, as if a spell had passed from memory.

Again, said the mind-voice of Mystra. Another flame writhed, opened, and flared up. At its passing Elmara felt stronger and more at ease from pain, and hung basking in the growing warmth of the now-golden mists.

Do this yourself now, the voice said, and El trembled in sudden awe and nervousness. She knew somehow that a slip could tear her mind apart . . . but the flames were unfolding, coiling, as her will surged through her and out to guide them. Brighter, now . . . aye! Thus, and—'tis done!

A golden radiance seemed to roll outward through the mists as the fires of the spell dissipated. Elmara felt stronger, as if the pain that numbness had shielded from her was suddenly gone, falling away from her like a tattered cloak that has split asunder . . . and the burning weight of spells in her mind eased again.

Mystra had shown her how to turn her memorized spells into healing energy and guide that raw force to work her own restoration. Hanging in the bright amber mind-void, El gasped

at the beauty and intricacy of the process . . . the chill darkness
seemed far away now. She found she could identify particular
spells if she stared at the flames long enough. She floated, con-
sidering, the remaining pain like an aching mantle around her,
until she'd chosen the least useful magic.

To spend it was the act of but a brief moment now, and the
pain eased still more. She was going to live!

With that thought, El found herself wanting to rise—and
then she was in motion, ascending smoothly through golden
mists into the light. . . .

There was a sudden rocking burst of noise and radiance.
Through a swimming golden haze she could see clouds in the
bright blue sky of morning—and darker and nearer, a ring of
gawking faces, staring openmouthed at her. El recognized the
anxious face of Asmartha the innkeeper, and smiled up at her.

"A-Aye," she said, finding her voice thick with blood, "I live."

There was more than one shriek, and gaps appeared abruptly
in the circle of heads. El smiled thinly . . . but her heart swelled
when the innkeeper matched her smile, and stretched down one
strong hand to touch her.

"I saw it," the woman said, voice husky in wonder. "You were
dead—cut open like a slaughtered hog—and now are whole. The
gods are *real* . . . they must be. I saw you heal, right in front of
me. The gods were *here!*"

Asmartha's face broke into a wide, wild laugh, and tears ran
down her face. She traced El's cheek with a gentle finger, shook
her head, and said, "I've never seen the like. What god smiles on
you, lady?"

"Mystra," Elmara said. "Great Mystra." She struggled to sit
up, and there were suddenly strong arms at her shoulders, helping her. "I am a priestess of the Lady of Mysteries," El told the
innkeeper—and then, as a sudden realization came to her, added
slowly, "Yet I must learn to be more."

"Lady?"

"If I am to battle magelords and their armsmen, face to face
and spell to spell," El said softly, frowning, "I must become a
mage in truth."

"You're *not* a sorceress?"

Elmara shook her head. "Not yet." Perhaps never, she
thought suddenly, if I can't find a wizard willing to train me . . .
and where in the world could she find one to trust? Not in Athalantar, where every sorcerer was a magelord . . . nor in the Calishar. There must be wizards in the other lands around, aye, but
where to start looking?

Wh—Braer. Of course. Go to the High Forest and ask her teacher. Whatever he said, it would be an answer she could trust. "I must leave," El said, scrambling to her feet.

The world wavered and swam around her, and she swayed, but one of the men of Narthil put a steadying hand on her shoulder, and she stayed upright. "The magelords can find me with their spells," El said urgently. "Every moment I stay here, I endanger ye all." She drew a deep, shuddering breath, and then another, reaching into the mists to uncoil another flame.

Asmartha drew back a pace as Elmara stiffened, and glowing white light emanated from her. Then it faded, and the innkeeper saw that the young, hawk-nosed woman stood at ease despite her blood-drenched clothing and the pale, drawn look on her face.

"My pack," she murmured, and turned back toward the inn. The innkeeper stepped hastily to her side to guard against her falling, but El smiled and said reassuringly, "I'm fine now . . . and happier than I've been in some time. Mystra smiles on me."

"That I can well believe," the stout woman said, as they went into the Rest. The door banged behind them.

* * * * *

Elmara walked off as she had come, alone, her pack on her back, heading northeast over the rolling fields. The innkeeper watched her march out of sight, hoping no ill would befall her. Once Asmartha had dreamed of a life of adventure, seeing all the fabled sights of Faerun and befriending elves . . . and there went a lass who'd done just that.

The innkeeper smiled at the crest of a far-off hill as the tiny dark figure of her guest disappeared over it. She shook her head. Perhaps the gods would smile enough on the reckless maid to keep her alive through her fight against the mighty magelords, and she'd come back to Narthil one day with time enough to spare to tell a fat and aging innkeeper where she'd gone and what she'd seen . . . but more likely that would never happen.

Asmartha sighed, wiped her hands absently on her apron, and went back into the Rest. She'd best stir some of the men to drag those bodies away, or the whole street'd stink by nightfall, and beasts'd come down into Narthil to feed.

* * * * *

And so, a grumbling goodman of Narthil found himself bend-

ing over the dead prince. He reached out to take the warrior's
sword for his own—and then hissed in fear, stumbling backward. The sword shivered, moving by itself. The runes on the
steel pulsed and rippled with sudden light. Then the blade rose
from the ground as if taken up by unseen hands, hung for a moment in front of the terrified townsman's eyes, and flew away,
sliding slow and smoothly through the air, point-first and
straight, like an arrow shot from a bow. Northeast it went, toward the grazing hills.

The man watched it go, swallowed, and muttered a prayer to
Tempus, Lord of Battles. What were things coming to, when
even swords held magic? And in the end, what good had that
fancy blade done this carrion at his feet? Nay, magic wasn't
something to be trusted, ever. The townsman looked down. The
dead warrior stared unseeing at the sun. The townsman shook
his head, spat on his hands, and took hold of the Athalantan's
feet. Hmm . . . the blade might be gone—but those boots, now?

Unseen, the enchanted blade crested a certain hill and flew
on, northeast. A spell from afar was bidding it rejoin the being
whose blood it had last spilled, a young sorceress hitherto un-
known to the magelords. A woman who defied armsmen, heralds, magelords, and princes of Athalantar alike—and for that,
she must die. The blade flew on, seeking blood.

Thirteen

SPELLS ENOUGH TO DIE

*Think on this, arrogant mageling: even the mightiest archmage
has no spells strong enough to let him cheat death. Some take the
road of lichdom . . . a living death. The rest of us find graves, and
our dust is no grander than that of the next man. So when next
you lord it over some farmer with your fireballs, remember: we all
master spells enough to die.*

> Ithil Sprandorn, Lord Mage of Saskar
> said to the prisoner wizard Thorstel
> Year of the Watching Wood

Flamerule had been warm and wet in this Year of Bloodflow-
ers, and if the gods sent rain sparingly in the fall, a plentiful har-
vest could be expected all down the River Shining.

Phaernos Bauldyn, keeper of the Ambletrees Arms, leaned
against his doorpost and watched the last light of the setting sun
fade over the hills to the west. A beautiful land, this . . . though
he'd be happier if it weren't ruled by wizards who swaggered
wherever they went, treating folk as slaves or cattle . . . or worse.

He sighed. So long as they didn't get foolish or arrogant
enough to face the elves of the High Forest spell to spell or of-
fended some god sorely enough to all be struck down on the spot,
there was no way he could see that Athalantar would ever be
free of the magelords. Phaernos frowned, sighed again, and
turned back for his candle. It was fast growing dark now. He
reached up, with the ease of long habit standing clear of the
dripping wax, and lit the over-door lamp. As he drew the candle
down and blew it out, he saw her coming wearily up the road to
his door: a lone girl, tall, dark haired, slim, and drenched, with
her clothes clinging to her and her sodden cloak trailing river
water behind.

"Fall in, lass?" he asked, coming forward to offer his arm.

"I had to swim the river," she replied shortly, and then raised
her head and smiled at him. She was thin and hollow-eyed, but
her blue-gray eyes were keen and bright above a sharp nose.

Phaernos nodded as he turned to lead the way in. "A bed for
the night?"

"If I can get dry by a fire," she answered, "but my coins are few. Are ye master of this house?"

"I am," Phaernos said, pulling open the wide front door. His guest peered at the old shields nailed to it and seemed almost amused.

"Why d'you ask?" he asked her as they came into the low-beamed taproom. A few farmers and village folk were sitting by the fire, cradling tankards of ale and mugs of broth. They looked up with mild interest.

"I can pay ye with spells," the wet girl said calmly.

Phaernos drew away from her in the sudden silence and said shortly, "We haven't much use for mages hereabouts. Most wizards in this land don't use their magic to help anyone but themselves."

"Then their magic should be stripped from them," she replied.

"And just how d'ye think anyone could do *that*, lass?" one of the drunker farmers demanded from his seat by the fire.

"Take their lives swift enough, and they've seldom any will left to work spells, I've found," the woman said calmly. "I'm no friend of magelords." The silence that followed her words was broken only by the faint, steady drip of river water from her clothes.

No one bothered her—or even spoke to her—after that. Phaernos led her wordlessly into the kitchen, pointed her to a bench by the hearth-fire, and brought her a cloak. The kitchen-women bustled over with rags for her to scrub dry with and food to eat, but then went on about their business. Elmara welcomed the peace; she was exhausted. Two hills away from Narthil, she'd made the mistake of using a spell that took her in a single step from where she'd stood to the most distant hilltop she could see. The magic had drawn on her own energy to do its work, leaving her exhausted. After that, the swim across the river hadn't helped—and it'd left her too chilled to just roll herself in her cloak and go to sleep in the open.

Elmara dried off as best she could, wrapped herself in the cloak, and dozed off, dreaming of shivering in a dripping hedge while magelords in the shape of wolves howled and bounded past, seeking her with sharp and hungry jaws agape.

It was much later when, at a gentle touch, she awoke; the innkeeper was bending over her. His guest tensed and looked up alertly as if she might spring up in a moment to give battle or flee.

Phaernos gazed down at her expressionlessly and said, "The house is closed for the night and the drinkers've gone home . . .

you're the only guest to sleep here tonight. Tell me your name, and what you meant about . . . paying me with magic." At his words, two of the women drew nearer to listen.

"I'm Elmara," his guest said, "a traveler from afar. I'm no mage, but I can work a few spells. Would ye like a larger storage cellar?"

Phaernos looked at her silently for a breath or two, and then the beginnings of a smile crept onto his face. "A larger cesspit would be more useful."

"I can do that, or both," Elmara said, rising, "if ye'll let me sleep here this night."

Phaernos nodded. "Done, lady . . . if you'll come with me, I'll show you a bed where no magelord will find you."

The woman gave him a sharp look and asked softly, "What d'ye know of me?"

The innkeeper shrugged. "Nothing . . . but a friend asked me to watch out for Elmara, if she should pass this way."

"Who was this friend?"

"He goes by the name of Braer," answered the innkeeper, looking steadily into her eyes.

El smiled and relaxed, her shoulders slumping wearily. "Show me the cellar and the pit first," she said. "It may befall that I'll have to slip away before daybreak."

Phaernos nodded again, saying nothing, and they went out together. As the door swung closed, the two kitchen-women exchanged looks—and with one accord made the warding sign against Tyche's disfavor, and turned back to their dishes.

In the morning, Elmara awoke to find her wet things had been dried and hung, and atop her battered pack sat a cloth bundle. It proved to contain sausage, dried fish, and hard bread. She smiled, dressed swiftly, and went out, to find the innkeeper slumped asleep in a chair by the bedchamber door, an old sword across his knees.

Swallowing to drive down the sudden lump in her throat, Elmara slipped down the stairs and out by the kitchen door, past the cesspit and into the trees behind. Perhaps it would have been wiser not to have said anything about magelords or spells last night . . . but she'd been wet and exhausted, and it was done.

It would be best to be well away from Ambletrees before any word of a sorceress spread. Elmara kept to the trees as long as possible before stepping out into the back fields, heading north toward Far Torel. She took care to keep well out of sight of the road. Phaernos had said many armsmen had marched up it this last tenday, gathering for he knew not what—an attack on the elves of the High Forest, he half-hoped and half-feared.

Elmara doubted the magelords would risk themselves as the innkeeper hoped. No, they'd more likely order the woods set afire, and tell their armsmen to use crossbows to fell any elves who came to fight the flames. She sighed and strode on. She might have to spend years slipping across Athalantar like a shadow, evading the clutches of the wizards and their swaggering armsmen while learning all she could of what magelords ruled where. If she were ever to avenge her parents and free the realm, she'd have to find some way to fell a few of the stronger magelords in the backlands so watching eyes would be fewer and she could make their deaths seem the work of enemy magelords or ambitious apprentices.

Perhaps she could seduce a magelord to gain his confidence and learn all he knew before destroying him. Elmara sighed, came to a thoughtful halt for a moment, and then went on. Not only did the idea make her stomach heave, she hadn't the faintest idea of how to act enticing . . . enough that a wizard who could have any maid he wanted would spare her more than a passing glance. A spell to change her shape might be noticed, and she wasn't particularly beautiful. She slowed her customary brisk stride and swayed her hips, gliding along with the lynxlike allure of an evening-lass she'd once seen in Hastarl, and then burst into high, helpless laughter at the very feel of it, shaking her head at how she must look.

Creep up on magelords like a thief, then. . . . Aye, that she still knew how to do, though this lighter, softer body, with its breasts and hips, balanced differently and lacked some of the strength she'd had as a man. She'd need to practice skulking again.

Soon, she thought suddenly. If Far Torel was an armed camp, they'd have patrols and watchers . . . and she'd blunder right into them if she went on walking in the open without a care. On the other hand, if she were seen, someone skulking along would look suspicious indeed, where a traveler who trudged openly would not. Time to walk in and embrace doom again, Elmara thought to herself and smiled wryly. Out of habit she glanced all around, and so saved her life one more time.

A gleaming rune-carved sword was speeding through the air toward her from behind, a sword she'd never forget. The horrible memory of her impalement flashed into her mind, and through the steely taste of fear that rose into her mouth, Elmara shouted the words she'd never forget. "Thaerin! Osta! Indruu hathan *halarl!*"

The blade shivered to a halt, turned aside, and darted uncertainly around in the trees. It reached an open space as El watched, her thoughts racing desperately, and then slowly turned until its glittering point was toward her again.

As the blade leapt at her face, she stammered out the only prayer to Mystra she had left that might work.

"Namaglos!" she shouted its last word desperately—and the blade burst into flashing shards right in front of her. Elmara shuddered in relief and sank to her knees, discovering that tears were running down her cheeks. In angry haste she wiped them away and gasped the words of another prayer.

Tyche smiled upon her, too, it seemed. There was no magelord near. This blade must have been sent after her by someone back in Narthil, or even a wizard distant from that town, perhaps in Athalgard. Whatever its origin, there was no magical scrying upon her, and no intelligent being within spell-sight.

El thanked both goddesses because it seemed the right thing to do, then rose from her knees and went on cautiously. Perhaps she'd best seek a place to hide and pray to Mystra for spells.

* * * * *

Othglar spat thoughtfully into the night, shifted his aching behind on the stump, and then grunted in sudden impatience and got to his feet, kicking at the air to ease the stiffness in his legs. These wizards were all crazed—who in Athalantar would dare to attack almost four thousand swords? Out here in the proverbial chill back of beyond, too, weary miles of marching away from Hastarl and the lower river posts.

Othglar shook his head and walked to the edge of the stone bluff, looking down. Scores of campfires glimmered in the vale below. He reflected on how depressingly familiar they looked as he scratched at his ribs, spat into the night, and then unlaced his codpiece, leaning his halberd against a tree.

He was thoughtfully watering the unseen trees below when someone gave his halberd back to him, swinging it hard into his ear. Othglar's head snapped to one side, and he toppled forward into the night without a sound.

A slim hand propped the halberd back where it had been as the brief, rolling thudding of the guard's landing began, far below.

The owner of the hand drew her dark cloak around herself against the chill of the night and peered out at the same view Othglar had been so unimpressed with. Elmara's mage-sight found only three small points of blue light—possibly enspelled daggers or rings. None was near, or moving about.

Good. She counted campfires and sighed soundlessly. There were enough armsmen here to start a war against the elves that might ruin both Athalantar and the High Forest. She must act . . . and that meant using one of the most powerful, lengthy, and dangerous prayers she knew.

Crawling cautiously on hands and knees, Elmara found a hollow a little way down the cliff, a place where someone coming to the guard's post wouldn't immediately fall over her. She knelt in it and undressed, putting everything that had metal in or about it in her pack, and then setting her pack well back behind her.

She faced the campfires, softly whispered a supplication to Mystra, spread bare feet for better balance, and began her spell.

Taking up the least favored of her several daggers, she pricked the palms of both her hands so they bled and held the dagger out horizontally before her, pinioned between her bloody palms.

As she murmured the incantation, she could feel blood running down to drip off her elbows and strength ebbing out of her as it was stolen by the spell.

Trembling with weakness, Elmara held the dagger up higher so it gleamed in the moonlight and watched it darken and begin to crumble. When it dissolved into rusty shards, she brushed off her hands and sank down, satisfied. Before dawn, every piece of metal between her and the forest would be useless, powdery rust. That would give the magelords something to think about. If they decided elven magic was the cause, the attack on the High Forest might never come.

Elmara curled her hands into fists and stared up at the moon as she whispered another prayer to Mystra, to heal her slashed flesh. It did not take long, but she was numb with weariness when she was done. She turned back to her pack. Put on cloak and boots, at least, and then best be gone from here, before . . .

"Oho! What've we here, eh?"

The voice was rough but delighted, pitched low so as not to carry far. "Heh," it chuckled, as its owner reached out of the night-shadows by the trees to clutch her firmly by the arm, "I c'n see why Othglar was in no great hurry to report in . . . come here, lass, and give us a kiss."

Elmara felt herself dragged into an embrace. The unseen lips that kissed her were ringed by rough, prickly stubble, but when she could breathe again she did not pull away. At all costs, she must keep this man from raising the alarm.

"Oh, yesss," she moaned, the same way that girl in Hastarl had done so long ago. "He sleeps, now, leaving me so *lonely*. . . ."

"Ho-*ho!*" the armsman chuckled again. "Truly, the gods smile tonight!" His arms tightened around her.

El fought down a rush of panic and murmured, "Kiss me again, Lord." As those bristled lips sought her own, Elmara put one arm around the corded muscles of his back, shuddered at the taste of the horrible ale the guard had been drinking—and found what she'd been seeking: the dagger sheathed at his belt. She slid the blade free and held the man's lips with her own as she swung the hilt of the dagger as hard as she could against his head.

The armsman made a surprised sound and fell away from her, landing heavily in the brush. The hilt of the dagger was wet and sticky; Elmara fought down a sudden urge to be sick and threw the weapon down. Rolling the senseless man across the rock was hot work, even naked as she was. "Ye were *great*," she hissed fiercely in his ear as she rolled him over the edge.

Her cloak was around her and her pack on her back by the time she heard the body crash through branches below and start to roll.

El stepped into her boots and carefully went forward onto soft moss before she stamped them firmly onto her feet. Then she crept into the darkness, heading back the way she'd come, hoping no new guardposts or patrols had been set. She'd a few spells left, aye, but scarce the strength to stand and cast them. She dare not try to go through this encamped army to reach the forest—elven patrols might slay her before they knew who she was, even if by some gods-sent miracle she got past all the armsmen.

No, 'twould be best to go back to the place of the goddess, that little pool, and seek Braer from there. It lay well west of here. . . .

Stumbling with weariness, Elmara made her slow way down through the night, wondering how far she'd get before she passed out. It would be interesting to see. . . .

* * * * *

By the end of her second day in the loft, Elmara was still as weak as a newborn kitten. She'd fallen twice on the ladder, and finally struggled up here hissing in pain from a bruised or broken forearm. It was healed now, but the working of that prayer had left her with a splitting headache and a sick, empty feeling within, and she'd lain dreaming for a long time.

She didn't feel ready to move even yet. "Mystra, watch over me," she murmured, and sank again into slumber. . . .

* * * * *

"Gods above!"

The awe-struck voice jerked her awake. Elmara turned her head.

The bearded head of an astonished farmer was staring at her from an arm's reach away, a candle-lantern trembling in his hand. She struggled not to laugh at his expression; she supposed she'd look something like that if she found a lass wearing only a cloak and boots and lying in *her* hay-loft. He handled it well, she thought.

As she burst into helpless giggles, he wiped a hand nervously across his mouth, found it was open, closed it, and cleared his throat with the same sort of sound sheep made in the meadow above Heldon. Fresh giggling seized Elmara.

The farmer blinked at her, clearly finding her mirth almost as startling as her presence, and said, "Uh . . . er . . . aghumm. Fair even, uh . . . lass."

"Fair fortune to this farm and all in it," she said formally, rolling over to face him. Redness stole across his face, and he dragged his eyes reluctantly away and hastily descended the ladder.

Oh, aye—*these*. Elmara pulled the cloak over herself and rolled up to one knee to peer over the edge of the loft. The farmer looked up at her as if he expected her to change shape of a sudden into some sort of forest cat and leap down on him. He caught up a pitchfork and brandished it uncertainly.

"Wh-Who are you, lass? How came you here? Are . . . are you . . . all right?"

The slim, sharp-nosed lady smiled wanly down at him, and said, "I am an enemy of the magelords. Hide me, if you will."

The farmer stared at her in horror, gulped, drew himself up, and said, "Ye'll be as safe here as I can make it." Then he added awkwardly, "If there's anything I . . . or my men . . . can do . . . uh, we daren't fight them, with their magic an' all. . . ."

Elminster smiled at him. "Ye've given me shelter and friendly words, and for me that's enough. It's all most of us need, and lack, in Athalantar."

The man grinned up at her suddenly, as delighted and proud as if she'd knighted him, and shifted his feet. "Be back, Lady," he said hesitantly.

"Tell *no one* I'm here!" Elmara hissed urgently.

The farmer nodded vigorously and went out. Not long after, he returned with a cup of fresh milk, an end of bread, and a slab of cheese.

"Did anyone see ye?" Elmara asked, chin on the edge of the loft.

The farmer shook his head. "Think you I want armsmen or magelords crawling all over my farm, burning down what they don't tear apart, and using magic to make me tell things? No fear, lass!"

Elmara thanked him. He didn't see her hand, glowing with gathered fire inside her cloak, fade again to its normal appearance. "Gods keep ye this night," she said huskily, moved.

The man shifted his feet, bowed a little in embarrassment, and answered, "An' ye, lass. An' ye." He gave her the raised-hand salute that men in fields use, one to another, and hurried out.

When he was gone, Elmara clutched the cloak to her and stared out the loft window, eyes very bright. She watched the moon riding high in the sky, and thought about . . . many things.

She was gone from there before dawn—just in case.

* * * * *

Her way west had been swift, as she fled to get well away from any report of her. Far Torel was emptying of troops, the armsmen returning to safer posts to the south. It seemed the magelords' plans to spill elven blood were abandoned . . . for now at least. That news gave Elmara great satisfaction as she went, earning blisters she healed when she could bear them no more.

She traveled mainly at dawn and at dusk, across country. When she turned north toward Heldon, she found her way blocked by several encampments of armsmen, and a band of magelings being trained by several watchful magelords—and with a weary sigh, decided to go west into the Haunted Vale, and try to reach the High Forest from that direction. She'd never thought fighting magelords would involve so much *walking*. . . .

* * * * *

It was late one day when she found battle again. She trudged up a hill, frowned curiously at a trampled, fresh-broken gap in a farm fence, and went through it. The field was empty, but the hilltop in the field beyond it was a crowded place. A large band of Athalantan armsmen stood in a large ring about a lone figure— a woman in robes—firing at her with crossbow quarrels.

A farmer stood leaning on a stout cane at the gate where the two fields met. His lips quivered in anger as he watched, eyes

blazing. He turned his head like an angry lion as Elmara came
up beside him, and put out his cane to block her path.

"Stay back, lass," he warned. "Yon dogs are out for blood—
and they won't care who they slay. They'd not have dared when I
was younger, but the gods and the passing years have taken all
from me but my smart mouth and this farm. . . ."

The woman on the hilltop knew sorcery; crossbow quarrels
were bounding aside from unseen shields, and she was conjuring
small balls of fire, and hurling them to consume some of the
bolts leaping at her. Her shoulders sagged in weariness, and
when she tossed long, tangled hair out of her eyes, the movement was tired. The armsmen were wearing her down fast.

Elmara patted the old man's arm, stepping around his cane—
and strode briskly off into the field, heading for the ring of armsmen. As she approached, a bolt took the sorceress through the
shoulder. The woman reeled and then fell to her knees with a
sob, clutching at the dark, spreading stain where the quarrel
protruded.

"Take her," the battlelord outside the ring snapped, waving at
his warriors with one imperious gauntlet.

The armsmen rushed in, but the sorceress was muttering
something and gesturing hastily with one bloody hand. The trotting soldiers slowed, and one slumped bonelessly to the trodden
turf, followed by another. Then a third, and a fourth.

"Back!" the battlelord roared. "Back, before she has all of you
asleep!" When the armsmen were back in an unsteady ring,
leaving many of their fellows sprawled on the ground, the commander glared around at them, and snarled, "Shoot her down,
then. Bows ready!"

The sorceress knelt with bleak eyes, watching helplessly as
crossbows were wound, loaded, and made ready all around her.

Elmara sat down hastily on the muddy ground and spoke one
of the most powerful prayers she had, timing it carefully.

"Loose!"

At the battlelord's command, the armsmen let fly their quarrels, and Elmara bent forward, eyes blazing, to watch her spell
take hold. Abruptly the battlelord was standing in the midst of
the ring, and the sorceress was slumped on the ground where
he'd stood, outside it. A score of bolts thudded home. Not a few
pierced the opulent armor and found the face that the raised
visor did not cover. The battlelord staggered, roared, transfixed
by many shafts, lifted his hand—and then slowly toppled onto
his face, and lay still.

The armsmen were still gaping at the body of their commander when Elmara's hasty second prayer-spell took effect. All around the field, armor glowed a dull red, and men began to grunt, squirm, and cry out, dancing in frantic haste and clawing at their armor.

Hotter it glowed, and hotter. Men were screaming now. The stink of burning flesh and hair joined the metallic reek as armsmen flung their armor desperately in all directions, howling and rolling about naked in the field.

Elmara turned and walked back to the farmer. He flinched at her approach, clutching his cane up in front of his chest like a warding weapon, but stood his ground.

"Ye should be able to deal with them now," she said calmly, looked back at all the writhing, shrieking men, and added, "I fear I've ruined much of your planting."

From empty air she plucked a handful of gems, put them into the astonished old man's hand, and embraced him. Into one large and hairy old ear she murmured, "Ye seem a good man. Try to stay alive; I'll need thy service when this land is mine." Then she turned away.

Darrigo Trumpettower stood with the gems glittering in his hand like so many fallen tears, and stared after her.

The slim woman in the tattered cloak strode off across the field, walking west. The bleeding sorceress floated along in the air behind her, as if she were being towed on an invisible, weightless bed.

Only one armsman moved to stop her, winding his bow into readiness, loading it, and setting it to his shoulder. He felt the hand that struck his bow aside but never felt the stout cane that smashed him to the ground, or anything else. His quarrel leapt toward the sun, and no one saw whether it reached there or not.

Darrigo Trumpettower stood fierce-eyed over the dead armsman and growled, "At least I can be proud of *something* before I die. Come on then, Wolves! Come and cut down an old man, and tell yerselves what mighty heroes ye are!"

* * * * *

This was the time to use a prayer she'd always wanted to try but had never found the right occasion for. Mystra's dictates were quite strict: her priestesses could never call on her for their own benefit, and Braer had warned her how few riches he'd made ready for her to call on. Yet she felt that now was the right time.

The bloodstanch litany was not one Elmara used often, so she had to take time to pray to the goddess for it. Night had come to

the Haunted Vale when Elmara took the fallen sorceress in her
arms and said the words of her last useful prayer, the one that
would transport them both to the only enclosed refuge she could
think of: the cave below the meadow, overlooking ruined Heldon.

As the moon-drenched hills vanished and familiar earthy
darkness was suddenly all around, Elmara smiled wearily. She'd
never heard of a female magelord, nor were armsmen likely to
dare turn on one. If this lady sorceress lived, she could be the
teacher and ally El would need in her fight to free Athalantar.

"All alone, I cannot defeat the magelords," she murmured, ad-
mitting it at last. "Gods above know, I can barely deal with one
enchanted sword!"

* * * * *

Much later, Elmara sighed despairingly. The sorceress hadn't
awakened, and her newly healed flesh felt burning hot under
El's fingers. Had the crossbow bolt been poisoned? El's prayers
had melted that dart away, stopped the bleeding, and drawn together the woman's torn shoulder . . . but in truth, she knew few
healing charms—the prayers Mystra gave her faithful included
many barriers and spells that blasted foes apart and hurled
things down, but were shy on magics that mended and healed.

Still unconscious, the woman lay on a bed of cloaks. Her
fevered flesh was drenched with sweat, and from time to time
she murmured things El couldn't catch, and moved her limbs
feebly about on the sodden cloaks. Her skin—even to her lips—
was bone-white.

Elmara's best efforts to gather her will and force healing into
the body of the sorceress failed utterly. El might be able to turn
memorized prayer-spells into healing energy for herself . . . but
Mystra hadn't given her the means to aid anyone else.

The sorceress was dying. She might last until morn or a little
longer, but . . . perhaps not. Elmara didn't even know her name.
The woman's body moved restlessly again, wet with a sheen of
sweat that returned however often El wiped it away.

Elmara stared at the woman she'd rescued, and wiped mois-
ture from her own forehead. She must do more, or she'd be shar-
ing her cave with a corpse in the morning. With sudden resolve,
she took the woman's purse—which held a good handful of
coins—and crawled out of the cave, casting a ward against
wolves across its mouth.

There had been a shrine to Chauntea, Mother of Farms and
Fields, south of Heldon. Perhaps for wealth enough the priest

who tended its plantings could be persuaded to come hence and
heal. It was too much to hope he'd keep his mouth closed about
the cave and the two women; whatever befell, she'd have to find
a new lair.

Elmara sighed grimly and hastened down from the meadow,
hurrying as much as she dared in the nightgloom. From days
when she'd played here often, her feet easily found gaps in the
trees. Just how long ago had those days been?

Then she was out of the trees, into the ruins of Heldon—
where she came to an abrupt halt. There were lights ahead:
torches burning where there should be none. Not moving as if
held by men searching for something, but held fast on high, as if
they blazed here always. What had befallen the ashes of Heldon?

Weariness gone, Elmara stole forward in cautious silence,
keeping to the deepest shadows. A palisade rose in front of her, a
dark wall that ran for a long way, enclosing—what? Looking
along it, she saw a helmed head at a corner where the wall
turned.

Carefully, El drew back, and retraced her steps in the night
until she found a certain boulder she'd climbed often as a child.
Shielded from anyone watching from the palisade, she cast a
spell that turned her into a silent, drifting shadow, and went to
the walls.

In this form, she could glide along swiftly, without worrying
about noise. She hurried around the walls. They enclosed a
square and were pierced by two gates. The gap under one of
them was large enough for her to pass in shadow-shape . . . and
she was inside. She reared up in the darkness of the wall and
looked around hastily. This spell did not last long, and she had
no desire to fight her way out of a camp defended by gods-alone-
knew how many aroused armsmen.

For there were armsmen here in plenty: two barracksful, at
least, by the look of things . . . guarding loggers, it seemed. Cut
timber lay piled everywhere; Elmara shook her head sourly. If
she were an angry elf-mage, one fireball over the palisade would
turn this torchlit camp into a huge funeral pyre. Perhaps someone should suggest it to them.

Later. She had work before her, as always. Where there are
lots of armsmen, there are always priests of Tempus, or Helm, or
Tyr, or Tyche, or all four . . . Tempus, at least.

The shadow scudded along behind the barracks and warehouses, seeking a corner where a sword would be standing upright in a wooden block as an altar. Ah . . . there. So where was
the priest? Elmara drifted toward the nearest building. Within

was a plain room hung with battered armor—trophies of Tempus, no doubt—and the unwashed man sleeping beneath them reeked of ale. If that was the priest, she thought in disgust, her venture here had failed, and she'd best be out and seeking the shrine to Chauntea before her spell ended.

But first . . . there was one splendid house in the center of the rest. The lair of the local magelords, doubtless, but she could hear a faint din of laughter and talk from this far off; perhaps they were drinking the night away . . . and a priest might be there.

The house had guards, but they were bored and resentful of the feasting within, and one soon strolled over to the other to share a jest. The shadow slipped through the spot where he'd stood and in at the door. Thence it ghosted past curtains and hurrying servants into a large, noisy room beyond.

A drifting globe of magical radiance competed with many candles to light up this grand chamber, which was crowded with men in rich robes and women in nothing but gems. All of this drunken company were lolling about on pillows and lounges, spilling as much wine as they were quaffing and talking far too loudly and grandly about what they'd do in the days and hours ahead, and how they'd do it.

To Elmara's magesight, the place was awash in the blue light of magic, but an inner room, partly visible past one of the many open doors at the back of the chamber, glowed even more brightly. Not wanting to risk her shadow-shape being stripped from her by some defensive spell or ward, or being seen by someone in the room who had the power to pierce spell-disguises, El glided swiftly around the edge of the feast and made for the beckoning doorway.

The room beyond the door was richly furnished and so overlaid by spells that it seemed one thick blue murk to Elmara's eyes. She stole quickly across the carpet and through an arch, into a bedchamber almost entirely filled by a huge canopied bed.

Now, if I were a mage and had lots of magic to hide, where would I . . . ? Under the bed, of course.

The skirts of the high bed were no barrier to a shadow, and the space within was almost another small room one could sit in. The blue glow was near blinding now, spilling from a chest and two coffers that sat beneath the bed. As Elmara bent forward to peer at them, her shadow-spell ran out, and she thumped down onto the dusty carpet on hands and knees. She froze, listening tensely—but there came no sound of alarm, or of anyone coming into the room.

The small coffer probably held gems and coins; the larger one and the chest were more likely to hold healing potions, if any were to be found here. There were apt to be some, if things she'd heard in Hastarl were true. With them, a magelord could rescue injured men and earn their gratitude, or bargain with them and force their service . . . and without them, a magelord could find himself at the mercy of priests and lesser men who might have healing magic, and could do the same to him.

Which chest or coffer held them, though? Elmara drew her dagger, and felt in the hair over her ear for one of the two lock-picks she still carried. A few deft turns and probes, and the lid of the coffer clicked once. She laid down on the floor beside the coffer, and carefully lifted the lid with the point of her dagger.

Nothing happened. Cautiously she raised her head to peer into it—and saw only coins. Bah!

She was working on the chest when someone came into the room—no, two people, a man who was laughing in anticipation and someone else. A maid for his pleasure, doubtless. The door slammed shut, and a bolt clacked into place.

The bed creaked just over Elmara's head. Ducking involuntarily, she pursed her lips and paused in her work on the lock. It would make a loud clicking sound when she forced it open.

She did not have to wait very long—when the man was roaring with laughter at his own jest, he made more than enough noise to drown out the sound of the chest opening. Unloading it onto the carpet while the couple bounced and rolled around on the bed just above her was a long, sweaty business, but Elmara's care was rewarded: along one side of the chest, under a robe that shimmered blue to her gaze with its own magic, were a row of metal tubes, each stoppered with a wax-sealed cork, and neatly labeled. One gave the power of flight, and the others were all for healing. Aye!

With a triumphant smile, El slid them into her boots and carefully repacked the chest, casting a longing look at the spell-book fastened into the lid. Nay; her task now was to begone from here, as fast as she could without raising an alarm.

Not so easily done. She could hardly hope to cast a spell right underneath a magelord—even a magelord in the throes of passion—without being heard.

And then she heard him grunt, above her head, and say, "Ahhh, yes, by all the gods! Now out, girl—out! I've work to do yet ere I sleep! Stay, mind—I'll be back out for you later!" The bolt was opened, and then the door, and then she heard both being put back again.

Elmara tensed under the bed. She had a few slaying spells—
but a sphere of flames is little use if one wants to survive a fight
in a small room . . . still less if one wants to do it without alerting
a fortress full of armed men.

She also had something smaller; a fleshflame. Hmmm.

And then the curtains in front of her were jerked aside, and a
kneeling man thrust his head in under the bed, seeking his
riches.

He stared in amazement at Elmara, as her hands shot out
and grasped his head by both ears, drawing her toward him.

"Greetings," she purred, murmured the few words that called
up the magic, and kissed him.

Flame spat from her parted lips into the incoherently struggling magelord. He stiffened, clutched at her convulsively, and
then sagged to the carpet, teeth clicking as his chin hit the floor.

Smoke drifted from the dead wizard's mouth and ears as she
dragged the chest over to him, opened it again, and left him
kneeling with his head in it. When he was found, perhaps they'd
think something inside it slew him.

Coolly, Elmara rose from under the bed. The door was closed
and bolted. Good. She ducked back under the bed, and took out
the spellbook. Flipping through it rapidly, she found the wizards'
spell she wanted.

It was very similar to the prayer-spell that Braer had taught
her. Kneeling with the book open before her, she prayed fer-
vently to the Lady of Mysteries.

Brightness seemed to flare inside her—and abruptly she was
standing just outside her ward in the meadow, the spellbook in
her hands. "Thanks be, Mystra," she told the stars, and went in.

* * * * *

The spicy scent of turtle soup wafted through the cave. Intent
on keeping it from burning, Elmara barely heard the faint voice
from behind her.

"Who—who are you?"

She turned to see the sorceress truly awake for the first time.
Large, hollow eyes stared into her own. The sorceress reached
up a hand to brush matted hair aside, and that hand trembled.
There must have been *something* on that crossbow quarrel. Even
with the potions, the sorceress had been a long time recovering.

Elmara went on stirring the soup with a long bone—all that
was left of a deer her spells had brought down days ago—and
said, "Elmara of Athalantar. I . . . worship Mystra." Those large

eyes held her own as if clinging to a last crumbling handhold, and El added, "And I will be a foe of the magelords of this realm until they are all dead, or I am."

The woman let out a long, shuddering breath, and leaned back against the wall of the cave. "Where—what place is this?"

"A cave in the north of Athalantar," El told her. "I brought ye here more than a tenday ago, after I rescued ye from armsmen in the Haunted Vale. How came ye to be there, in a ring of quarrels?"

The woman shrugged. "I . . . was newly arrived in Athalantar, and met with a patrol of armsmen. They fled, gathered more of their fellows, and came to slay me. From some things they said, it seems they're under orders to slay any wizards they meet who aren't magelords. I was tired and careless . . . and was overwhelmed."

She smiled and stretched out a hand to touch Elmara's own. "My thanks," she said softly, eyes very large and dark in her beautiful bone-white face. "I am Myrjala Talithyn, of Elvedarr in Ardeep. They call me 'Darkeyes.' "

Elmara nodded. "Soup?"

"Please," Myrjala said, sitting back against the cave wall. "I have been wandering," she said slowly, "in my dreams, and have . . . seen much."

Elmara waited, but the sorceress said no more, so she dipped a drinking-jack—all she had—into the soup, wiped its dripping flanks, and handed it to Myrjala. "What brought ye all the way to Athalantar?" she asked.

"I was riding overland to visit elven holds up the Unicorn Run when I first met with the armsmen, and they slew my horse. After, I walked to where you found me," Myrjala replied, and looked around. "Where am I now?"

"Above the ruins of Heldon," Elmara said simply, licking soup from her fingers.

Myrjala nodded, drank deep of the steaming soup, and shuddered at its heat. Then she raised her black, liquid eyes again to meet Elmara's gaze, and said, "I owe you my life. What can I give you in return?"

Elmara looked down at her hands, and found them trembling with sudden excitement. She looked up, and blurted, "Train me. I know some spells, but I'm a priestess, not a mage. I need to master sorcery in my own right, to hope to hurl spells well enough to destroy the magelords."

Myrjala's dark brows arched upward at El's last words, but she said only, "Tell me what you've mastered thus far."

Elmara shrugged. "I've learned to blast foes, and to use their anger against them. . . . I can create and hurl fire, and jump from place to place, take shadow-shape, and rust or master steel. But I know nothing of wise spell-strategies against a clear-headed foe, or the details of just what most wizards' spells do, or how one can best use one spell with another, or . . ."

Myrjala nodded. "You've learned much . . . most mages never even notice they lack such skills—and if someone dares point it out to them, they lash out in anger to slay the one who revealed it to them, rather than giving thanks."

She took another sip of soup and added, "Aye, I'll train you. Someone had better; there're wild wizards in plenty out roaming Faerun already. When you've come to trust me, you might tell me why you want to slay all the magelords in this land."

Elmara's thoughts raced. "Ah," she began, "I . . ."

Myrjala held up a restraining hand. "Later," she said with a smile. "When you're ready." She made a face, and added, "And when you've learned just how much salt to put into soup."

They laughed together then, for the first time.

Fourteen

NO GREATER FOOL

Know this, mageling, and know it well: there is no greater fool than a wizard. The greater the mage, the greater the fool, because we who work magic live in a world of dreams, and chase dreams . . . and in the end, dreams undo us.

Khelben "Blackstaff" Arunsun
Words To Would-Be Apprentices
Year of the Sword and Stars

Fire was born, swirling into furious life where the air had been empty moments before. Swiftly it grew in two places in the huge cavern, until Elmara's intent face was lit by two huge spheres of flame. A double-throated roar began, rising in tone and fury as the spinning spheres grew larger. El stared from one whirling conflagration to the other, sweat running down her face like water over rocks and dripping steadily from her chin. Across the chamber, Myrjala stood unmoving, watching expressionlessly. The twin fireballs grew even larger, seeming to pluck flames from the air as they rolled over and over.

"Now!" El whispered, more to herself than to her teacher, and brought her trembling arms together.

Obediently the two huge spheres of flame moved, pinwheeling across the cavern toward each other. Elmara took one careful pace backward without looking away from the flames, and then another. It was as well to be far away when the two fiery spheres—*touched!*

There was a blinding flash of light, as tortured tongues of flame leapt wildly out in all directions; the cavern rocked with the force of the mighty blast. Heat rolled over Elmara, and the force of the explosion smashed into her, plucked her from her feet and hurled her spinning back into—nothing. The fury of the blast roared past her, and slowly died away. El found herself floating motionless in midair as the echoes of the explosion boomed and rolled around her and rocks and dust fell on her from the unseen ceiling far above.

"Myrjala?" she asked the darkness anxiously. "Teacher?"

"I'm fine," a calm voice replied from very near at hand, and El felt herself turning in the air to look into the dark, intent eyes of the older sorceress, who was floating upright in midair beside her. Myrjala's bare body was as dusty and sweat-dewed as her own; around them, the cavern was still uncomfortably hot.

Myrjala leaned forward and touched El's arm. They began to descend. "To protect us both," she explained, "I had to spin my spell shield around you, then make it pull me into it; my apologies if I startled you."

El waved that away as they sank to the cavern floor together. "My apologies," she said, "for working too powerful an inferno for this space—"

Myrjala smiled, and dismissed those words with a wave of her own. "This was what I intended. You followed my instructions perfectly—something many apprentices never manage in twice the years of study you've had."

"I had experience in following dictates in my time as a priestess," Elmara said, settling to the still-warm stone floor.

Myrjala shrugged. "As much as any adventurer-priestess, perhaps. You were given a goal, and forged your own way toward it." She bent to pluck up her robe from the floor and mop her face with it. "True obedience is learned by folk who spend years drudging away at some endless task, with little hope of betterment or reward, following petty orders issued by small folk who've mastered the tyrant's whip or tongue without any real power to deserve such swagger."

"Was that thy experience?" El asked teasingly, and Myrjala rolled her eyes.

"More than once," she replied. "But seek not to divert my attention from your schooling—you can hurl spells as well as some archmages, but you've not yet mastered them all." She leaned forward, speaking earnestly. "One who has truly mastered sorcery *feels* each magic, almost as a living thing, and so can control its effects precisely, using it in original and unexpected ways or to modify the enchantments of others. I can tell when a pupil develops such a feel for a spell . . . and so far, you've acquired this intimate control over less than half the spells you cast."

Elmara nodded. "I'm not used to talking about magic in this way . . . but I understand ye. Say on."

Myrjala nodded. "When you revert to prayer, calling on Mystra to empower you, I see that attunement in every magic, but that's a feel for the goddess and the flow of raw spell-energy, not a mastery of the structure and direction of the unfolding magic."

"And how shall I acquire this mastery over all spells I use?"

"As always, there's only one way," Myrjala said, shrugging. "Practice."

"As in, 'practice until ye're sick of it,'" El said with a wry smile.

"*Now* you understand aright," Myrjala replied. Her answering smile was eager. "Let's see how well you can shape a chain lightning to strike and follow the light-spheres I'll conjure . . . green is untouched, and a change to amber means your lightning has found them."

Elmara groaned and gestured down at the bright rivulets of sweat on her dust-coated body. "Is there no rest?"

"Only in death," Myrjala replied soberly. "Only in death. Try not to remember that when most mages do . . . too late."

* * * * *

"Why have we come here?" Elmara asked, staring around into the chill, dank darkness. Myrjala laid a comforting hand on her arm.

"To learn," was all she said.

"Learn what, exactly?" El asked, looking around dubiously at inscriptions she could not read and strangely shaped stone coffers and chests of glassy-smooth stone that bristled with upswept horns. However odd the shapes she was seeing, she knew a tomb when she stood in one.

"When *not* to hurl spells and seek to destroy," Myrjala replied, voice echoing from a distant corner of the room. Motes of light suddenly danced and whirled in a cluster around her body—and when they died away, Myrjala was gone.

"Teacher?" El asked, more calmly than she felt. From the darkness near at hand there came an answer of sorts: inscriptions that had been mere dark grooves in the stone walls and floor filled with sudden emerald light. El turned to face them, wondering if she could puzzle some meaning out of these writings—and then, with a sudden touch of fear, saw wisps of radiance rising from them, thickening and coiling to coalesce into . . .

Elmara hastily readied her mightiest destroying spell—and paused, waiting tensely.

In front of her, the wraith of a man was building itself out of the empty air—tall, thin, and regal, robed in strange garb adorned with upswept horns like the chests, and standing on nothingness well above the rune-graven floor. Eyes that were two emerald flames fixed Elmara with a powerful, deeply wise gaze, and a voice spoke in her head. "Why have ye come to disturb my sleep?"

"To learn," El said quickly, not lowering her hands.

"Students seldom arrive with ready slaying spells," was the reply. "That is more often the style of those who come to steal." Vertical columns of emerald radiance suddenly leapt into being all over the chamber, and from the ceiling jumbled bones descended into each shaft of light, to drift therein lazily. A score or more skulls stared at Elmara. She looked at them and then back at the wraith.

"These are what remains of thieves who've come here?"

"Indeed. They came seeking some glorious treasures of Netheril . . . but the only treasure that lies here is myself." The voice paused, and the wraith drifted a little nearer. "Does this change the purpose of thy visit?"

"I have been a thief, but I did not come here hoping to bear anything away but lessons," Elmara replied.

"I shall let ye keep that much," the cold voice replied.

"Let me keep lessons? Ye can deny them?"

"Of course. I mastered magic in Thyndlamdrivvar . . . not as the wizards of today seem to, plucking spells from tombs or foolish tutors the same way small boys steal apples from others' trees."

"Who are ye?" El whispered, eyes straying to watch the skulls drift and dance.

"I now go by the name of Ander. Before I passed into this state, I was an archwizard of Netheril—but the city where I lived and the great works I wrought seem to have all vanished 'neath the claws of passing years. So much for striving . . . and there's a valuable lesson for ye to bear away, mageling."

El frowned. "What have ye become?"

"I have passed beyond death by means of my art. I understand from such conversations as these—so my knowledge may be clouded by untruths said to me—that all the wizards of today can manage is to preserve their bodies, shuffling about as crumbling, putrefying wreckage until they collapse altogether . . . ye call them 'liches,' I believe?"

Elmara nodded uncertainly. "Aye."

The green eyes of the wraith glowed a little more brightly. "In my day, we mastered our bodies, so we can become solid or as ye see me now, and pass from one state to another at will. With long practice, one even learns to turn only a hand solid, and leave the rest unseen."

"Is this something that can be taught?"

The emerald eyes danced in mirth. "Aye, to those willing to pass beyond death."

"Why," asked Elmara softly, "would anyone want to pass beyond death?"

"To live forever . . . or to finish a task that drives and consumes one's days, as vengeance on magelords consumes thine . . . or to—"

"Ye know that about me?"

"I can read thy thoughts, when ye are this close," the Netherese wraithwizard replied.

Elmara stepped back, raising her hands with fresh resolve, and the undead sorcerer sighed in her mind.

"Nay, nay—cast not thy petty spell, mageling. I've worked ye no harm."

"Do ye *feed* on thoughts and memories?" El asked in sudden suspicion.

"Nay. I feed on life-force."

El took another step back, and felt a light touch on her shoulder. She turned and stared into the endless grin of a floating skull, bobbing inches away from her nose. She leapt back with a little cry. The sorcerer sighed again.

"Not the life-force of intelligent beings, idiot. Think ye I've no morals, just because ye see bones and all the trappings of death? What is so evil about death? 'Tis something that befalls all of us."

"What life-force, then?" El asked.

"I have a creature imprisoned on the other side of that wall . . . called a deepspawn, it gives birth to creatures it has devoured—stirge after stirge after stirge, in this case."

"Where's the door to this room of monsters?" El asked suspiciously.

"Door? What need have I of doors? Walls are no barrier to me."

"Why are ye revealing all this to me?"

"Ah, there speaks a living wizard, fearful and mistrustful of all others, jealous of power, hoarding learning like precious stones, to keep it from others. . . . Why not tell ye? Ye're interested, and I'm lonely. While we speak, I learn what I want to hear from your mind, so it matters not what we talk about."

"Ye know all about me?" El whispered, looking around for Myrjala.

"Aye—all thy secrets, and fears. Yet be at ease. I shan't reveal these to others, nor attack thee. Improbable as it seems, I can see ye truly did not intend to steal from me, or hurl magic against me."

"So now what will ye do with me?"

"Let ye go. Mind ye return, in ten seasons or so, and talk with Ander again. Thy mind'll have fresh memories and learning for me by then."

"I—I'll try to return," El said uncertainly. Though she'd now mastered her fear, only the gods above knew if she'd live that long, or still be able to work magic . . . and not be a twisted prisoner of some magelord or other.

"That's all any mortal can promise," Ander said, drifting nearer. "Take this gift from me, sith ye did not come to seize anything."

A shaft of light descended in front of Elmara's nose, and within it hung an open book, a book of circular pages, open at one. As El stared at the crawling runes on that page, they seemed to writhe and reform until she could suddenly read them. It was a spell that completely and permanently transformed the gender of the wizard casting it. El swallowed. She'd almost grown used to being a woman, but . . . The page was tearing itself free of the book, right in front of her eyes. Involuntarily she cried out at this destruction, but the wraith answered her with a laugh.

"What need have I of this spell? I can assume any solid form I choose! Take it!"

Numbly, El reached forth her hand into the light and took the page. As she did so, she was abruptly plunged into darkness. The emerald glows, the wraithwizard, and the bones and all were gone.

All that remained in the silent room was her own feeble mage-fire, and the crumbling page in her hand. She stared around for a moment, and then carefully rolled the parchment and thrust it into her bodice.

Then she stiffened as a quiet chuckle sounded deep in her mind, followed by the words, *Remember Ander, and return. I like thee, man-woman.* El stood for a long time in the gloom, silent and unmoving, before she said, "And I thee, Ander. I *will* come back to visit thee." Then she walked to where Myrjala had disappeared. "Teacher?" she called. "Teacher?"

All was dark and silent. "Myrjala?" she said uncertainly, and at that name, motes of light sparkled into being in front of her, and she saw her tutor's dark and friendly eyes for a moment, before the light specks swirled around her too, and took her from the tomb.

* * * * *

"This is very important to ye," El said, standing on a barren hill in the westernmost reaches of the Haunted Vale.

"And even more to you. This is your greatest test of all," Myrjala replied, "and if you succeed, you'll have done something more useful to Faerun than most mages ever accomplish. Be warned: this task will take at least a season, and drain some of your life-force."

"What is the task?"

Myrjala waved an arm at the ravine below them—a place of bare stones, weeds, and the ashen stumps of trees consumed in a long-ago fire. "Bring this place back to life, from where this spring rises to where it joins the Darthtil half a day's walk hence."

El stared at her. "Bring it to life with spells?"

Her teacher nodded.

"How shall I begin?"

"Ah," Myrjala said, rising into the air. "Trying, and setting right mistakes, and trying again is the best part of the task. I shall meet with ye on this spot, a year from now."

Then brightness flared about her, and she was gone.

El closed her mouth on now-useless protests and questions, then opened it again to say quietly, "Gods smile upon ye, Myrjala," and then looked down at the barren gully. Learning its ways had to be the beginning of the task.

* * * * *

The dragon's talons enfolded Elmara. She calmly watched them close around her, doing nothing . . . and the gigantic claws faded away an instant before touching her. Then the quickening breeze blew the last spell-mists away, and she was facing Myrjala across a bare hilltop, on this rainy, windswept day in Eleint, Year of the Disappearing Dragons. Clouds raced past, low in the heavy gray sky.

"Why didn't you strike at me?" her teacher asked, eyebrows raised. "Have you thought of some other way to shatter a dragontalons spell?"

Elmara spread her hands. "I couldn't think of any way not to hurt ye sorely," she said, "with the spells I have left. I knew I could take the harm and survive—just. The other way, I might have lost a teacher . . . and worse, a friend."

Myrjala looked into her eyes. "Yes," she agreed quietly, and waved her hand in an encircling gesture.

Abruptly, the two women were standing in a hollow in the lee of the hill, where their camp was. They were facing each other across a campfire that had lit itself; Myrjala's doing, of course.

Sometimes El mused about how little she knew of her tutor's life and powers, though time and again in their long training together she'd realized just how mighty in magic the sorceress known across Faerun as 'Darkeyes' must be. Right now, she felt a curious foreboding as she stared across the fire at Myrjala.

The older sorceress stood looking into the flames, sadness in her eyes. "Your work on the ravine was superlative . . . much better than my own when I was set the same task. You are stronger than Myrjala now in might-of-magic." She sighed, and added, "And now you *must* go adventuring on your own to try new ways of using spells, and of altering those you know to make them truly your own . . . so you can come to full mastery of what you wield and not stand forever in the shadow of a mage-mentor."

Unshed tears glimmered in the dark eyes she raised to meet Elmara's horrified stare. "Otherwise," Myrjala added slowly, "the days and the years will pass, and both of us shall be the weaker for it—each forever clutching the other's skirts for support, neither growing in her own right."

Elmara stood staring at her in silence.

"Being a mage is a lonely thing," Myrjala said gently, "and this is why. Do you hear my words and agree?"

Elmara looked at her, trembling, and sighed. "So we must part," she whispered, "and I must go on alone . . . to face the magelords."

"You aren't ready to resume your vengeance yet. Live, and learn a little more first. Find me when you feel ready to challenge for the Stag Throne, and I'll aid you if I can. Yet if we do not part," Myrjala said softly, "you will have won nothing alone, and *that* you must do."

Silence hung heavily over the fire for a long time before Elmara nodded reluctantly. Then she said slowly, "There is a secret I have kept from ye; I would not have it lying between us longer. If we are to go separate ways, it is wrong to keep the truth from thee."

She undid the ties of her gown and let it fall. Myrjala watched as Elmara, standing nude in the firelight, murmured the few words she'd held in her memory since that day in the tomb—and her body changed. Myrjala let fall hands that had risen to weave a swift spell if need be, and stared across the fire at the naked man.

"This is my true self," the hawk-nosed man said slowly. "I am Elminster, son of Elthryn . . . prince of Athalantar."

Myrjala regarded him soberly, her eyes very dark. "Why took you a woman's shape?"

"Mystra did this to me to hide me from magelords, for my likeness had become known to them . . . and, I think, to force me to learn to see the world through a woman's eyes. When I tended ye, ye came to know me as a maid . . . I feared that seeking my true form would upset thee and smash the trust between us."

Myrjala nodded. "I have come to love you," she said quietly, "but this—changes things."

"I love ye, too," Elminster said. "It is one of the reasons I . . . stayed a maid. I did not want to change what we share."

She came around the fire then, and embraced him. "Elminster—or Elmara, or whoever you are—come and eat, one last time. Nothing can change the good work we've done together."

* * * * *

It was dark, and the fire had died down low. Myrjala was a shadow across the flames as she turned her head and asked quietly, "Where will you go?"

Elminster shrugged. "I know not . . . west to see the Calishar, mayhap."

"The Calishar? Take care, Elminster—" her voice caught on the unfamiliar name, forming it with difficulty "—for Ilhundyl the Mad Mage holds sway there."

"I know. It's why I'll go. There's a score I must settle there. I can't go through life leaving *everything* unfinished."

"Many do."

"I am not many, and I cannot." He stared into the fire for a long time. "I will miss ye, Lady . . . take care."

"Gods keep you safe, too, Elminster." Then they both dissolved in tears and reached for each other.

When they parted, the next morn, both of them were weeping.

* * * * *

Ilhundyl let the lions into the maze when he saw the intruder—but they froze in midsnarl as the intruder's spells caught them. The hawk-nosed mage who'd paralyzed the beasts strode on without even slowing, finding his way unerringly through the illusory walls and around portal-traps to stalk across the terrace before the Great Gate, toward the hidden door. Ilhundyl's lips thinned, and he spoke words he never thought he'd have to use.

Stone statues turned, creaking. Clouds of dust fell from their joints as lightings leapt from their palms. The blue bolts leapt at the hawk-nosed man, who ignored them. The lightnings struck something unseen around the walking man and encircled it, crackling harmlessly.

One of Ilhundyl's long-fingered hands tapped the table before him. Then he raised the other hand, made a certain gesture, and muttered something. Golems stepped out of the solid stone walls of the Castle of Sorcery and lumbered toward the walking wizard. As they came, the lone intruder spoke an incantation. The air in front of the hawk-nosed stranger was suddenly full of whirling blades. In a flashing cloud, they spun over to strike sparks from the armored colossi—who strode stiffly and ponderously through the storm of steel.

Ilhundyl watched the scene expressionlessly, then leaned forward to ring a bell on his table. When a young woman in livery hurried in, face anxious, he said in calm, cold tones, "Order all the archers to the wall by the Great Gate. They are to bring down the intruder by any means necessary."

She hurried out as the golems closed in on the intruder, lifting massive arms to smash him like a rotten grape against the stones. The wizard raised his hands. Invisible forces cut a slice of stone away, severing one moving leg from its foot, and slowly, but with awesome, quickening force, the first golem fell.

The Castle of Sorcery rocked, and Ilhundyl started up from his seat in rage, in time to see the second golem fall over the broken remnants of the first, and topple in its turn.

Gods take this intruder! He was perilously close to the walls already. Where were those archers? And then arrows lashed on the terrace like hard-driven black hail, and the Mad Mage smiled as the wizard's body jerked, spun around, and fell, transfixed.

Ilhundyl's smile collapsed into a frown as the screaming body was suddenly upright again. Another arrow took it through the head, which flopped loosely, and the corpse reeled and fell headlong, only to appear upright again with no shaft standing out of its mouth. Two arrows sped into it and the body spun, legs kicking—to jerk erect again in different garb. . . .

"Stop!" Ilhundyl snarled. "Stop firing!" His hands stabbed for the bell, knowing it was too late. By the time his orders were heard and relayed, all the archers were dead. His foe was using some spell that switched one person for another, in a double teleport!

That was a spell he *had* to learn ... this young mage must be taken alive. Or at least destroyed in a way that left his spellbook intact.

Ilhundyl strode out of the room and down the Wind Cavern, where smooth shapes of glass stood on all sides, pierced by many holes that sang mournful songs when the wind blew. Taking down this mage might cost him all of his Winged Hands—but it would be done, whatever the price. He could always make more. . . .

He was still a few hurrying paces short of the archway that led into the north tower when the horned suit of armor beside it clanked down from its pedestal and strode toward him, raising its weapons. Ilhundyl spoke a soft word and turned one of the rings on his hand, then cast a spell with a few swift, snarled phrases. Acid burst out from between his fingers in a sphere of acrid purple flames that expanded as it flew. The hissing sphere crashed over the armor and spattered to the floor beyond. Smoke rose from flagstones as it ate away at them; the molten blobs that had been the armor crashed down into the widening pits in the stone, breaking into vapors and droplets.

Another suit of armor was already coming through the door from the next chamber. Ilhundyl sighed at this childishness and hurled his second—and last—acid sphere spell. There was a flash this time as the purple flames struck something in the air and rebounded on the master of the Calishar. Ilhundyl had time for a single pace back before the acid drenched him.

Smoke hissed, and Ilhundyl fell without a sound, dwindling into vapor rather than blood and bone. Out of the air on the far side of the gallery, the Mad Mage faded back into view, and said scornfully, "Fool! Think yourself the only wizard in all Faerun to use images and spells of deceit?"

He waved an imperious hand, and stone spikes suddenly erupted from the air to his right. He pointed, and obediently they flew toward the armored figure. Long before they reached it some force dragged them aside—to smash through the many-curved glass figures. Ilhundyl's wind sculptures toppled into ruin, and the Mad Mage's eyes blazed in fury.

"Seven months to fashion those!" he snarled. "*Seven months!*"

Rays of amber radiance leapt from the archwizard's out-thrust hands toward the armored figure. His target abruptly vanished, and the rays stabbed past where it had been, to touch the far wall of the chamber. The stones of the wall seemed to boil briefly as the rays sheared through them, opening a large hole, and continued on across empty air to bore through the distant wall of the north tower in the same manner. Outside, an unseen guard shouted a startled warning to his fellows.

The furious ruler of the Calishar was still staring at the destruction he'd caused when the armored figure winked into view a little behind him and well to the right, at the spot the stone spikes had appeared from—and its armored fists swung down, striking apparently empty air with solid smacks. The visible Ilhundyl fell to the floor without a sound and winked out of existence. An instant later, the Mad Mage reappeared at the far end of the gallery in a blind, snarling fury. "You *dare*—?"

He growled out a stream of words that echoed and rolled with power, and the Castle of Sorcery shook around him. Impaling spikes shot up from the floor, transfixing the armored figure from below, and then with a thunderous roar, a score of stone blocks crashed down from the high ceiling and smashed the intruder flat. As the dust of their landings rolled lazily across the floor, wall-panels opened all along the gallery. From behind the panels drifted three dead-looking, rotting beholders, eyestalks questing stiffly back and forth for a foe. A glowing cage on a chain plunged down from a ceiling trapdoor, burst open as its spell-glow faded, and six winged green serpents boiled out of it, jaws snapping angrily as they swooped around the gallery, seeking prey. Here and there on the gallery floor, stone blocks turned over with slow uneasiness to reveal glowing magical glyphs.

The hard-eyed Mad Mage waited with hands raised to unleash more destruction as the chamber settled into slow silence. The undead eye tyrants floated menacingly about, finding nothing to turn their beams on, and the flying snakes darted excitedly here and there. One snake dived at Ilhundyl, and he crisped it in the air with a single muttered word. Silence fell again. Perhaps he really had managed to destroy the intruder.

The Mad Mage spoke another spell to raise the stone blocks from the shattered armor. They drifted upward obediently—and then rose to one side. Ilhundyl's jaw dropped. He watched in horror as the blocks, undead beholders, snakes, glass shards, and all began to move in a slow spiral before him.

"Cease!" Ilhundyl cried, and called up the strongest shatter-spell he knew. The spiral's rotation faltered for one breath-stopping moment . . . and then resumed, quickening until things were whirling rapidly around the chamber.

Ilhundyl backed away, for the first time in years knowing the cold taste of fear. More wind-sculptures shattered as the aerial maelstrom swept blocks or undead beholders through them. Their shards glittered in a rising circle to join the spiral, now sweeping down the gallery at Ilhundyl.

The Mad Mage backed away, then turned and ran, hands flashing through hasty and intricate spell-passes. Abruptly there were running Ilhundyls all over the chamber, flickering here and there in a complex dance. The whirlwind swept them all up. One body was promptly dashed against a wall; it crumpled like a broken doll and was gone. Another Ilhundyl suddenly appeared on a balcony high in the gallery, and cast a glowing crystal down into the storm below. The gem flashed once—and in that flash of radiance it and all the whirling items vanished, leaving the chamber empty save for the shattered glass spires on their pedestals.

Ilhundyl looked down on them and said coldly, "Be revealed."

The hawk-nosed mage melted into view—on the balcony beside him, *inside* his protective spellshields!

Ilhundyl recoiled, frantically trying to think of a spell he could safely use against a foe so close. "Why have you come here?" he hissed.

The intruder's eyes met his own coldly. "Ye tricked me, hoping to send me to my death. Like the mages of Athalantar, ye rule by fear and brutal magical might, using thy spells to slay or maim folk—or entrap them in beast-shape."

"So? What do you want of me?"

"Such a question is more appropriately asked *before* attacking," Elminster replied dryly, and then answered, "Thy destruction. I would put an end to all mages who behave as ye do."

"Then you'll have to live a long, long time," said Ilhundyl softly, "and I've no interest in your doing so."

He spoke three words, his fingers moved—and lightning leapt from a shield set high on the far wall of the gallery. Its bright, many-stroked crackling web raked the balcony. Ilhundyl pulled at his magical shieldings as the blue-white bolts danced and spat around him, dragging them aside to expose his foe to the furious energies. The edge of the shield rolled back, lightnings snapping over it viciously, and the Mad Mage saw Elminster stagger.

The ruler of the Calishar roared in triumph and leveled his

left hand to unleash a bolt from the ring on his middle finger. There was no way he could miss this upstart wizard, barely three paces away. His life-leeching bolt stabbed out—and rebounded!

Ilhundyl screamed as his own spell tore at his innards, and tried to flee, struggling toward the archway that led off the balcony. Then Elminster's hand touched the stone floor—and the balcony broke off and plunged down the wall. Ilhundyl fell with it, roaring out a desperate word.

A few feet from the floor, his magic took effect; their crashing plummet slowed to a gently drifting descent. In the tumult, neither man noticed a glowing, floating pair of eyes appear low down at one end of the gallery, to calmly survey the battle.

Ilhundyl turned to the wall and raised his hand again. Another ring winked. And the wall slowly sprouted a massive arm, reaching out for Elminster with stony fingers. Elminster spat out a spell, and the hand shuddered in a burst of force and rock shards that hurled the hawk-nosed mage out of the settling balcony. He skidded across the floor, toppling another glass sculpture.

Ilhundyl snarled out an incantation, stabbing his thumbs forward at Elminster. The prince felt himself plucked up from amid the glass and thrown across the room. El spread his hands in a grand, sweeping gesture, and an instant before he would have smashed with bone-shattering force into the gallery wall, the wall suddenly wasn't there any more. With a grinding rumble, the ceiling began to fall. Ilhundyl stared up at tumbling stone blocks for a moment, and then broke into a run, gabbling the words of another spell.

Outside the Castle of Sorcery, Elminster drifted to the ground, upright and alert. His feet touched the stones of the terrace, he turned toward the north tower, and then felt slashing pain as something unseen cut him across the ribs!

It felt like spreading fire! El sprang back, doubling up in agony, and threw up his hands to protect his face. The next sweep of the invisible blade took the tip off one of his fingers. He could see its edge now, a shimmering line of force edged with his own blood. Ilhundyl faded into view behind it, grinning, and slashed down with his conjured blade again at Elminster's hands.

"A handless man casts few spells," the Mad Mage laughed cruelly, chopping and slashing. Elminster hissed out a spell as he dodged and ducked, and with a wild, tortured shriek, the sorcerous blade shattered into bright stars of force.

The blast sent him rolling helplessly away, head ringing. El writhed and groaned. For a breath or two the hawk-nosed prince could do no more than lie on the stones twisting in pain.

Ilhundyl shuddered and wrung his hands, willing away the pain the blast had wrought in them. When he'd mastered control of his trembling fingers again, he raised a shield-spell around himself and stalked forward. His lips curved from a thin line of pain into a cold smile of anticipation.

When he was close enough to touch the writhing intruder, the Mad Mage carefully cast the most powerful and complex spell he knew—and leaned forward to hook one finger into Elminster's ear.

If the soul-drain succeeded, he would gain all the spells and knowledge this intruder possessed. Entering the helpless man's mind, Ilhundyl bore down through the roiling pain he found there, seeking to find and break this upstart's will. Instead, he felt his probe pounced on and slashed at. He threw back his head, hissing in pain, but did not break the contact . . . yet. It would take hours to memorize this spell again, and if his prisoner died, it would all be for nothing—or if the mage recovered, the fight would begin anew.

Suddenly he was falling, plunging into a dark void in the other man's mind, and out of nowhere and everywhere a blade of white flame was stabbing and cutting him, shearing through his very self. Screaming, Ilhundyl fell away from the sprawled mage, breaking contact. Gods, the pain! Shaking his head to clear it, he crawled away through a yellow haze.

When it cleared, he turned . . . and saw Elminster struggling to his own knees, vainly raking through his own gore to recover a ring with fingers that had been chopped away. Angrily, Ilhundyl hissed the words of a short, simple spell and stepped back to watch his foe die.

The spell manifested. Bony claws coalesced out of empty air into sudden, harsh reality, and swarmed over Elminster—a score or more of them, raking and gouging with needle-sharp talons.

Ilhundyl smiled as they did their gruesome work . . . and then his jaw dropped. They were fading away! The claws were ebbing back into the air, leaving the bloody wreck of a man still living.

"What befalls?" the Mad Mage angrily asked Faerun at large as he strode forward.

"Doom," said a low voice from behind him. Ilhundyl whirled. A dark-eyed woman was *growing* from his own front door, stepping smoothly out of the dark wood to confront him. She was tall and lithe, and wore robes of dark green. Black, liquid eyes under arched brows met his own . . . and Ilhundyl saw his death in them. The Mad Mage was still stammering an incantation when white fire, brighter than anything he'd ever seen, leapt from one of her slim-fingered hands at him.

Ilhundyl stared helplessly at her beautiful, merciless face. And then the roaring flames swept into and through him, and her bone-white face and the sky behind it darkened in his failing gaze.

Through the blood dripping into his eyes, Elminster saw the Mad Mage swept away and consumed in a single roaring moment.

"Wha-What spell was that?" El croaked.

"No spell, but spellfire," Myrjala told him crisply. "Now get up, fool, before all Ilhundyl's rivals arrive to seize what they can. We must be gone by then."

She turned and blasted the Castle of Sorcery with that same all-consuming fire. The Great Gate vanished, and the halls beyond collapsed in flames.

Elminster struggled to his feet somehow, spitting blood. "But his magic! Lost, now, all—"

Myrjala turned back to him. The slim hands that had hurled magical fire an instant before now held a thick, battered old book. She thrust it into Elminster's mangled hands; the pain of the contact nearly made him drop it. "His important work is here—now we must go!"

Elminster's eyes narrowed as he looked at her; somehow her tone seemed different. But perhaps he was just too hurt to hear aright . . . he nodded wearily.

Myrjala touched his cheek, and they were suddenly elsewhere: an echoing cavern. Fungi on its walls glowed a faint blue and green here and there.

Elminster stumbled and with an effort caught his balance, cradling the spellbook. "Where—are we?"

"One of my hideaways," Myrjala said, peering around alertly. "This was once part of an elven city. We're deep under Nimbral, an island in the Great Sea."

Elminster looked around and then down at the book in his hands. When he raised his watery eyes to meet hers, they held a strange look. "Ye knew him?"

Myrjala's eyes were very dark. "I know many mages, Elminster," she said, almost warningly. "I've been around a long time . . . and I did not live this long by recklessly challenging every archmage I heard of."

"Ye don't want me to go to Athalantar yet," Elminster said slowly, eyes on hers.

Myrjala shook her head. "You're not ready. Your magic is still unsubtle, brutal, and predictable—doomed to fail when greater force contests against you."

"Teach me wisdom, then," Elminster said, swaying on his feet.

She turned away. "Separate paths, remember?"

"Ye were watching over me," Elminster said to her back, desperately. "Following me . . . why?"

Myrjala turned back to him slowly. Tears glimmered in her eyes. "Because . . . I love you," she whispered.

"Stay with me, then," Elminster said. The book fell forgotten from his hands, but it took all his strength to stride forward and put his ravaged arms around her. "Teach me."

She hesitated, her dark eyes seeming to look deep into him. Then, almost shuddering, she nodded.

A dark, triumphant fire rose in his eyes as their lips met.

* * * * *

Mirtul was a dry, windy month in the Year of the Wandering Leucrotta—especially in the hot, dusty lands of the east.

Elminster stood hard-eyed atop a wind-scoured cliff, glaring down at a castle of the sorcerer-kings far below. To reach it, he and Myrjala had ridden for a tenday or more past dead slaves stinking in the sun.

Here at last were their slayers. Through his eagle-eyes spell, Elminster watched bloody whips rise and fall in that courtyard, laying open the bodies of the last slaves. All life had fled already, but the sorcerers flailed on, weaving an evil magic with the fading life-forces of the men and women they'd slain.

In anger, El lashed out with spells of his own devising. The magics fell through the air in a bright web, and Elminster stepped off the cliff to follow them. He was striding along on empty air over the castle when it began to topple. He stopped to watch, standing angrily above the dust, screams, and tumult.

Something rose up out of a shattered window, with men in robes riding it. Elminster fired a bolt down to blast them. The enchanted flyer shattered amid explosive brightness; the men on it jerked like flung dolls and fell back into the ruins. They did not rise again. Stones tumbled to a halt, and the rumble of their falling slowly died. When the dust had settled, Elminster

turned, face grim, and walked back through the air to join Myrjala on the heights.

Her dark eyes lifted from the ruined castle, and she asked
softly, "And was that the wisest, least wasteful thing to do?"

Anger glinted in Elminster's eyes. "Aye, if it'll make the next
band of fools think twice about using such fell magic."

"Yet some wizards'll do so anyway. Will you murder them,
too?"

Elminster shrugged. "If need be. Who is to stop me?"

"Yourself." Myrjala looked down at the castle again. "Re-
minds one of Heldon, doesn't it?" she asked quietly, not looking
at him.

Elminster opened his mouth to refute her—and then closed
his mouth again in silence, watching her step calmly off the
height and walk steadily away, treading softly on the air. His
gaze fell to the ruin below, and he shivered in sudden shame.
Sighing, El turned from what he had wrought—and then looked
helplessly down again at the castle. He did not know any spells
to put it back up again.

* * * * *

It was a warm night in early Flamerule, in the Year of the
Chosen. Elminster awoke drenched with sweat, flinging himself
upright to stare with wild eyes at the moon. Myrjala sat up in
bed beside him, hair flowing around her shoulders, eyes dark
with worry. "You were shouting," she said.

Elminster reached for her, and she folded him into her arms
as a mother cradles a frightened child.

"I saw Athalantar," El whispered, staring into the night. "I
was walking the streets of Hastarl, and there were sneering
wizards wherever I looked. And when I stared at them, they fell
over dead . . . terror on their faces. . . ."

Myrjala held him and said calmly, "It sounds as if you're
ready for Athalantar at last."

Elminster turned to look at her. "And if I live through purg-
ing it of magelords—what then? This vow has driven me for so
long . . . what should I do with my life?"

"Why, rule Athalantar, of course."

"Now that the throne comes into my reach," Elminster said
slowly, "I find myself wanting it less and less."

The arms around him tightened. "That's good," Myrjala said
quietly. "I've grown weary waiting for you to grow up."

Elminster looked at her and frowned. "Outgrowing blind

vengeance? I suppose . . . why go through with it all, then?"

Myrjala looked at him steadily in the darkness, her dark eyes large and mysterious. "For Athalantar. For your dead mother and father—and all who lived and laughed in Heldon before the dragon came down on them. For the folk in the taproom of the Unicorn's Horn, and those in Narthil . . . and for your outlaw comrades who died in the Horn Hills."

Elminster's lip's thinned. "We'll do it," he said with quiet determination. "Athalantar shall be free of magelords. I swear before Mystra: I'll do this or die in the trying."

Myrjala said nothing as she held him, but he could feel her smile.

PART V
KING

Fifteen

AND THE PREY IS MAN

In mighty towers they quake with fright
for the man who kills mages is out tonight.

Bendoglaer Syndrath, Bard of Barrowhill,
from the ballad ***Death to All Mages***
Year of the Bent Coin

Eleasias was a wet month that year. On the fourth successive stormy night, Myrjala and Elminster were thankful to duck out of the rain into a tavern on a muddy back street in Launtok.

"That's the last of the Athalantan envoys put to flight. Their masters have certainly noticed us by now," Myrjala said with some satisfaction as they settled into a corner booth with their tankards.

"On to the magelords, then," Elminster said, rubbing his hands together thoughtfully. He leaned forward. "Ye've warned me often against charging in with fireballs blazing in both hands . . . so do we spread a few rumors of plots and unrest, sit back in hiding, and let them kill each other for a while, trying to see who'll sit in the best spell-tower?"

Myrjala shook her head. "While we sat, they'd destroy Athalantar along with each other." She sipped her ale, winced, and gave the tankard a dark look. "Besides, that'd work only if we'd destroyed the most powerful archwizards, the leaders of the magelords . . . thus far, we've only foiled the buffoons and the most reckless fools."

"What next, then?" Elminster asked, taking a deep drink of ale.

Myrjala arched one shapely eyebrow. "This is *your* vengeance."

Elminster set down his tankard and licked foam from the beginnings of a mustache. Myrjala looked amused, but her companion was intent on his thoughts.

"I never thought I'd feel this," he said slowly, "but after Ilhundyl and those slave-sorcerers . . . I've had a bellyful of vengeance." He looked up. "So how should we work it? Attack

Athalgard, trying to slay all the magelords we can before they know a foe's come calling?"

Myrjala shrugged and told her tankard, "Some folk get a thrill out of destroying things. With most, the delight fades quickly. The gods don't suffer the others to live all that long—if a mage goes about just hurling spells, he eventually runs into someone else doing the same thing, with just a few more spells up his sleeve."

She lifted her eyes to meet Elminster's. "If you tried a hurl-all-fireballs attack on the magelords, bear in mind how much countryside you'd destroy—and all of it'd be Athalantar, the realm you're fighting for. They won't all obligingly challenge you one after another, each one politely awaiting his turn to die."

Elminster sighed. "Stealth and years in the doing, then." He sipped from his tankard. "So tell me how ye think we should go about this. Ye're the elder of us two; I'll do as ye say."

Myrjala shook her head. "It's past time to think for yourself, Elminster; look at me as your teacher no more, but an ally in your fight."

El looked at her grave expression, nodded slowly, and said, "Ye're right, as always. Well . . . if we're to avoid huge spell-battles, magelords must be lured into situations where we can fight them alone and they won't be able to call on all their fellows for aid. We'll have to lay some traps—and if just the two of us go up against them, sooner or later we *will* end up in a mighty spell-contest. If we and the magelords both hurl flames at each other, there's going to be a fire."

Myrjala nodded. "And so?" she asked quietly.

"We need allies to fight with us," El said, "but who?" He stared at the table in frowning silence.

Myrjala took up her tankard again and stared thoughtfully at her reflection in it. "You've said more than once you wanted fitting justice to befall the magelords," she said carefully. "What could be more right than calling on the elves of the High Forest, and the thieves in Hastarl, and Helm and his knights? 'Tis their realm you're fighting to free, too."

Elminster started to shake his head, then grew very still, as his eyes slowly narrowed. "Ye're right," he said in a small voice. "Why am I always so blind?"

"Lack of attention; I've told you before," Myrjala said crisply—and when he looked at her in irritation, she grinned at him and extended gentle fingers to stroke one of his hands. After a moment, El smiled back at her.

"I'll have to travel about the realm cloaked in magic and speak to them," he said slowly, thinking it through, "because they know ye not." He sipped ale again. "And as a magelord may notice me and 'tis never wise to reveal all one's strengths too soon, ye'd best stay out of sight."

The dark-eyed sorceress nodded. "Yet in case the magelords come down on you in earnest, I'd best accompany you—in other shapes than my own, of course—to fight at your side if need be."

El smiled at her. "I'd not want to be parted from ye now, to be sure. Should we try to raise the common folk of the realm to our cause?" Then he answered his own question. "Nay, they'd flee before the first spell hurled against them, and once roused would strike out blindly until as much ruin is spread across the realm as if enraged magelords were using spells without restraint . . . and whether we won or lost, they'd die by the hundreds, like sheep led to slaughter."

Myrjala nodded. "You were first trained in magic by the elves . . . they would seem the most important allies to gain."

El frowned. "They use their magic to aid, nurture, and reshape, not to blast things in battle."

Myrjala lifted her shoulders in a shrug. "If all you're seeking in allies is folk to stand beside you and add battle-spells to your own, much of the realm *will* be riven in the struggle. You need to find folk with strengths you lack . . . and their decision to aid you or not will shape everything; you need to know if they'll stand with you before you contact the others. Moreover, you know where to find the elves . . . with less likelihood of a magelord watching than in Hastarl or the Horn Hills."

Elminster nodded. "Good sense. When should we begin?"

"Now," Myrjala replied crisply.

They traded grins. A moment later, two tankards settled onto an empty table. The tavernkeeper, frowning anxiously, hurried over to the sound—and glumly collected the two tankards from the bare board. They rattled.

He peered in. A silver coin lay at the bottom of each. He brightened, shrugged, and tipped the coins, sticky with beer-foam, into his hand. Juggling them, he headed back for the bar. These wizards' coins'd spend as well as any . . . and as fast, more's the pity. . . .

* * * * *

El stopped when he came to the little knoll in the heart of the High Forest, knelt and murmured a prayer to Mystra, and then sat down on the flat stone beside the little pool. Almost immediately his spell-shield flickered as something unseen—an elf, no doubt—tested it, seeking to learn who he was. El stood, looking around at the duskwood, shadowtop, and blueleaf trees that pressed close about the knoll. "Well met!" he called cheerfully and sat down again.

In patient silence he waited, so long a time that even an elf could grow restive. From the gloom beneath the trees strode a silent elf in mottled green, a strung bow in his hand. His face was still, but his eyes were not friendly.

"Magelords aren't welcome here," he said, setting a shaft to his bow.

Elminster made no move. "I am a mage, but no magelord," he replied calmly.

The elf did not lower his bow. "Who else would know of this place?" As he spoke, seven more elven archers stepped out of the trees all around the knoll. The points of their aimed arrows glowed a vivid blue—too much magic for even the strongest shield to withstand.

"I dwelt here a year and more," El replied, "learning magic."

The silvery eyes hardened. "Not so," came the swift reply. "Speak truth, man, if you would live!"

"Yet I dwelt here as I told ye, and what is more, six elves swore to aid me should I try to destroy the magelords."

The elf's eyes narrowed. "I swore such aid, but to a woman, not to a man."

"I am that woman," Elminster said firmly, and kept to his seat amid the merry laughter that followed.

Then he looked mildly around at their scoffing faces. "Ye use magic mightier than most mages but don't believe a wizard can take the shape of a man or a maid?"

The elf's eyes flickered. "Not can't—won't," came his reply. "Humans never do such things for more than a night's lark, or a desperate escape. 'Tis not in their natures to be so strong in themselves."

Elminster spread his empty hands slowly. "Tell Braer—Baerithryn—that I am stronger now than I was then . . . and the master of a few more spells."

The elf's eyes flickered again before he turned his head. "Go," he said to one of the other archers, "and bring Baerithryn to us. If this man is who he claims to be, Baerithryn will know it—and tell us all we need to know of him, too." The archer turned and slipped back into the mushroom-studded dimness under the trees.

El nodded and peered into the depths of the crystal-clear pool. For a moment, he thought he saw a pair of thoughtful eyes looking up at him . . . but no, there was nothing there. He sat calmly, ignoring the arrows trained tirelessly on him, until his spell-shield flickered again. He let it drop deliberately, and immediately felt a feather-light touch in his mind. Then the probing contact was gone, and Braer was striding out from under the trees, looking just as he'd done when El had last seen him.

"Time seems to have wrought some small changes in you, Elmara," he said dryly.

"Braer!" El sprang to his feet and rushed down the slope to embrace his old teacher, who kissed him as if he'd still been a maid and then slipped free of Elminster's arms and said, "Easy there, Prince! Elves are far more refined—and delicate—than men."

They laughed together, and the watching elves put away their shafts. Braer looked keenly into Elminster's eyes—and then nodded as if he'd seen something there. "You've come for our aid against the magelords. Sit and tell us your desires."

When they returned to the stone, El found himself surrounded by almost a score of silently watching elves. He looked around at them, found no answering smile to his own, and drew a deep breath. "Well," he began—but got no farther.

The elf who'd first challenged him held up a hand. "First, Prince, be aware that Braer and we who pledged to thee hold it our duty to do whatever you ask of us . . . but we are reluctant indeed to hazard others of the People. Outside the forest, elves are all too easily slain, and when we die, so do the last of our folk in this fair corner of Faerun. Men—even mages—spring up like so many weeds in spring. Elves are rarer flowers . . . and so the more precious. Do not expect a marching army, or a score of elven archmages flying at your shoulder."

Elminster nodded and looked at Baerithryn. "Braer, d'ye feel the same way?"

His old teacher inclined his head. "I would not like to lead a march on Hastarl under the open skies of day, with mounted hosts of armsmen and dragon-riding magelords waiting to harry us . . . that is not our way of war. What have you in mind?"

"That you shield folk—primarily myself and another mage, but also a few knights and street folk of Hastarl—from slaying spells cast by the magelords . . . and perhaps a few seeking and farspeaking magics, too. Shield us, and we'll fight."

"How powerful are you?" one of the archers asked. "There are a lot of magelords, and it would be folly indeed to support you in an attack on Athalgard . . . only to find ourselves beset by all the angry wizards after you've fought one or two—and then fallen."

"I destroyed the archmage who ruled the Calishar not so very long ago," El said calmly.

"We've heard several tales as to how he met his end—even the magelords have claimed to have worked his destruction, though they say several of them had to work together to do it," said another elf. "With respect, we must see your powers for ourselves."

El did not sigh. "What sort of a test d'ye have in mind?"

"Slay a magelord for us," another elf said firmly, and there was a murmured chorus of agreement.

"Any magelord?"

"One—Taraj, he's called—keeps watch over our forest and amuses himself by taking beast-shape to hunt. He slays for the love of killing, and mauls not only his prey, but any creatures of the forest he meets. He seems to have some protection against our spells and arrows. If you could destroy Taraj, most of the People would feel beholden to you . . . and you'd gain more aid than the bows and veiling spells of a handful of foresworn."

"Take me to where Taraj hunts, and I will destroy him," Elminster promised. "What does he like to hunt?"

"Men," Braer replied quietly, as he set off down the slope into the forest. Without ceremony the other elves followed. Elminster rolled his eyes once, but kept pace among them, feeling a strange exultation rising in him. The familiar weight of the Lion Sword bumped against his chest, and El's fingers sought it and gripped it almost fiercely. At last—at long last—the scouring of Athalantar had begun. . . .

* * * * *

"Release him," the magelord ordered, swirling the dregs of the wine in the depths of his goblet.

"Sir," the servant said with a bow and hurried away. Taraj watched him go and smiled. He was the magelord who'd come the farthest to rule in this splendid land of forests and grass-girt hills . . . lovely hunting country. If only Murghom had been like this, he'd never have to endure these accursed winters.

He went to the window to watch the terrified peddler from far Luthkant flee across the courtyard into the brush beyond. Sometimes he hunted his prisoners as if they were stags, felling them with lances hurled from horseback. He scorned armor, but always rode shielded with warding spells. Today though, he felt like a beast run. He'd take the shape of a lion, perhaps, or . . . yes, a forest cat! 'Panther,' they were called back home.

Taraj set down the empty goblet, threw off his robe, and strode naked into his spell-chamber to study the shape-change spell. It would give the man more time to run.

* * * * *

The spell coiled and burned comfortably in his mind. Taraj felt the same quickening excitement he always did when a hunt was about to begin. He bowed to his reflection in the wall-glass. "Taraj Hurlymm from far Murghom, magelord and cruel man," he introduced himself to an imaginary feasting-company, smirking. His image smirked back, looking just as satisfied as he was. Taraj winked and moved his arms so the corded muscles of his shoulders rippled. He admired them for a moment, then slid on a robe and rapped with his knuckles on a wall-gong. The servant was slow; Taraj told himself to remember to rake her with a claw when he returned, to put a little fear into her.

"See that a feast awaits me at my return," he said, "at moon-rise. And at least four women I've not seen before, to share it."

He waved a hand in dismissal, and watched her bow and hurry away. Well, now . . . make her this night's fifth consort, and teach her fear that way. Being abed with a man who can change his shape has its own delights—and dangers.

Taraj grinned and strode down the steps to the garden. He liked to begin every hunt here, under the watchful statue of the Beastlord. As usual, he hung his robe over its snarling head and strolled down the many-flowered grassy paths, speaking the spell slowly, savoring the moment when his body would flow, surge, and change. The moment came. Teeth lengthened to fangs, thighs sank and thickened, shoulders shifted powerfully, and a glossy black panther leapt away into the tall grasses at the end of the garden.

At the garden door, the watching servant shivered. The magelord liked to hunt down and devour men who'd displeased him . . . and deal with women in other ways. She was sure he'd withdrawn from the intrigues of Hastarl to make his home here in far Dalniir at the edges of the realm because it offered him a countryside to hunt in. That peddler was doomed, and any woodcutters or hunters her master met with, too. She hoped he'd find none, and be a long, wearying time at his chase.

She sighed and went in to order the feast made ready . . . and then to the south wing to personally choose the maids who might die tonight. More than once she'd seen that bed and the carpet beneath it awash in blood and torn to shreds . . . sometimes with a gnawed foot or other remnant left tauntingly for the staff to find. She shuddered and prayed silently to whatever gods might be watching that Taraj Hurlymm would meet his own doom this night.

Folk would pray much harder to the gods, she thought to herself as she got up off her knees, if they gave proof that they listened to the fervent desires of mortals more often. Tonight, for instance.

She sighed. That peddler was doomed.

* * * * *

The Calishite's fine silk shirt was soaked through with sweat; it stuck to him, dark and slick, as he puffed wearily up a slope, forced a way through bushes that clawed and tore at his finery, and hurried on, gasping for breath. The man wasn't in very fine form . . . and now, covered with sweat and grime and with his long mustache drooping with sweat and smudged with dust, the magelord liked his looks even less.

The man's appearance had been the reason Taraj had ordered this trader seized in the first place. That and the appeal of the exotic; merchants from as far away as Luthkant found Athalantar seldom and ventured out of Hastarl even more rarely. This exotic prey, however, didn't look to be able to provide him with much sport at all . . . already the trader was wobbling along in exhaustion, his breath coming in fast, sobbing gasps.

Skulking along a ridge not far behind the terrified man, Taraj decided he was becoming increasingly bored. Time to make his kill.

He bounded down into the brush, a sleek black panther feeling fast and deadly and alive! Exulting in his power, he leapt across a narrow, deep gully, his paws scrabbling in crumbling earth for one exciting moment on the far side before they gripped . . . and then he was safely across and into the thicket beyond.

Bursting out of cover atop a bank, he soared right over the Luthkantan, who howled in fear and snatched out a belt-knife, slashing uselessly at the air, well in his wake.

So that was the only fang the man had? Well, then . . . Taraj turned, sleek coat rippling, and rushed back at the man, dead leaves rustling as his racing paws hurled them aside.

The Calishite dodged, eyes wide and white with terror, slashed wildly at Taraj's nose—and then turned and ran.

Taraj gave him a throaty snarl and bounded after him. The man heard and spun around to prevent being hamstrung, that tiny blade gleaming again as he brandished it desperately. Taraj snarled and kept coming, not slowing . . . and the terrified man backed away.

After a few hurried, unseeing paces, of course, he stumbled on something underfoot, and fell hard on his behind. Taraj leapt at him, jaws opening wide for that first playful bite, but the man kicked out with frantic savagery—and the magelord felt sudden tearing pain. He snarled and recoiled, bounding away and then whirling back to face his victim.

Gods curse the man! The trader's boots had suddenly sprouted toe-daggers. Vicious little blades; one gleamed at him as the exhausted man stayed on his back, feet up—and the other was wet and dark with Taraj's blood.

The magelord snarled again and loped off into the nearest tall grass. Dragon at the gate! You couldn't even trust fat Calishite merchant traders to fight fair these days! Well, you'd never been able to, he admitted wryly as the panther's body fell away, flowing and changing again. A brief visit to the Luthkantan in the shape of an acid-spitting snake should do away with the man's weapons so he could be killed slowly and enjoyably afterward. The snake reared up, coiling experimentally, shaking as the magelord settled into this new shape.

A black crow that had been scudding along unseen behind the panther dived earthward, starting to change even before it struck the grassy ground below.

Something huge and dark rose up out of the grass where it landed, batlike wings unfolding and long tail switching . . . a black dragon crouched amid the crushed grass, leaning forward over the suddenly hissing, coiling snake.

The snake spat. The smoking acid struck the dragon's snout and dripped; black dragons are never harmed by acids. The dragon smiled slowly and opened its own jaws. The acid that streamed from the dragon's maw consumed a tree and left the snake itself smoking and writhing in the scorched grasses beyond, throwing coils about in its agony. The dragon strode forward, slowly, heavily . . . and tauntingly.

From somewhere in the trees ahead came a despairing scream as the Calishite trader saw the dragon, and crashing sounds as he struggled through trees and thick brush in frantic flight.

The snake grew larger and darker, and wings began to sprout from it. As its shape built and stretched, it grew a human hand and mouth for an instant. The ring flashed, and the mouth cried, "Kadeln! Kadeln! Aid me! By our pact, *aid me!*"

The dragon lumbered forward, extending claws to rend the snake that was rapidly becoming another black dragon. Another pace, and another . . . and the dragon that was Elminster reached out and slashed with one black-taloned claw to rend still-forming scales. Blood spattered, and the magelord-turned-dragon squalled in pain.

Elminster extended his head to bite down hard on the other dragon's neck and end this wizard for good—but suddenly a mage stood beside the still-growing dragon, where the only crushed grass had been a moment before. Elminster had a glimpse of this new magelord's dark, glittering eyes as he reared and backed hastily away. The wizard was already casting a spell; there was no time to shift shape into something else.

Elminster beat his wings once to hurl the man off his feet and ruin his spell, but tree limbs got in the way. He was still struggling to lunge forward and bite down on the newcomer when something streaked from the mage's outthrust hand, and roaring fire erupted on all sides and rolled over him.

El's curse of pain came out as a rumble as he hastily backed away, turned, and lashed out with his tail so the magelord had to dive ingloriously into the dirt to avoid being struck. El grunted and bounded aloft.

This body was heavy and ungainly, but the large wings beat strongly. He put some effort into flight, and the wind was whistling past his head when he turned and plunged back down through the air in a dive, waiting for just the right moment to spit acid.

The other dragon was almost fully formed now, but thrashing about in pain, all tangled up under the trees. El could deal with this fire-hurling wizard first!

Snarling, Elminster roared down out of the sky, teeth flashing.

The wizard's hands were making complicated passes—and then he leapt back to watch in triumph . . . and Elminster knew sudden fear. He tried to unfold a wing and veer away—but couldn't! His wings were bound by magic!

Helplessly he plunged down into the trees, bracing himself for the crash he knew would come. The wind whistled past him. And then he saw his true doom. Before him a shimmering wall of bright, swirling colors was growing; a rainbow of deadly magic directly in his path. El could only turn his eyes in horror to look at the magelord who stood watching as he fell to death.

"Aid me, Mystra," he whispered, as the swirling colors rushed up to meet him.

* * * * *

Kadeln Olothstar, magelord of Athalantar, laughed coldly. "Ah, I *love* a good fight! Taming a mageling, too! My thanks, Taraj!"

The dragon hurtled helplessly down into his prismatic wall. Kadeln threw up a hand to shield his eyes from the blast he knew would come as the huge beast passed through his spell and they destroyed each other.

It came. The world rocked, and a blinding flash clawed at his eyes even through his tightly shut lids. Kadeln landed hard on his back and spat a curse at the gods for putting a hard tree-root under his spine. Then he blinked his eyes until he could see again and rolled to his feet. Broken trees and smoking grass surrounded him, with nary a dragon in sight . . . and stumbling sightlessly out of the smoke came a fat Calishite in tattered silks, a dagger clutched in one trembling hand.

Hah! He could even rob Taraj of his quarry this night! Kadeln smiled a thin, cruel smile and raised his hand to slay the man. It would take only the least of his spells. Then a dark form melted out of the air in front of him—Taraj, tattered and blackened with soot.

"Out of my way, Hurlymm," Kadeln said coldly, but his dazed fellow magelord seemed not to hear. Hmm . . . perhaps an accident might befall Taraj here, with no watching eyes to speak later of Kadeln's treachery. Or would it be wise to fell this lazy, blood-hungry idiot, and have perhaps a stronger mage rise to take his place in the councils of magelords?

Kadeln made his decision, sighed, and stepped around the bemused Taraj, raising his hand again to hurl a death bolt at the sobbing merchant. As he passed, the dark tatters seemed to ripple. Kadeln Olothstar had been a magelord for many years. He turned to see what shape Taraj was taking—just in case.

Cold blue-gray eyes swam out of the melting form to meet his own, around a hawk-beak of a nose, and a mouth that smiled at him without warmth or mirth.

"Greetings, Magelord," that mouth said, as one dark arm rose up to strike aside Kadeln's raised hand. The dark form's other arm streaked up to his mouth. "I am Elminster. In the

name of my father Prince Elthryn and my mother Princess Amrythale, I slay thee."

Kadeln was gabbling the words of a desperate spell as the
stranger, still smiling that steely smile, thrust a finger into the
magelord's mouth. Flame burst forth in a sphere that rolled
down the magelord's throat, and found no ready room to ex-
pand.

A moment later, Kadeln Olothstar burst apart in flames that
briefly outshone the sun . . . and then swiftly died away into
drifting smoke. Silence fell—followed a moment later by the
Calishite, who gave a despairing moan as his eyes rolled up and
he thudded limply to the scorched turf.

The lady who glided into view atop the nearest ridge made a
face at the blood covering Elminster. He looked up at her
quickly, raising a hand to blast another foe if need be—and then
relaxed, and called, "My thanks—again—for my life."

Myrjala smiled as she came up to him and spread her hands.
"What, after all, are friends for?"

"How did ye do it this time?" El asked, striding forward to
embrace her. She whispered something and made a small sign
with one hand—and the magelord's gore was abruptly gone. Elminster looked down, shook his head, and then wrapped his
arms around her and kissed her.

"Let me breathe, young lion," Myrjala said at last, pulling
her head back. "To answer you—I used that spell you're so fond
of, switching folk about. Taraj was the dragon who struck the
wall-spell, and I guided you into his semblance."

"I needed ye after all," Elminster said, looking into her dark,
mysterious eyes.

Myrjala smiled at him. "There's much more to do for Athalantar yet, O Prince . . . and I need you whole to do it."

"I'm—losing my thirst for killing magelords," Elminster said.

Myrjala's arms tightened around him. "I understand, and respect you the more for that, El—but once begun, we must take
them all . . . or all we'll achieve for the folk of Athalantar is
changing the names and faces of those who rule them iron-hard.
Is that all you want to have done to avenge your mother and father?"

When Elminster looked up at her, his eyes were bright and
hard. "Who's the next magelord we should slay?" he snapped.

Myrjala almost smiled. "Seldinor," she said, turning away.

"Why he, of them all?"

Myrjala turned back. "You have been a woman. When I tell
you his latest schemes, you will understand why, better than

most brash young men who call themselves wizards."

Elminster nodded, not smiling. "I was afraid ye'd say something like that."

Elves were suddenly all around them, seeming to melt out of the trees. Braer met Elminster's eyes, and asked, "Who is this lady mage?"

Myrjala spoke for herself. "Al hond ebrath, uol tath shantar en tath lalala ol hond ebrath."

El looked at her. "What did ye say?"

"A true friend, as the trees and the water are true friends," Myrjala translated softly, her eyes very dark.

The elf who'd first challenged Elminster by the pool said, "A proud boast, lady, for one who lives and then is gone, while the trees and streams endure forever."

Myrjala turned her head, as tall and as regal as any elf, and said, "You may be surprised at my longevity, Ruvaen, as others of your folk have been, before."

Ruvaen drew back a pace, frowning. "How is it that you know my name? Who—?"

"Peace," Braer said. "Such things are best spoken of in private, one to another. Now we have much to plan and prepare. The test has been set and passed. Elminster may not have prevailed alone, but two magelords are no more, not one. Do any challenge this?"

Silence answered him, and he turned wordlessly to Ruvaen.

The archer looked at Braer, nodded, and then said to Elminster, "The People will fight at your side for Athalantar, if you hold to the pledge you made to us when we swore aid to you."

"I will," Elminster said, and extended his hand.

After a long moment, Ruvaen took it, and they clasped forearms firmly, as one warrior to another. Around them, the gathered elves of the High Forest shouted in exultation—the loudest sound of celebration any elf of Athalantar had made in many a year.

*   *   *   *   *

Old, wise eyes watched the elves and humans dwindle into the depths of the crystal, and then slowly fade. What to do?

Aye, what? The lad was just one more young spell weaver with glory in his eyes, but the woman. . . . He'd not seen spellmastery like that since . . . his eyes narrowed, and then he shrugged.

There was no time for idle memories. There never is.

He had to warn everyone, and then s—but no. No. Let these two destroy Seldinor first.

Sixteen

WHEN MAGES GO TO WAR

A star rushes past, to crash upon the shore
But the first of many many more
Stoke the fire and stout bar the door
For this is the night mages go to war.

Angarn Dunharp
from the ballad *When Mages Go to War*
Year of the Sword and Stars

Leaves rustled. At that slightest of sounds, Helm whirled, hand going to hilt. Out from behind the tree stepped the silent elven warrior he'd come to know as Ruvaen, the gray cloak that was so hard to see swirling around him. There was another elf with him. Their still faces somehow betrayed a mood darker than usual.

"What news?" Helm asked simply. None of the elves or the knights were wont to waste words.

Ruvaen held out something that filled his hand—something clear and smooth-sided and colorless, like a fist-sized diamond. A few clumps of moss clung to it. Helm looked down at it and raised his brows in an unspoken question.

"A scrying crystal. Used by human wizards," Ruvaen said flatly.

"The magelords," Helm said grimly. "Where did ye find this?"

"In a dell, not far from here," said the other elf, pointing off into the forest gloom.

"One of your men hid it under moss," Ruvaen added. "When he wasn't using it."

Helm Stoneblade let out his breath in a long sigh. "So they may know all our plans and be laughing at us now."

The two elves did not need to answer. Ruvaen put the crystal gently into Helm's callused hand, touched his shoulder, and said, "We'll wait above, in the trees . . . should you need us."

Helm nodded, looking down at the crystal in his hand. Then he lifted his head to stare into the forest. Who most often went off into the woods to relieve himself in *that* direction?

His battered face changed, hardening. Helm thrust the crystal into the breast of his tunic, turned, and made a short barking sound. One of his men, cutting up a deer some distance away, looked up. Their eyes met through the trees, and Helm nodded. The man turned and barked in his turn.

Soon they were all gathered around: the score or so knights he'd brought with him into the depths of the High Forest. All who still dared swing a blade in defiance of the magelords, clinging to the thin shield of elven mystery and providing the Fair Folk a front line of blades and bows to keep the woodcutter's axes from hewing out a new and larger Athalantar unopposed.

The magic of the elves cloaked them from the wizards who ruled Athalantar, but was ill suited to spell-battle . . . beyond quenching fires and hiding Folk, that is. The threat of greater elven spells had kept the magelords largely at bay, thus far, at least. Lending Helm time to plan a rising that might—just might, with the gods' own luck—shatter this rule of wizards, and give him back the carefree Athalantar he'd fought for and loved, so long ago. So they'd fought, by night and the quick blade, and vanished back into the trees or perished under spell-torment, while the long years dragged on and Helm became ever more desperate . . . as the Athalantar of his youth slowly faded away.

The hard winters and the dead friends had hardened him and taught him patience. This crystal, now, changed things. If the magelords knew their numbers, names, schemes, and camps, they'd have to strike swiftly, now, or not at all . . . to have any chance at anything more than an unmarked grave and feeding the wolves.

He waited, silent, stone-faced, until the most restless of his men—Anauviir, of course—spoke. "Aye, Helm, what is it?"

Wordlessly, Helm turned to Halidar, holding out the scrying crystal. Halidar's face went white. He sprang to his feet, whirling to flee—and then gasped and sagged slowly back against Helm. The old knight stood unmoving as the traitor slid slowly down his chest to tumble onto the forest floor. Anauviir's dagger stood out of Halidar's throat, just beneath his contorted mouth. Helm bent to pull it out without a word, wiped it clean, and handed it back to its owner. Halidar had always been quick . . . and Anauviir had always been swifter. Helm held up the crystal for them all to see.

"The magelords have been watching over us," he said flatly. "Mayhap for years." Faces were pale all around him now. "Ruvaen," Helm asked, holding the crystal up, "have ye any use for this?"

Some of his men looked up, involuntarily, though by now they all knew they'd see nothing but leaves and branches, as a quiet, musical voice replied, "Properly used, it can burn out one magelord's mind."

There was an approving murmur, and Helm tossed the crystal straight up, into the branches overhead. It did not come down.

Hand still raised, Helm looked around at his men. Dirty, dark-eyed, and armed like the sort of mercenary bodyguards short, fat men hire to give them grandeur. They looked back at him, haggard and grim. Helm loved them all. If he had another forty blades such as these, he could carve himself out a new Athalantar, magelords or no magelords. But he did not. Forty blades too few, he thought, not for the first time. Nay—forty-one, now . . .

"Stand easy, knights," Ruvaen's lilting voice came unexpectedly from the trees above them. "A man approaches who would speak with you. He means no harm."

Helm looked up, startled. The elves never suffered other humans to venture this far into the woods. . . . And then something faded into view behind a nearby tree. Anauviir saw it even as Helm did and hissed warningly as he raised his blade. Then the shadowy figure stepped forward and mists of magic fell away from it.

The old knight's jaw dropped.

"Well met, Helm," said a voice he'd never thought to hear again.

Out of sight for so long . . . surely the lad had died at the hand of some magelord or other . . . but no. . . . Helm swallowed, lurched, and then went to one knee, proffering his sword as he did so. There were mutters of amazement from his men.

"Who's this, Helm?" Anauviir asked sharply, blade up, peering at the thin, hawk-nosed newcomer. Only a wizard or an upperpriest could step out of empty air like that.

"Rise, Helm," Elminster said quietly, putting a hand on the old knight's forearm.

The old knight got up, turned to his men, and said, "Kneel if you be a true knight of Athalantar . . . for this is Elminster son of Elthryn, the last free prince of the realm!"

"A magelord?" someone asked doubtfully.

"No," Elminster said quietly. "A wizard who needs your help to destroy the magelords."

They stared at him unmoving—until, one by one, they caught Helm's furious glare, and went to their knees.

Elminster waited until the last knee—Anauviir's—touched
the leaf-strewn ground, and then said, "Rise, all of ye. I am
prince of nothing at the moment, and I need allies, not
courtiers. I've learned magic enough to defeat any magelord, I
believe—but I know that when any magelord gets into trouble,
he'll call on another . . . and in a breath or two I'll have forty or
more of them on my hands."

There were mirthless chuckles, and the knights unconsciously moved forward. Helm saw it in their faces and felt it
himself: for the first time in years, real hope.

"Forty magelords is too many for me," Elminster went on,
"and they command far too many armsmen for my liking. The
elves have agreed to fight with me in the days ahead, to cleanse
this land of the magelords forever—and I hope to find other allies in Hastarl."

"Hastarl?" Anauviir barked, startled.

"Aye . . . before this tenday is out, I plan to attack Athalgard.
All I'm lacking is a few good blades." He looked around at the
scarred, unshaven warriors. "Are ye with me?"

One of the knights raised hard eyes to meet his. "How do we
know this isn't a trap? Or if it isn't, that your spells are strong
enough not to fail once we're in that castle, with no way out?"

"I held that same view," Ruvaen's voice came to them from
overhead, "and demanded that this man prove himself. He's
slain two magelords so far this day—and another mage works
with him. Have no fear of their magic failing."

"An' look you," Helm added roughly, "I've known the prince
since the day the mage royal's dragon slew his parents, an' he
vowed to me—a boy an' all, mind—that he'd see the magelords
all dead someday."

"The time has come," Elminster said in a voice of iron. "Can I
depend on the last knights of Athalantar?"

There were murmurs and shufflings. "If I may," Anauviir
said uneasily, "one question . . . how can you protect *us* against
the spells of the magelords? I'd welcome a chance to hew down a
few magelings and armsmen—but how'll any of us ever get
close enough to *have* that chance?"

"The elves will go to war beside you," Ruvaen's voice came
again. "Our magic will hide or shield you whenever we can, so
you can stand blade-to-blade against your foes at last." There
were rumbles of approval at this, but Helm stepped forward
and raised his hand for silence.

"I've led you, but in this every man must choose freely. . . .
Death is all too likely, whatever grand words we toss back and

forth here." The old knight spat thoughtfully into the leaves at his feet, and added, "Yet think you: death is coming for us if we say no and go on cowering in the forest. The magelords're wearing us down, man by man . . . Rindol, Thanask; you know all of us who've fallen . . . and not a tenday passes that the armsmen aren't seeking us in every cave and thicket we run to. In a summer, or two at most, they'll have hunted down us all. Our lives are lost anyway—why not spend them to forge a blade that might actually take a magelord or two down with us?"

There were many nodding heads and raised blades among the knights, and Helm turned to Elminster with a grin that held no mirth at all.

"Command us, Prince," he said.

El looked around at them all. "Are you with me?" he asked simply. There were nods, and muttered "Ayes."

Elminster leaned forward and said, "I need ye all to go to Hastarl—in small groups or pairs, not all together where ye may attract notice or be all slain together by a vigilant magelord. Just outside the wall, upriver, is a pit where they burn bodies and refuse; traders often camp near it. Gather there before a tenday's out and seek me or a man who gives his name to you as Farl. Dress as peddlers or traders; the elves have mint wine for you to carry as wares. . . ." El grinned at them and added dryly, "Try not to drink it all before ye get to Hastarl."

There were real laughs this time and eagerness in their eyes.

"There's a supply train bound for the eastern fortresses just leaving the fort at Heldon," Helm said excitedly. "We were debating whether to risk striking at it . . . it'll gain us clothes an' mounts an' pack beasts an' wagons!"

"Good!" Elminster said, knowing he couldn't hold them back now if he wanted to. A hunger for battle was alight in their eyes; a flame he'd lit that would burn now until they—or the magelords—were all dead. There were shouts of eager approval. Helm collected the gazes of all the knights with his own eyes, turning as he drew his old sword and thrust it aloft.

"For Athalantar, and freedom!" he cried, voice ringing through the trees. Twenty blades flashed in reply as they echoed his words in a ragged chorus. And then they were gone, running hard south through the trees with their drawn swords flashing in their hands, Helm at their head.

"My thanks, Ruvaen," Elminster said to the leaves overhead. "Watch over them on their way south, won't ye?"

"Of course," the musical voice replied. "This is a battle no elf or man loyal to Athalantar should miss . . . and we must keep

sharp watch in case there are other traitors among the
knights."

"Aye," Elminster said soberly. "I hadn't thought of that. Well
said. I go." He wove a brief gesture with one hand and vanished.

The two elves descended from the tree to make sure one of
the knights' cooking-fires was truly out. Ruvaen looked south,
shook his head, and rose from the last drifting tendrils of
smoke.

"Hasty folk," the other elf said, shaking his own head. "No
good ever comes of hot haste."

"No good," Ruvaen agreed. "Yet they'll rule this world before
our day is done, with recklessness and neverending numbers."

"What will the Realms look like then, I wonder?" the other
elf replied darkly, looking south through the trees where the
men had gone.

* * * * *

Eight days later, the golden sun of evening saw two crows
alight in a stunted tree just inside the walls of Hastarl. The
branches danced under the weight of the birds for a moment—
and then were suddenly bare. Two spiders scuttled down the
scarred and fissured tree trunk, and into cracks in the wall of a
certain inn.

The winecellar beneath the streets was always deserted at
highsun—which was a good thing, for the two spiders crawled
out into a musty corner, moved a careful distance apart . . . and
suddenly two short, stout, pox-scarred women of elder years
stood facing each other. They surveyed each other's tousled
white hair, rotting clothing, and sagging, rotund bodies—and in
unison reached to scratch themselves.

"My, but ye look beautiful, my dear," Elminster quavered
sardonically.

Myrjala pinched his cheek and cackled, "Oh, you say the
sweetest things, lass!"

Together they waddled through the cellars, seeking the
stairs up into the stables.

* * * * *

Seldinor Stormcloak sat in his study, thick tomes on shelves
all around him, and frowned. For two days now he'd been trying
to magically graft the cracked, severed lips of a human female—
all that was left of the last wench he'd seized for his pleasure—

onto the unfinished golem standing before him. He could make them knit with the purple-gray, sagging flesh around the hole wherein he'd set the teeth, yes. . . . To make them move again, as they should and not of themselves, though, was proving a problem. Why now, after so many successful golems? *What* had cursed this one?

He sighed, swung his legs down from the desk, and sprang to his feet. If he left the fleshcreep spell hanging and brought it down *as* he sent lightnings through the thing . . . well, now. He raised his hands and began to speak the complicated syllables with the swift sureness of long practice.

Glowing light flashed, and he leaned forward eagerly to watch the lips bind themselves to the raw, knotted flesh of the faceless head. They trembled. Seldinor smiled tightly, remembering the last time he'd seen them do that . . . she'd pleaded for her life. . . .

He brought down his most special spell of all—the one that mated the golem with the intellect of a limbless familiar he'd prepared last night. Hanging in its cage, it stared at him in helpless, mute horror for an instant before the spell took hold and the lights in its eyes went out. Now if things were right at last. . . .

The lips moved on the otherwise blank face, shaped a smile that Seldinor matched delightedly, and breathed the word, "Master!"

Seldinor stood before it triumphantly. "Yes? Do you know me?"

"Well enough," was the breathy, whistling reply. "Well enough." And the arms of the golem came up with frightening speed to grasp his throat. Strangling for air, hands frantically shaping spells out of the air, Seldinor had time for one last horrified glimpse of a magical eye appearing on the blank face of the golem and winking at him, before the golem snapped his neck like a twig—and then, unleashing its awful strength for a moment, tore the wizard's head from his shoulders in a bloody rain of death. . . .

* * * * *

Old, wise eyes watched Seldinor's head sail across his study. The lips of their owner thinned in a smile of satisfaction. He passed a hand of dismissal over his scrying crystal and walked away. It was time to prepare against this threat to them all, now that his hated foe was gone, and in such a fitting manner, too. . . .

He chuckled, whispered a word that kept guardian lightnings at bay, and grasped the knob atop a massive wooden stair.
It swung open at his touch, and from the hollow within he drew
two wands, slid them up his sleeves into the sheaths sewn into
his undertunic, and then drew out a small, folded scrap of cloth.
Carefully he unfolded it and lowered it onto his head: a skullcap
set with many tiny gems. He went back to stand over the crystal, closed his eyes, and gathered his will. Tiny motes of light
began to sparkle and pulse in the web of jewels.

Lights played back and forth among the gems as the old
man mouthed silent words and traced unseen sigils . . . and the
skullcap slowly faded into invisibility. When it was entirely
gone, he opened his eyes. The pupils had become a flat, brightly
glowing red.

Staring unseeing into the distance, the old man spoke into
the crystal. "Undarl. Ildryn. Malanthor. Alarashan. Briost.
Chantlarn."

Each name brought an image into the air above his head.
Looking up, he saw six mages approach their own crystals and
lay hands on them. They were his, now. He smiled, slowly and
coldly, as the magic of his crown reached out to grip their wills.

"Speak, Ithboltar," one wizard said abruptly.

"What befalls, Old One?" another asked, more respectfully.

"Colleagues," he began quietly, and then added, "students."
It never hurt to remind them. "We are endangered by two
stranger-mages." From his mind rose images of the young,
hawk-nosed one and the tall, slim woman with the dark eyes.

"Two? A boy and a woman? Old One, have you plunged asud-
den into your dotage?" Chantlarn asked scornfully.

"Ask yourself, wise young mage," Ithboltar said, his words
mild and precise, "where Seldinor is now? Or Taraj? Or Kadeln?
And then think again."

"Who are these two?" another magelord asked curtly.

"Rivals from Calimshan, perhaps, or students of Those Who
Fled from Netheril and flew far to the south . . . though I've seen
the woman a time or two before, riding the lands west of here."

"I've seen the boy," Briost said suddenly, "in Narthil . . . and
thought him destroyed."

"And now they are killing us, one by one," Ithboltar said with
velvet calm. "Done scoffing, Chantlarn? We must act together
against them before others among us fall."

"Ah, Old One—another frantic defense of the realm?" Malanthor's voice was exasperated. "Can it not wait until the morrow?" They all saw him look over his shoulder and smile

reassuringly at someone they could not see.

"Amusing your apprentices again, Malanthor?" Briost snorted.

Malanthor made a rude gesture and stepped back from his crystal.

"Until the morrow, then," Ithboltar said quickly. "I'll speak with all of you then." He broke contact, shaking his head. When had all his students, once eager to bend the world to their wills, become such spineless, self-indulgent fools? They'd always been reckless and arrogant, but now . . .

He shrugged. Perhaps they'd learn the error of their ways on the morrow, if the two strangers continued to strike down magelords. At least he could now compel the wizards of Athalantar into battle with the crown . . . so these foes wouldn't find too many more of them alone and unsuspecting. And nothing this side of the archmages' tombs of Netheril, short of a god, could hope to stand against the magical might of the gathered magelords of Athalantar. And gods interested in the Kingdom of the Stag seemed in short supply these days.

* * * * *

"Yes," Elminster said softly. "In this building here." Braer and one of the other elves nodded silently, and stepped forward to touch El's shoulders. As he faded into wraith form, he heard them muttering softly, weaving cloaking magics more powerful than anything he knew.

They alone could still hear him, so he thanked them before stepping off the rooftop and flying through the moonlight to the window below. A single amulet glowed in his mage-sight, but his experienced eyes saw more: a trap Farl had rigged elsewhere in earlier days. A heavy cleaver had been set on a trap-thread to chop down onto the sill. Elminster's mistlike form drifted past it, and then he was in the room, moving unthinkingly to one side of the window to avoid being silhouetted against the moonglow—and to avoid the sleep-venomed darts set to fire when the floorboard below the sill was stepped on.

The elves had made his insubstantial form completely invisible; Elminster drifted across the room toward familiar snores. They were coming from within a close-canopied bed larger than some coaches El had seen. The prince raised his eyebrows at such wealth. Farl had certainly come up in the world.

There was another trap-thread just inside the draperies. El slipped past it and settled into a comfortable sitting position on the foot of the bed. The sleepers had thrown aside the covers in the warm night, and lay exposed to his view: Farl on his back, one arm spread possessively over the small, sleek woman who lay curled against him: Tassabra.

Elminster looked longingly at her for a moment. Her beauty, sharp wits, and kindness had always stirred him. But . . . we make choices, and he'd chosen to leave this life. At least she and Farl had found happiness together, and hadn't died under the blades of the Moonclaws.

They might well find death in the nights ahead, of course, because of him. Elminster sighed, spoke a word that would let them see and hear him, and said quietly, "Well met, Farl. Well met, Tass." Farl's snores ended abruptly as Tass tensed, coming instantly awake. Her hand slipped under her pillow, seeking the dagger El knew must be there.

"Be at ease," Elminster said, "for I mean ye no harm. 'Tis Eladar, come back to plead with ye to save Athalantar."

By now Farl was awake, too. He sat up and gaped, open-mouthed, as Tassabra let out a little shriek of surprise and leaned forward to stare at him. "Eladar! It *is* you!" She lunged forward to embrace him, and fell through his sitting form, to land on her forearms at the end of the bed. "What?"

"A sending—just an image," Farl told her, rising with blade in hand. "El, is that really you?"

"Of course it's really me," El told him. "Were I a magelord, I'd not be just sitting here, would I?"

Tassabra's eyes narrowed. "You're a mage, now?" She passed her hands through his form. "Where are you, truly?"

"Here," El told her. "Aye, I'm something of a mage now. I took this shape to get past all thy ah, friendly traps."

Tassabra put her hands on her hips. "If you're right here, El," she said severely, "make yourself solid! I want to feel you! How can I kiss a shadow?"

Elminster smiled. "Right then. But for thine own safety, stop waving thy hands about in me."

She did so, he murmured a few words—and was suddenly heavy and solid again. Tassabra embraced him eagerly, smooth skin sliding against his dark leathers. Farl put his arms around them both, hugging tightly. "By the *gods* I missed you, El," he said huskily. "I never thought to see you again."

"Where were you?" Tassabra demanded, running her hands along his jaw and through his hair, noting the changes the years had wrought.

"All over Faerun," El replied, "learning enough magic to destroy the magelords."

"You still hope to—?"

"Before three dawns have come," El told them, "if ye'll help me."

They both gaped at him. "Help how?" Farl asked, frowning. "We spend much of our time just evading casual cruelties cast our way by those wizards. We can't hope to withstand any sort of deliberate attack by even one of them!"

Tassabra nodded soberly. "We've built ourselves a good life here, El," she said. "The Moonclaws are no more; you were right, El—they were tools of the magelords. We run the Velvet Hands together now and shrewd investments and trading make us more coins than we ever got slipping into windows of nights."

Elminster sent a thought to Braer and knew he was cloaked again. He caught an appreciative "Nice lass, there," from the other elf before he turned his attention again to the pair facing him.

"Can ye see me now?" he asked. Farl and Tass shook their heads.

"Nor can ye touch me—even with spells," Elminster told them. "I have powerful allies; they can cloak ye even as they're shielding me now. Ye could steal from magelords and stab at them without fearing their magic!"

Farl stiffened, eyes shining. "No?"

Then his eyes narrowed. "Just who are these allies?"

Elminster flicked a thought at Braer: May I?

Leave this to us, came the warm reply. A moment later, he heard the bed-hangings rustle behind him. Tass gasped, and Farl's hand tensed on the blade he held beneath the covers.

El knew both elves had appeared behind him even before he heard Braer's musical voice. "Forgive this intrusion, Lord and Lady," the elf said. "We do not make a habit of intruding into bedchambers, but we feel this chance to free the realm is most important. If you'll fight beside us, we would find it an honor."

El saw his old friends blink; the elves must have vanished abruptly. He heard the bed-hangings fell back again. Tass closed her gaping mouth with an effort. "An honor?" Farl said wonderingly. "*Elves* would take it as an honor to fight with *us*?"

"Elves," Tassabra murmured. "Real elves!"

"Aye," Elminster said with a smile, "and with their magic, we can defeat the magelords."

Farl shook his head. "I want to—gods, I want to!—but . . . all those armsmen . . ."

"Ye would not be fighting alone," El told them. "Beside ye,

when it comes to open battle, will stand the Knights of the Stag."

"The lost knights of Athalantar?" Tass gasped.

Farl shook his head in disbelief. "More children's legends! I—this seems a dream . . . you truly intend this. . . . " He shook his head again to clear his wits, and asked, "How did you manage to get the elves and the knights to follow you?"

"They are loyal to Athalantar," El said quietly, "and answered a call from its last prince."

"Who's that?"

"Me," El said flatly. "Eladar the Dark is also—Elminster, son of Prince Elthryn. I am a prince of Athalantar."

Farl and Tass stared at him, and then, shakily, Farl swallowed. "I can't believe it," he whispered, "but oh, I want to! A chance to live free, and not have to fear and bow to wizards anywhere in Athalantar . . ."

"We'll do it," Tassabra said firmly. "Count on us, El—Eladar. Prince."

Farl stared at her. "Tass!" he hissed. "What're you saying? We'll be killed!"

Tassabra turned her head to look at him. "And what if we are?" she asked quietly. "We've made a success of things here, yes . . . but a success that could be swept away in an instant at a magelord's whim."

She rose. Moonlight outlined her bare body, but she wore dignity like a grand gown. "More than that," she went on, "we can be satisfied about what we've done . . . but Farl, for once in my life I want to be *proud!* To do something that folk will always respect, whatever befalls! To do something that . . . *matters*. This may be our only chance."

She looked out the window, stiffened as she saw the elves standing on a nearby rooftop, and then made what might have been a sob as they waved to her in salute. Solemnly, feeling her heart rising within her, she waved back, and spun from the window in sudden fierceness. "And what better cause can there be? Athalantar needs us! We can be free!"

Farl nodded, a slow smile building on his face. "You speak truth," he said quietly, and looked up at Elminster. "El, you can depend on the Velvet Hands." He raised his blade in salute; it flashed as moonlight leapt down its steely length. "What will you have us do?"

"Tomorrow even," El said, "I'll call on ye. I need Tass to make contact with the knights—'tis best if she looks like a pleasure-lass, to go to the camp outside the walls by the burning pit.

Then, all the night through, I'll need your folk to work with the elves . . . stealing magic items and the small things they use to work spells—bones and rust flakes and gems and bits of string, ye know—from magelords all over the city. The elves'll cloak ye and guide ye as to what to take."

All three of them grinned at each other. "This is going to be *fun*," Farl said, eyes shining.

"I hope so," Elminster replied quietly. "Oh, I hope so."

* * * * *

"Have they attacked us yet, Old One?" Malanthor's tone and raised eyebrow were sardonic. "Or did I miss it? I did spend a few moments in the jakes this morn."

Ithboltar's smile was thin and wintry. "The threat is real, and remains so. You would do well to set aside a trifling amount of that arrogance, Malanthor. Pride usually precedes disaster, especially for mages."

"And old men start to see things, until the shadows of their dreams seem more real than what is truly around them," Malanthor replied cuttingly, "if we're trading platitudes."

Ithboltar shrugged. "Just be sure to prepare yourself with spells, wands, and the like as if for battle against mage-foes, in the days ahead."

"Athalantar under attack again?" Chantlarn's tone was breezy as he strode into the room. "Armies at our gates and all that?"

"I fear so," Malanthor said, putting a hand to his brow and affecting the broken tones of a hysterical matron. "I fear so."

"And I do too," Chantlarn said heartily. "How does the morning find you, Ithboltar?"

"Surrounded by idiots," the old wizard said sourly, and turned back to the spellbook on the table in front of him. The two younger magelords exchanged amused glances.

* * * * *

"How do I look?" Tassabra asked, lifting her arms and twirling. Small brass bells chimed here and there on the web of leather straps that displayed, rather than clothed, her body. Strips of ruby-hued silk proclaimed her trade to any eye; even her thigh-high boots were trimmed with red.

Elminster licked his lips. "I should never have gone away," he said sadly, and she laughed delightedly.

El rolled his eyes and settled her ruby-red cloak around her shoulders. As he'd suspected, it was pierced by many daring cutouts, and trimmed with lace. Tass strutted, bare knees peeking through the cloak as she approached him.

"Ye're supposed to look as if ye can't make enough coins in Hastarl, and have to go to the traders' camp," El protested, "not bring the whole city to a tongue-dangling halt!"

Tass pouted. "This was supposed to be fun, remember?"

El sighed and took her in his arms. Her eyes widened, and then she reached up her head eagerly and kissed him. Their lips were about to touch when he whispered the word that whirled them away from the dim room to behind a pile of barrels in the garbage-strewn alley along the walls.

Tass clung to him, wrinkled her nose, and then teased, "I've never been kissed like *that* before!"

"Let it be a first, Lady," El said with a bow, as his form faded from view. "My likeness of Helm—'tis still clear in your mind?"

Tass nodded. "Vivid . . . a wonderful spell, that."

"Nay, lass; it takes years to learn magic enough to cast it— and the teleport, too. Tyche smile upon ye . . . try not to get yourself killed or half-crushed under the rush of amorous men before ye find Helm and his knights."

Tass made a very rude gesture in his direction, and then strutted off through the gathering dusk.

Elminster watched her go and then shook his head. He hoped he'd not be looking at her again sometime soon—and seeing a contorted corpse.

He sighed and turned away. There was much else to do tonight.

* * * * *

Tass absently slapped aside another groping hand and snapped, "Coins first, great lord."

A rueful chuckle answered her. "Three silver, sister?"

"Your sister is all you'll get for three silver," Tass agreed pleasantly, moving on. This way and that she peered in the gathering shadows, seeking the face Elminster had left hanging in her mind. He wasn't a noble-looking man, this Helm Stoneblade.

"Swords from Sarthryn, Lady?" a voice whined at her.

She looked scathingly in that direction. "What would I want with a sword, man?"

"To go with your tongue, lass?" another voice rumbled in

quiet amusement. Tass turned to glare across a campfire at its
owner—and stopped dead. This was the man. She looked
quickly around at the ill-garbed men oiling and sharpening
blades. Of course . . . what better way to account for many weapons, without warriors boldly bearing them?

"It's you I've come for," she said calmly, striding toward
Helm. The battered old warrior looked her up and down—and
the blade in his lap swept up like a striking snake to touch her
breast. Tass came to a sudden halt, swallowing. She'd never
seen a sword wielded so fast—and the steel was very cold and
firm against her flesh.

"Stand back," its owner ordered, "and tell me who you are,
an' who sent you."

Tass stepped smoothly back and parted her cloak to put her
hands on her hips. One of the men craned his head for a good
look at what she was displaying, but Helm's eyes were fixed on
her hands, and his blade was raised and ready.

"I speak for Elminster . . . or for Farl," Tass told him calmly.

The blade flashed in the firelight as it dipped smoothly away.
"Well," Helm rumbled, taking up a tankard and offering it to
her, "why don't you decide which one, an' we'll talk?"

* * * * *

"The mage royal is elsewhere," Farl whispered, face glistening with sweat. "Or I'd never have kept my life." He was trembling.

"Easy," Elminster said. "Ye did, that's the important thing."

"For now," Farl hissed back. "Who knows if that mage left
spells that capture my looks, for him to view later—and come
after me?"

The elf beside them shook his head in silence. Elminster indicated the silent elven mage with a nod. "I'd trust him to sense
anything this Undarl could cast."

Farl shrugged, but seemed more at ease as he thrust a var-
ied assortment of gems, vials, and pouches into Elminster's
hands. "Here. He's got something built into his bed, too, but I
couldn't find the way to it, and forgot to bring my axe with me."

"Next time," El replied soothingly, and after a breath or two,
Farl grinned at him.

"There were so many thieving apprentices trying to get past
Undarl's ward to steal spell scrolls that I kept falling over them!
I still don't know how they missed seeing me . . . this shadow of
mine must be *good*." He frowned. "How—how're my Hands

doing?"

Elminster scratched his nose. "The headstrong lass—Jannath, d'ye call her?—ran into a servant and slew him before she gave herself time to think . . . but her elven shadow flew the body out and gave it to the river. Otherwise, all is quiet, unfolding as we foresaw."

"Who's left to do?"

"We leave the tower of Ithboltar alone," Myrjala's voice came quietly out of the night beside them. "So that leaves only Malanthor for you."

Farl nodded. "Right . . . where's Tass?"

Elminster grinned. "I made her change out of her ruby-red costume—"

"I'll *bet* you did," Farl and Myrjala said in unison, and then looked at each other and laughed.

"—so she was a trifle late getting started," Elminster continued smoothly, as if the interruption hadn't occurred. "She's in Alarashan's turret now; her shadow hasn't reported anything amiss."

Farl sighed in relief, and sprang to his feet. "Lead me to this Malanthor, then."

Myrjala raised her eyebrows, and gestured at Elminster to cast the first spell. Obediently El stepped forward, pointing across the dark rooftops of the city. "See ye that turret, there? We're going to fly you across to the window . . . the smaller one; it's his jakes, whereas the other is sure to have alarm spells and probably traps."

"Fly me?" Farl said, and rolled his eyes. "I'm still not quite used to you being a mighty mage, El—or a prince, for that matter."

"That's all right," Myrjala said soothingly. "El's not really used to being either of those things himself, yet."

"You surprise me," Farl said dryly, striding to the edge of the roof. Behind him, the two mages exchanged an amused glance.

* * * * *

Farl reached for the ring. This was almost too easy. "The wine's all gone," a pettish female voice complained, from the bath on the other side of the curtain.

"Well, get some more," the magelord replied from the other end of the bath. "You know where it is."

Water splashed. Farl's fingers closed on the ring—and a wet, long-fingered hand reached through the curtain, closing on . . .

Farl's knuckle! Farl snatched his hand away and spun. The time for stealth was past. The woman screamed piercingly. Yes, long past.

Farl heard the magelord's startled curse as he sprinted for the jakes. "Get me *out* of here!" he snarled, vaulting a low chair. "Now!"

There was a chorus of splashing sounds from behind him, and a man's voice, chanting quickly.

Farl cursed despairingly. "Elminster!" he cried, dodging around a table. Then he felt a tingling in his limbs. He faltered, saw light flickering around him like dancing flames, and then fell through the door into the jakes. *Lie still,* a calm elven voice said in his mind. Farl shivered, and did so. What other chance did he have?

"Shielded!" the magelord spat in disbelief. "A spell-shielded thief in my own chambers! What's this realm coming to, anyway?"

Dripping, he strode across the room, tiny blue lightnings playing between his hands. "Well, I think I'll get a few answers before he dies . . . Nanatha, bring me some of that wine too!"

Oh, gods help me, Farl prayed, forehead on the floor. El, where are you? I *knew* this would h—

There was a sudden burst of light, and then a disgusted sigh. "*Right* in the chamberpot," Elminster told the room angrily. "It's not that small a room, but I have to appear right in the—"

"Who in the Nine Blazing Hells are *you?*"

Malanthor was flabbergasted; there were not one, but two intruders in his jakes, and with no sign of how they got there. He shook his head, but decided not to wait for a reply. Blue lightnings spat from his fingertips. They struck the hawk-nosed man—wait! This was one of the mages Ithboltar had been gibbering about!—and rebounded, leaping back at the magelord before he had time to do anything. They struck home. Malanthor grunted as his body was hurled back, jerking and spasming uncontrollably, and fell backward over a couch. Nanatha screamed again.

"Alabaertha . . . shum*gol*nar," he gasped, writhing on the carpet. Chantlarn'd demand a high price for this aid, but it was call on their pact-link or die!

"Myr?" El called. "Are ye ready?"

"I'll come for him," was the soft reply. "We've got a patrol of armsmen up here."

"Is that why I'm visible?" El said, suddenly realizing that the magelord had seen him instantly.

El stepped out of the chamberpot, deciding not to look down at whatever mess he must be making, and strode toward where the magelord had vanished. A bottle sailed across the room at his head; he ducked, and it touched his shoulder and shattered against the door behind him.

"Yes, that's why," Myrjala answered him calmly. "Next time, just pour me a glass, all right?"

El stared at the frightened woman who'd hurled the bottle—did all these magelords walk about naked? Nay, she was dripping wet, just as the man had been: bath time, then—and then turned back to see Myrjala touch Farl.

"Be back," she said to El, and the two of them vanished. El looked back at the woman, and then over to where the magelord was struggling to his feet.

"For the deaths of my parents," he said softly, "die, Magelord!" And a spell roared out of him. Silver spheres poured across the room and began to burst, one after another, shaking the room. The magelord tried to scream.

"My, what a dramatic speech," said a new voice at El's elbow. Elminster turned, and a smug-looking, mustachioed man in purple robes who hadn't been in the room two breaths before smiled pleasantly at him and triggered the wand in his hand. The world went dark, then red. Dimly El heard a splintering crash, his own body striking a wall and demolishing a mirror. He heard bones shattering as he bounced back out into the room, half-crushed, and fell forward into oblivion. . . .

Chantlarn of the magelords nodded in satisfaction and sauntered forward to inspect the stranger's body. Perhaps there'd be some salvageable magic . . . he didn't spare a single glance for the sobbing apprentice or the smoking ruin of the couch, where Malanthor's contorted, blackened bones were still writhing in an eerie, futile struggle to stay upright.

"Elminster?" The voice from the doorway of the jakes was low and quiet, but definitely female. Chantlarn turned, and heard the speaker gasp. The other intruder Ithboltar had warned them of! He smiled tightly and triggered his wand again, aiming at her face. The wand flashed again, and Chantlarn opened his eyes. He'd have to stop firing at folk so close to him, or . . . it was his turn to gasp.

The woman still stood in the doorway, eyes alight in fury and grief. The magic had done nothing to her! Chantlarn gulped and triggered the wand again. She reached right through its blaze to touch him. Chantlarn had time for one strangled cry before his hurtling body crashed out through the balcony window. He

was still high above the castle courtyard when he thrust the
wand into his own mouth, thrashing and struggling as he
fought the terrible compulsion, and triggered it again.

The bloody explosion set the wand into a wild discharge. Its
bolts burst in all directions, hurling flaming spell forces at the
castle wall, and scattering a terrified patrol of armsmen.

The apprentice screamed again. Myrjala looked up at her
tear-streaked face once, and then turned back to Elminster
again, murmuring an incantation. A blue-white glow rose
around her hands and flowed out to envelop Elminster's twisted
form. She gestured, and he rose into the air, lying limply as if on
a bed. The blue-white glow brightened.

Nanatha backed away, moaning in fear. Myrjala turned
again to face her . . . and smiled. The dumbfounded apprentice
watched her features swim and flow, reshaping themselves
into—the mage royal! Undarl Dragonrider sneered at her,
dropped his cold gaze down her nakedness and then up again,
and then waved a mocking salute. The light flared until it
blinded her . . . and when she could see again, they were gone.

There was a pattering sound from across the room. Nanatha
looked there in time to see Malanthor's bones collapse and
topple down into the ashes. It seemed like a good time to faint—
so she did.

* * * * *

"You'll be all right, my love," Myrjala said softly.

El tried to nod . . . but seemed to be floating back from somewhere far away, on a succession of gently rolling waves that left
him powerless to move.

"Lie still," Myrjala said, laying a hand on his brow. Her fingers were cool. . . . Elminster smiled and relaxed.

"Did ye . . . clean my boots?" he managed to ask.

She exploded with laughter, mirth that ended in a sob that
betrayed just how worried she'd been.

"Aye," she said, voice steady again, "and more than that. I
took the semblance of the mage royal and let Malanthor's apprentice see me. She thinks the whole thing's his work."

"One magelord against another," El murmured, satisfied. "I
hear ye. . . . "

A moment later, it was obvious he didn't. Sleep had claimed
him, a deep, healing sleep that left him oblivious when Myrjala
burst into tears and embraced him. "I almost lost thee," she
sobbed, her tears falling onto his face. "Oh, El, what would I

have done then? Oh, why couldn't your vengeance have been something lesser?"

Seventeen

FOR ATHALANTAR

*In the name of a kingdom
many fell things are done.
In the name of a love
fairer things are won.*

Halindar Droun, Bard of Beregost
from the ballad *Tears Never Cease*
Year of the Marching Moon

The magelord's words made Tassabra bite her lip. She froze, listening, her fingers only inches away from the glowing armlet.

"I have her with me," the Magelord Alarashan went on almost jovially as he leered at the trembling Nanatha, "and she insists the woman revealed herself as the mage royal—and Undarl even waved farewell to her before he left, taking the other one with him."

"That hardly seems possible." The sour old voice coming from the scrying-crystal grew stronger. "Bring her to me."

Alarashan bowed his head. "Of course, Old One," he said, taking hold of Nanatha's wrist. "It shall be done."

He touched the crystal, murmured a word, and they both vanished. Tassabra risked a peek around the edge of the table to stare at the empty air where they'd both been a moment before.

She was alone. She sighed and then shrugged, swept the armlet and a scepter she'd been eyeing earlier into her sack, turned away—and then turned back, gave the scrying-crystal an impish grin, and tipped it into the sack too.

"All done here," she said gaily, and felt the tingling of a spell flood through her as her elven shadow brought her home. . . .

* * * * *

The last failing rays of moonlight were falling into the cobbled courtyard as Hathan strode across it, toward the tower where his spell chamber waited. Those useless idiots of apprentices had better be standing ready at their places around the circle when he got there. . . . Farjump spells always held risk, even without three ambitious young wild-wands and their clever little plots in—

Hathan stiffened in midstride and came to a sudden halt. His face paled, and then he spun around and stared up at the highest tower of Hornkeep, frowning in concentration. He'd never heard the Old One sound so insistent before; something bad had happened.

In a dark chamber high in that tower, glowing water splashed. Its reflections danced across the intent face of Undarl Dragonrider, mage royal of Athalantar.

The griffons struggled in the water, fighting his spells. If he could ever get them to mate in this vat of enspelled giant crab fluids, a few simple spells afterward should give him what he was after. The offspring would be flying armor-plated killers ruled by his will . . . and he'd have taken his first step beyond what the most powerful sorcerers of his family had ever achieved. The gods above knew he was growing weary of waiting, though. Undarl sighed and sat back in his chair, listening to the water surge up over the edge of the vat, the overflow slapping against the wall beyond.

He dare not waste many more days here with that lizard-kisser Seldinor and the others so hungry for his high seat, and . . . Undarl froze as Hathan's mindsend stung him. It was loud because his senior apprentice was only in the courtyard below, and high with excitement and a little fear. He'd have a headache for sure. The mage royal listened, curtly bid Hathan return to his own affairs, and broke the contact.

Forgotten, the creatures splashed and gurgled in the tank behind him as he strode out. Undarl hastened down a dark passage to a certain spot where he laid one hand on the bare wall and murmured a word. The wall swung open with the faintest of rumbles; he reached into the revealed darkness, felt the iron lid, and laid his hand on it. It glowed briefly, tracing his hand, and then swung open, its interior glowing with a faint radiance of its own. Undarl took four wands from it, thrust them into his belt, and reached into a pocket on the lid of the chest. He plucked out the handful of gems he felt there, closed the chest and closet with two quick gestures and a word, and went on down the passage.

One of his junior apprentices looked up, startled, from the scroll he was copying. "Lord Master?" he asked uncertainly.

Undarl strode past him without a word and stepped around a motionless four-armed gargoyle squatting on its block, to mount the stairs beyond. They rose to a dusty, seldom-used balcony, where a bare stone pedestal stood among strange hanging things of wire and curved metal and winking glass. Undarl halted before the pedestal, laid his handful of gems on it, traced a certain sign around them with a finger that left a glowing trail behind, and murmured a long, complicated incantation under his breath.

The apprentice half-rose in his seat to get a better look at what Undarl was doing, and stiffened in that awkward pose, swaying, as the spell took hold.

Undarl smiled tightly and left the chamber. Three rooms away he found another apprentice sprawled on the floor, a key he wasn't supposed to have had fallen from his hand, the other clutching a scroll he'd been forbidden to read. Much good might it do him now.

The spell that brought down the sleep of ages would hold until Undarl ended it, the pedestal broke or crumbled away to break the sigil, or the magic consumed the gems—and that would take a good thousand winters or more. Anyone save Undarl himself who entered the Dragonrider's Tower would fall into enspelled stasis, a sleep that held them unchanged as the world aged around them.

Perhaps he'd leave them all that long and stay away from his tower for a time to see if Seldinor or other ambitious rivals would be tempted into entering it and be caught in his trap. It would be a simple matter to arrange things so that the spell that broke the stasis also slew them before they could arrange any defenses.

Musing, Undarl strode down the winding stone stair and out into the courtyard, the floating, empty suits of armor raising their halberds to let him pass through the door. "Anglathammaroth!" he called. "To me!"

A step later, he was gone. When the huge shadow fell over the courtyard two breaths later, all it found were a few dwindling motes of light. It beat its wings once, the sound of a thunderclap breaking over the Horn Hills, climbed toward the stars, turned, and soared southeast.

* * * * *

The warm, sweet smell of bread rolled out over the armsmen. They sniffed appreciatively and hauled open the door of the bake shop, striding straight over to Shandathe, who was bent over pans of cooling loaves. One grabbed her arm; she looked up and screamed.

Her husband stepped through the door from the kitchens. He took two quick, furious steps toward his struggling wife, and was brought up short by two blades at his throat.

"Keep back, you!" one of the armsmen at the other end of those weapons ordered.

"What're y—"

"Silence! Keep back!" another armsman snarled, snatching up a loaf of bread from the nearest pan. "We'll have this, too."

"Shandathe!" the baker roared, as the two jabbing sword tips forced him back a step.

"Keep back, love!" she sobbed as she was dragged roughly toward the door. "Back, or they'll slay you!"

"*Why* are you *doing* this?" Hannibur snarled in bewilderment.

"The king has seen your wife and fancies her. Be honored," one of the armsmen said with cruel humor. Another armsman backhanded the baker's head from behind with a heavy, gauntleted fist. Hannibur opened his mouth in a last, trailing snarl, and crashed headlong to the floor. . . .

* * * * *

"Get used to it," Farl said with a grin. "The sewers are the only way under the castle walls."

"Don't you know about the secret passages?" Helm rumbled, glaring around at the dripping walls. Scum floated past his chin; he wrinkled his nose as one of the other knights, to the rear, started to retch.

"Yes," Farl said sweetly, "but I fear the magelords do too. Folk who try to use them always end up in the wizard's spell chambers as part of some fatal magical experiment or other. We lost a lot of competitors that way."

"I don't doubt it, clever-tongue," Helm said sourly, trying to keep his sword dry. Filth swirled and rolled past him as he forged ahead in the chest-high waters, wondering why it was that the elves, who could have pushed back the waters, had chosen to hide nearby, and do their cloaking from their hideaway . . . which was somewhere drier.

"Here's the place," Farl said, pointing up into the darkness. "There're handholds cut into this shaft, because at its top is a chamber where six glory-holes meet and things sludge up; it all has to be raked clear every spring. Now remember, Anauviir: the Magelord Briost's chambers can be reached up either of the glory-holes off to the left . . . that's *this* hand. . . ."

"*Thank* you, thief," Anauviir growled. "I do know right from left, you know."

"Well, you *are* knights," Farl said merrily. "And if the nobles of Hastarl are anything to go by . . ."

"Where do the other holes up there lead to?" Anauviir interrupted. Helm grinned at his fellow knight's expression.

"Two rooms used by apprentices," Farl said, "but it's morning; they'll be up preparing morningfest and baths for their masters . . . and the last hole runs to a sort of reading-chamber, which should be empty. . . . Helm and I will go on to the next shaft, which leads to Magelord Alarashan's rooms; and Prince Elminster's promised to show himself if the castle is roused, to draw the magelords into attacking him—and *not* attacking *us*. . . . Any questions?"

"Aye," one of the knights said, spitting into the water. "How do thieves ever steal anything in Hastarl? Do they only rob deaf folk?"

* * * * *

The apprentice let out a little shriek. Alarashan frowned. He preferred willing wenches, but Undarl had forced this one idiot male youth on him . . . doubtless a spy, and the man was hopeless at magic. When he wasn't breaking things, he was busily miscasting spells all over the place, and . . .

The magelord looked into the jakes. Ortran was slumped over on the seat, trousers around his ankles, and . . .

Alarashan stiffened. His apprentice was being thrust aside, by something—someone!—underneath. He strode forward, snatching a wand from his belt, as Ortran's body fell against the wall and the bloody blade that had slain him withdrew down the privy hole.

Alarashan aimed the wand, then stopped. What was to stop someone thrusting a blade into his face, if he showed himself over the hole? No, let them emerge, and slay them as they appear. . . . He crouched low, waiting.

And part of the wall behind him slid smoothly aside. Alarashan had time to whirl around and gape at the secret panel he'd never known about, before the cudgel came down on his shoulder with numbing force, and his wand fell from nerveless, burning fingers.

* * * * *

Briost didn't waste any time being shocked when the man in filthy armor burst out of his garderobe, sword raised. He lifted a hand, triggered his ring, and stepped smoothly aside to give the dying man room to fall.

The second attacker brought a surprised look onto the mage-lord's face, but his ring winked a second time. Something flashed over the falling man's shoulder, though—*gods!* The hurled dagger nearly took out Briost's eye. He ducked aside and felt a numbing blow on his cheek. The dagger spun on, and as he straightened to meet the men now pouring out of the jakes, he felt wetness on his face.

He'd put his hand up to feel, and brought it away with the fingertips crimson with his own blood, when he realized he hadn't time for such luxuries. . . .

And by then, as the blades came at him from all sides, it was much too late.

* * * * *

The scrying crystal flashed. Ithboltar looked over at it and waved an imperious finger at the thoroughly frightened apprentice, bidding her sit. Nanatha sat in hasty silence as the Old One, one-time tutor of most of the magelords, got up and glared at his crystal.

Obligingly, it flashed again. "Either . . . no . . ." Ithboltar growled and leaned forward to touch something Nanatha could not see, on the underside of his desk. He uttered one soft word, and the room rocked under the sudden tolling of a great bell.

"We're being attacked," the Old One hissed fiercely as a chorus of bells echoed and boomed all over the castle. "Briost? Briost, answer me!" He leaned forward over the crystal, muttering—and then his eyes widened at what he saw in its depths, and he thrust a hand into the breast of his robes, tearing them open in his frantic haste. Nanatha saw white grizzled hair on a sunken chest as Ithboltar found what he was seeking—some sort of gem-adorned skullcap—and pulled it onto his head, hair sticking out wildly in all directions. At another time the apprentice might have giggled inwardly at the old archwizard's ridiculous appearance—but not now. She was too terrified . . . of whatever might put such fear into the Old One, mightiest of all magelords.

Ithboltar fumbled speedily through the gestures of a spell he'd hoped he'd never have to use, and the room whirled amid the ringing sounds of shattering crystals. Nanatha gasped.

Ithboltar's chamber was suddenly full of five startled magelords.

"What did y—?"

"How did you brin—?"

"Why—?"

Ithboltar held up a hand to quell them all. "Together, we
stand a chance against this threat. Alone, we are doomed."

* * * * *

The bells boomed again, and the armsmen rose with a chorus of curses. "This *never* happens," Riol protested, his boots
scattering dice underfoot as he skidded past the table and raced
for the stair.

"Well, it's happening *now*," First Sword Sauvar growled,
from right behind him. "And you can bet that anything that can
scare a dozen or more magelords is going to be something we
should be scared about, too!"

Riol opened his mouth to answer, but someone reached out of
a dark side-passage and put a sword into it. The blade glistened
as it came out of the back of Riol's head; Sauvar ran right into it
before he could stop, and reeled back with a startled oath.

"Who in all the—?" he started to ask.

"Tharl Bloodbar, knight of Athalantar," came the crisp reply
from a wild-bearded old man whose armor seemed to be made of
cast-off, flapping remnants scavenged from a dozen battlefields,
which is what in truth it was. "*Sir* Tharl to you."

The bright blade in the old knight's hand skirled against
Sauvar's own steel and then leapt over it—and the First Sword
joined his fellow armsman on the passage floor. The thunder of
hurrying boots coming up the stairs slowed, and the old man
grinned fiercely down into the gloom and snarled, "Right then—
which one o' you heroes is most eager to die?"

* * * * *

Jansibal Otharr sighed in perfumed exasperation. "Why, in
the name of all the gods, does this have to happen *now*?"

He finished at the chamberpot, turned with his elaborate
codpiece dangling to look longingly at the woman waiting on the
bed, and then sighed and reached down to buckle himself up.
He knew what the penalty would be if one of the magelords discovered he'd ignored their precious warning bell for a little rutting.

"Stay," he ordered, "but avail yourself not *over*-heavily of the wine, Chlasa. I'll be back soon." Snatching up his bejewelled blade, he strode out.

The torchlit passage beyond, in the part of the castle reserved for noble visitors, was usually deserted except for the occasional scurrying servant. Right now it was crowded with hurrying bodyguards in livery, an envoy in full Athalantan tabard, and Thelorn Selemban, his hated rival. Thelorn was striding along toward him, his slim-filigreed blade drawn.

Jansibal's face darkened, and he struggled to belt on his own blade and get it out into his hand before Selemban reached him—in such chaos, "accidents" could all too easily happen.

Thelorn's eyes were dancing with amusement as he bore down on Jansibal. "Fair even, lover mine," he said lightly, knowing his reference to that little embarrassment in the Kissing Wench would enrage the only scion of the noble house of Otharr.

Jansibal snarled and jerked his blade free—but Thelorn was past him with a mocking laugh, and hurrying down a broad flight of stairs toward the guard room below. A twisted, sneering smile slid onto Jansibal's face, and the perfumed dandy hurried after his rival. Accidents could happen, yes, especially from behind . . .

* * * * *

"What befalls?" Nanue Trumpettower set down her glass, real alarm in her eyes. Ah, thought Darrigo delightedly, the lass is such a delicate little flower . . . wasted on young Peeryst, come to think of it . . .

The old farmer stumped to his feet. "Well, now," he growled, "them's the alarm bells, calling out the guard. I'll just have a—"

"No, uncle," Peeryst interrupted grandly, drawing his blade with a flourish. "I've brought my steel with me. . . . *I'll* go and look. Guard Nanue until I return!"

He shouldered past Darrigo without waiting for a reply, jaw set and eyes bright. Aye, trust him to leap on any chance to show off before his wife, Darrigo thought, and reached out to keep the door from banging into a table the magelords might be rather fond of, as Peeryst flung it wide.

Almost immediately, he gave a startled cry. Darrigo saw a rushing armsman crash into the youth, reel, and keep on running. Peeryst wasn't so lucky; he hit the wall nose-first and groaned.

Darrigo groaned. Of *course* blood was leaking from the idiot's

over-delicate beak when he got up . . . and of course, little
Nanue would have to get up and rush out to see what had befallen her light-o'-love. . . . On cue, Nanue rushed past him,
skirts rustling, and shrieked in earnest.

Darrigo peered out in time to see a well-dressed noble shove
Nanue off his blade, snarling, "Step *aside*, wench! Can't you
hear the alarm?" Nanue fell back against the doorway with a
sob of fear. The man's blade had gashed her arm, and blood was
running freely down her skirts. That was enough for Darrigo.

Two strides took him to Peeryst. With one hand he snatched
the dainty little blade out of his nephew's hand. With the other,
he shoved the young hope of the Trumpettowers at his wife.
"Bind her wounds," he snarled, setting off down the passage
after the hurrying noble.

"But—how?" Peeryst called after him desperately.

"Use yer shirt, man!" Darrigo snarled.

"But, but—'tis new, and—"

"Then use yer hose, stonehead," Darrigo roared back, as he
took a flight of stairs three at a time.

He was wheezing and stumbling by the time he reached the
bottom, but he caught up with the hurrying noble there. His
quarry was just raising his blade, looking for all the world like
he was going to plant it in the ribs of another dandified fellow a
little farther along the hall. Darrigo smacked him across the
back of the head with his sword. Thankfully, the dainty weapon
didn't break. The dandy whirled, the reek of his perfume
swirling about him.

"You *dare* to touch me, old man?" The noble's blade was darting at his throat before Darrigo could have uttered any reply.

Snarling, the old farmer beat it aside and shouldered forward. "Set steel to a Trumpettower lass, would you? And her
unarmed, yet! *You* don't deserve to live three breaths longer!"

Jansibal leapt backward just in time. The old man's ornamental sword hissed past his nose. His urge to laugh died
abruptly . . . this graybeard was serious!

Then a clear laugh rang out from behind him: Thelorn, damn
him before all the gods! Jansibal snarled and slid aside, forcing
his way past the old man to get his unprotected back away from
the reach of his rival.

"Attacking old men now, Jansibal? Younger ones starting to
refuse you?" Thelorn called interestedly. In sudden fury, Jansibal lunged at Darrigo. Their blades crashed together—once,
twice, and thrice . . . and Janisbal's codpiece clanged to the floor,
both of its tiny straps cut.

The old man gave him a mirthless smile. "Thought perhaps you'd be able to move a mite faster without all that weight down there," he remarked, advancing again.

Jansibal stared at him in astonishment, and then that little blade was sliding in at him again, and he was forced into a desperate flurry of parries. Thelorn laughed again, enjoying his rival's humiliation. Jansibal snarled and attacked, and almost casually the old man's blade floated in over his guard and drew a line across his nose and cheek.

Jansibal spat out a startled oath and backed away. Darrigo lumbered after him, and the perfumed dandy turned and ran down the dark hall, away from them all. The old man raised an incredulous eyebrow. "Fleeing a challenge? And you think yourself *noble?*"

Jansibal Otharr made no reply but a gasp, and a moment later Darrigo saw why. A blade was protruding from his back, dark with the nobleman's blood. The blade shook, a booted foot kicked, and Jansibal Otharr slid down to his knees on the floor and sagged back into a silent heap.

"That's an Athalantan noble?" said the battered old warrior who held the bloody blade. "We should have cleaned out this place earlier!"

Thelorn Selemban strode forward, past the staring Darrigo. "Just who are you?" he demanded.

Helm Stoneblade eyed the noble's ruffed open-to-the-waist silk shirt, its puffed sleeves adorned with many crawling dragons.

"A knight of Athalantar," he growled, "but by the looks of you, it seems I'd've done better down the years as your tailor."

"A knight? What idiocy is this? There are no—" Selemban's eyes narrowed. "Are you loyal to King Belaur and the magelords?"

"I fear not, lad," Helm said, striding forward. There were ten or more warriors in motley armor behind him.

Thelorn Selemban flourished his blade. It glittered in the torchlight as he said excitedly, "Come no farther, rebels, or die!"

" 'Tis certainly a day for grand speeches," Helm responded, moving steadily forward. "Let's see if you're any better with that blade than your aromatic friend was . . ."

"Friend?" Thelorn snorted. "He was no friend of mine—despite anything you may have heard. Now stand back, or—"

"Or you'll wave your sword at me?"

Helm's voice was heavy with sarcasm, but it trailed away as Thelorn jerked something from around his neck, raised it to his lips, and sneered, "Or I'll slay you traitors with *this!* I'm told i—"

It was then that Darrigo Trumpettower made his decision. He took two shuffling steps forward and thrust his blade into the young nobleman's ear.

Thelorn gurgled, dropped blade and bauble, reeled, and fell on his face.

Darrigo peered past him at the grim-faced men beyond. "Helm?" he asked, squinting. "Helm Stoneblade?"

"*Darrigo!* You old lion! Well met!"

A moment later they embraced, keeping their swords out of the way with the ease of old veterans.

"I heard you were an outlaw . . . what've you been doing, Helm?"

"Killing armsmen," the knight said, "but I've found killing magelords more fun, so I'm doing that right now. Care to join me?"

"Don't mind if I do," Darrigo Trumpettower growled. "Thank you—I will. Lead the way."

Helm rolled his eyes. "You nobles," he said in disgust, and strode forward. . . .

* * * * *

The magelords stared at the Old One and then at each other. There was reluctance in their words of agreement, and suspicious looks in plenty were exchanged. These pleasantries were yet incomplete when the tall window at the far end of Ithboltar's vast spell chamber shattered from top to bottom.

Through the opening strode the grand figure of a mage as tall as two men, white-bearded and crowned with fire. He moved purposefully toward them, walking on air and holding high a staff as tall as he was. Its shining length glowed with pulsing, moving radiances. Every magelord shouted out a spell, as one—and the very air seemed to shatter.

The end of the Old One's chamber vanished, raining dust down into the inner courtyard of Athalgard. Unseen behind them all, Ithboltar's crystal winked into life.

* * * * *

El let the crystal Tass had taken fade into darkness once more. "Beautifully done, Myr . . . each one wasted a powerful spell."

Myrjala nodded. "We'll not catch them that way again,

though—and they're together now, whisked away from their chambers where the knights and Farl's folk could outnumber them."

El shrugged. "We'll just have to do this the hard way, then."

* * * * *

Armsmen clattered up the stairs by the score. Tass wasn't that good with a crossbow, but it wasn't easy to miss striking *something* in that river of armored humanity. As they watched, an elf spread his hands in a spell, and the foremost armsmen stumbled, clutched at their eyes, and ran on blindly into the wall. Their fellows running right behind them tripped over the sightless, falling armsmen. Curses arose, and a thief leaned out from his perch high on a stair to slip a dagger into one open helm and bellow, "We're under attack!" Another thief uttered a gurgling scream from somewhere near the head of the stair. A breath later, the entire stairway was a tumult of slashing blades and screaming men. Farl watched it with a widening grin on his face.

"How can you *smile* at that?" Tassabra said, waving down at the men mistakenly killing each other.

"Every one dead is one less guard to chase us, Tass—men I've itched to strike down for years, and dared not for fear of magelords' seeking magic. And here they are chopping and hacking at each other—they've no one to blame for their deaths but themselves. Let me enjoy it, will you?"

Braer smiled thinly but kept silence. The tall elf felt much the same way, though he didn't like to admit it even to himself. Whatever befell hereafter, they'd got in a few good sword thrusts right through the might of the magelords this night. Nay . . . this day, by now. . . .

Braer looked up out the great window into the gray sky of breaking dawn—and stiffened. A warning spell he'd set three days ago had just been triggered, sending its cry into his mind. He stepped back in haste; as his battle comrades turned startled faces his way, he waved at them to keep away from him.

"My own battle begins, I fear," he murmured, and started to grow taller, his body darkening swiftly. Wings sprouted and spread, scales shone silver in the flickering torchlight, and a dragon shifted its bulk experimentally for a breath before bounding up through the window. Glass and timber flew in all directions, and a long tail switched once as it slid out of the room.

Tassabra stared openmouthed as those great wings beat once, and the dragon that had been Braer surged up into the sky out of their sight. She turned her head a little to catch the last possible glimpse of him, and then her eyes rolled up in her head, she gave a little sigh, and toppled sideways.

Farl gathered her against him with one long arm. "She never used to do this," he complained to no one in particular. One of the elves—Delsaran was his name, Farl thought—leaned over and stroked her hair tenderly, just once.

* * * * *

Undarl Dragonrider's face was set in anger as Anglathammaroth flew swift and strong across the realm, heading for Athalgard. Something was seriously amiss. Magelords fighting magelords, a rebel mob inside the castle . . . didn't those fools know hated rulers will be attacked by commoners the moment they show weakness? This is what comes of letting ambitious magelings do as they pleased. . . . If it hadn't been for Ithboltar, Undarl could have kept them all in a tight harness!

The mage royal snarled in frustration as the great black dragon dived down over Hastarl, and then gaped in utter astonishment as the breaking dawn showed him a dragon rising to meet them!

A silver dragon . . . Undarl's eyes narrowed. This must be some trick set by a magelord who knew the mage royal would come to the city on dragonback . . . a trap to intercept him. Undarl smiled tightly and cast the strongest spell he carried. Spheres of black, chilling deathflame rolled out from his outflung hands, expanding as they rolled through the air.

The silver dragon sheared away to one side, and Undarl's death flames vanished. The mage royal stared at the empty air in disbelief, and then snatched out one of his wands and fired it. A green bolt of ravening radiance tore along the silver wyrm's side. It shuddered and circled away. With a short laugh of satisfaction, Undarl urged his own dragon after it.

* * * * *

"By all the gods!" a carter swore. Folk around him followed his incredulous gaze, and there was more than one shriek of terror. One man fell to his knees on the cobbles and began babbling a prayer; many others decided to pray on the run, sprinting away down the street—away from the battle raging in the air overhead as two mighty dragons circled and roared in the first bright rays of morning.

Magic flashed, and the carter snarled a bitter oath. Of course one of the two would be the mage royal, not caring if death rained down on the citizens below—but who was the other? A silver wyrm, now! The carter peered up into the sunlight, seeing the black dragon breathe out acid in a curling cloud. That would fall as a stinging rain on . . . the docks, he judged, and wondered if he should be elsewhere, somewhere safer.

But where? There was no place that the two battling wyrms might not imperil . . . no safe place to run to. The carter stared helplessly at the house and shops all around as more screams broke out from their windows. Down on the street folk began to run. He looked at them sprinting in all directions, and then turned his gaze back up to the sky. He shrugged. If fleeing won no safety, he might as well stay here and see all he could. He'd never see such a thing again . . . and if he lived to tell about it, he could always say he'd been there, and watched it through to the end.

* * * * *

The black dragon roared out a challenge. Baerithryn of the High Forest wasted no breath in reply. He was working a magic as he rose in a tight spiral, banking and curling his tail to avoid the bolts of death the wizard was firing repeatedly from his wand.

"Stand and fight!" Undarl snarled. A moment later, a bolt caught the wheeling silver dragon's tail. It convulsed and plunged down below him, wind rippling in its wings, followed by the mage royal's triumphant laughter.

Something flickered in the air around him, but Undarl felt no pain. A failed spell, he thought, dismissing it with a shrug, and urged Anglathammaroth into a dive. If its claws could rake the silver wyrm's wings, this battle could be ended right now.

The black wyrm's shoulders surged powerfully. Undarl exulted in its might as the wind streaming past his ears rose into a wail. Aye, let it be *now!*

The silver wyrm was beating its wings frantically, trying to evade Anglathammaroth's dive. Undarl snarled at his steed to turn, turn, and not let their foe escape . . . but the smaller, lighter silver dragon was turning tightly back in and under them. They were going to plunge past it. . . .

Anglathammaroth twisted violently; only the harness kept

Undarl from falling helplessly out of his high saddle. The black dragon's limbs curled as he tried to rake or bat at their foe with at least one cruel claw, but the silver wyrm was arching away from them. It was going to slide completely clear! As the rooftops of Hastarl rushed up to meet them, Undarl snarled in anger and triggered his wand again, aiming at the silver dragon's face. Its eyes, proud and sorrowful, met his own: it knew he could not miss.

The green bolt leapt out—and there was a flash as it struck a hitherto unseen barrier, a sphere around Undarl that . . . *gods!*

The mage royal roared out in helpless fear as the rebounding bolt crashed into him. Faerun seemed to explode around him. The torn ends of harness-straps slapped his face and shoulders, he spun in agony and felt a new, greater pain as one of the other wands in his sleeve exploded, blasting that arm to nothing and flinging him out of the saddle. . . . Then, mercifully, Undarl Dragonrider lost all sight of sky and twisting dragons and rooftops below. . . .

The black dragon screamed, a raw sound of horror and agony that echoed back from the city below, awakening every citizen of Hastarl who still slept. The wyrm arched and writhed, but its back was broken, the torn flesh where the saddle had been streaming gore into the wind. Nerveless wings trembled helplessly. Unable to turn, Anglathammaroth dived on toward Athalgard.

The crash shook all Hastarl. Flying raggedly, curled around his own weary agony, Braer saw those black wings crumple like those of a crushed insect—and the castle tower they'd struck shifted, cracked, and with a thunderous roar, toppled over into the courtyard below. Doomed armsmen screamed as they saw death coming down on them; Braer closed his eyes so as not to see the destruction.

Pain ruled him now. Braer felt his magic failing, his torn and bleeding body shifting and dwindling. As his wings receded back into the slim shoulders of an elf, he began to fall.

The rooftops were very close; he hadn't much time for a last prayer. "Mother Mystra," he gasped, fighting to open his eyes. He had a brief glimpse of smoke trailing from his own limbs, and then he was caught by something and cradled gently, the rushing wind around him slowing. Tears were blinding him. Furiously Baerithryn blinked them away and stared up into the face of his rescuer.

Dark eyes glowed with power in the face bent so close over

his own. It was Elminster's colleague, Myrjala, and yet—
Braer's eyes widened in recognition and awe. *"Lady?"*

* * * * *

It was dark and cold this deep in the dripping cellars of
Athalgard. Here below the sewers, the solid stone walls sweated
water, and things long undisturbed scuttled or slid away as the
sudden fire blazed in their midst. Blood and formless flesh
curled and flowed at its heart; flesh that blurred and coiled and
spasmed, as all that was left of Undarl Dragonrider fought to
rebuild his body. A long time the mage royal struggled, the light
flickering and waning as the man shaped one arm onto the
shoulder, head, and back that had survived. Then he fought
with all his will, panting, to give himself legs again.

Several times he slipped toward his true form, but each time
regained the semblance he wanted—a taller, more regal Undarl. The pain ebbed as his confidence grew. . . . He was win-
ning. . . . He could weave all matter to his will, given time
enough.

A second arm lengthened into a hand and fingers. Undarl
fought to control its thrashing, but could not. Not yet. Give me,
gods, just a little more time. . . .

* * * * *

The magelords were arguing bitterly as Elminster rose like a
vengeful wraith from Ithboltar's crystal. Bits of the ceiling
broke off here and there to fall and shatter on the floor below.
Proud wizards stepped back hastily. El's hard eyes were on the
Old One as he whispered the last careful words of a mighty incantation.

It ended—and the stone floor of the chamber split from end
to end with a crack that deafened them all. Gems, blazing like
tiny fireballs, flew in all directions from the Old One's crown.

Ithboltar staggered, screamed in pain, and clutched his
head.

A few of the magelords saw Elminster as he vanished back
into the crystal, but their angry and disbelieving gazes were
caught by the flickering forces spiraling out from the shattered
skullcap on Ithboltar's head. Smoke was rising from their staggering ex-tutor's eyes. The crown pulsed, spinning a vortex of
gathering force out into the chamber.

Hasty incantations were being chanted all over the shat-

tered chamber as the vortex shivered, throwing off roiling
waves of force that swept the wizards into each other and
dashed them against the walls . . . and the crown exploded,
white bolts of destruction stabbing out in all directions. Magelords wailed and flickered in and out of visibility as contingencies took effect.

Watching the scene from a balcony across the courtyard,
Myrjala murmured the last words of a spell of her own. A
bloody, disheveled Elminster appeared out of the air beside her,
gasping.

They stared together into the shattered chamber. Ithboltar's
headless body swayed for a moment, took one unsteady step forward and fell. Over against one wall, a magelord was gibbering
on his knees, and another of the mages had become a smoking
heap of bones and ashes.

The other wizards were struggling to escape, hands moving
in frantic spellcastings. The vortex, adorned with the swirling
bolts the crown had spat into it, gathered speed and strength
like an angry cyclone as it swept across the chamber toward
them. A roar like a deep, unending roll of thunder grew and
moved with it, throwing back echoes from the walls and towers
of Athalgard. The entire castle began to shake.

Myrjala frowned and made a pulling motion with her hands.
The seeing eye she commanded slid through the ragged gap in
the wall to hang just outside the tower. "The crown," she murmured, "must be holding them in the room."

The vortex struck the mages—and whirled through them to
the back wall of Ithboltar's spellchamber. It smashed into those
old stones, the tower shuddered . . . and slowly, with terrible
purpose, the shattered room folded in on itself and collapsed,
bringing down the upper reaches of Ithboltar's tower in a titanic
crash and roar of falling stone.

An earsplitting explosion burst from where the chamber had
been, flinging stones out of the avalanche of falling rock, and
among them, one magelord was dashed across the courtyard
like a rag doll. He was still struggling weakly to work a spell as
his body smashed into another tower. The face of a servant,
watching in fascinated horror from a window, was spattered
with the wizard's gore. What was left of the mage slid limply
down the stone wall . . . and then vanished in a little cluster of
winking lights as a last contingency magic awoke. Too late.

Stones were cascading down the walls of the riven tower
when the courtyard itself rocked and shuddered. Gratings,
paving stones, and dust leapt aloft, borne on sudden geysers of

magical radiance, as something exploded in the unseen dungeon depths of the castle.

The shattered stump of Ithboltar's tower swayed, sagged sideways, and crashed into utter ruin. Flames leapt up here and there about the courtyard, amid the frantically running armsmen. The soldiers of Athalantar stumbled on through smoke and dust vainly waving their halberds about as if cleaving the air would fell some invisible foe and set all to rights again. Somewhere a raw screaming arose and went on and on, amid fresh rumblings.

"Come," Myrjala said, taking Elminster's hand and slipping up to the balcony rail. Elminster followed, and she stepped calmly off it into the air. Hands clasped, they drifted slowly down through the tumult. Athalgard was erupting with running, shouting soldiers. The two mages were still a few feet above the paving-stones when a band of armsmen sprinted around a nearby corner and swept down on them.

The guardcaptain saw wizards in his path and slowed, throwing his arms out to signal his men. "What befell?" he bellowed.

Elminster shrugged. "Ithboltar got a word or two of a spell wrong, methinks."

The officer stared at them, and then at the fallen tower, and his eyes narrowed. "I don't know you!" he said sharply. "Who *are* you?"

Elminster smiled. "I am Elminster Aumar, Prince of Athalantar, son of Elthryn."

The guardcaptain gaped at him. Then with a visible effort, he swallowed and asked, "Did you—cause this?"

Elminster gave the wreckage around a pleasant smile, then shifted his gaze to the halberds blocking his way and said, "And if I did?"

He raised his hand. Beside him, Myrjala had already raised her own. Small lights spun and twinkled above her cupped palm.

The armsmen cried out together in fear . . . and an instant later were in full flight, flinging down their halberds and slipping and sliding on the stones underfoot in their headlong haste to get back around the corner.

"You may go," Myrjala grandly told the empty courtyard where they'd stood. Then she chuckled. After a moment, Elminster joined in.

* * * * *

"We can't hold on much longer!" Blood from a gash left by the axe-stroke that had split his helm was dripping into Anauviir's eyes as he shouted desperately at Helm.

The old knight roared back, "Tell me something I don't know!"

Beside him, a red-faced Darrigo Trumpettower was panting as he swung a heavy blade he'd snatched from a dead hand. The old farmer was protecting Helm Stoneblade with his faltering right arm and his life. That was a price, it seemed, soon to be paid.

The surviving knights stood together on the slippery, blood-smeared cobbles of Athalgard's outer courtyard. Armsmen were charging in at them from all sides now, streaming in the gates from barracks and watchtowers. A few old men in motley armor couldn't stand against such numbers for long.

"We can't hold!" one knight cried despairingly, hurling an armsman to the ground and wearily stabbing the man in the face.

"Stand and fight!" Helm roared out, his raw voice rising above them all. "Even if we fall, every armsman we take with us is one less to lord it over the realm! Fight and die well for Athalantar!"

A First Sword got through Darrigo's guard, laying the old man's cheek open with the point of his blade. Helm lunged forward and ran the man through, his sword buckling against the man's spine and the armor plate behind it. He let go of his weapon and tore the man's own blade out of failing hands to fight on. "Where *are* you, Prince?" he muttered as he slew another armsman. Aye, the knights of Athalantar couldn't hold out much longer. . . .

* * * * *

King Belaur was wont to partake of evenfeast at about the time lesser men sought their morning meal. He would dine heavily on fresh fish slathered in fresh-frothed cream, and then turn to venison and hare cooked in spiced wine. When he felt full to bursting, he'd retire to the royal chambers to sleep his belly's load off. He awoke now, stretched, and strolled naked into his larger, more public bedchamber. Belaur expected to find there fresh minted wine and warmer, livelier entertainment.

This day, rising to the waking world amid the thunders of a strange dream of shakings and rumblings, he was not disappointed. In fact, he was pleased to see two women waiting in the ornate and gigantic bed. One was the woman who'd led that Moonclaws thieving band. Isparla 'Serpenthips' glittered, languorous and dangerous, amid the cushions. Smiling at him in her collar and hip-string of jewels, she looked like a cat strung with diamonds, and trembling beside her was the new wench he'd noticed the evening before outside a midtown bakery. Unclad, the new arrival was even more entrancing than he'd hoped. She wore only the spell-chains magelords used to make defiant prisoners more biddable, and for the occasion someone had polished the links and the collars encircling her wrist, ankles, and throat so they gleamed as bright as Isparla's jewels.

Belaur met her eyes with a savage grin, snatched up a goblet and a decanter from the shining row atop a nearby board, and expressed his approval with a long, rumbling snarl as he strode to the bed. Like a purring lion he lowered himself between them, quaffing wine lazily, and wondered which pleasure to enjoy first. The new treasure . . . or save her, turning first to familiar delights?

Isparla gave a low, throaty purr of her own, and moved her body against him. The king cast a look at Shandathe, lying anxious and still in her chains, and then smiled and turned away from her. He laid a cruel hand on a rope of jewels, and pulled. Serpenthips hissed in pain as the stones cut into her and she was dragged against him. Belaur bent his mouth to hers, intending to bite. He remembered earlier tastes of her warm, salty blood. . . .

There was a sudden flash and a singing sound, and Belaur looked up, startled, into a gaze as frowning as his own. The mage royal of Athalantar stood beside the bed. Belaur cast a quick look down the room at the still-barred doors and back at the master of magelords before he roared, "What are you playing at *now*, wizard?"

"We're under attack," Undarl snarled at the king. "Come! Up and out of here, if you would live!"

"Who *dares*—?"

"We'll have time to ask them who they are later. Now *move*, or I'll blast your head from your shoulders . . . all I *need* to take is the crown!"

Face dark with fury, Belaur heaved himself up from the bed, spilling wenches in both directions, and snatched down the sword that hung on the wall. For an instant, he considered thrusting it into the back of the mage royal, who was striding down the room to a painting that could be swung aside to reveal a way up into the old castle. Undarl turned with more speed

than the swiftest sword in Belaur's bodyguard, drawing aside
from the extended point of the blade, and said in a cold, clear,
menacing voice: "Don't. Ever. Even. Think. Of. Such. A. Deed."
He leaned closer, and added in a harsh whisper, "Your daily sur-
vival depends on my magic."

The blade in the king's hand turned into a snake that reared
up and hissed at him, throwing coils around his wrist.

As he stared at it in frozen horror, it slid back into sword
shape, and flashed mockingly once. Belaur shuddered, reluctantly turned his gaze to meet the hard points of the magelord's
cold eyes, and managed a nod. Then he moved forward obediently as Undarl gestured at the passage door.

* * * * *

"Ye know I must do this alone," Elminster said quietly as
they stood together in the darkened passage.

Myrjala laid a hand on his arm, and gave him a smile. "I
shall not be far. Call if you want me."

El saluted her with the stump of the Lion Sword and strode
away down the passage, exchanging the remnant of his father's
sword for a more serviceable blade.

The last prince of Athalantar had very few spells left, and
lurched in weariness as he went. In his tattered tunic and
breeches, drawn sword in hand, he could not have been a usual
sight in the grand central rooms and halls of Athalgard as he
made his way to the throne room. Servants he passed—and
there were many—kept their eyes downcast and stepped
smoothly out of his way, as if long used to making way for swaggering warriors. Courtiers tended to stare, and then quickly
looked away or turned down another passage or hastened
through the door and closed it behind them.

Save for many glances back over his shoulder, Elminster
seemed out for a casual walk. Guards stiffened at their posts as
he approached, but he'd cast a certain spell before parting from
Myrjala. The guards tensed for battle . . . and then froze, held
motionless by his magic as he strode past.

When El approached seven armsmen with their backs to
high arched double doors, and drawn swords in their hands, he
murmured an incantation that sent creatures slumping into
slumber beneath a magical cloak that stilled all sound.

The blades raised against him fell to the floor in eerie silence,
followed by their owners. El stepped calmly over the doorguards,
drew one of the doors open a little, and slipped within.

The high room beyond was hung with banners and encircled by a high gallery; the walls were richly tapestried. Pillars flanked a carpet of deep forest green that ran straight from where he stood to a high seat alone at the other end of the room.

The Stag Throne. What he'd fought his way toward—not just the chair, he reminded himself, but a land around it free of magelords. Men and a handful of women were milling about just within the doors, all around him, talking and shifting their feet rather wearily: courtiers, merchants, and envoys nervously awaiting the return of the king for early court.

Elminster ignored their curious looks, stepped around several in his path, and strode confidently along the green carpet.

The steps leading up to the Stag Throne were guarded by a mountain of a man in gleaming coat-of-plate, standing patiently with a warhammer as long as he was tall in his hands. He wore no helm, and his balding head gleamed in the flickering torchlight as he glared coldly at the intruder, his gray mustache bristling. "Who art thou, stripling?" he asked loudly, taking a step forward, the warhammer sliding up to rest ready on one shoulder.

"Prince Elminster of Athalantar," was the calm reply. "Stand aside, if you would."

The warrior sneered. Elminster slowed his pace and gestured with his blade for the armsman to step aside. The guardian gave him a mirthless, disbelieving smile, and stood his ground, waving the hammer warningly.

El gave the man a brittle smile and lunged with his blade. The warrior smashed it aside with the warhammer, twisting his wrists so the mighty weapon's backspike would lay open this arrogant fool's head on his return sweep. Elminster stepped smoothly back out of his reach and murmured something, raising his free hand as if throwing something light and fragile.

It raced from those delicately spread fingers, and the guardian of the throne blinked, shook his head as if disagreeing violently with something, and crashed to the polished stone tiles beside the carpet. Elminster calmly walked past him and sat on the Stag Throne, laying his blade across his knees.

A murmur arose from the stunned court, then broke off in a fearful hush as sudden light blazed into being from above. In the heart of the pulsing purple-white radiance, the mage royal appeared in the hitherto-empty gallery—flanked by a dozen armsmen or more, loaded crossbows in their hands.

Undarl Dragonrider's hand chopped down. In response, seven crossbow bolts sped at the man on the throne.

The young intruder watched calmly as those bolts cracked and shivered in the air in front of him, striking something unseen and falling aside.

The magelord's hands were moving in the flourishes of a spell as the senior armsman ordered, "Ready bows again!"

Elminster lifted his own hands in quick gestures, but the folk watching saw the air around the throne flicker and dance with sudden light. El knew no magic would take hold where he sat now; he could raise no barrier to stop missiles or blades seeking his life.

The mage royal laughed and ordered the armsmen who hadn't fired their quarrels yet to loose them. Elminster sprang to his feet.

A fat merchant standing under a pillar suddenly flickered and became a tall, slim woman with bone-white skin and large, dark eyes. One of her hands was raised in a warding gesture—and the crossbow bolts leaping toward the Stag Throne caught sudden fire as they flew. They flared and were gone.

The senior armsman turned and pointed at Myrjala. "Shoot her down!" he ordered, and two crossbows cracked as one.

Dodging around the throne, deciding which spell to use when he got far enough away from Undarl's magic-rending field, Elminster watched those bolts streak across the throne room at his onetime tutor. They glowed a vivid blue to his mage-sight.

He stared in horror; spells flared out angry radiance around them. Undarl laughed coldly as a sudden burst of light marked the destruction of a shield spun around the sorceress. It was followed by a second flash, an instant later, as an inner shield failed—and Myrjala staggered, clutched at her breast where one bolt stood quivering, turned sideways so he saw the second bolt standing in her side—and fell. Undarl's harsh laughter rang out loudly. Elminster started down the steps at a run, his own safety forgotten. He was still three running paces short of Myrjala's sprawled form when she vanished.

The green carpet where she'd lain was empty. Elminster turned from it, eyes blazing, and spat a spell. He was a single snarled word away from the end of the incantation when the mage royal's cruel eyes, fixed triumphantly on his own, faded away into empty air. The wizard had vanished, too.

Elminster's completed spell was already taking effect. Sudden fire raged along the gallery, and armsmen screamed hollowly inside their armor, writhing and staggering. Crossbows crashed down over the rail, followed by one guard, armor blackened and blazing, who toppled over the gallery rail and crashed down atop a merchant, smashing him to the flagstones. There were fresh screams from the courtiers as they rushed for the doors.

The portals they sought were flung open then, bowling over more than one hurrying merchant, and into the throne room strode King Belaur, naked but for a pair of breeches. His face was dark with anger, and a drawn sword glittered in his hand.

Folk fell back before him—and then fled in earnest as they saw who was behind the king. The mage royal was smiling coldly as he walked, his hands weaving another spell. Elminster went white and spat out a word. The air flashed, and that end of the throne room shook, but nothing happened . . . except that a little dust drifted down from above.

Undarl laughed and lowered his hands. His shield had held.

"You're on *my* ground now, Prince—and fool!" he gloated. Then his face changed, he gasped—and fell forward with a howl of pain.

Behind him, belt knife red to the hilt, stood a certain baker, brows trembling in fury. Hannibur had come to Athalgard to find his wife. Courtiers gasped. Hannibur reached down to cut the magelord's throat, but Undarl's hand darted out in a gesture.

The air pulsed and flowed, and the baker's raised dagger shattered. From the whirling sparks of its destruction rays of light leapt out in all directions: a protective spell-cage flashed into being around the fallen mage.

Elminster glared at Undarl and spoke a clipped, precise incantation. A second cage, its glowing bars thicker and brighter than Undarl's, enclosed the first. The mage royal struggled up to one elbow, face pinched in pain, and his hand went to his belt.

Hannibur stared down at the purposeful magelord and the radiances that had just consumed his only blade, shook his head in slow anger, and turned away. It was only two steps to the nearest courtier. A quick jerk freed the startled man's sword from its jeweled scabbard. Holding it like a toy, the baker turned slowly to survey the room, like a heavy-helmed knight peering about in search of foes. Then, implacably, he started down the green carpet toward the king.

A courtier hesitated, and then followed, drawing his own belt knife. Elminster spoke a soft word, and the man froze in midstep. Overbalanced, the motionless man fell over on his face. A second and third courtier, who'd also reached for their blades, stepped back, suddenly losing interest in defending their king.

Elminster sat down again on the Stag Throne to watch his angry uncle come for him. It seemed a fitting place to wait.

King Belaur was furious, but not so rash as to rush right onto the unwavering point of Elminster's waiting sword. He advanced with menacing care, his own blade held high, ready to sweep down and smash aside Elminster's steel. "Who are you?" he snarled. "Get off my throne!"

"I am Elminster, son of Elthryn—whom you had that caged snake over there murder," Elminster replied crisply, "and this seat is as much mine as yours." He sprang down the steps, sword flashing, and went to meet Belaur.

Eighteen

THE PRICE OF A THRONE

How much does a throne cost? Sometimes but one life, when sickness, old age, or a lucky blade takes the life of a king in a strong kingdom. Sometimes a throne costs the life of everyone in a kingdom. Most often, it takes the life of a few ambitious, grasping men, and the more of those the Realms is rid of, the better.

Thaldeth Faerossdar
The Way of the Gods
Year of Moonfall

Their swords crashed together, ringing loudly. Both men reeled back from the numbing impact, and Elminster carefully declaimed words that echoed and rolled around the room. The two men were suddenly encircled by a wall of white radiance that seemed to be a whirlwind of flashing phantom swords.

Belaur sneered. "More magic?"

"It's the last I'll unleash in Faerun until ye're dead," Elminster told him calmly, and strode forward.

They met in a whirling clash of steel. Sparks flew as king and prince tried to hack through each other's guard, teeth set and shoulders swinging. Belaur was a heavy-shouldered warrior of long years, run to fat but wary as a wolf. His challenger was younger, smaller, lighter, and quickly on the defensive, as Belaur used his weight to smash through Elminster's parries. Only the young prince's swiftness kept him alive, ducking, dodging, and diving aside from thirsty steel as the furious king rained a flurry of sword-blows on his foe.

When Elminster's arms grew too numb to take the onslaught, he was forced to give way. He stepped back and circled to the right. Belaur turned to press him, grinning savagely, but Elminster spun away and ran, heading behind the throne.

"Hah!" Belaur shouted triumphantly, striding forward. He was only a few steps away when Elminster stepped out from behind the throne to hurl a dagger at the king.

Belaur's blade flashed up to smash whirling death aside. The unharmed king did not even slow his rush. He sneered in triumph as he charged in to cut his enemy down.

Elminster parried desperately, dodging around in front of the throne again. The king leapt after him and lunged, but his swifter foe slid out from under the blade. The king snarled, bent to his boot, plucked a dagger from it, and threw it all in one swift flurry and grunt. Elminster ducked away—too slowly. The dagger burned across his cheek and spun on its way . . . and Belaur was at him again, blade flashing.

El's parry was almost too late. The impact jarred his hand, and he shook it to banish numbness and then hastily put both hands to his blade, thrusting it up just in time to smash aside the king's next attack. Belaur's leaping steel seemed to be everywhere.

The Sword of the Stag, Elminster had heard it called—a new-forged blade said to be enchanted by magelords. El was beginning to believe that. Their weapons crashed together again. Sparks flew as steel shrieked and then caught, guard to guard.

The two men snarled into each other's eyes, shoving, both refusing to leap back. Belaur's shoulders, now glistening with sweat, rippled and bunched . . . and Elminster's blade was slowly forced back and around. Belaur bellowed exultantly as his greater strength forced the locked blades into Elminster's neck, and blood flowed. Gasping, Elminster dropped suddenly to the floor, wrapping his legs around Belaur's as their blades flashed over his head.

Overbalanced, the king crashed heavily to the tiles, elbows smashing down hard. The locked swords spun far away as Elminster kicked himself free. They were on the floor on their sides now, face to face. Belaur rolled and reached for Elminster's throat. Elminster tried to knock those strong hands aside, and the two men grappled for a moment. Then the prince was overpowered again.

Hard, gouging fingers stabbed at his throat. Spitting in Belaur's face, El arched his head away, struggling. The king smashed his fist against Elminster's forehead, then got a good firm hold on the prince's throat. El clawed vainly at the hairy arms that were choking him and tried to wrench himself free by kicking on the slippery tiles. He managed only to drag the king a little way. Belaur bore down, grunting triumphantly. Elminster's lungs were burning now. The world slowly began to spin and grow dim.

His desperately scrabbling fingers touched a familiar hardness—the Lion Sword! Carefully, as the darkness rushed up to claim him, Elminster drew out the sharpened stub of his father's blade and slid its uneven edge across Belaur's throat. He closed his eyes as the king's hot blood drenched him. Then Belaur was gurgling and thrashing feebly, hands falling from Elminster.

Free to rise at last! Elminster rolled to his feet, shaking his head to clear it, coughing weakly for air, and peering about to make sure no armsmen were near.

A courtier was just retreating from his barrier, hissing in pain from a webwork of cuts welling forth bright fresh blood. Another man who'd tried to breach the barrier lay on his face on the tiles, unmoving. The prince shook his head and turned away.

When he found breath and balance, and stood wiping Belaur's blood from his face, Elminster saw that the courtiers were huddled back along the walls under the gallery. A few had swords out, but none of them wore the faces of men eager for battle. The king made a last wet, rattling sound . . . and then it died away, and he lay still, facedown in his own blood. Elminster drew a deep, trembling breath and turned, the Lion Sword in his hand. It seemed a long way down the green carpet to where Undarl Dragonrider, who'd obviously managed a spell to heal himself, was trying everything he knew to break Elminster's spell cage.

A spell flashed out from the caged wizard, clawed vainly at the radiant cage, and then rebounded on him. The mage royal shuddered. Elminster smiled tightly and waded into the cage he'd spun. Its energies raged briefly along his limbs like hungry lightning, surging through him until he trembled uncontrollably.

Undarl's hands were flicking faster than those of any mage El had ever seen, but Elminster had a very short distance to reach. The Lion Sword stabbed down into the wizard's fast-muttering mouth. Undarl made a choking sound, then Elminster leapt on him, sobbing, and stabbed the mage royal repeatedly.

"For Elthryn! For Amrythale!" the last prince of Athalantar cried. "For Athalantar! And—for me, gods blast you!"

The body beneath his blade started to flow and twist. Suddenly fearful of contingencies, Elminster sprang clear. The blood that sprayed from his dripping weapon as he did so was . . . black!

El stared in horror at the bloody ruin of the master of the magelords. The wizard Undarl swayed up to his feet, took one sagging step, and clawed weakly at Elminster—with hands that were suddenly scaled and taloned. His pain-twisted face lengthened into a scaled snout as the wizard fell, and a long, forked tongue flopped onto the tiles before his writhing body was suddenly surrounded by twinkling lights. Amid those lights, the scaly thing slowly and quietly faded from view, leaving behind only a black pool of blood on the tiles.

Elminster stared down at where his greatest enemy had lain, feeling suddenly so weary that he could scarce . . . stand . . . The prince toppled to the floor, the jagged stub of blade that had slain both the king and the mage royal clattering from his hand. The glowing barrier of blades faded swiftly.

Silence fell. It was several long, still moments before a courtier hesitantly stepped out from behind the pillars, warily drawing his slim court sword. He took a cautious step forward, and then another . . . and raised his blade to stab the fallen stranger.

Steel flashed at his throat, and the courtier leapt back with a scream. The king's blade gleamed in the light as the baker who held it glared around the throne room. "Keep back!" Hannibur snarled, "all of ye!"

Merchants and courtiers alike stared at the stout, disheveled figure standing over the fallen stranger, waving the Sword of the Stag a little uncertainly but with fierce determination . . . until a great light streamed into the room. Their staring faces turned to it, only to goggle all the more.

Through the open double doors walked the source of the radiance: a tall, slim, regal lady with bone-white skin, dark eyes, and a confident manner. She was leading another woman by the hand, a bewildered, barefoot maid wearing a fine gown that did not fit her, who shrieked as she saw the baker and burst into a headlong run. "Hannibur! *Hannibur!*"

"Shan!" he roared, and the Sword of the Stag clattered forgotten to the floor. Sobbing, they rushed into each other's arms.

A bright glow seemed to shine from the regal lady's body as she smiled at the embracing couple and walked calmly along the bloodstained carpet to where Elminster lay on the tiles. She waved her hand, and something suddenly shimmered and sang in the air around them both. Standing there in the light she'd conjured, the woman looked like some sort of sorcerous goddess as she lifted her chin and stared around the chamber with those dark, mysterious eyes. Folk who met that gaze fell still and stared helplessly; Myrjala looked around the chamber until all the watching folk were in her thrall.

Then she spoke, and every man and maid there swore until their dying day that she'd spoken to them, and to them alone.

"This is the dawn of a new day in Athalantar," she said. "I want to see folk who were welcome in this hall when Uthgrael was king. Bring them here to the throne before night falls. If Belaur and his magelords suffered any to live this long, bring them, and bid them fair welcome! A new king summons them!"

Myrjala snapped her fingers, and her eyes darkened. Suddenly folk were moving, pushing toward the doors in urgent haste.

When she snapped her fingers again, only Hannibur and Shandathe, smiling through their tears, were still in the room to turn and see an ornate coffer obediently appear from empty air.

Myrjala looked up, smiled, and waved at them to stay as she drew a flask from the coffer. As she knelt beside Elminster and unstoppered it, the bright glow began to fade from her skin.

* * * * *

The streets were soon full of curious folk, some still smelling of hastily abandoned evenfeast. Hesitantly entering the gates of Athalgard, they skirted a battle between the magelords' armsmen and some unfamiliar warriors and crowded on into the hall of the throne by the score. There were children peering excitedly at everything, shopkeepers looking about warily, and bright-eyed old men and women who tottered and shuffled about, leaning on sticks or the arms of younger folk.

Proud and lowly alike they pushed into the throne room, gawking at the blood and the blackened, dangling bodies of the armsmen, and most of all at King Belaur, sprawled bloody and half-naked by the Stag Throne.

A young, hawk-nosed man they did not know sat on that throne, and a tall, slender woman whose eyes were very large and dark stood beside him. He looked like an exhausted vagabond despite the Sword of the Stag across his knees—but she looked like a queen.

When the room grew so crowded that the press of bodies drove Shandathe up against the shimmering barrier and she gave a little cry of alarm, Myrjala judged the time was right. She stepped forward and gestured at the weary-looking man on the throne. "Folk of Athalantar, behold Elminster, son of Prince Elthryn! He has taken his father's throne by right of arms—do any here deny his right to sit on the Stag Throne and rule the realm that was his father's?" Silence answered her. Myrjala looked around the chamber. "Speak, or kneel to a new king!"

There were uneasy stirrings, but no one spoke. After a moment, Hannibur the baker knelt, drawing Shandathe down with him. Then a fat wine-merchant went to his knees, and then a horse-trader . . . and then folk were kneeling all over the room.

Myrjala bowed her head in satisfaction, a long labor ended, and said, "So be it."

On the throne, Elminster sighed. "At last, 'tis over." Sudden tears spilled down his face.

Myrjala looked out over the kneeling crowd, at the older folk at the back of the chamber, searching among the faces—until she suddenly smiled and raised her hand in greeting.

"Mithtyn," she said to an old, bearded man, "you were herald in Uthgrael's court. Be it so recorded that none contested Elminster's right to the throne."

The old man bowed and said in a voice dry from little use, "Lady, it shall be . . . but who art thou? Ye know me, and yet I swear I've ne'er seen thee before."

Myrjala smiled and said, "I looked different, then. You said once, after you saw me, that you had not known I could dance."

Mithtyn stared at her and turned very pale. He found his mouth had fallen open, swallowed, and staggered back a pace, overcome with awe. Then he fell to his knees, trembling.

Myrjala smiled at him and said, "You do remember. Be not afraid, good herald. I mean you no harm. Rise, and be at ease."

She turned back to the throne. "As we agreed, El?"

He nodded, smiling through his tears. "As we agreed."

Myrjala nodded, and strode down the green carpet until she was in the center of the room. The folk of Hastarl parted before her as if she were preceded by a row of leveled lances. "Stand back, folk of the court!" she said pleasantly. "Clear a space, here before me!"

Their retreat became a hasty rush . . . and when a large area of tiles was clear, Myrjala snapped her fingers and spread one hand.

The empty space was suddenly filled. Some twenty sweating, bleeding armed men were standing before her, reddened blades raised, looking around wildly.

"Peace!" Myrjala said. She seemed suddenly taller, and a white radiance pulsed and played again around her. Such was the force of her voice that the warriors did not move. They stood silent, staring around in unmoving wonder at each other and at the hall around them.

"Behold, folk of Hastarl!" Myrjala said. "Here stand men who

have remained true to Athalantar—men who want freedom for
their realm and an end to the rule of cruel magelords. They are
the knights of Athalantar, and mark he who leads them—Helm
Stoneblade, a true knight of Athalantar!"

Elminster rose from the throne and came to stand beside
her. The two glanced at each other, smiled, nodded—and the
hawk-nosed man strode into the midst of the dumbfounded
armed band. Blades swung to point his way, but no one struck a
blow.

Elminster walked up to Helm. "Surprised, old friend?"

Helm nodded, unspeaking. His dirt-smudged, sweating face
wore a look of astonishment and a little awe. Elminster smiled
at him, and then looked around at the crowd and said loudly,
"By right of arms, and my lineage, the Stag Throne is rightfully
mine! Yet I know well that I am not suited for it. One better
suited to rule stands here before you! Folk of Athalantar, kneel
and do homage to your new king—Helm of Athalantar!"

Helm and his men stood amazed. A ragged cheer rose and
then died away again. Even in Hastarl, clasped most tightly in
the fist of the magelords, folk had heard of the daring rebel of
the backlands.

Elminster embraced Helm, tears in his eyes, and said, "My
father is avenged. The land I leave to you."

"But—why?" Helm asked in disbelief. "Why give up yer
throne?"

Elminster laughed, traded glances again with Myrjala, and
said, "I'm a mage, now, and proud of it. Sorcery is . . . well, it
feels right to me. Working with it is what I do, and was meant to
do. I'll have little time for the care a realm needs, and even less
patience for intrigue and pomp." He smiled crookedly and
added, "More than this: I think Athalantar's had enough of wizards ruling things for a long time."

Heartfelt murmurs of agreement were heard all around the
chamber, as the doors burst open and a band of ruffians stared
into the chamber, swords glittering in their hands. Farl and
Tassabra stood at the head of the thieves of the Velvet Hand. El
waved merrily to them; Helm shook his head, as if seeing
troubles in the days ahead, sighed—and then, as if he could not
stop himself, smiled.

"There is one thing we would like before we go," Myrjala
purred as she stepped up to them both.

Helm eyed her warily. "Aye, Lady?"

"A feast, of course. If you're of like mind, I'll work a spell that
forces all cold iron out of this hall, so that none need fear weap-

ons—even arrows—here tonight, and we can all make merry!"

Helm stared at her. Then he suddenly threw back his head and shouted with laughter. "Of course," he roared, " 'tis the least I can do!"

Mithtyn was pushing through the crowd toward them, leading a young, trembling page, who bore the crown of Athalantar on a cushion. Elminster smiled, took up the circlet with a bow, and placed it on Helm's head. Then he cried, "Kneel, folk of Athalantar, before Helm Stoneblade, Lord of Athalantar, King of the Stag Throne!" There was a thunder of movement as everyone in the hall—except Elminster and Myrjala—knelt.

Helm bowed his head, grinned at the two of them in thanks, and clapped his hands. "Rise, all!" he roared. "Bring food and wine and tables! Call out the minstrels from all over this city, and let us make merry!" His men threw down their swords and roared back their approval, and the great chamber was suddenly full of happy, shouting people. They wavered in Elminster's sight . . . and he found his face was wet with tears again. "Mother . . . Father . . . " he whispered, unheard in the tumult, "I have done the right thing."

Myrjala's arms were suddenly around him, warm and comforting, and he leaned his face into her bosom and wept. It is a glorious thing to be free at last.

* * * * *

More food had vanished than Helm had thought possible. He grinned around at snoring folk sprawled on the benches . . . and his smile broadened as he looked down the carpet to where most of his men were dancing, whirling flush-faced lasses of Hastarl around the floor as weary minstrels played on and on. Among them, the dark-eyed sorceress who'd accompanied Elminster was treading the measures, dancing with first one of his men and then another. She still looked as fresh and as serene as if she were a queen newly arrived from her chambers of a morning.

There on the floor, as they whirled and stepped to the music, a stubbled and dirty warrior bowed over Myrjala's hand and turned her through the intricate steps of the sarad. As he dipped past her, he asked curiously, "Lady, I mean no offence— but why did ye not kneel to the new king?"

"I kneel to no man, Anauviir," Myrjala said and smiled. "If you would know why, ask Mithtyn in the morning."

She left the warrior wondering how she knew his name, and

turned away through the dancing folk to find Mithtyn.

He was standing with most of the older folk by the pillars, watching the dance. As she glided toward him out of the whirling dancers, the old man went pale and turned to hasten away, but found himself surrounded by folk pressed forward for a good look. He had nowhere to go.

Myrjala took him firmly by the hand. "After your praise for my dancing, you don't want to measure this floor with me? I'm hurt, brave Mithtyn! You'll not escape me tonight!"

There were chuckles and half-jealous, half-teasing words from the folk standing around as the sorceress dragged the old herald out into the dance—but when he returned to his place later, he stood tall and smiled, and walked as if he were a much younger man.

Elminster was tired, and his throat hurt . . . but Tassabra had firmly whirled him into the midst of the dancers and guided him deftly through a dance of many avid kisses and caresses—and when Farl had smilingly reclaimed her, clapping El on the back so hard that the prince had almost fallen to his knees, the ladies of the court had pressed in.

El found that the night fled slowly before his stumbling feet, but always another beautiful, eager lady of the court, eyes shining with excitement, was waiting for his hand, and the dances went on.

His feet were beginning to hurt as much as his raw throat, and sweat was trickling down his back under his already-soaked shirt . . . and still the music went on, and still he was surrounded by eager ladies. Shaking his head, Elminster peered past whirling shoulders and laughing faces, seeking a tall, regal face with serene dark eyes. Then he was looking into them, and though half a hundred folk were dancing between them, Myrjala's voice seemed a soft whisper in his ear: "Go, and enjoy! Meet me here at dawn!"

Elminster asked the air, "But what will ye be doing?"

A few whirling turns later, Myrjala swept up to and past him and winked. El watched her dance up to Helm, deftly pluck him from the very arms of Isparla, and turn her head back to meet his wondering eyes. "I'll think of something!" Myrjala said to her pupil, and set off across the room, towing Helm by the hand. The old knight shook his head, grinned at Elminster, and shrugged.

Elminster stared across the room at them, astonished at the bubbling laughter in her voice—and then, helplessly, started to laugh. He was still rocking with mirth as smooth hands drew

him away through a door into less-well-lit antechambers, where
there were couches, and wine, and eager lips to share it
with. . . .

*   *   *   *   *

In the first gray light of dawn, Elminster staggered back
into the throne room. His head was pounding and his mouth
very dry. Something seemed to be wrong with his balance, and
he was still belting and adjusting the tattered remnants of his
clothing when he came through the double doors, and looked
straight into Myrjala's amused eyes. She stood in front of the
Stag Throne looking immaculate, her dress and regal appearance unchanged from the evening before. "Has Athalantar
thanked you properly?" she asked teasingly.

Elminster gave her a look. His fingers, still busy fastening
and adjusting, encountered smooth silkiness, and he drew a
lady's veil from where it been caught up under his belt. Shaking
his head, he held it out to Myrjala. "Ye want me to pass this
up?" he asked mournfully.

She laughed. "You'd be sick of plots and betrayals inside a
tenday. . . . One doesn't have to be king to eat and dance and
love a night away, you know."

Elminster sighed and looked around the throne room at the
shields and banners of his ancestors. His gaze came very slowly
back to her from looking on distant memories, and he stirred.

"Let's to horse, then," he said briskly, "and be out of here before Helm's awake."

Myrjala nodded and stepped forward to link her arm with
his. They went out of the throne room together.

The stables were huge and dimly lit, but quiet; it was well
before the first feeding. Myrjala calmly chose the two best
horses, and ordered a drowsy-eyed groom to saddle them.

"Here, now—" he protested, frowning. "Thos—" He broke off
hastily, staring into her stern eyes. His eyes fell to her hands,
beginning to shape a spell, and he gulped and said, "A moment,
Lady—they'll be ready'n' but a breath or two!"

Myrjala smiled dryly, then turned to Elminster and snapped
her fingers. Bulging saddlebags melted slowly out of thin air beside his feet. Elminster gave her a questioning look.

"I took the liberty," she said with a serene and innocent
smile, "of assembling these early this morn. Folk who conquer
kingdoms and then give them away deserve to eat well, at
least."

Elminster hefted one of them and found it was gods-cursed heavy . . . and that it clinked. Coins, or he'd never been a thief. He deftly undid the knots and opened the throat of the bag wide. It was full of gold coins.

Myrjala smiled at him innocently and spread her hands. "How much gold can one king spend? We'll need something to see us along the trail to our next adventure . . . "

"And just where is that, if I may ask?" Elminster cupped his hands, and she put a toe of one soft, pointed boot into them, springing lightly up into the saddle.

"*This* adventure's not quite done yet, I fear," Myrjala replied in a warning tone. Elminster looked at her thoughtfully, but she said no more as she urged her mount on toward the stable gate.

They went out into the mists of the morning and found Mithtyn leaning on his stick waiting for them. He looked up at them, swallowed, and managed a smile. "Someone of Athalantar should thank ye both properly. I fear I have not the words . . . but I would not want thee to ride away without even a salute!"

Myrjala gave him a little bow from her saddle, and said, "Our thanks, Mithtyn. Yet I see something troubles you . . . and I would know what it is, if you will."

Mithtyn stared up at her for a moment, and then his words come in a rush. "Alaundo's prophecy, Lady! He's ne'er been wrong yet, and he said 'the Aumar line shall outlive the Stag Throne'! That can only mean Athalantar won't survive without an Aumar as king . . . and yet ye ride away!"

Elminster gave the anxious old man a crooked smile. "While I live, the Aumar line lasts. Let this land grow in strength and happiness, as I hope to, in the days ahead."

Mithtyn said nothing, face troubled, but bowed low. They raised their hands to him in farewell, and rode away up the street in silence. As they went, the risen sun touched the rooftops with rose-red light. The old herald stared after them, still and silent.

They paused at the top of the lane. The hawk-nosed young man looked toward the old burial ground and said something to the tall lady who rode with him, pointing. The herald peered, trying to see what the prince who was giving up his kingdom had indicated . . . and could just make out a lump of cloth.

'Twas . . . a cloak, drawn over a sleeping man and woman. Mithtyn cleared his throat in embarrassment, but by then he'd recognized them: the smiling man called Farl and his lady, the beautiful little one. Aye, Tassabra, that was her name. And be-

hind them, someone was sitting, staring right back at him! An
elf! A tall, silent male elf, with a staff of wood across his knees
. . . Mithtyn gulped, raised his hand in an awkward salute, and
saw it returned.

Then the elf turned his head. Mithtyn looked in the same direction in time to see the prince and the—sorceress, if she
wanted to be known so—vanishing around a corner behind the
old stone of a proud house. When they were gone, Mithtyn shivered once. Then he turned back into the castle, his eyes wet
with tears. He knew he'd not see anything of like importance for
the rest of his days. Such knowledge is a heavy thing to bear
early in the morning.

Perhaps after a good dawnfry, a few hot mugs, and his wife
to tell it all to. Mithtyn hoped—not for the first time—he'd live
long enough for his daughter to be old enough to heed, and hear,
and appreciate what he told her. He'd tell her about this morning perhaps a hundred times.

As he crossed the courtyard, one of Helm's knights approached and hesitantly told the old herald what the Lady Myrjala had said about herself while dancing the night before.
Mithtyn looked into the man's eyes and discovered he did have
someone to tell about it, after all. He led Anauviir toward the
kitchens, feeling much better.

* * * * *

"Whither now?" Elminster asked, as Myrjala reined in
where the trail crossed the shoulder of a little knoll west of the
city. He looked around curiously; from Hastarl, one couldn't see
this was a grave-knoll. A stone plinth stood within a low wall,
overgrown with shrubs and low-branched trees that cloaked the
stone from all but the closest eyes.

"In all your struggle, you've gained none of the spells wielded
by the magelords," Myrjala replied. "As it befalls, I know where
the mage royal kept a cache of magic—spellbooks, healing potions, and items held ready in case he was hounded from Hastarl, or ever found the city held against him. Here in this old
shrine of Mystra, where no thieves come for fear of the guardian
ghosts of dead mages, is his cache."

"Is it guarded?" Elminster asked warily, as they dismounted
amid the trees.

"*Of course it is, fool mageling!*" someone snarled from behind
him.

Elminster whirled around—in time to see the rearing body

of his horse flow and twist . . . into the familiar shape of Undarl, mage royal of Athalantar. Myrjala's mount screamed in terror, and they heard the frantic drumming of hooves as it fled.

Elminster gulped and plucked at his belt for the things he'd need to cast what paltry battle-spells he had left. Undarl's gloating grin told him he was not going to be in time. The master of the magelords raised his hand and began to murmur something, but Myrjala sprang between them, skirts swirling. The lightning that cracked forth from Undarl split before her upraised hands and splashed harmlessly off to either side.

The mage royal screamed in anger. When he could find words through his fury, he snarled at her, "*You!* Always, it is you! *Die*, then!" His next words were a hissed incantation, and streams of fire burst from his fingertips in a crimson web that crackled and clawed the air, but was turned back by Myrjala's conjured shield. Elminster had no spells left to match such magics; he could only stand anxiously in the lee of Myrjala's barrier.

The web of fire Undarl had spun began to glow a dull, angry red. The mage royal lashed at the shield with his fading flames, and called out a name that echoed among the stones of the shrine.

His call was answered by a vast bestial roar. Something huge and dark rose up from behind the trees behind the mage royal . . . a red dragon! It unfurled batlike wings and hissed, eyes glinting with cruelty. Then its shoulders surged and it leapt through the air toward the prince and the dark-eyed sorceress. It breathed fire as it came, a roaring torrent of flame that poured over Myrjala's shield . . . but could not consume it.

The sorceress said something long and awkward, and the dragon's flame doubled back on itself, coiling and turning from red to an eerie bright blue before it became white-hot. To Elminster's mage-sight it seemed even brighter; Myrjala had transformed it into something awesome. It rushed back at the dragon like a hungry wind. El glimpsed dark wings beating frantically amid the roiling flames for a moment, and then, in an explosion that rocked the knoll and hurled him from his feet, the dragon burst part.

Scales and blackened scraps of flesh flew past the last prince of Athalantar as he struggled to his feet and saw Undarl snarling and lashing at the sorceress with his whip of flames, seeking to pierce the shield. Fire roared and rumbled.

Myrjala stood unmoving against the fury of the flames, and spoke a single calm word. The edges of her shield began to grow, lengthening into long, lancelike tips that reached toward Undarl, pulsing with power.

The wizard laughed contemptuously. His arms were growing longer, too, stretching into tentacles. The tips of his snakelike limbs hardened into sharp, red, long-taloned claws. The lance-tips of the shield reached him and passed harmlessly through. Undarl's laughter grew more shrill, and his face had begun to stretch forward horribly into a snout. The talons of his hands ended in small bulbous things, now, each with its own snapping mouth.

"My spell can't touch him!" Myrjala exclaimed, amazed.

The mage threw back his head, and his ever-wilder laughter echoed back from the stone plinth behind him. "Of course not! I am no puny mortal of Faerun, to be mastered by your magic—I walk the shadows where I will on many worlds. Many think themselves mightier than me, only to learn the depths of their folly in the moments before they perish!"

Undarl's ever-larger tentacle-heads suddenly swooped around the shield and were upon her, darting and biting like writhing snakes. Myrjala shrieked as one bit off her raised hand—but her scream was abruptly cut off an instant later when the wizard's head, dragonlike now, breathed out fire that burst through the shield without pause. The sorceress vanished from the waist up, collapsing in a smoking welter of ashes and blackened bones.

"*No!*" Elminster cried, leaping on the dragon-thing the magelord had become. He clawed at its eyes, kicking and weeping.

Undarl shook him off. El fell heavily, saw the fanged snout turn just above him to breathe down devouring fire, and rolled in under it with desperate speed, rising beneath those snarling jaws.

Undarl's flame roared skyward, useless, as the prince snatched out the stub of the Lion Sword and stabbed at its throat repeatedly, forcing the dragon-thing to recoil. Even as its head arched back away from his blade, hissing, Undarl's biting claws clutched and tore El's back and face. Elminster crooked an arm around the dragon-thing's throat and swung around behind it, scrabbling for balance. Those clattering claws swarmed in on him, but he drove his blade deep into one of the dragon's golden eyes.

Undarl convulsed and shuddered, tearing free. Its newly grown tail smashed El away. He rolled in the dirt as the dragon-thing squalled and thrashed in agony. Elminster scrambled to his feet and carefully cast a lash of lightning, a feeble spell that might not do more to a dragon than singe its scales—but he cast it not at Undarl, but at the hilt of the Lion Sword, where it stood quivering in the dragon's eye.

Lightning leapt and flashed. The dragon-thing stiffened, jerked its tail, and sank limply back across the low stone wall, its brain cooked. Smoke rose in lazy curls from its eyes and nose.

Weeping in fury, Elminster hurled every battle-spell he had left. Before his streaming eyes the scaly body of his foe was chopped apart and then frozen. He stood over the riven carcass until he could force his trembling lips to shape the words of his very last battle-spell. Small, stinging bolts of magic lanced out at the pieces of Undarl, hurling them aloft. El did not stop until only tangled lumps of flesh remained amid blood . . . blood everywhere.

Still weeping, Elminster turned to where Myrjala had fallen. Fallen defending him—again. He tried to embrace her ashen bones, but they crumbled and he was holding only drifting dust . . . and then, nothing.

"No!" he sobbed brokenly, on his knees before Mystra's shrine in the brightening morning. *"No!"*

He stood up, mouth working, and shouted at the uncaring sun, "Magic brings only *death!* I'll wield magic *no more!*"

The ground rumbled and rocked at his words, and something slithered around his feet. Elminster looked down . . . and froze, watching in stunned silence. The ashes around him began to glow and drift together over the overgrown stone, rising and re-shaping themselves into . . . Myrjala!

Honey-brown hair swirled as the glow became her bone-white body, lying on the stones. The hair wavered as if disturbed by an ebbing wave, and fell aside to reveal his teacher's familiar, pert face, and those large, dark eyes. They opened and looked up at him.

Elminster stood gaping in shock as Myrjala said gently, "Please, Elminster . . . never utter such words again—please? For me?"

Dumbly, Elminster fell to his knees again, reaching out wondering hands to touch her shoulders. They were solid, and smooth, and so were the hands that lifted to him and pulled his mouth down to hers. The sharp smell of burnt hair was strong around them as Elminster pulled back in alarm, wary of another magelord trick, and stared down into the eyes of the sorceress.

Their eyes met for a long time, and El *knew* he was facing Myrjala. He swallowed, tears falling from his cheeks onto her own, and said, "I-I promise. I thought ye dead . . . ye *were* dead, burned to ashes! How can this be?"

Fire rose and raged, deep in those dark eyes staring up into his. The ghost of what might have been a smile passed over her lips as she said softly, "For Mystra, anything is possible."

Elminster stared down at her, and then at last, he realized who—what—his teacher truly was.

In real fear, he tried to pull away. A hint of sadness crept into those dark eyes, but then their gaze sharpened and, as much as the firm arms around his neck, held him motionless. The goddess Mystra held him captive with her eyes of dark mystery, and said softly, "Long ago, you said you could learn to love me." Suddenly her eyes held a challenge.

Face white, wordless, Elminster nodded.

"Show me, then, what you've learned," the Lady beneath him said softly, and cool white fire rose up around them both.

Elminster felt clothes and all burn away as they rose into the air amid searing flames, up into the morning sky above the weathered stone plinth. Then her lips met his, and the burning began, as power such as he'd never known before surged into him. . . .

* * * * *

The cart squeaked loud enough to rouse the sleeping dead, as usual. Bethgarl yawned as he pushed it up the bumpy slope before the long descent into Hastarl . . . but then, he was all too used to it.

"Awaken, Hastarl!" he muttered, spreading his arms grandly and yawning again. "For Bethgarl Nreams, famed cheese merchant, cometh, cart loaded high with wheels of sharpcrumble, whitesides, and re—" something moved and caught his eye off to the left, by the old grave-shrine. Bethgarl looked in that direction, then up—and a third yawn died forever as his jaw dropped open in wonder.

He was looking—nay, staring—at a rising ball of blue-white flame, flaring so bright he could scarce bear it . . . but he *had* looked, eyes burning, and seen two folk floating half-hidden in its heart! A man and a maid, and they were. . . . Bethgarl stared, rubbed his watering eyes, stared again, then let fall his cart and ran back the way he'd come, for all he was worth, howling in fear.

Gods, he'd *have* to stop eating those snails! Ammuthe had been right, as usual . . . oh, gods, why had he ever doubted her?

* * * * *

Sated, they floated in each other's arms, hiding from the brightness of highsun in the shade of an old and mighty tree.

The white flames were gone, and Mystra seemed only a languid, beautiful human woman. She rested her head on his shoulder and said softly, "Now your road must be alone, Elminster, for the more I walk Toril in human form, the more power passes from me, and the less I become. Thrice I died as Myrjala, watching over you—here, in Ilhundyl's castle, and in the throne room in Athalgard . . . and with each death I am diminished."

Elminster stared down into her dark eyes. As he opened his mouth to speak, she put fingers over his lips to still him, and went on. "Yet you need not be alone—for I have need of champions in the Realms: men and women who serve me loyally and hold a part of the power over Art that is mine. I would very much like you to be one of my Chosen."

"Anything, Lady," Elminster managed to say. "Command me!"

"No." Mystra's eyes were grave. "This you must freely agree to—and before you speak so quickly, know that I am asking of you service that may last a thousand thousand years. A hard road . . . a long, long doom. You will see Athalantar, with all its folk and proud towers, pass away, crumble into dust, and be forgotten."

Those dark eyes held his, and Elminster floated, looked into them, and was afraid. Staring into his eyes, the goddess went on. "The world will change around you, and I shall command you to do things that are hard, and that will seem cruel or senseless. You will not be welcome in most places . . . and your welcome in others will be born of fawning fear."

She drifted a little apart from him and turned them both, until they hung upright in the air, facing each other. "Moreover, I will not think ill of you if you refuse. You have done far more already than most mortals ever do." Her eyes glowed. "More than that, you fought at my side, trusting me always, and never betraying me or seeking to use me for your own ends. It is a memory I shall always treasure."

Elminster began to weep again. Through the tears, he managed to say huskily, "Lady, I beg of ye—command me! Ye offer me two things that are precious indeed, thy love and a purpose for my life! What more can any man ask than those? I would be honored to serve ye . . . make me, *please,* one of thy Chosen!"

Mystra smiled, and the world around seemed brighter. "I thank you," she said formally. "Would you like to begin now, or have some time to ride your own way and be yourself first?"

"Now," Elminster said firmly. "I want no waiting for doubt to creep in . . . let it be now."

Mystra bowed her head, exultation in her eyes. "This will hurt," she said gravely as her body drifted in to meet his again.

As their lips touched and clung, lightning leapt from her eyes into his, and the white fire was suddenly back, roaring up around them deafeningly, searing him to the bone. Elminster tried to shriek with pain, but found he could not breathe, and then he felt himself torn, tugged, and swept away into the rising flame, and it did not matter anymore. . . .

* * * * *

"Such tales you tell!" Ammuthe was working herself up into a fine temper as she walked. She tossed her head, and that magnificent hair swirled in the sunlight. "Always such fancies—so, well enough, my husband dreams when awake as well as when he snores! I give the gods thanks for that, and in silent despair put up with it! But *this* time—a whole cart of our cheeses let fallen to be snatched up by who knows who? Too much, indeed, my lazy sluggard man! You shall feel *more* than the edge of my tongue, if every single one of those chee—"

Ammuthe broke off in midtirade, staring up at the grave-shrine on the hill. Trembling with renewed fear, Bethgarl nonetheless allowed himself a small, leaping moment of satisfaction as Ammuthe shrieked, spun about, and ran headlong into his chest.

Bethgarl staggered back, but held her firmly. "None o' that, now," he said, not too loudly, casting a wary eye up at the streaming, roiling sphere of white fire above the shrine of Mystra. "We'd gather up all the cheeses, you said . . . I'd not eat at our table again until you'd seen the money for them, you said . . . well, presently, good wife, I shall grow hungry. I know I will, and—"

"By all the gods, Bethgarl! Shut thy mouth and *run!*"

Ammuthe made as if to jerk free of him. Bethgarl sighed and let her go, and she was off like a rabbit, bounding down the hill again, hair streaming behind her. Bethgarl watched her go, fought down a sudden wild desire to laugh, and turned back to his cart. One of the cheeses had fallen off into the grass. He dusted it thoughtfully, put it back, picked up the handles, and pushed the cart on toward Hastarl, ignoring the sudden cries of his name from far behind.

As he passed the shrine, he looked up at the ball of fire, and winked at it. Then he swallowed. Cold sweat trickled down his back, and he struggled against rising fear. Carefully he pushed the cart on down the hill, not hurrying. He could have sworn that as he stared at the flames, a pair of dark, knowing eyes had met his—and winked back at him!

Bethgarl reached the bottom of the hill and looked back. Fire still pulsed and glowed. Whistling, he pushed his cart on to Hastarl, and frowned curiously at the hubbub by the gates. There seemed to be a lot of folk out in the streets today, all of them excited. . . .

Epilogue

There are no endings save death, only pauses for breath, and new beginnings. Always, new beginnings . . . it's why the world grows ever more crowded, ye see. So remember, now—there are no endings, only beginnings. There; simple enough, isn't it? Elegant, too.

Tharghin "Threeboots" Ammatar
Speeches of a Most Worthy Sage
Year of the Lost Helm

Elminster floated back from somewhere far away indeed, and found himself lying naked on a slab of cold stone, smoke rising from his limbs. As the last gray wisps curled up and drifted away, he raised his head and looked down. His body was unchanged, unmarked. A shadow fell across him, and he turned his head. Mystra knelt over him, nude and magnificent. Elminster took one of her hands and kissed it.

"My thanks," he said roughly. "I hope I serve thee well."

"Many have said that," Mystra replied a little sadly, "and some have even believed it."

Then she smiled and stroked his arm. "Know, Elminster, that I believe in you far more than most. I felt the Lion Sword's enchantment stripped away by dragonfire that day when Undarl destroyed Heldon, and looked to see what befell, and saw a young lad swear vengeance against all cruel wizards and the magic they wielded. A man of great wits and inner kindness and strength, who might grow to be mighty. So I watched over him as he grew, and liked the choices he made, and what he grew to become . . . until he came to confront me in my temple, as I knew he would in the end. And there he had the courage and the wisdom to debate the ethics of wielding magic with me—and I knew that Elminster could become the greatest mage this world has ever known, if I only led him and let him grow. I have done that—and El, lovely man, you have delighted me and surprised me and pleased me beyond all my hopes and expectations."

They stared into each other's eyes, and Elminster knew he'd never forget that calm, deep gaze of infinite wildness and love and wisdom, however many years might lie ahead.

Then Mystra smiled a little and bent to kiss his nose, her hair brushing his face and chest. El breathed in her strange, spicy scent anew for a moment and trembled with renewed desire, but Mystra lifted her head and looked southeast, into the quickening breeze. "I need you to go to Cormanthor and learn the rudiments of magic," she said softly.

Elminster raised an eyebrow. " 'The rudiments of magic'? What have I been hurling about so far?"

Mystra looked down at him with a quick smile. "Even knowing what I am, you dare to speak so—I love thee for that, El."

"Not *what* you are, Lady," Elminster dared to whisper, "but *who* you are."

Mystra's face lit up with a smile as she went on, "Power, yes, but without discipline or true feeling for the forces you're crafting. Ride south and east from here to the elven city of Cormanthor . . . you'll be needed there in time to come. Apprentice yourself to any archmage of the city who'll have you."

"Aye, Lady," said Elminster, sitting up eagerly. "Will the city be hard to find?"

"Not with my guidance," Mystra said with a smile, "yet be in no haste to rush off. Sit with me this night and talk. I have much to tell you . . . and even gods grow lonely."

Elminster nodded. "I'll stay awake as long as I can!"

Mystra smiled again. "You'll never need to sleep again," she said tenderly, almost sadly, and made a complicated gesture.

A moment later, a dusty bottle stood between them. She wiped its neck clean with one hand, teased out the cork with her teeth like any serving-wench, took a sip, and passed it to him.

"Blue lethe," she said, as Elminster felt cool nectar slide down his throat. "From certain tombs in Netheril."

Elminster raised his eyebrows. "Start telling," he said dryly, and then glowed in the midst of her tinkling laughter.

It was a sound he treasured often in the long years that followed. . . .

Thus it was that Elminster was guided to Cormanthor, the Towers of Song, where Eltargrim was Coronal. There he dwelt for twelve summers and more, studying with many mighty mages, learning to feel magic, and know how it could be bent and directed to his will. His true powers he revealed to few—but it is recorded that when the Mythal was laid, and Cormanthor became Myth Drannor, Elminster was one of those who devised and spun that mighty magic. So the long tale of the doings of Elminster 'Farwalker' began.

Antarn the Sage
from ***The High History of Faerunian Archmages Mighty***
published circa Year of the Staff

Saga

The sweeping saga of honor, courage, and companions begins with . . .

The Chronicles Trilogy

By *The New York Times* best-selling authors
Margaret Weis & Tracy Hickman

Dragons of Autumn Twilight
Volume One
Dragons have returned to Krynn with a vengeance.
An unlikely band of heroes embarks on a perilous
quest for the legendary *Dragonlance!*

ISBN 0-88038-173-6

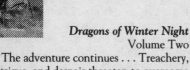

Dragons of Winter Night
Volume Two
The adventure continues . . . Treachery,
intrigue, and despair threaten to overcome
the Heroes of the Lance in their epic quest!

ISBN 0-88038-174-4

Dragons of Spring Dawning
Volume Three
Hope dawns with the coming of spring, but then
the heroes find themselves in a titanic battle
against Takhisis, Queen of Darkness!

ISBN 0-88038-175-2